Faoii Ascended

Tahani Nelson

For My Father

Who taught me I could be anything, not the least of which was loved.

1

For as long as humans have built cities, they've been aware of something just outside the ring of torchlight.

Jacir Harkins, the Royal Arcanist of Clearwall, stood alone in the highest tower in Clearwall Keep, staring at the Eternal Tapestry. There was something ominous beneath Imeriel, hidden from the light of the Starlit Throne, and he could not place it. Inky tendrils snaked across the Weave, but he could never see the full specter of whatever darkened the strands. The being slithered away from his mind like a shadow.

The Royal Arcanist pulled away from the Tapestry. What he could not see unnerved him, and what he could see was so wrapped in the murky tendrils that he could not act without pulling on the threads and alerting those that lurked in the darkness.

They were at a stalemate. He would have to be crafty.

Jacir smiled as he absentmindedly picked up a fallen pen and returned it to its place. He could be shrewd if that's what Clearwall needed of him. He'd learned from Ilahna, after all.

Ilahna. His devious, impetuous, overprotective, courageous, possibly insane older sister. Jacir wondered if the former urchin would like Clearwall if she could see it now. So much had changed. On the surface, it seemed that the jewel of Imeriel was everything she'd hoped for in life. Queen Isolde Clearwall I sat on the Starlit Throne, following the plans that Ilahna and Jacir had helped her great-grandfather set in motion almost a century before. The Maze was no longer the cesspool it had been when Ilahna had known it, and magic was celebrated. More than that, people were not only allowed—they were encouraged to see the world outside the city's walls, and many citizens took pilgrimages called kintars to the Faoii monasteries and beyond when they came of age. It was everything Ilahna had wanted for him. For everyone.

The Faoii, too, had changed. Their numbers had been decimated by Madame Elise during the War of False Prophets, and between her destruction of the monasteries and the decades of witch burnings, few had believed the Faoii Order capable of rebuilding. But Aurelius had believed in the Faoii and had raised his descendants to honor them. Between the resources of the Starlit Throne and the hope borne of legends, a new Faoii Order was being built on the ruins of its predecessor, almost as feared and revered as they had been before the Godfell War.

Few still remembered, but his sister had been part of the Faoii's resurgence. The Faoii Order had grown under her mantra, though she herself had never taken up the bronze breastplate and ivy helm. *Hope. Rise. We are stronger together.* His sister's words had been enough to bring an entire civilization back from the brink of despair.

Again. Jacir had once tried to see the number of times the Faoii monasteries had been burnt and rebuilt across all the Tapestries, but he'd lost count. Images of leather breastplates and mud huts falling as thoroughly as the developed monasteries that had graced the Weave more recently clouded his memories for a moment. He shook them away. Refused to let himself get tangled in the threads that reached out constantly now and focused.

The Faoii monasteries had been little more than polished spittoons in Kaiya the Emancipator's time—filled with women stuck in tradition who felt entitled to their power while the rest of Imeriel lay in their shadows or, as the Croeli had been, pushed beyond the fringe altogether. And in Madame Elise's time, no one had been allowed to shine at all. Both generations had fallen to ash and ruin. But just as he had told Madame Elise once, long ago, the monasteries weren't what mattered; they were temporary buildings built around an idea. They never truly fell for long.

The true strength of the Faoii Order came from an ideal that had spurred a million people, his sister included, through the centuries: Justice and truth tie us all together, and we are stronger with that bond unbroken.

But every now and again, a shadow fell across the Weave, just beyond his sight. And Jacir did not know if the monasteries were enough to hold it back.

Jacir looked at the ring of torchlight around Clearwall and knew that something ancient watched them from the dark. There was a rot below Imeriel, and it was attached to the tonicloran in his veins that writhed and twisted where no one else could see. Dark roots holding the Tapestry in place like a wicked, poisoned loom. The keys to a locked door the darkness did not want opened.

He did not know for sure what was trapped beneath those threads, but he knew it had to do with the rot under his feet and the eyes that peered from shadows that mortals dared not face. It had to do with children dying. With the curse of the Maze. With

Tapestries carried on four shoulders and ancient voices that whispered on the wind. Kaiya had started something when she'd killed a Goddess three hundred years ago. Madame Elise had woken something when she sacrificed the Faoii to the Old Gods. And now... now he didn't know what those combined stories had created. Something dark.

He'd find the source of all of it. He'd make it right. But he would need help. And the shadows could never know that he was circling.

Jacir sighed as he used eyes that were no longer mortal to watch a girl at the edge of the Starlit River. It would be hard, nearly impossible.

But that's what hope was for.

***

Far below the tower of Clearwall Keep, Ehryn stood at the edge of the Starlit River, watching the inky water slide through the night. The scent of silkstrand moss and dead fish filled her nose, but she was used to it. She'd spent the majority of her life here at the docks, watching the water roll by, wrapped in blankets and thoughts as she watched the waves.

Clearwall was a hub for passenger ships and trade vessels, and she loved to watch the ships sail in, filled with travelers and strange furs and intricate pieces of jewelry. She'd always been intrigued by whatever waited beyond the waves, but her mother's sad eyes and her love for her parents kept her feet on shore. She had no desire to leave Clearwall.

But things were different in the night.

In the night, the winds shifted, and the waters grew as black and endless as her eyes. It was in those quiet moments beneath the stars that the Call was loudest. It came from something deeper than the ships or the waves or the far-off oceans. It was a longing and nostalgia for something she'd never experienced, wrought from the stardust between her bones. It felt like it had carried through her entire line, through the existence of every civilization. And when she sat beneath the stars Ehryn could almost tell where the Call came from, could almost walk across the Starlit River to whatever voice it was that beckoned from deep within her soul. It begged her to be more than she was.

Ehryn shivered and pulled her blanket around her shoulders, already knowing what the Voices on the Wind would say.

Help us.

2

There was screaming in the square. Chants of anger and demand. Cries of fear.

Ehryn looked up from the cobblestones at her feet. Violence in Clearwall was so rare she didn't even know what she was supposed to do. Run? Try to call the guards? Hide? But as a man wove unsteadily towards her, carrying a child and bleeding from his forehead, she found she couldn't do anything at all.

"Run! The Elisians are in the square!" he gasped out over the sound of his crying daughter. "Why are you just standing there? Move!" He pushed her roughly with his free hand as he tried to get around her, and Ehryn realized others were running past her too, screaming or crying as they shoved her aside. Ehryn shook herself awake, clutched her father's laundry basket to her chest, and started running the way she'd come, letting the crowd carry her along.

STOP!

The command was so powerful, so urgent that Ehryn slid to a halt on reflex, not noticing or caring as the mob jostled her in their haste to get by.

Help us!

The Call. She'd heard that quiet whisper of direction and encouragement for years. The Voices on the Wind had been her constant companions, always pushing her to be more than she was. Giving her small whispers of reassurance or empathy during the day and stories of far-off lands at night. But this was different. This was a command laced with fear.

She'd never heard them express fear before.

The Tapestry is shifting!

We smell Her on the air.

She Who Demands the Blood.

You must stop Her servants.

Go, Ehryn! GO!

The last word was another command, and it came from a voice older and stronger than the others that Ehryn usually had for company. A voice that felt bigger than the sea or sky, and infinitely more powerful.

Go!

Ehryn's heart thundered in her chest. The Voices on the Wind had never led her astray, but they had also never led her into danger. She'd never had reason to hesitate before. But this was different. The cries in the square were getting louder, and she was afraid. She didn't want to go. Didn't want to--

GO!

And Ehryn's feet were moving. Towards the square. Towards the shouts and the smell of blood. She was scared of what might be at the end of her path, but the idea of disappointing the chorus of voices that urged her on scared her more.

Ehryn sprinted into the square, nearly deafened by the shouts and chants and cries. Normally this was a festive place, where storytellers would stand at the base of towering statues depicting the Called, sharing elaborate tales of everything those heroes were doing at the behest of the Starlit Throne. But today there were no stories, and it seemed wrong that someone would choose this place to make their mischief. To spread fear or chaos beneath the hard gazes of those who were tasked with leading Clearwall to greatness.

There were so many people gathered here now, screaming frantically, many garbed in white robes and waving holy symbols. Ehryn recognized those robes. *Elisians.* Religious fanatics that lived in enclaves outside the walls. A few of Clearwall's citizens huddled in the center of their circle, bound and beaten. Others shouted at the Elisians to let the hostages go.

Ehryn didn't know what to do. The Elisians had never taken hostages before. The Voices on the Wind chittered behind her eyes, but without direction. Without orders. Had they led her here only to abandon her? She nearly choked on the smell of rot that she sometimes caught whiffs of in Clearwall. Had the Elisians brought it with them?

"We demand to see Queen Isolde! Imeriel is in danger!" one of the Elisians screamed over the yelling citizens. "The Starlit Throne is harboring a Hollowed! Our Lady Mavrikal tastes it on the wind!"

The crowd was suddenly quiet. Ehryn's heartbeat was loud enough she couldn't hear what else the Elisians were saying. Couldn't tell if the Voices on the Wind were still chattering at her. Even the word "Hollowed" was enough to drive terror into her bones and silence into the throats of those around her. This was a mistake. She shouldn't have come here. The Elisians were dangerous. They only brought trouble. And the Hollowed were more dangerous still.

But there couldn't be a Hollowed in Clearwall. They were all safely locked up in the Faoii monasteries.

Right?

But the Voices on the Wind trembled.

Mavrikal returns.

She Who Demands the Blood rises.

The Hollowed are Hers.

Help us.

Ehryn didn't know what to think. Didn't know why she was standing here with a laundry basket while Elisians kicked hostages and screamed about Holloweds. Why had the Call brought her to this place?

Wait. The Tapestry is about to change.

You must be here.

This is your destiny, Ehryn.

Ehryn didn't know anything about destiny. She only knew that she was frightened. And now the shouting behind her was getting louder again.

Suddenly a stone flew towards the center of the Elisian mob. "Go back to your enclave!" someone from the Clearwall crowd yelled. The Elisians responded with arcs of lightning, and everything broke at once. There were more screams. More rocks thrown by angry citizens. A flash of silver and the thunder of hooves from between the buildings up ahead. There was blood on a few of the white robes. Yells. Curses. More cries. Bodies surging into each other as spells and fists and rocks collided. Ehryn tried to break away. Tried to hide.

Stay, Ehryn!

Then there was suddenly the glint of sunlight on breastplates as two armed Faoii and someone wearing the Clearwall crest rode into the courtyard. The fighting slowed.

"Citizens of Clearwall! Return to your homes! This raucous gathering is a disturbance of the peace!"

Ehryn knew that voice. It was Princess Namaoii, Queen Isolde's only daughter. The Wolf Pup of Clearwall. Her shout was hard and strong and rang with all of the authority of the Starlit Throne, and Ehryn felt almost comforted.

Most of the people not clad in Elisian robes broke away from the scuffle at the princess's command, and even Ehryn felt compelled to leave. To go home. The Faoii could handle the Elisians. They would make Clearwall safe again. She didn't have to be here.

But the Call was stronger than the compulsion.

No! Don't go! Don't let them get her.

Everything is about to change.

Destiny, Ehryn! Destiny!

And suddenly the mob of white robes and symbols were surging forward, the Elisians yelling over each other as they shoved incense burners and relics in the Faoii's direction, gathering their magics into their hands, moving as one in a coordinated attack.

"You cannot silence the Goddesses! You cannot silence the truth!" they cried.

A flash of fire. The smell of burnt hair and skin. One of the horses went down, and Ehryn couldn't see what happened to the rider. Surely she couldn't have survived that? Surely the Elisians had her? But then there was a terrifying, beautiful cry as the Faoii on the ground drew her blade. Her mounted sister followed suit, and their swords' battle songs twisted and shone, a dazzling ballet of light and bloodlust that sounded like the chorus of angels. A few of the Elisians fell away, their heads bouncing across the cobblestones.

Ehryn saw Namaoii's face harden as she bellowed again, drawing her own sword as she fought to keep her steed under control. Her blade did not scream like the others did, but Namaoii didn't need it to. "Leave Clearwall and return to your enclaves! NOW!" The Wolf Pup's voice was like fire and iron, filled with power and fury. A few of the Elisians began to break away.

"No!" another Elisian screamed, his voice commanding the same tones that the princess's had. "We WILL be heard!"

The commands clashed in the air like untuned notes from a violin. For a moment, Ehryn thought that between the magic voices and the blade songs, the noise would rend the sky. But as other Elisians added their shouts to their leader's chorus, Namaoii's yells were drowned out. Even the fantoii seemed muted. And when their combined might finally broke through whatever veil the three women had woven above the square, all of the sound together shattered like glass in a falling pane. Those that remained of the Elysian mob rushed the princess and the Faoii in the silence.

Get her. Don't let them take her.

Go! GO!

Ehryn didn't know what she could do against a mob fueled by fanaticism. She especially didn't know what she could do that two armored Faoii and the Wolf Pup of Clearwall couldn't. But she ran anyway, driven by adrenaline and command. The sound started again as she moved, but almost in slow motion. The Faoii tried to hold the horde back with their screaming swords. Namaoii swung her blade in a wide arc against those who tried to pull her from her mount, then yelled as she fell away from the saddle.

Then Ehryn was there, and everything seemed to move too quickly. Ehryn was not a Weaver. She did not know what the future held. But she had felt the power in that ancient voice and knew better than to question its orders.

So when the Call demanded that she swing her father's basket of folded laundry forward, showering clean linen over the Elisians just as they reached the princess… she did.

Momentarily blinded and confused, the fanatics fumbled, and Namaoii tore away from their grasps, kicking one Elisian hard in the stomach and bringing the hilt of her sword down against another's skull. Ehryn was dismayed to see the blood on her father's newly-cleaned tunics, but there was nothing she could do.

The concern was quickly forgotten, though, because now the Elisians were turning towards *her*. Ehryn panicked. She didn't have a sword. She didn't even have more laundry to throw. What had she done? Why was she even here? Why--?

Lend me your voice, Child.

It was the voice that sounded like waves on rocks and wind through mountains. The voice of fire and earth and sea. Calm, but unyielding.

Lend me your voice!

Ehryn opened her mouth to give her approval, to beg that ancient queen who came from across stars and centuries to help her…but no sound came. The Elisians were still coming at her, and she couldn't speak, couldn't move.

"What are you doing? Get out of here!" Princess Namaoii yelled, shoving another attacker aside. "Move!"

Lend me your voice! NOW!

And Ehryn let go.

The primordial scream that came from her throat when she opened her mouth again was laced with power, and the Elisians in front of her were knocked to their knees, grabbing their heads as the Voice on the Wind took control.

"LEAVE, IMPUDENT WORMS! RETURN TO YOUR FALSE MASTER! AND KNOW THAT WE WILL COME FOR SHE WHO DRAINS THE BLOOD! FOR ALL OF YOU!"

The Voice was so loud that Ehryn thought she would go deaf or blind with the force that burst from her skull, and for a moment there was nothing. Then the Elisians were trying to clamber to their feet, running in every direction. Even Namaoii and the Faoii took several moments to stand back up, a string of colorful curses spilling from the princess's mouth.

From there, the Faoii made short work of the Elisians that remained, who were either too wounded or too frightened to flee. They rounded up those left standing and released the fanatics' frightened hostages back into the safety of Clearwall's streets. Ehryn thought that the freed citizens would cheer as the Elisians were herded towards Clearwall Keep, but instead they only stared at her, faces white and frightened. It wasn't until the princess ordered them back to their homes that they began to disperse, still casting fervent glances over their shoulders.

Ehryn knelt shakily to gather the laundry from Clearwall's cobblestones, dismayed by the blood and dirt that now soiled the fabric. Her father would have to rewash all of these. She was trying to decide what she would say to him when she was interrupted by a large hand blocking her view. Ehryn looked up and found herself staring into the stern eyes of Princess Namaoii.

"Why did you do that?" the Wolf Pup growled. "Better yet, how did you do that? That wasn't commanding magic or honeyed words. That was something older and deeper than a whelp like you should be capable of."

Ehryn didn't know how to answer. She didn't even know how to point out that Princess Namaoii was only a year older than her. Instead, she lowered her head. "I am one of the Called," she finally responded. "The Voices on the Wind did not want you to be harmed."

The princess narrowed her eyes and gruffly pressed one of the fallen linens into Ehryn's hands. "I figured that power couldn't come from someone as puny as you. It had to be something bigger stepping in. Stupid…whatever they are. Voices on the Wind."

Ehryn couldn't hide her surprise at the princess's disdain. "But… but they just saved you."

Namaoii snorted. "No, they saved *you*. We would have been just fine if we hadn't had a gaping laundry girl to worry about." The princess turned away. "Don't get into fights anymore. You're just in the way and a burden to those who have to save you. I hope the Call watches your bony ass when you finally abandon Clearwall, because I sure as the Broken Blade won't be there next time."

Ehryn tried to protest. Tried to explain that she had no plans to ever leave the city she loved. But Namaoii, the Wolf Pup of Clearwall, was already mounted again and riding away, her bright breastplate glinting in the sunlight.

3

Now that the Elisians had been rounded up and the crowd dispersed, the square was quiet. Ehryn finished gathering up the laundry she'd spread across the cobblestones, wondering what her father would say. He'd probably just be happy that she was safe, even if he had to rewash some of the garments. Her mother, on the other hand… she'd want to know about the Elisians. About Ehryn's brother, Dhruv. And Ehryn had no information for her. She could already picture the disappointment in Everly's eyes.

The Voices that would normally offer her little songs or words of comfort were quiet. They felt distant in a way Ehryn had never experienced before.

We rest.

You lent Her your voice.

She sleeps.

You must, too.

Ehryn wasn't sure what the Voices meant until she stood up and her head swam. Her throat hurt. Her legs were shaky. Whatever the Voice on the Wind had done to frighten the Elisians away, it had taken its toll. But it seemed a small price to pay to know that she was alive. Slowly, quietly, Ehryn turned to make her way home.

By the time she'd made it a block, Ehryn had decided she wouldn't tell her parents what had happened in the square. She wouldn't say anything about having stepped in to help the princess and her Faoii guards. Her parents, Cole and Everly, knew she was one of the Called, of course, but so far, the Voices on the Wind had not affected their lives in any significant way. Her parents would be worried if they thought being a Called was dangerous. Ehryn's abilities already made them afraid of the future. Of what would happen when the Call got loud enough to pull her away from Clearwall like the others who had come before.

Ehryn wondered at what Namaoii had said, though. About the Called abandoning Clearwall. The other Called that Ehryn had heard about had gone to follow the destinies the Voices on the Wind had whispered into their ears. Queen Isolde had commissioned statues of them, and the bards told of their greatness in the square. Plays were created in their honor. The Called were considered heroes, and their legacies added to the greatness of Clearwall.

Ehryn hated it. She knew that if more people found out that she could hear the Voices on the Wind, they'd push her to find her destiny. But she couldn't imagine leaving her family. Her home. Not like the other Called. Not like her brother.

The Voices on the Wind were quiet now, and Ehryn couldn't figure out why they'd been so insistent that she step up against the Elisians. It didn't feel like she'd made any difference in that fight; the Faoii could have protected the princess even if

Namaoii wasn't more than capable of protecting herself. Why had the voices been so insistent when the Elisians made their stand?

Why had the Elisians made a stand at all?

This, in particular, was unsettling to Ehryn. Clearwall had always been a place of tradition. The entirety of Imeriel was built on old beliefs that had never quite died. But they had… dimmed, with time. Religion, in particular, had become a soft picture in the background of most people's lives, rather than the forefront of their focus. People still honored the goddesses, of course, but it was more out of inherited habits than anything else. A goddess had walked among humans only a few generations ago, but Her life and death had been followed by a very dark period in Clearwall's history. Now things were changing. People were making grand strides in science. Medicine. Arcana. Machinery. People went on kintars in their youth—went out into the world to bring back information, experiences, and new ideas to Clearwall, and everyone benefited from this knowledge. But very few people thought to thank the gods in all of this. Rarely gave deities more than a cursory thought at dinner or when passing a temple. And that's what the Elisians hated most.

The Elisians were different from the rest of the people in Imeriel. They warranted caution. There was always a level of frightening uncertainty with fanatics, but the Elisians were an entirely different level of unknown. No one—not even the Weavers or the Queen or the Royal Arcanist—knew for sure what was coming when it came to the Elisian enclaves. Their communes were a blank spot in the Weave, and out of it came whispers of goddesses returning to the world and names of deities old enough to have been forgotten. And now they spoke of Hollowed in Clearwall.

Ehryn shuddered and walked a little quicker towards home, the leaden exhaustion in her limbs deepening. She didn't want to think about it. She didn't want to know what implications the last hour had held. She just wanted to sleep.

She should have known, however, that news had already spread. She should have realized she'd meet her mother on the way, rushing down the street, eyes wide and desperate.

"Ehryn! Daughter! The Elisians are in Clearwall!"

"No, Mother," Ehryn responded kindly. "The Elisians are gone."

Everly stopped and peered at Ehryn uncertainly, almost like she didn't recognize who was talking to her. Ehryn tried to smile. Her mother barely recognized anyone or anything when she was thinking about Dhruv.

Ehryn's older brother had gone on his kintar as soon as he was old enough, but he had never come home. Those who accompanied him said that he'd joined one of the Elisian communes. That he'd found enlightenment. They'd seemed happy for him. Tried to assure her that he hadn't fallen to the firstborn curse of the Maze. But Mother had never been the same afterward.

Everly had gone to every enclave within riding distance. Each commune let her in, of course. Those who spread the word of the Goddesses felt obliged to let outsiders see their good work. But she had only been admitted into the chapels and courtyards. Never into the private buildings or communal kitchens. "For our family's privacy," they'd said.

They'd looked down their lists of charters, both past and present. "There is no one named Dhruv here. Are you sure you are in the right place?" But Mother couldn't read the dialect they wrote in. Couldn't tell for sure. Could only take them at their word.

There was nothing else to be done. She had no way of knowing which commune had enfolded her son. So she'd left heartbroken every time. And now she didn't always seem like she was looking at the world that everyone else saw. Something inside of her had dimmed.

Ehryn tried again. "The Elisians are gone, Mother. They… they took hostages this time. There was a scuffle in the square. The

Faoii and the Wolf Pup dealt with them and took them to Clearwall Keep."

"The Faoii? Did they hurt them? Did they hurt Dhruv?" Everly seemed wild in her panic, and Ehryn put her hand on her mother's arm.

"Dhruv wasn't there, Mother. He wasn't with them."

"We must look. We must! He is out there somewhere. We have to see!"

Ehryn nodded. She'd accepted already that anytime the Elisians came to Clearwall, her mother had to at least see where they'd stood. Like some part of her would be able to tell if her baby boy had stepped on one of the cobblestones. Ehryn shifted the basket of laundry onto one arm and took her mother's hand. When they returned to the square, she tried to ignore that the few Voices on the Wind still there were now singing a sad chorus of lost children.

Do you want to spare others this pain, Ehryn?
Help us.

4

Weeks passed, and the incident with the Elisians faded from being the talk of Clearwall to being just another example of "fanatics can't be trusted." Once more the Elisians and their enclaves fell into the back of people's minds, though sometimes one could hear old women arguing over whether they should be eradicated by the Faoii or be allowed to spread their gospel peacefully.

Ehryn had no opinion on the matter either way, and she was just grateful that fewer and fewer people talked about the girl whose voice held galaxies.

But it didn't seem like everyone forgot completely. As much as Ehryn never wanted to leave Clearwall or fulfill any of the unspoken obligations of the Called, some part of her always knew she couldn't hide it forever. There were no laws or edicts declaring that she or anyone else had to go on their kintar—but there were societal expectations. Everyone knew that the kintar was how you gave back to Clearwall. How you kept society from stagnating. Ehryn knew that eventually she would have to decide for sure if she wanted to live up to that idea or skip her kintar altogether.

She'd never thought the question might come all the way from the Starlit Throne.

Nearly a month after the incident in the square, Ehryn approached the steep winding road leading to Clearwall Keep on top of its dais high above the rest of the city. She didn't know what to expect. While technically anyone was allowed to hike the twisted path that led to the jewel of Clearwall, old traditions died hard, and there was still a sense of foreboding when it came to approaching the great stone building that had been forbidden to the public for generations. Queen Isolde and her Faoii guards had tried to change that. People were allowed to approach the Starlit Throne with news, concerns, or even celebrations. Fledgling Weavers and children with strong magic in Clearwall were often brought to the Keep to be properly trained in a monastery or paired with a mentor of similar gifts. The Gracious Queen took a special interest in giving her most talented subjects every chance to reach their full potential. Clearwall Keep was not supposed to be a frightening place any longer.

But Ehryn's heart hammered in her chest, and she readjusted her sack, trying not to notice the way the ground felt almost spongy under her feet. The rot no one else noticed or acknowledged. The Voices on the Wind chittered as she approached the Faoii at the gates. The warriors looked at her expectantly.

Ehryn shifted nervously. Was she supposed to bow? Introduce herself? She'd seen some people make an inverted triangle with their hands before, but it wasn't common and she wasn't sure what it meant. Would it be offensive if she tried?

"Good morning, citizen," one of the Faoii said after a few moments of awkward silence. "Can I direct you?" She sounded kind, but Ehryn didn't feel any calmer.

"I… I have a summons from Jacir Harkins of Clearwall Keep," she finally stammered out.

The other Faoii frowned. "The Royal Arcanist? May we see your summons?"

Ehryn fumbled with the parchment, tried to hand it to the Faoii without anyone noticing her sweaty, shaking palms. She wasn't very good at reading. Was it possible that she'd gotten the words wrong? Would they arrest her if she had? Or would they be angry that she'd wasted their time? But she'd recognized the symbol of the crown and star over a river. She knew it meant Clearwall Keep. The symbol was on the gate in front of her. On the flags that fluttered above the parapets. She was at the right building, if nothing else. So maybe they wouldn't be too upset.

It was the other symbol she was worried about. An inverted triangle with a clockwise spiral that had been literally woven on to the parchment with multicolor thread. The Faoii at the library had said that was Jacir Harkin's mark. She'd been so careful. She couldn't have messed this up. She couldn't—

The Faoii handed back her parchment, interrupting Ehryn's anxious internal monologue. She finally realized that the Voices on the Wind were trying to calm her, but she hadn't heard them over the sound of her own heartbeat.

Ehryn must have looked as scared as she felt, because the Faoii smiled kindly. "Do not worry, Citizen. Everything seems to be in order. Would you like someone to escort you to the Royal Arcanist? The Keep can be confusing to those who are not used to it."

Ehryn swallowed hard and nodded uncertainly. "Yes, please," she stuttered.

The Faoii gave her another warm smile before reaching up and sounding the great bronze bell hanging by the side of the gate. After a few moments, a young boy ran up to meet them. "Greetings, Faoii. How may I assist?" he asked, making his hands into an inverted triangle and bowing his head as he approached.

"Hrotul, this is Mistress Ehryn, special guest to the Royal Arcanist. Please escort her to his tower."

The young boy turned to Ehryn and did something she never would have expected.

He bowed.

"If you'll follow me, milady?"

Stunned and not fully sure that she was experiencing reality, Ehryn nodded and followed silently. The Faoii at the gate fisted their hands one over the other as she passed them and resumed their post. Hrotul ran ahead to pull open the grand wooden door for her, bowing again as she went inside.

Ehryn had never seen such a building before. Its walls were built of gleaming white stone, and high, multicolored windows of actual glass cast beautiful patterns on the tiled floor and thick rugs and rich blue wall hangings. The Clearwall Crest—the crown and star over the Starlit River—was on almost everything, the silver thread bright and eye-catching against the deep blue that Queen Isolde favored. Ehryn wanted to reach out and feel the soft velvet of the tapestry closest to the door but refrained. She didn't want to be asked to leave.

As gorgeous as the building was, though, it felt… cold. Distant. The blues and silvers reminded her of the Starlit River at twilight, but there was nothing of the coursing pull to explore the grandeur of a distant continent from within these stone walls. Clearwall Keep was a monument unto itself, closed off from all the moving, binding cords that surrounded the rest of Imeriel. There was no room for anything outside of Clearwall in this monument to her greatness.

Ehryn shuddered at the sudden disconnect of threads she hadn't even been aware of until they'd been cut off. The Voices on the Wind whispered that it felt like a prison. A mausoleum. But she saw it more like the fishbowls that some of the other children kept. One's entire world in too small a space, completely unaware of oceans.

Hrotul waited patiently to one side for a few minutes before he cleared his throat softly, drawing Ehryn back to the present. She smiled sheepishly and hurried to him as he led her up the grand, carpeted staircase in the center of the room. Ehryn couldn't help but run her fingers across the beautifully carved banister.

At the top of the stairs Ehryn got a glimpse of the grand throne room with its astonishing chandeliers and stately, highbacked throne. There was a small crowd of people inside, waiting for their turn to speak with Queen Isolde. As Hrotul led her past the open doors, Ehryn had the quickest glimpse of the powerful ruler and her rich, flowing robes. But then Hrotul was already leading her away from the main entry hall and up another, smaller staircase.

The further they got from the entrance of Clearwall Keep, the less extravagant the decorations became, though there was still no lack of luxury in the tapestries and beautiful paintings. Ehryn had seen such things before—many people decorated their homes with beautiful items made by Clearwall's many talented craftsmen— but she had never been somewhere where *everything* was so delicate. So… untouched and pristine.

It was only after Hrotul finally led her across a parapet and to a lone tower that Ehryn felt that she could breathe again. Until the inside took her breath away.

The home of Jacir Harkins, Royal Arcanist of Clearwall, was so much more than just a tower. It was filled with a stunning, gorgeous variety of plants, carvings, and paintings, most of which Ehryn could not name or place. The ceilings and walls were covered with constellations that Ehryn had never seen and beautiful landscapes she'd never dreamed of.

Suddenly all the beauty and luxurious splendor of the Keep proper was forgotten, the velvet hangings and carpets no more important than the stable her mother kept their donkey in. Surely this—whatever this was—was what it meant to be rich.

Hrotul cleared his throat, once again pulling Ehryn from her reverie. She turned to him to apologize and realized he was bowing towards the stairs. She followed his gaze to see the slippered feet of the Royal Arcanist descending towards them. She hit her knees on reflex, bowing her forehead until it touched the woven rug on the floor.

The Royal Arcanist laughed softly. "There's no need for that, Mistress Ehryn. You may stand." Cautiously, Ehryn raised her head, but did not move from her kneeling position. "Please. Please. Stand up," the Royal Arcanist said again, motioning her up with his hands. She did and, still smiling, Jacir took the last few steps towards her.

"Thank you for your assistance, Hrotul. You may go," the old man said without looking away from Ehryn. Hrotul nodded and backed quietly out of the room.

Ehryn fidgeted with the hem of her tunic, not sure what she should do. Should she make eye contact? Keep her head bowed even if she was standing? Had it been a mistake to come here? Or someone here must have made a mistake by inviting her. There was no reason for the Royal Arcanist to request her presence. He must have thought she was someone else. She'd just explain it to him and then go home.

Ehryn opened her mouth to speak, but Jacir had turned away from her, hands clasped behind his back, looking across the span of portraits and constellations that covered the walls and ceiling.

"I saw you admiring them when you first came in," Jacir said quietly, the same way one might speak to a timid horse. "Tell me, Mistress Ehryn. What do you see?"

Ehryn looked at the pictures again, wishing she knew what he expected her to say. "They're lovely," she finally whispered. "They look like... dreams." The words escaped her mouth before she could even really realize what she was saying, and Ehryn was immediately embarrassed. "I mean... they look... it's just that..." She choked on air, coughed several times, and tried again. "They're very pretty." She lowered her head, flustered. The tall man beside her chuckled softly, though the sound was not unkind.

"Pretend for a moment that you weren't ashamed of the first thing you said. They look like dreams. What did you mean by that?"

Ehryn's face felt hot. "Sir?"

"I'm being serious, Mistress. Tell me why that was the first thing you thought of."

"It's just... I feel like I've seen them before. Like I've been there. I know I haven't, but they remind me of dreams. Memories of things that aren't real. That slip through your fingers when you try to grasp at them. They drift like clouds through the sky, ethereal and ghostly... And... like clouds... I... I know they're real. I just can't reach them." Ehryn wasn't sure she'd ever sounded so dumb before. She wanted to go home.

The Royal Arcanist didn't seem to notice. "Do you *want* to reach them?" he asked with a smile.

"Sir?" Was he making fun of her?

"If you could. If you had the ability to reach out to these paintings and walk on the sands and grasses and beside the oceans they present. If you could talk to the people you met or smell the flowers you found, would you?"

Ehryn frowned. "Why are you asking me this, Sir?"

The Royal Arcanist smiled. "Because I want to know what you'll say."

Ehryn bit her lip and looked up at the paintings that were both real and not. They seemed so alien to her. So distant. The prospect of seeing anything outside her little walled city and her ever-moving Starlit River was frightening. Overwhelming. She enjoyed the comfort of her home. Of the life she knew.

And the light in her mother's eyes would extinguish completely if Ehryn left, too. Forever.

"I don't know, Sir," she finally whispered, afraid to deny him outright. "It... scares me, knowing how big the world is and how little of it I understand or can control. There are streets in Clearwall I've never ventured down. Alleys I've never looked at. I could spend my entire life in this city and never see all of it. Never know everyone who lives here. That should be enough."

"Is it?"

"What?"

"Is it enough?"

Jacir looked at her so intently, so knowingly that something broke in Ehryn's heart beneath his gaze. Words started tumbling from her lips before she could stop them. Her eyes were wet and she didn't know why.

"I don't want to leave, Sir. It would kill my mother. It would break my father. They need me. But... but..." She was sniffling now, and Jacir was still looking at her so calmly, so wisely, that she couldn't think of anything she could say that he didn't already know. Something in his eyes asked simply for the truth, and she could not deny him. "But at the same time... it feels like I already know all of the people here. Like I've already experienced everything that life has to offer in this this little bowl. And I *am* afraid of what lies beyond the walls, but... they call to me. Sometimes at night it feels like every blade of grass and scrap of bark are screaming out for me to come. They sound so pained. So trapped. Like they just want to be heard."

Ehryn pressed her hand over her mouth, surprised and ashamed and feeling guilty about everything she'd said. She was crying and she didn't even know why, and the frustration made it harder to stop her tears. The Royal Arcanist produced a silk handkerchief and offered it to her.

"Don't be embarrassed, Miss. Sometimes the truth is hard, but you should never be ashamed of acknowledging it. Though I think normally you would not be so outward about it. I apologize for that; my sister used to spend a lot of time in this tower with me, and I think parts of her might have seeped into the walls." He smiled brightly at that, but Ehryn didn't understand the joke.

After she'd had time to compose herself, Jacir spoke again. "About these pulls you say you feel. And the Voices on the Wind."

Ehryn's heart beat faster in her chest. She was certain she had not mentioned those who sounded the Call by name. "Sir, how did you--?"

"I've watched the Weave since before you were born, Mistress. I know how to recognize a Called in the strands." He looked very sage for a moment, but then he laughed. "I'm just kidding, Mistress. It isn't anything as mystical as all that. The Princess Namaoii told me a laundress had introduced herself as one of the Called after that unfortunate incident in the square. I'm sure she didn't say so herself, but what you did was very brave."

"It was nothing, Sir."

"On the contrary—I know how much you strive to blend in. I can see it in your face and the way you hold yourself. That must have been very frightening for you, to strike out from the crowd. Especially when there were so many others who could have saved the princess instead. But none of them did. What made you step forward so readily when no one else dared try?"

"The… The Voices on the Wind told me to. They said it was my destiny. And they were… very frightened, Sir. I'd never heard them afraid before."

Jacir nodded and stroked his beard. "There are a great many things that we know nothing about, Ehryn. Secrets buried for centuries. Powerful beings lost in slumber. They were silent for so long that most of us forgot they existed, but it seems that now they are finally finding their voices again. That they speak of destinies and fear would be enough to make even the Faoii tremble, but no one else can hear the whispers enough to be afraid. I'm so sorry, Miss. It is a burden you do not deserve."

Ehryn stared at the Royal Arcanist. He looked older than he had a few minutes before, his eyes reflecting centuries beyond what any ordinary person had ever seen. She drew away, trying to find out where the joke was. She had the sudden, undeniable certainty that he was making fun of her, but couldn't figure out how or why. She looked at the pictures again, felt the calling from below the wind and waves and grass, and for a moment she was certain that all of it was simply a trick. Some sort of illusion so that this powerful, reclusive man could draw her here and make fun of her. And it didn't help that the Voices had been silent since she'd entered this tower with its walls steeped in magic she didn't understand.

"…Sir?" she repeated again, her voice quivering.

Jacir's eyes returned to normal at her whisper, and he looked embarrassed. "Oh dear, I've frightened you. I'm sorry, Mistress. I forget sometimes that such grand things must be broken into smaller chunks. Let me try again. If, Mistress Ehryn, I gave you the means to travel to these places that call to you, would you want to go? I need nothing from you—only your eyes to see them. Your ears to hear them. I simply want you to explore the earth that pulls you forward and, when you are satiated with it, to return and tell me what you learned."

Ehryn stared at him, caught off guard by the sudden change in the air. But the Royal Arcanist just continued to look at her hopefully, the aura of centuries and secrets gone. The air was lighter, and his words finally started to make sense.

"Sir? Are you offering to sponsor my kintar?"

"I am, indeed, Mistress. You are of the proper age, and you are one of the few people in Imeriel with the ability to hear the Voices on the Wind. The Starlit Throne and I are both interested in learning more of your abilities, and we would be happy to fund your kintar, as well as pay your family for any information you bring back with you. Knowledge helps all of Clearwall, after all."

Ehryn didn't know how to respond. She knew what her parents thought of the kintar. Thought of her brother and how he'd never come home from his. But to be offered sponsorship by the crown? By the Royal Arcanist? Were you allowed to just… say no to that?

If she refused, would he be angry? Would he talk to her again about destiny and sleeping gods? Would the Queen force her to go or imprison her or worse? Ehryn's heart began to beat faster. She had spent her entire life doing whatever she could to please those around her. She was not the type of person to say no. But saying yes to this… she pictured her mother's lightless face.

Finally, not knowing how to respond, Ehryn groped for something—anything else—to talk about, and she found herself staring at the pictures again. They seemed too close now, like the walls were nearer than they should be. Struggling to breathe, she focused on the painting, trying to count each brushstroke. "What's this one?" she asked, trying not to let her voice break.

The Royal Arcanist followed her pointing finger to a strange machine. It looked like a bloated fish with too many fins. Even without seeing him, she could hear that his eyes lit up with excitement when he answered. For a moment, the Royal Arcanist sounded like an excited child.

"Isn't it wonderful? It's an airship! It can fly like a bird. Well… sort of. It's more like it swims like a fish but in the air. It uses heat and fire and water all at once to propel itself. Truly a marvelous thing to behold! After centuries of not being able to do anything, the people of Imeriel are fairly bursting at the seams to create and invent! And look at what they're capable of! That's not the product of gods or chants or oaths. That is the ingenuity of mortals!" He laughed out loud, and the sound was warm. Despite everything, it made Ehryn feel comforted. "Of all the gifts the Faoii praise, intuition and curiosity are some of the most magical, and hardly anyone remembers to marvel properly! Isn't it amazing?"

"Is it here in Clearwall?"

"Not yet. But someone will create it soon enough. You watch and see. Or maybe they'll make something even better. So hard to know ahead of time. The Weave is filled with possibilities."

Mention of the Weave and the unknowable future brought the anxiety back again, and Ehryn didn't respond, her mouth dry. Jacir must have noticed because he put a hand on her shoulder. "This is a lot to process, I know. But I haven't forgotten why I asked you here. Why don't you go home and think it over? If you decide you want to accept the sponsorship and go on your kintar, come back to me. I will be happy to oblige you." He smiled again and turned to head back up the stairs, then paused. "Wait. Let me give you something… here." He produced another piece of parchment like the one she had been issued by the messenger at her door this morning, then frowned. "Where did I put that ink pen? Do you see one around here?"

Ehryn carefully picked one up from a low table and offered it to him. The Royal Arcanist's eyes sparkled as he saw it, holding it like a precious gem when he took it from her.

"Fancy that this would be the pen you find amongst all of the clutter in here. I thought I'd lost it."

Something about his voice reminded Ehryn of a garden for some indiscernible reason, but before she could piece it together, Jacir had already scribbled something onto the scroll and handed it back to her. "Here you are. This will direct the Faoii at the gate to lead you here again. You don't have to speak to them at all if you don't want to. Nor do you have to return, should you choose not to. I don't mind. This will be the last you hear from me if that is your decision, do not fear. I understand what it's like to feel uncomfortable in strange situations. Not a pleasant feeling at all." He winked, gave her a slight bow, and turned to the stairs again. "Take care of yourself, Ehryn of Clearwall. May the Voices on the Wind either quiet or lead you somewhere grand."

5

Ehryn walked home and thought about what the Royal Arcanist had said. Wondered what her mother would say. Thought about Dhruv's kintar and the empty spot at their table. And when she finally made her way back through the twisted streets of Clearwall to the little house near the Starlit River with its hand-carved shutters and quaint porch, she listened outside the door. Even after all these years she still expected to hear her mother singing from inside, but there was only silence. Ehryn wasn't sure the chandler would ever sing again, but she still waited outside the door for a few extra moments each day, hoping for a sound that never came.

Finally, Ehryn pushed open the door, hanging her cloak on its peg with the Royal Arcanist's scroll still shoved into the pocket sleeve. "I'm back."

The light was back in Everly's eyes as she smiled around the wick in her mouth, her hands covered in peeling wax. Ehryn's heart sighed in relief. As much as the Elisians pulled Everly to a place no one else could go, she was still a bright and happy woman when she had other things to occupy her thoughts. She was still Ehryn's mom. Ehryn didn't want to jeopardize that by going on her kintar. She didn't want to be another Dhruv.

But the Voices on the Wind still pulled her north, begging. Pleading.

She'll be alright.

We need you.

Help us.

Ehryn shook away the Call and returned her mother's smile. Similarly, Ehryn's father hummed from above the wash tub on the other side of the kitchen. The shirt he was scrubbing was nicer than anything they'd ever cared to own, and the new patronage of one of the most famous acting troupes in Clearwall had the entire family in high spirits. No one was able to get stains out of linen quite like Cole could, and his abilities were being recognized. It was not easy work, but both of Ehryn's parents took pride in being good at what they did.

"How did it go, Ehryn? How many did he buy?" Ehryn's mother asked cheerfully as she set the wicks in two freshly-poured candles and hung them above their wax-crusted table.

Ehryn stopped. She'd forgotten about the candles in her sack. She hadn't even taken them out to show the Royal Arcanist.

"None," she finally replied. "He didn't buy any, Mother."

Everly frowned. "None? Was there something wrong with the quality? I was very proud of that batch. Surely the Royal Arcanist doesn't have a better supplier? What did he say?" She peeled the flaking wax from her hands and returned it to the bucket where she'd later melt it down again for other pieces. Ehryn shook her head.

"He wasn't looking for candles at all. He was looking for… me."

"For you?" Cole pinned the fine shirt near the silkstrand furnace to dry and wiped his hands on his apron. "Sit down, Daughter. You look so frightened. Tell us everything."

Ehryn did, doing her best to describe the Royal Arcanist with his tower and the portraits on the wall. Her parents listened in awe, and as she detailed the amazing sky fish and the beautiful, impossible landscapes, her heart began to lighten. The fear was gone now that she was out from beneath Jacir's watchful gaze, and she was left with only the amazement at everything she'd seen. She thought her mother would enjoy the tale, but Everly's face only became gloomier until finally Ehryn fell silent.

"What is it, Mother?" she finally asked, ashamed that she'd gotten so excited that she'd missed her mother's hollow eyes.

"He wants to take you away from me. He wants you to leave. We can't deny the Starlit Throne. The Queen and the Faoii and the Royal Arcanist… we can't tell them no. But he wants to take you away from me. I lost one child to the kintar. I won't lose you, too."

Ehryn clutched her mother's hand, paintings and ceiling constellations forgotten. "He said I don't have to go, Mother," she said quickly. "I won't go. I'll stay here with you." Her heart twisted at the anguish on her mother's face. "I'll stay, Mother. It will be okay. I promise."

Everly was sobbing now, and it was Cole who reached across the table to place a hand over Ehryn's as she desperately tried to console her mom. "Wait a moment, Daughter." Cole hadn't spoken at all while Ehryn laid out everything she had seen, but his eyes had filled with wonder at her descriptions of the tower room and its collage of art and song. More than that, though, Ehryn thought she'd seen pride in his smile.

Everly turned to her husband. "Wait? What do you mean, 'wait?' You heard her! The Royal Arcanist wants to take our baby! Wants to send her to gods-know-where!"

Cole frowned softly and shook his head. "I didn't hear that at all, Everly." He reached out and took her other hand, brushing a piece of wax off her thumb with his soap-scented fingers. "I heard our daughter speak with excitement and joy for the first time in years. I heard her marvel at places we'd never dream of seeing. I heard the waves in her voice and saw the changing of leaves in her eyes." He smiled at Ehryn. "I understand your reluctance to take the Royal Arcanist up on his offer, Daughter. Such a wonderful opportunity must surely come with a catch. But to hear you speak just now... there's something more in those pictures than what you're saying, isn't there?"

"Father?" Ehryn didn't know what to say.

Cole squeezed her hand. "You've always been a timid thing. But that girl—that woman I saw a few moments ago—that was not the Ehryn I know, who stares longingly at rivers and twists leaves from distant trees into her hair. That was the Ehryn I always thought I saw hiding below the surface. And she was quite a wonder to see, just now." He leaned over and kissed her forehead. "I thought she'd been lost. I want you to have the chance to find her, Daughter. If that's what you want."

"Cole! You can't be serious! We can't lose her, too! We can't—"

But Ehryn's father was still staring at her. "There's something out there, isn't there, Ehryn?"

"The Call—" Ehryn began, but Cole shook his head.

"No. I don't care what the Voices on the Wind say. Or what the Royal Arcanist said or anything else. What do *you* want to do?"

Ehryn looked past her father to her mother's stricken face, watching the tears flow down her withered cheeks from eyes that had lost their sparkle. She swallowed. "I don't want to leave you," she whispered. "I don't want to be another Dhruv." And she didn't. She didn't want the responsibility of everything Jacir had said, nor the responsibility of her mother's heartache. It was too much.

Couldn't they just stay how they were and catch a few wisps of happiness as often as possible? Wasn't that enough?

Cole's face fell a little, and he looked between Ehryn and Everly. Finally, he wrapped his arms around both of them, giving each a kiss on the forehead.

"You are a good daughter, Ehryn. I wonder sometimes that we have not been good parents. You have always framed what you want from the world through the question of what you think would make us happy. Even now you answered the question of "what do you want" with an answer about what you don't. But if the world is offering you so much... as parents, we should want you to experience that, too."

Ehryn's mother cried harder, the floodgates opened after Ehryn's mention of Dhruv. Cole rubbed her back soothingly as she wept into his shoulder, but he held Ehryn's gaze. "Think on it, Daughter. If no one's happiness but your own mattered, what would you want?"

"I couldn't be happy if the people around me were not, Father."

"And we shouldn't be capable of joy if you do not find it yourself, Ehryn. That is what family is." He kissed the top of Everly's head again as her sniffles faded. "Think on it for a few days. And for once, I want you to think only of yourself. Promise me that?"

But Ehryn looked at her mother's worn, broken expression and made up her mind immediately. She'd never leave them and give her mother a reason to look that way again.

That night, Ehryn sat on the docks and watched the Starlit River flow by in the darkness. She'd tried to sleep, but the space between her bones had pulled her forward in the twilight. In her dreams she'd watched the Starlit River flow through rocky canyons and lush valleys. She'd witnessed offshoots of it twist their way through forests and swamps. Had gazed upon flowers even more beautiful than the ones she and Dhruv had planted in their youth and smelled scents other than those of fish and woodsmoke. And eventually, all of those rivers and streams led to the sea.

The sea. Where beasts bigger than houses floated in serene darkness. Where sunlight filtered through water and danced on shells and sand and creatures that others would call monsters. Where ships so unlike the ones that came to Clearwall sailed.

At last she'd woken and padded barefoot to the docks, hoping that seeing the real waves would release her from the ethereal ones. But she could not be free of them.

There was something else, too. Something that pulled across the earth in the same way that the sea pulled the rivers and streams forward. Something far to the north, past the inlets and the forests and the cities she knew about. It was where the Voices came from, crying out from somewhere dark and cold and ancient. Ehryn felt that she could follow those coursing threads of power forward if she truly wanted to, following them in her dreams like she followed the rivers. But even with the encouragements and promises of safety from the Voices on the Wind, she was afraid. Whatever waited at the end of that journey was bigger and deeper than even the sea was. Greater than the air and the sky and the earth. She did not want that responsibility, but it urged her forward. And some deep part of her, through the fear, yearned to answer the Call.

As Ehryn walked back home late that night, listening to the whispers of the wind and stars, she was resolute that she would not leave her mother to cry alone in their house over candles that would not hold their shape when softened by salty tears.

But she still felt that flicker of candlelight that her father had offered her—the smallest spark of dreams and hope for what was out there, fanned by the idea that she would not be disappointing her loved ones. It grew in her chest until it almost erupted into a bright blue flame that she knew could burn out all of her uncertainty. But she beat it down again—drenched it with her mother's sadness.

Ehryn was happy in Clearwall. She loved her parents and could live here until the end of her days. It was enough. It had always and would always be enough.

But the tiniest ember refused to die.

6

Alathi saw a speck form on the Tapestry and watched with interest. Just a smudge at first, barely noticeable. But then it grew. It moved. And eventually it began to color the strands.

Alathi was fascinated.

They were young, these mortals who had clawed their way from mud and ash. They had grown from the Tapestry and now wove their threads across it in a beautiful array of potential and promise. But they were young. Unformed. They were like animals, caring only about their own survival, without plan or fear of what the future might bring. They did not know yet how to expect a future at all.

Alathi pitied their weakness. Their need. It seemed cruel that the Tapestry would let such creatures rise this far without spines or claws or fangs. Such an unjust existence. Surely they would be wiped out quickly by a world that was better equipped than they were, despite such promise. A pity.

But the mortals were tenacious things. Stubborn. Angry. And they grew enough to call for aid against all that would oppose them, for the tools to defeat that which would kill them. They screamed their challenge and asked for help against beasts and cold and famine.

The mortals called for War.

And Alathi heard them.

Amazed that such little things could tap into the power of the Weave enough to make themselves known within the threads, Alathi chose a worthy form and went to them. Cared for them as one does a favored tool. At first, they were nothing without Her arm to guide them, but neither was the hammer or the blade.

The mortals grew beneath Her call. Became stronger than the monsters that stalked them. Became worthy instruments against elements and beasts.

Now She stood before Her first hunters, bathed in ice and snow. Furry creatures with long fangs and claws circled warily, growling in fury and hunger. Alathi lowered Her spear, released Her cry. She drew the magic of the Tapestry and all its power up through the ground. Through Her lungs, Her vocal cords. The mountains shook when She released Her roar into the night. The beasts stopped circling, standing on paws that shook with something more than cold.

Behind Her, Alathi's first warriors released their own primitive war cries, following Her path. She felt the magic rise up through their feet, their arms, their screams. The howls twisted around each other. Knotted. Tightened. Flew through the air, sharp and cold and gleaming.

The beasts scattered, whimpering in fear. All except for one, which fell to its side. Its blood and flesh spread across the snow, shredded by battle magic. The first to fall before Her warriors' spells.

Alathi nodded at Her followers, pleased, and turned Her little humans against the monsters that could not hear Her call. Those animals that could be used for food or warmth. Steppingstones for Her little mortals' ascension.

She taught them how to call upon the magic of the Weave with grunts and roars. Primitive battle cries.

They were the Danhaid.

Her claws.

7

Ehryn hummed while folding the pile of freshly cleaned napkins her father was adding to. While Jacir had been telling the truth—no Faoii had come forward to demand Ehryn's return to Clearwall Keep—a different representative of the palace had sent for her father the day before. Ehryn's heart had climbed into her throat. Would they hurt her parents in a desperate effort to convince her to take the kintar? Would they break up their little family one way or another in their bid to know about the Call?

But the Starlit Throne had only come with an offer of work for Cole. To wash the linens of the royal palace! He'd even be allowed to work in Clearwall Keep if he desired, though Cole had refused.

"It's peaceful here," he'd said when Ehryn asked why he didn't want to work in the splendor of the palace. She'd tried again to describe what she'd seen to her father, but Cole didn't seem interested. "There's no splendor the palace can offer me that would be more beautiful than doing my work surrounded by my family," he'd replied.

Ehryn respected her father's devotion and pride. There were grand stories of people whose magical gifts had shifted the world and everything in it. It was said that members of the Clearwall family were graced with voices that inspired thousands. The Royal Arcanist could navigate paths through the Eternal Tapestry that no one else could see. The Faoii of old had been able to turn the tides of battle with a song.

Most people saw these people and thought that that was what it meant to be great, but Cole believed that every person's abilities, no matter how small, should be considered equally important. "Why else would the goddesses give them to us if they weren't meant to be grand in someone's life? Your mother's candles can burn for hours during a thunderstorm. Without her, we would have never been able to find that little boy when the Starlit River flooded. Who knows how many other lives she's changed, even though we'll never know about it? There is no insignificant magic."

Queen Isolde seemed to agree. There had never been a war during Ehryn's lifetime, and she did not know what the people who knew war magic did during the regular day-to-day, but Clearwall, under the Gracious Queen's guidance, seemed to make a conscious effort to look for the value in every person's gifts. Those who could coax life from the earth or mend bones were as important to Clearwall's infrastructure as those who painted or sang. The libraries that the Faoii had founded in the past (before Elise the Queen of Dark Iron had desecrated them) were open again, and craftsmen and artists were encouraged to hone their skills.

Inventions, however, were most often backed by the coffers of Clearwall Keep. Grand mills outside the city proper were used to manufacture steel and iron, which was then used to create elaborate equipment and tools that Ehryn couldn't even name. Homes were finely decorated with beautiful tapestries or carvings and warmed by silkstrand furnaces that hummed pleasantly at night. As the buildings of Clearwall rose higher and sturdier, as the ships that left her docks came back more often and more quickly, and as farmers produced higher quality crops with less waste, Ehryn truly understood what Queen Isolde meant when she spoke about the greatness of Clearwall.

But as the people of Clearwall grew more inventive and industrious, so did the Voices on the Wind grow louder.

And the stern, ancient voice that the others trembled before was the loudest of all.

None of this is the work of goddesses, Child. This is what has come after you've broken free of those who trap you and others beneath the Weave. Is it not grand? What might you do if the grip of the False Children was loosened further? I can show you the benefit of true divinity. But you must help us.

Help us.

Come.

Ehryn shook the Call away. Tried to bury it deep within herself as she dove into helping her parents with their duties. Tried to ignore it the same way that everyone else ignored the rot beneath Clearwall. She'd already decided not to go on her kintar. Had chosen not to give her gift to the Starlit Throne. She would help her parents excel in their own abilities, and they would all be happy. The Voices could quiet now. She did not need them.

But they didn't. Instead, the Voices and the pull and the desperation on the wind got louder. Stronger. Ehryn couldn't sleep at night, her dreams yanking her to the north with desperation and fury. It was not the sweet, gentle rolling of a stream towards the ocean that she had always followed before. It was the gale of ice through mountain passes, howling like tortured souls, and she'd wake, shivering in the darkness, her entire being begging her to follow the pull. To silence the cries.

Help us.

Sometimes it would get quieter if she walked through the twisted streets of Clearwall or sat beside the black waves of the Starlit River in the dark. Sometimes, she could almost pretend that things were like they used to be before she'd heard the Voices on the Wind for the first time. When she and Dhruv could spend hours in the garden, unbothered by anything other than their seedlings and the stars.

The wailing screams were so desolate that sometimes Ehryn thought she would go mad if she could not silence them. Sometimes she wondered if it was the sound of every person who had heard the plea and ignored it, cursed to call others forward for all eternity.

And when she glimpsed her reflection, her eyes had become as empty as her mother's.

You trade the suffering of one for that of two.
Nothing gained. So much lost.
Not just for you. For everyone.
Help us.

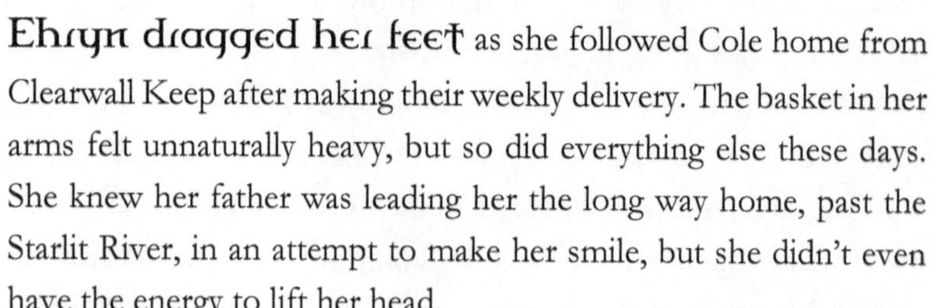

Ehryn dragged her feet as she followed Cole home from Clearwall Keep after making their weekly delivery. The basket in her arms felt unnaturally heavy, but so did everything else these days. She knew her father was leading her the long way home, past the Starlit River, in an attempt to make her smile, but she didn't even have the energy to lift her head.

There was no longer any relief. Every moment of her consciousness was consumed by the image of her mother's distraught face and the wailing Voices on the Wind competing for her attention. She could not sleep. Could no longer taste food. Didn't know anymore what was right or if anything was. If a Hollowed walked up to her, Ehryn thought she would let it touch her, steal her magic, empty her… Maybe then the Call would stop. Being magicless could not possibly be any worse than where she was now.

She hadn't even realized they'd made it home until her father stopped her from walking up the front steps as she would have normally done. Gently, he took her basket from her and set it by the door, then tilted her chin up until she was facing him. His eyes were sad as he studied her face.

"Come with me, Daughter."

Ehryn did, following her father through the little gate that led to the garden. He sat on the carved bench that he'd made with Dhruv when she was young and put one arm around her shoulders. She leaned into him, breathing in the scent of soap and clean linen.

"It's been a long time since we sat out here." Cole's voice was kind, but Ehryn couldn't bring herself to meet his eyes. She brushed her hand over a persistent ivy twisted through the bench's armrest, still alive despite her lack of attention to it in recent years. The rest of the garden was barren, a graveyard of crushed leaves and her brother's forgotten laughter.

"I remember when this garden was filled with grand, exotic plants," Cole mused. "You and Dhruv created a paradise within this little picket fence. The colors and smells—we'd never seen anything like it before, nor have we seen anything so splendid since. Do you remember?"

Ehryn's heart clenched at the mention of her brother's name. She wasn't sure if it was easier or harder hearing her father speak of his only son. He never sounded sorrowful when he spoke of Dhruv. Only proud. His eyes twinkled in a way that her mother's didn't when he discussed the past.

"I know that you stopped gardening after we lost your brother, and I understand. But sometimes I miss the beauty you coaxed from the ground here. The way your eyes lit up when you talked about finding new seeds and breeding new flowers. It was magical, the way you sought new things just for the chance to share them with your mother and me. The way you found things that no one else knew the name of. That no one else had ever seen." His eyes roamed the garden like he could see every plant that had ever flourished within its barren planters. "I wish I knew how to help you find that again, Daughter. I don't care about a voice that beckons you or a queen who orders you. I care about the things that bring you joy. In the end, that's all that matters. The world has so many sad people. Too many." He looked towards the house as though listening for a song. When it was silent, his shoulders drooped, and he faced the untended garden again. "I want you to know that it's okay if you only ever bring one person happiness, my Daughter. And I would be proud if that one person was you."

Ehryn froze, not sure how to respond. Because she knew that it would make her mother sad if she left… but she wasn't sure that staying would actually make her *happy*. Was it enough to simply not take anything from the universe? Or was it her duty to add something back to it?

Ehryn sat there, completely encircled by her father's strength and love. She wasn't sure she wanted to leave the safety of her home. Of Clearwall. Of her father's embrace and her mother's hearth. She wasn't sure she wanted to know what waited for her in the void that called her forward.

But she felt the truth in her father's words. Her family had lost something deep when Dhruv had disappeared on his own kintar. She personally had lost the joy she'd once had in this little home with its little porch and little garden. She'd convinced herself she was content here…but she was not. And when she thought of the impossible landscapes and infinite faces she'd seen on Jacir's walls, she thought that maybe the joy that would set her soul on fire was out there somewhere. Possibly in the journey. Or in the discovery. Or just in the hope.

And in that moment Ehryn wanted to find it again. She wanted to try.

Somewhere on the wind, quiet voices whispered of distant mountains and stars. Of adventures yet untaken. And for once, the stories did not end with a plea for help.

Together, father and daughter watched the sun set and the stars appear. Nearly an hour passed before Ehryn finally broke the silence. "I need to tell Mother."

Cole kissed the top of her head and nodded into her hair. "Do you want me to do it, Daughter?"

"No, thank you. I want to do it myself."

Together they walked into the little home where Everly was setting the table. She smiled at them both, and for a moment Ehryn lost her nerve, afraid to dim the sparkle in her mother's eyes. But her father squeezed her shoulder and the Voices on the Wind whispered encouragement. With a deep breath, Ehryn stepped forward.

"Mother. We need to talk."

8

Ehryn tried to convince herself that she was sure of her decision as she made the winding trek back to Clearwall Keep. Eventually Everly had come out from wherever she went when she stared at nothing, though every second of watching her mother's faraway gaze had been torture to Ehryn. Eventually, though, Everly had hugged her daughter, making a valiant effort to hide her sniffles. "I can't lock you in the house forever, Ehryn. If this is really what you want to do, then… be safe. Come home again. Please, please come home. And…" She'd paused, her eyes wet with tears. "Don't go to any of the Elisian communes. I don't know what happens there. But I don't think people come back out."

Now Ehryn stood in front of the gates to Clearwall Keep again, and the same two Faoii that had been stationed there before greeted her. Hrotul once again led her to the solitary tower with its gorgeous, beckoning paintings. The Royal Arcanist smiled brightly as he descended the stairs.

"Ah, Ehryn! I thought I would see you today. Everything is packed and ready for your journey."

Ehryn frowned. "You knew I would come today?"

"I knew it was a possibility! Isn't it lovely when the threads are easy to read? Are you ready to set off?"

"Where am I to go?" Ehryn asked timidly. She looked over the paintings in the room again. Was her destination already set? Did the Royal Arcanist know something she didn't?

But Jacir only laughed, clapping his hands beneath the wide sleeves of his flowing robes.

"Wherever you want to, of course! This is your story to tell! I am only providing the means of travel and protection. I am your sponsor, not your guide."

"Will you… will you be coming with me, then, Sir?"

"How I wish I could! But I have much to do here, and the Infinite Tapestry ties me to other duties. Threads sure feel like ropes when you're entangled, don't they? But I'm sure you'll have many wonderful stories about your discoveries and adventures when you return. Take care, young Ehryn. We'll paint pictures of everything you experience when you come home."

Ehryn smiled at that. "You can see the Tapestry. You know that I'll come back, Sir?"

Jacir's smile flickered a little, and his eyes turned into infinite pools. "You know that no one can guarantee something like that. We weave the Tapestry even as we see it, and none of the threads are set before we place them. Just know that I have taken every precaution to make sure that your safety is the most likely outcome that the Tapestry has to offer. Which reminds me…" His eyes cleared, and he beckoned Hrotul forward. "Go tell the lady's escort and Kant that they should make sure preparations are ready for tomorrow. I'll inform the others." Hrotul trotted out the door.

"Escort? Others?" Ehryn frowned.

"Oh, the 'escort' is a guide more than anything. Someone who knows the land and the perils it offers, who can help you find the clearest paths to wherever you decide to go and keep you warm and safe outside the city walls. It's a big world out there, and there are rarely markets in the forest. You will need someone who can trap and hunt, and who knows how to traverse whatever path you choose."

Ehryn nodded, wringing the hem of her tunic. She hadn't thought about any of that.

Jacir smiled again. "Do not worry, Mistress. I promise you are in the best of care. If you feel compelled to follow the Voices on the Wind wherever they take you, then I will make sure you are accompanied by someone who can help clear the way."

"Who are the others? Are they Called, too?"

"No, no. Simply a few other young people asked to travel the world on Clearwall's behalf. You didn't think you were the only one who wants to see outside Her walls, did you?"

"No, Sir. Just… won't they want to go somewhere else?"

"I suppose you won't know for sure without asking them, but the stories of the Called are always some of the grandest, and you might be surprised at how eager other people are to find what greatness lies along that route. Queen Isolde often finances kintars, and I dare say that this group has particularly caught her eye. She was very careful in selecting your traveling companions."

Ehryn paled at the idea of the Queen having a vested interest in her kintar. Of being considered important to the Starlit Throne.

Jacir smiled kindly. "Don't look so worried, Miss. I think you'll get along just fine. One of them is quite an interesting lad who has been my personal servant for a few years now. It's going to be so dull around here without his company, but I'm sure I'll make do. He'll be a fine traveling companion. You'll see." He smiled and clasped his hands behind his back, looking over the collage of paintings that covered his walls.

"The kintar really is a wonderful thing, Ehryn. Nearly all of these amazing paintings and inventions have come to Clearwall because of kintars. Or they will someday." He stroked a painting that depicted a herd of animals Ehryn had never seen. When he spoke again, his voice was quieter. "We've come so far in such a short amount of time. And still we know so little. It is an honor that our ancestors never knew, these kintars. And it strengthens us as a society. As a culture. Our… ambassadors…" He chuckled slightly like it was a joke he thought she'd understand. "They quite often come back with ideas or inspiration or philosophies they couldn't have created within these walls. It's good for all of us, I assure you. But we also have to make sure you are safe." He smiled and turned towards the door. "And thus we must meet with your escort and your benefactor."

"My… benefactor?"

"Of course! You don't think I personally am paying for your supplies and guide, do you? No, no. I assure you that I spend everything I have on pens. Constantly losing the things." He laughed again. "Come along!"

Ehryn's heart dropped nearly into her stomach as Jacir the Royal Arcanist led her out of the tower and back through Clearwall Keep. But he did not turn to go down the grand staircase and out the towering doors she'd entered at her arrival. Instead, he turned and went through the ornate archway that led to the Starlit Throne.

Queen Isolde sat atop the throne that stretched towards the vaulted ceiling, its silver sheen catching the torchlight. She wore a long gown of deep blue velvet, nearly black in the places the sun and torchlight didn't touch, save for the silver threads that seemed to produce their own light tracing through its deep folds. Ehryn almost gasped at its beauty. Even her mother's most gorgeous candles couldn't compare to the splendor she found here.

Queen Isolde was speaking, and Jacir stood patiently to one side of the throne room, hands clasped behind his back, bouncing on his toes every now and again. Ehryn stayed behind him, head down, trying desperately not to make a single breath or noise while the Gracious Queen was speaking.

"Send your men to the Monastery of the Infinite Choir. I will have other forces waiting there. Then, rendezvous with the scouts watching the Elisian enclave outside of Elmswitch. I expect a full report within three weeks."

"Yes, your majesty." The armed soldier at the foot of the throne clicked her heels together and saluted before turning and marching away, several other armed guards following behind. Unlike the Faoii from outside, these soldiers had the Clearwall crest emblazoned on their breastplates.

Queen Isolde watched them go, and the sunlight from the windows behind the throne caught the sapphire pin in her hair. Its light bounced around the crystals in the chandelier and across the walls for a moment as she moved her head to speak.

"What is next, Daughter?"

Namaoii, the Wolf Pup of Clearwall, leaned forward on her own seat. It was not as grand or imposing as the Starlit Throne was, and Ehryn had not even realized she was there, even though Namaoii's armor shone nearly as much as the throne itself did.

Namaoii looked nothing like her mother. While Isolde was fair-skinned with high cheekbones and pointed features, Namaoii had her late father's tanned skin and square jaw. The Wolf Pup had her mother's dark hair, however, but wore it braided with thick iron rings. The style was similar to what Ehryn had seen the Faoii wear, though Namaoii kept her head shaved on the sides, more akin to what her father's people, the Danhaid or Alathi—Ehryn didn't know which—sported. It made the woman look fierce and powerful, more so than even the fantoii belted at her side.

The Wolf Pup looked over the few people left in the throne room until her eyes fell upon Jacir and Ehryn. Something in that piercing gaze made Ehryn want to cower even further behind the old man, but she refrained.

"Royal Arcanist Jacir. Come forward." Namaoii's barking voice demanded obedience, and Ehryn's first instinct was to scuttle forward with bowed head. Jacir, however, stepped forward with a bouncing gait.

"Your Majesty. Princess. What a lovely day, would you agree? I've brought you the final kintar candidate."

Queen Isolde smiled pleasantly, but Namaoii scowled. "Really, Mother? This one? This… urchin?"

Isolde turned a sharp eye on her daughter. "Namaoii. All citizens are *your* citizens. Your disrespect tarnishes the Starlit Throne. It is our duty to lead our people to greatness, and you dare doubt the worth of any who would help us on that path?" Isolde's voice reminded Ehryn of ice—cold, pristine, and sharp.

Namaoii raised her chin, looking like she was going to argue, but reconsidered.

"I… apologize," she finally ground out. "Royal Arcanist, please tell us who accompanies you. Introduce her to the Starlit Throne."

Isolde's eyes darkened, and she held up a slender hand. "Shame on you, Daughter. We know this girl, even without the conflicting reports I received from you and your escorts during the Elisian incident." She turned her full gaze on Ehryn, and Jacir stepped to one side to give the queen a better view. "Your name is Ehryn, is it not? The chandler's daughter. I believe we have some of your mother's work in the dining hall."

Ehryn swallowed hard. Now she'd been directly addressed by the Queen. She had to say something. Should she bow? Kneel? Introduce herself again, even though Isolde had just addressed her by name? She didn't know. And now she'd already been standing here for too long looking like a scared colt, and the queen was still looking at her. Ehryn wanted to sink into the ground.

"Yes, Ma'am… Your Majesty. Yes, Your Majesty," she finally stammered. "My mother… my mother makes good candles." Her face flushed, and all she could hear was the blood rushing in her ears and Namaoii's laughter.

"This is who you want to accompany me, Mother? Let's hope the voices in her head sound more intelligible than the one from her throat!"

Ehryn didn't say anything; she was too afraid to look up from her worn slippers that looked so ugly against the beautiful, intricately woven rug she was standing on. Her face burned in the wake of the princess's laughter.

"This is exactly the type of person I want you to accompany on your kintar, Namaoii. Perhaps she can teach you humility. To dare laugh at an untrained girl a year your junior who saved your life with a laundry basket despite the fantoii I had crafted for your hand. For shame." Namaoii stopped laughing abruptly. Ehryn still didn't look up from the floor, but she knew the Wolf Pup was glaring in her direction. You could cut the tension in the air.

It seemed like far too long before Isolde spoke again. "Step forward, Ehryn, and meet my daughter under better circumstances." Ehryn took a small step forward, and Jacir cleared his throat.

"I present Princess Namaoii, the Wolf Pup of Clearwall, Daughter of the Gracious Queen Isolde and Amanji, White Wolf of Alathi, Goddesses grant him peace in death and his daughter strength in life, heir to the Starlit Throne."

Ehryn waited a few moments to see if the Royal Arcanist was going to add anything else to the absurdly long title. When he didn't, she bowed in the direction of the smaller throne. "It is an honor, Princess Namaoii."

The princess didn't respond, and it was Isolde who broke the silence. "Since she evidently will not, I would like to formally thank you for coming to my daughter's aid, Ehryn. She might very well owe you and your laundry basket her life."

Namaoii straightened quickly. "Mother! You know that's not what happ--"

Isolde cut her off without raising her voice. "The Faoii that were with you gave me a more accurate report of what transpired than you did, Daughter. They don't know what you and this girl spoke about, but suffice it to say that there *are* people in this city who tell me the important things that happen within my domain, even if you do not." Namaoii looked like she was going to protest, but Queen Isolde turned away from her to look at Ehryn and Jacir again. "It is one of the reasons I will be sending Kantilieh with you as well, if you'll allow us to complete the formalities of this process."

"Mother! You can't expect a Called and someone like Kant worthy of--"

"Be *silent*, Daughter. We are in court. Mind your appearance, or you may leave." Namaoii clutched both arms of her chair with white knuckles but did not say anything else. Isolde gave her a long look before turning back to Jacir. "Royal Arcanist, it is my main goal in life to lead Clearwall and her citizens to greatness. The stories of the Called are some of our most honored tales, reported to the Starlit Throne by the very gods. Do you, in your wisdom, believe that sponsoring the young woman before me would facilitate this honored duty?"

Jacir nodded. "I've taken great pains to ensure that she will be able to find the source of the mysterious Call if she so chooses, Your Majesty. I humbly submit my formal recommendation that Mistress Ehryn of Clearwall be a candidate for your patronage on the kintar."

Ehryn stared at her shoes again, memorizing where the leather was beginning to wear. She envisioned those shoes turning and carrying her out of this room as quickly as they could.

"Very well. Come here, Ehryn of Clearwall. Let me look at you."

Ehryn took a deep breath and took a few more trembling steps to the foot of the dais. She raised her head until the light of the sun from the ceiling-high windows behind the Starlit Throne nearly blinded her. The silhouette of the Gracious Queen seemed to nod.

"Kneel."

Ehryn did.

"Do you, Ehryn of Clearwall, promise to use this kintar to learn more of the world, its people, and of your blessed gifts? Do you promise to use what you learn on this kintar to serve Clearwall and her people to the best of your abilities?"

Ehryn tried to swallow, but her mouth was dry. "Yes, Your Majesty."

"As a more personal question—do you promise to, should the need arise, do everything you can to protect my daughter and keep her safe on this journey?"

Namaoii barked out a harsh, incredulous laugh. Ehryn looked between the two living members of the royal family, eyeing Namaoii's sturdy frame, polished armor, and glinting fantoii. Uncertain, she glanced to Jacir for guidance, but he only smiled encouragingly.

"Your Majesty, I'm… I'm not a fighter," she managed to protest.

"Obviously," Namaoii snorted.

Isolde's face didn't change, however, and she remained straight and regal in her seat. "Nor were you that day in the square, but it did not seem to matter then. Answer the question."

"Yes, Your Majesty. I promise."

"Mother, that day in the square was a fluke. You can't possibly believe that this girl can do anything to protect *me*. Look at her."

"I never presume anyone's abilities just by looking at them, Daughter. You would be wise to learn the same." Namaoii didn't respond, and Isolde clapped her hands twice. "Very well. So shall it be. Arise, Ehryn of Clearwall."

Ehryn stood on shaking calves, and Queen Isolde nodded towards the door. "I hope that no one here expects that I would send my only heir, one of my Called, and one of the royal servants out into the vast world on a kintar without proper guidance and protection? It occurs to me that you've yet to meet your escort."

There was the faintest sound behind Ehryn, and Namaoii's gaze shot to the entrance of the throne room. Uncertain, Ehryn turned to look over her shoulder, surprised by the towering figure who greeted her gaze with an understated smile. His graceful movements reminded Ehryn of an ebony willow tree, and yet the strength that radiated from him made her think of a pillar of black quartz. But his ice-blue eyes were kind.

"Ah, yes. Here he is." Jacir smiled brightly and gestured the stranger forward. "Princess. Mistress Ehryn. Allow me to introduce you to one of Clearwall's most honored heroes." The monolith of sword and stone stepped forward.

"This is Faoli-Tendaji."

9

The next day, Ehryn waited near the docks and fidgeted with the heavy pack Jacir had gifted her. Tendaji was nearby, leaning casually, apparently at ease in the swarm of the Maze, but Ehryn could see his eyes watching every movement as they waited.

Ehryn was about to ask if she should go back to the palace and get the princess when the crowd parted with a murmur of surprise and appreciation. The Wolf Pup of Clearwall approached on a well-bred gelding, flanked by a Faoii on either side. The crowd around her knelt, their eyes drawn to the finely-crafted saddle and bright armor. Clearwall had grown into a rich city, and its citizens were comfortable, but few people left the town on foot or by horse when boat was faster, and horses within the walls were rare. Even those who had steeds on their land or stabled outside the Maze rarely spent money on such luxurious tack.

Ehryn knelt too, suddenly feeling grungy and awkward in her plain travel attire. Tendaji, on the other hand, didn't seem to be bothered at all as he stood up from where he'd been leaning, brushing the dust off his plain leather breeches.

"Namaoii. It is good to see you. We are waiting on young Master Kant, and then we may depart. We'll take a boat downstream."

"We're not riding?" Namaoii seemed disappointed as she dismounted.

"Not immediately, Your Majesty. The kintar is supposed to be a chance to explore things outside of Clearwall's influence. We can travel further on the water in a short time, and then disembark beyond the forests that you've all doubtlessly explored a thousand times already. Also, the Queen thinks you need more experience with watercrafts." Ehryn wasn't sure, but she thought she saw a bit of mirth in the old warrior's features at that last part.

Namaoii rolled her eyes. "Of course she does. Doesn't matter that Father taught me to pilot a skiff even before he died. I could probably take over any one of these heaps before she got wind of it. Twice as quickly if the Called got us some worthy help." She turned towards Ehryn, who sank into the wall behind her in response. "How about it, Almighty Called? Do your Voices on the Wind want us to become pirate queens right away or wait until we're outside the archers' range?"

"Wh… what?" Was the princess being serious? Was she allowed to flat-out deny one of the royal family if they were being crazy? Wouldn't Ehryn be the one blamed when they were ultimately caught? She looked between Tendaji and the Faoii escorts for help.

Namaoii rolled her eyes. "Broken Blade. It was a *joke*. I hope you're not like this the entire trip." She turned her back on Ehryn and addressed her still-mounted Faoii guards. "You may go back to the Keep. I'm more than safe with the Faoli." The two Faoii fisted their hands and departed, leading Namaoii's fine steed back along with them.

"Where the blades is Kant?" Namaoii fumed after the Faoii were out of sight and the crowd around them had begun to go about their business once more. "He couldn't have gotten lost, could he? Not already. We haven't even left the blasted city." Namaoii looked around the crowd impatiently, barely aware that the other people around were doing everything in their power not to look like they were noticing her, peering through the corners of their eyes.

"Do you know him? This…Kant?" Ehryn asked. Jacir and the queen had both mentioned a palace servant, but she didn't know anything else about their mysterious traveling partner. The Wolf Pup didn't respond, still scanning the crowd, and Ehryn tried again. "Princess?"

"Don't call me that!" The words were harsh and Ehryn was momentarily taken aback, not sure what she'd done to offend the other girl. Namaoii huffed through her nose and tried again. "I mean… call me Namaoii."

Ehryn just nodded, worried about saying anything else to this girl who was wound so tightly. She glanced at Tendaji, but he was scanning the crowd, arms loosely crossed over his chest. She noticed that the stance brought one hand right next to his sword hilt, and she couldn't remember if it had been like that before Namaoii's sudden outburst. She thought it hadn't been.

A few moments passed in awkward silence before Namaoii sighed and spoke again, softer this time, but still more brusquely than Ehryn thought she deserved.

"Your name is Ehryn, right? I assume you'd rather I call you that than the Almighty Called."

Ehryn nodded. "Yes, please. I know… I know you don't like the other Called. You said they abandoned Clearwall. I just… I want you to know that I don't plan to do that. I'm not like them."

"I'm sure they all said that at one point, too. But now they don't even come back to Clearwall, and we have to wait to hear about their exploits from my mother's sources." She shook her head angrily. "Did you know my father's ancestors were the first to hear those calls? The White Wolves of the Alathi were the first to call them the Voices on the Wind, and the Danhaid called them Dream Speakers. Both tribes followed the Call and now they're all gone. A few people born here followed it, too, and they never came back afterward, though my mother gets reports from time to time. Always saying that the Called bring greatness to Clearwall even if they're not here."

"You don't believe her?"

"Doesn't matter what I believe. We're all about to find out for sure, anyway. And this time, I'm going to be there to see for myself what happens at the end of the path. And I'll drag you back with me if I decide that's what's best for Clearwall." She turned away before Ehryn could respond. "Where is that blade-cursed boy?"

Tendaji nodded towards the crowd. "We need not wait for much longer, it would seem."

At first, Ehryn didn't see anything, but then there was the smallest ripple in the sea of bodies moving between the docks and the market. After a minute, a slight, wiry boy popped out.

He was quite small, and his large, untucked tunic and overflowing backpack did nothing to make him seem bigger. Between his long, gawky arms, pointed nose, and tiny frame, he looked to Ehryn like a wet mouse. His smile was the biggest thing about him.

"Hello!" the gawky boy exclaimed, giving an awkward bow to Namaoii and then waving at the other two. "I'm Kantilieh. But everyone calls me Kant. Which is strange, because they also say there's nothing I can't remember, so I don't really know why they call me that. I'm very excited to be here! We're going to see a lot of new things. And then when we get back I'll tell my baby sister all about them. Or I will as soon as she's born! Isn't that wonderful?" He beamed happily, shaking Ehryn's hand fervently. "It's so nice to meet you. Hello again, Princess!"

Namaoii rolled her eyes. "Don't call me princess. And they call you Kant because it's the first syllable of your name."

The little boy's smile broadened even more. "Oh! I never thought of that! That must be much easier for all of them. Short things are easier to remember if… if you're not like me, right?"

"Sure, Kant. I'm sure that's why they do it." Namaoii crossed her arms over her chest. "Why are you so late, anyway? Your mother said you were already packed when she served breakfast   this   morning."

Kant fidgeted with his hands. "I'm sorry, Princess Namaoii. I couldn't decide what to wear."

"Don't call me princess. And how is that possible? You only own three tunics!"

"I didn't know which one was best for this." Kant looked down at his feet. "I packed all three. Should I change?"

"No, no," Ehryn interjected, bothered by how quickly his wide smile had changed to the face of a kicked puppy. "You look lovely, Kant."

Kant's face brightened again, and he smiled up at Ehryn. "Thank you! Are you Ehryn? The Called? I heard Master Jacir mention you. I can track my lineage all the way back to some of the first people in Imeriel and then back up again. You and I are distant cousins! We had the same great-great-great-grandmother! It sounds really neat, but my family is related to most of the people in Clearwall somewhere along the line, so maybe it's not that interesting." He fisted his hands in front of him in greeting. "Anyway, I'm your cousin Kantilieh. But everyone calls me Kant."

Namaoii snorted in disapproval again. "You already said that, Kant. And the Royal Arcanist should know better than to speak about such matters in front of you. I will take it up with him when we return."

"Aw. But, Princess—"

"Namaoii."

"Aw, but Namaoii... please don't! He has the greatest stories! One time he even told me about this huge monster with scales and fire and eyes of gemstones..."

The small mouselike boy dove into a long story describing every detail of the mystical monster, and Namaoii took the opportunity to pull Ehryn aside.

"Be careful what you say around him," she ordered. "Do you understand?"

Ehryn pulled her arm from Namaoii's grasp. "Why?"

"He works in the palace. He's actually your age, but he's… touched. Gifted, definitely, but… well, look at him." She gestured to Kant, who was now telling the story to one of the goats in a nearby pen. "You see? He can remember every detail of everything he's ever seen or heard and can recite it back to anyone without error. It's a very useful sort of magic that we haven't seen anywhere else, but it's dangerous when it's poured into a mind like that."

Ehryn looked over to the little boy, who had now chosen a pig for his audience. She thought her mother's fat donkey was more dangerous than Kant could be. Namaoii caught her gaze.

"Maybe not physically, but Kant doesn't have the ability to make his own thoughts or opinions on what he knows any more than a toddler can. He can recite something back word for word, and he likes some stories more than others. But once he has information, he doesn't really know what he should or shouldn't do with it. He's incapable of lying. Of inventing stories. He can recite a thousand poems and never make up one of his own. And he doesn't understand why some stories shouldn't be shared with strangers. I'm not even sure he should be with us, but Mother wouldn't listen."

"I can see why your mother would send him with you, Princ—Namaoii. The world will want to chronicle your kintar and all that you do while on it. I think it's nice."

"Right." Namaoii spit to one side. "I'm *sure* I'm the one my mother wants to immortalize in tales. Just remember what I said, okay? Kant's magic is a priceless tool that some people would turn into a weapon. It cannot fall into the hands of Clearwall's enemies."

"Then we must be grateful that there are no enemies to the crown on this kintar." Tendaji smiled from behind the gossiping girls, making them both jump. Neither had realized he was there. "The kintar is a rite of passage, children. You have the opportunity to learn about your magics and about yourselves, but your shared experiences will help the others grow as well. Young Master Kant will need you on this journey, as you will undoubtedly need him. After all, there is always much to learn." He set a hand on both of their shoulders, then called to Kant. "Come along now. The boat awaits."

Jacix stood at the top of his tower and watched the little group board the passenger vessel that would take them away from Clearwall. At this point, he could no longer tell if he was watching them with normal eyes or through the Weave. It didn't matter. He knew what it meant to leave the safety that the twisted streets of Clearwall offered. Most people were okay. But that group below him—they weren't most people.

He thought about something his sister had taught him long ago about the safety of the Maze. Ilahna had taught him to escape guards and angry merchants. She had seen it as a place to get lost. Ilahna had been a master Mazer and could outpace anything once she was within the twisted labyrinth of Clearwall's jumbled streets. But she hadn't realized how right she was.

"There's safety in the Maze," Jacir whispered. "For as long as humans have built cities, they've known it. We learned it from the rivers first. The way they twist and turn and break up magic. Our ancestors knew that sinister creatures followed us in darkness. They made fires and burnt offerings, trying to keep those things at bay, but they were always there, just outside the ring of light. You could lose them in the rivers if they were of the land. You could lose them in the forests if they were of the water. You could lose them on the twists and turns that broke up magic and auras. So we built our cities and our walls to match the streams and forests and the natural mazes of the world. And it worked."

It worked.

But Ehryn and the others weren't staying in the Maze. Weren't protected by the twisted walls and constructed safeguards. He, Tendaji, and a dozen others had prepared for this. Had done their best to help Ehryn hide her threads from those creatures that would follow her once she stepped foot out of Clearwall. They would seep after her in darkness, drawn forth by the beacon of light that even she did not understand. How many others had left through one of Clearwall's gates to find the source of those whispered calls? No others had returned, though the Queen and whoever supplied her with their so-called exploits tried to hide such shameful failures. He'd pulled every string he could find to help ensure that Ehryn would be successful where they had not. She'd hate him if she knew. But it was necessary.

Because even now, as they crossed the threshold and sailed away from Clearwall, he knew that They knew.

And They would follow.

And worse yet, he thought that Ehryn had woken something with her Call in the square, and they might have waited too long before leaving to escape it. He hoped it was still far enough away that they would have time.

But his eye was drawn to the darkness of the forest and then the black shimmer of the Starlit River. He didn't know which was safer, if either was. He'd tried to protect them by choosing the river path.

But They would follow.

10

Ehryn wasn't sure what she'd expected from her kintar. Her mother had taken her and Dhruv camping when they were young, and she remembered sitting outside a canvas tent staring up at a million stars. She remembered going deeper into the forest with Dhruv and coming back with an array of amazing seeds and saplings neither had ever seen before. Part of her remembered meeting a woman well away from the path who smiled and laughed and had given her new seeds to plant. Part of Ehryn had always assumed that the kintar would be similar to those experiences.

Instead, however, they boarded a small passenger vessel and made their way upstream, something Ehryn had never done before despite all her time on the docks. She thought she liked this more than she would have enjoyed horseback riding, which it was obvious Namaoii was already proficient at while Ehryn had never had cause to learn. She didn't want to give the older girl yet another reason to mock her.

Besides that, Ehryn was comforted by the steady rocking of the boat and the rhythmic way the waves lapped against the sides. The seats and beds were comfortable, and the captain didn't mind that she spent most nights lying on her back on one of the deck's many benches, staring at the stars.

Tendaji was usually on the deck when she was, watching the dark waves, contemplative and silent. Some nights, however, he would sit cross-legged near the prow of the ship, describing to Kant a vast array of fish that could be found in the Starlit River and beyond. Ehryn liked these nights, thinking about the beasts as big as houses that she had sometimes seen when she followed her dreams out past the edges of the Starlit River. Other nights, Tendaji and Namaoii would practice swordsmanship, testing their balance on the uneven deck, or would discuss matters of foreign trade.

The others sought out these personal lessons whenever they could, but Ehryn was grateful that Tendaji seemed content to let her just experience the kintar at her own pace. Her heart still hurt from leaving her mother behind, and even the Voices on the Wind were no comfort as they released their continuous mournful plea.

Help us.

During the days, the deck was more crowded. Most of the other passengers were small trinket traders rather than farmers, whose perishable produce was transported by the faster cargo ships with silkstrand engines that burned hot and smelled terrible, but that moved much more quickly than anything else on the Starlit River. These other passengers—the traders and crafters—held Ehryn's attention more than Tendaji ever could. She was fascinated by watching old men with gnarled hands carve animals from wood while their grandchildren painted them. She liked listening to merchants' wives trade stories about towns they'd visited recently, and she liked hearing news of babies born and festivals planned.

Even on a small merchant ship that only sailed between Clearwall and the other communities along the Starlit River, Ehryn was surprised by the variety of lives and people outside the capital.

The most fascinating person on the ship, however, was definitely Kant with his perfectly-recited stories. His infectious smile and amazing tales seemed to brighten everyone's days, and the other passengers often made requests, grateful for the change of scenery between their often-traveled route from the capital city to the small outlying towns and villages they served. Listening to someone who exuded such joy, Ehryn almost started to feel like herself again, blooming like a wilted wildflower after the first rain of summer.

Almost. Because there was something else here, too. Something beneath the tide, coming from far-off seas.

At first, Ehryn thought it was merely the smell of fish from the docks or the silkstrand from nearby vessels, but by the third day she couldn't deny it anymore. There was something gliding along the river's bottom towards them. And whatever it was, it scared her so much that even Kant's radiance could not break through the shell.

The Voices on the Wind were uncertain, too, and chattered about being followed. That it was coming for them.

Help us.

It came on the fourth day.

They were nearing their destination—a small settlement called Crested Fir where Tendaji said there would be horses stabled and they could continue the kintar inland.

Ehryn had seen fishermen haul huge fish the size of goats from the river and knew that, while they were not the beasts from her dreams, the Starlit River held strange creatures. But as she glimpsed unnatural ripples lapping against their boat, she knew in her heart it wasn't because of fish.

"Tendaji, Sir?" she called. Tendaji stood from where he had been listening to Kant's stories and was next to her almost immediately. "I…" But she didn't know how to continue. She didn't know how to explain that the Voices had started screaming when she'd seen the odd ripples in the water. Didn't know how to explain that her heart was in her stomach and that she tasted something sour on the wind. It reminded her of the rot that she'd so often smelled in Clearwall. She thought that they'd left it behind, but now… now it was stronger than ever before.

Ehryn thought she was suffocating. Thought she would be sick. Thought that there was something truly, truly *wrong*.

"Are you okay, Ehryn?" Tendaji asked, studying her face. "Some people do not sail well. It's nothing to be ashamed of. We will be on land again soon."

"It's not that. It's…"

But she couldn't hear the sound of her own voice over the screams of the Call.

We sense Her.

It's not the Middle.

We thought the river would be safe.

She's left the ocean.

She's found us.

Help us.

Help us!

Ehryn looked to the water, eyes fixated on the ripples that were moving faster now. Surely even Tendaji could see that something was wrong. Surely the captain would notice. Surely…

"Ehryn? Are you all right?" Tendaji repeated. He followed her gaze, tensing at the eerie waves. Then, in an instant, he was between Ehryn and the edge of the boat, his fantoii drawn. "Stay behind me."

Namaoii saw Tendaji's change in demeaner and crossed the deck, her hand also on the sword buckled at her side. "What is it, Faoli?" she asked as she approached.

Tendaji didn't answer, now staring above the waves and taking a few steps back, bringing his fantoii higher. Namaoii pressed again. "Faoli, there's nothing there!"

Lend me your eyes, Child.

The strongest Voice was kind but stern. Ehryn swallowed hard. She still remembered what it had been like to lend her voice in the square. She remembered what had happened the last time she'd given in to the commands of this ancient whisper. She wasn't sure she wanted to see whatever it was that made even Tendaji seem afraid.

We need you to see.

Help us.

Look! Look! She's coming.

Lend me your eyes, Child!

The strong Voice's command was louder now, edged with annoyance and impatience.

Lend me your eyes!

The order beat against Ehryn's skull urgently. With a whimper, she finally relented. "You may use my eyes," she whispered.

"What?" Namaoii demanded, but Ehryn couldn't answer.

The boat was surrounded by torrents of spray as tall and solid as the walls of the Maze. And within the murky ramparts, something ancient swayed, rippling through their currents, getting closer.

The primordial parts of Ehryn screamed and writhed in the same way her ancestors had run from the things that came from the dark. This was the thing that had taught her bones to fear swimming in water where you couldn't see the bottom.

She wanted to run. To get away. But where could they go on a boat so small? Even Tendaji straightened defensively, still positioned directly in front of Ehryn. Namaoii mirrored him, unafraid, and the other passengers of the boat watched them warily, completely unaware of what was happening just beyond the veil. If Ehryn had been less terrified herself, she might have wondered what this scene looked like to those simple people who saw only a calm river and sunny day. It was only out of respect for the Faoii Order from which Tendaji came that stayed their tongues. And Ehryn wished that she could sit beside them, blissfully unaware of what the Faoli was willing to face on their behalf.

But Ehryn saw. And when the waves at last parted, opening like a curtain of sea spray and foam, she couldn't repress her surprised cry. Could she be called a woman, this thing with eyes so dark and deep and cold, standing taller than the trees on shore? This primordial being with blue-black hair that twisted with seaweed and silkstrand moss, dark body festooned with shells and stones and scales that smelled of saltwater and shipwrecks? Whose voice was the color of storms?

"Tiny mortals. Fear Me. Know Me. Answer Me and you may live. You do not appear on the Tapestry as you should, and you cross My domain in silence, fleeing from the sound that woke Me from the depths. Can you see Me? Hear Me?"

Ehryn thought the question was directed at her, but Tendaji, still standing between Ehryn and the water's edge, answered instead.

"I can, Lady of the Tides. Why have you come so close to our side of the Tapestry, Jaladri? What do you want from us?"

"Jaladri? What? There's nothing there! What the blades is Jaladri?" Namaoii demanded.

"Oh! I know this!" Kant cried excitedly, completely unaware of anything amiss. "Jaladri is the Goddess of Oceans! There's a book in Jacir's library with a poem dedicated to her. 'Queen of the depths and tides, empress of shipwrecks and lungs without air…'"

"Not now, Kant!" Namaoii yelled. But the mousey boy's words seemed to affect her, because she did not try to get closer to the edge of the boat, and her dark eyes roamed the water, searching for something she couldn't see.

If Jaladri heard the two kintar-goers or even cared that they existed, She gave no sign. Instead, She spoke directly to Tendaji. "The waves speak of someone who uses a voice that is not theirs. I followed the ripples in the life pond to the city on My shores, and then the wave of that power to this vessel. If it was you, I would have you speak again."

Now the others on the boat were beginning to look troubled as Tendaji spoke to no one, but, like Namaoii, they drew no closer. They could sense something in the air. A presence that wasn't there before. The smell of storm clouds and seawater, even though the sky was clear and the Starlit River fresh. The captain caught the uncertain glances from his passengers and cleared his throat before Tendaji could speak again, and Ehryn watched both the Faoli and the Goddess turn to him.

The captain walked awkwardly to where Tendaji stood, fidgeting. After a moment, he turned towards the water and fumbled in his coat for a small, worn trinket. It took several tries before he could bring it out.

"My Goddess, Jaladri, Lady of Depths and Storms." The captain raised his eyes upward, far too high to actually be seeing the Goddess he was addressing. "We of… of the faith… worship You and ask Your blessing of safe passage as we… as we begin our journey across Your coursing pathways."

Ehryn frowned. It was a prayer that was traditionally offered at the beginning of a voyage. She'd heard sailors say it on the docks. It seemed out of place now that they were nearing their destination.

The captain evidently recognized his error, too, because he mumbled an apology. "I'm sorry I haven't worshipped You as I should. I pray You forgive my lack of respect and grant my passengers safe crossing despite my error. They have done no wrong."

In a deluge of water Jaladri of the Deep liquified and repooled directly before the captain, shrinking in size until She was only marginally taller than he. The captain still could not see the Goddess, but he saw the difference in the river and paled, clutching the token to his breast. The other passengers, too, gasped at the impossible swells. Several fell to their knees, begging forgiveness from gods they'd never truly believed in before.

Jaladri sneered and looked across the boat and its cowering passengers. "You speak boldly for one who did not drop gold over the side before departing. Who came across My road without blessing or praise until I arrived to demand it." Her eyes darkened like shadows, her voice and visage growing until She was towering again. "How *dare* you. How dare all of you?"

The thunderous rumble of Jaladri's voice was like a storm, and even the regular passages looked to the sky for lightning that wasn't there. The waves around the boat churned and roiled, and even people on other vessels within shouting distance released distressed cries at the sudden rocky waters. "You have all forgotten how to worship! You have all forgotten what it is to depend on Us! I will remind you."

"Jaladri! This is not necessary!" Tendaji yelled over the sudden gale. "We ask for safe passage. The captain will worship properly in the future! He swears!" Tendaji spun to the shaking man, who had fallen to his knees, still wringing his previously-forgotten trinket in his hands. "Swear it!" Tendaji demanded. "Swear you'll make reparations, or this craft will never make it to shore!"

"I swear! I swear! Everything I have will be yours, my Queen! I will dump it all into the Starlit River as soon as I return to Clearwall. Or even make the passage to Your blessed ocean and deposit it there! I swear!"

But Jaladri, the Queen of Storms and Swells, was not one to forgive transgressions. She towered ever higher above them, streams of water falling from Her clenched fists as She bellowed in a voice that Ehryn could barely believe no one other than she and Tendaji could hear.

"I am She Who Rides the Tides. I am The Goddess of the Icy Depths. Your people knew to worship me once. To fear Me. But I have been too lax. You will remember Me. You will *all* remember Me and kneel or lay littered on My shores."

Finally, desperately, Tendaji called upon his fantoii, and its ringing cry almost outmatched Jaladri's rising tempest. "Jaladri, I cannot allow that. Allow us passage. Leave us be!" His voice rose above the gale, filled with power that tinted the air with iron. The Goddess narrowed Her eyes.

"That blade," She nearly screamed, Her voice the sound of hurricanes and waves the height of cliffs. "I know that blade. How *dare* you brandish it at Me?" The Goddess's eyes took on the same color as the dark clouds that were now swirling behind Her head. "It was you who spoke in Alathi's voice! You who threatens all We are. You will all pay for your insolence. And remember that humans are nothing without Gods."

He cannot defeat her. Even with the Eternal Blade.

You must wield it.

Take it from him. Cut her down.

Help us.

Not yet. She's not ready.

She must! It's meant to be hers!

What do we do?

The False Child will crush the boat.

You will drown. We are lost.

And then the strongest Voice spoke. The Voice on the Wind that carried to Ehryn from across time and space, as powerful and eternal and deeper than the sea. Deeper than the eyes of the Goddess that rose above them. Larger than all the power Jaladri had ever wielded. The Voice that Goddess of Oceans had called Alathi.

Lend me your voice, Child. Now!

Ehryn didn't need to be told twice this time. She let go.

The scream that broke free of Ehryn's chest was not a song or word or phrase so much as a tidal wave of destruction and demand.

"YOU HAVE FORGOTTEN WHO BOWS TO WHOM, JALADRI. REMEMBER WHO TAUGHT YOU TO HARNESS SEA AND STORM. REMEMBER ME AND TREMBLE."

The cry tore across the boat, parting the waves like a fin slicing through the water. And Jaladri, Great Goddess of the Sea, shrank back in fear as it charged.

"No. No! We trapped you! We cannot—you cannot—No!" But Jaladri was already shrinking, Her shaking shoulders lower than the tide now. "Teilithia will know of this. Mavrikal will come. We will not relinquish what is Ours, Alathi. Never again."

It was never yours.

Ehryn heard the words but could not open her mouth to speak them. Instead, her body felt hollow, and her head spun in the aftershock of the wave that had broken free of her mouth.

Ehryn reached out an arm, looking for support, but there was none. There were only a few shouts of her name as she tumbled backwards, and the quiet whisper of the Voices on the Wind.

Rest. You did well. But you must rest.

You both must rest.

Our Queen, she is silent.

She'll be okay.

You'll be okay.

But we do need you.

Help us.

11

Ehryn caught snippets of conversation as she drifted in darkness.

"That captain didn't have to kick us off the boat." It was Namaoii's voice. Low and irritated. "I couldn't see what was happening, but everyone could tell you're the only reason that no one drowned. They should have been grateful."

"People do not often see logic when they are afraid." Tendaji's voice was calm in response. "And perhaps it's better that we're on land again, Namaoii."

Namaoii only continued to grumble about ungrateful merchants and having to walk to their destination. But there was an edge to her voice. A concern. "Is Ehryn going to be okay? Will Jaladri…" Ehryn didn't catch the rest before she drifted into silence again. But the question hung in her mind. Were they safe? Would Jaladri follow?

Ehryn floated in an ocean of headaches and whispers, simultaneously trying to remember every detail of what she'd seen on the Starlit River and begging whoever would listen to let her forget. It was too much. Too big. When she thought of Jaladri she could feel the rot beneath her back. Smell the decay that seeped up through the ground. She didn't want to face it. Didn't want to draw the Sisters' eyes.

But she didn't want to forget, either. And the Voices on the Wind would not let her.

You must know.

You must face Her.

All of Them.

Help us.

Ehryn slept again.

When Ehryn woke next, they were on the shore. Tendaji was sitting nearby, staring into the low embers of a fire, his face grim. He must have noticed some change in her, because he turned to her immediately as she pulled herself from sleep.

"Ehryn, how do you feel?"

Ehryn took stock of herself and sat up. "My head hurts a little," she finally admitted, "but it's not so bad." She looked around at the clearing they were in. Namaoii and Kant were sleeping in bedrolls on the other side of the small campfire, but Namaoii was already rustling at the sound of their voices. Looking down, Ehryn realized she, too, was wrapped snuggly in the bedroll Jacir had provided for their trip. "What happened?" she asked, trying to keep her voice low so the others could sleep.

"I was going to ask you the same thing." Tendaji knelt next to her, his face concerned. "Do you remember what happened on the boat?"

Ehryn did not need the Voices' suddenly excited chatter as they all at once tried to remind her, as though she could forget. Ehryn shook her head violently to silence them, the pain growing behind her eyes.

Tendaji must have seen it as her shaking her head no. "Maybe it's better that way," he said quietly. "But you deserve to know if powerful creatures are using you as their tools."

He doubts us.

He will try to silence us.

Do not trust him.

That one is full of secrets.

Take his blade.

It should be yours.

Take it! Take it!

"No!" Ehryn nearly yelled, stifling the sound too late. Namaoii cursed on the other side of the fire and was on her feet before Ehryn could apologize.

"What's wrong?" Tendaji was standing too, watching the edges of the firelight. "Do you see something?"

"No, Sir." Ehryn felt awful for waking Namaoii and scaring them both. "I'm sorry. I'm so sorry. I do remember what happened with Jaladri. I remember that the Voice on the Wind used my eyes to see Her and my voice to make Her leave. I… They get so loud sometimes, I can't drown them out. Even when the loudest one is silent."

"The loudest one is the one we heard, isn't it?" Namaoii asked, rubbing sleep from her eyes and looking surly as she crossed the campsite. "The power that burst out of you like a waterskin that's been filled too much." Ehryn nodded. "Then why aren't you dead?"

"What?" Ehryn was dumbfounded.

"You heard me. Why aren't you dead. That was too much power for anyone to hold onto, especially someone like you. I might not have seen Jaladri like you two did, but I sure as the blades felt Her. I've stood next to some of the most powerful mages in Imeriel and I've never felt anything like that. And whatever came out of your mouth was bigger still. It should have killed you, but it didn't. So what was it? And what are you?"

"I'm nobody," Ehryn replied defensively. "I don't know why the Voices on the Wind picked me or why they keep begging me for help or why no one else can hear them. I don't know what that power is or where it comes from. But I know it saved us from Jaladri."

"That's another thing!" Namaoii turned to Tendaji, her eyes filled with angry questions. "I had Kant tell me everything he could about the Ocean Goddess. What was She even doing here? The histories say that Illindria was the last Goddess to walk amongst mortals, and She got cut down by the Emancipator. It's been so long since any of the other Goddesses were around that basically everyone forgot that They existed. Even the Faoii. And now one of the Sisters is just… here? In the Starlit River demanding respect? How? Why?"

Tendaji spread his hands. "I do not know. Perhaps it has something to do with Madame Elise's rise and fall. Her actions brought a resurgence of old traditions and beliefs in Imeriel that had not existed outside the Faoii monasteries for generations. It is possible that, with all of her attempts, she succeeded in waking one of her blessed Old Gods in the end. Or it might have something to do with Illindria's death. Or perhaps the Sisters are impossible to know."

"And as powerful as They are, Jaladri was still overpowered by whoever's behind the Call."

"Jaladri called Her Alathi," Ehryn whispered. At the mention of the name, the air suddenly felt crisp, like the night before the first snowfall of the season. Namaoii narrowed her eyes. "There are a lot of Voices sometimes, but Alathi's different than the rest. She's the one that holds power. The others follow Her. Call Her their Queen."

"Alathi? The ancient Goddess of my father's people would choose to speak to *you?* Why not someone more worthy?"

"Namaoii," Tendaji chided. Ehryn shook her head.

"I don't mind. I've asked myself that many times. I don't know where the Voices come from or why Alathi wants my help. I wish She'd pick someone better."

"What kind of help does She want?" Namaoii demanded.

Ehryn shook her head. "I don't know. They never say. The Call comes from the North, and the Voices have often begged me to go in that direction. But they've never told me why."

Namaoii blew a burst of air out her nostrils. "North? Really? You couldn't say that before? Like, at any point when it would have been convenient? Before we started, maybe?"

"Namaoii. Be kind." Tendaji's voice was soft, but his eyes were harder than they usually were. Ehryn couldn't figure out if it was because of Namaoii's words or her own.

Namaoii seemed to notice that the Faoli was on edge, because she softened her voice. "Fine. We were going North anyway, so I guess it doesn't hurt that you waited this long to say anything. Kant and I want to know about the Call, too, so at least now we can be grateful we have some sort of information instead of just following a girl who's never seen the world outside her little picket fence." She gave an unexpected wolfish smile. "Besides. This is actually good. At least now we know we're following someone of worth. I'll follow the Goddess of Justice any day, like my father and his mother and all of their line."

"Is that who She is? The Goddess of Justice?"

Namaoii shrugged. "That's what the few stories we can still find say. It's an old religion. It was an old religion before the Faoii were formed and when the Danhaid still roamed Imeriel. It was an old religion when my ancestors crossed the sea to come here. It was nearly lost completely as they died out, and what we had left was destroyed by Elise and her holy crusade. But my father's people heard the Call in their bones, and their skalds spoke of deities who embodied something more than lines drawn in the dirt. Alathi was the name of Justice, and Her warriors were Her Wolves."

"I am impressed, Namaoii. Very few know of the Sisters anymore. Fewer still know of the Old Gods." Tendaji gave her an approving look, but Ehryn heard a hint of surprise under his voice.

"Yeah, well… I loved my dad. I'm glad he got a chance to teach me." Namaoii looked embarrassed for a moment before she cleared her throat. "Do you know anything else? About the Old Gods, I mean?"

Tendaji shook his head. "You know as much as I. We might be able to find more information in one of the Faoii monasteries. Some scholars debate that Illindrian prayers and Oaths from within the Order are not all about Illindria and Her sisters. They might be the repurposed relics of something much, much older."

"Yeah. My father always thought that the Faoii and the White Wolves sounded similar. Like branches off the same tree." A spark lit behind her eyes, and she cocked her head in Tendaji's direction. "Where'd you find out about the dissidents, Faoli? I thought the monasteries taught that anything other than the Faoii Oath was an affront to Illindria and the Sisters?"

Tendaji's mouth flicked in the barest of smiles. "I was an infiltrator once, tasked with learning about other cultures so my people might understand them better. The young lord Jacir once asked me to put those skills to use, and I spent a long time watching civilizations that most have never heard of, learning what I could of the past."

"Like the Danhaid? The Alathi?"

"Amongst others, yes."

Namaoii sat quietly for a long time, her eyes brooding. Finally she ground her teeth and stared at the ground. "In all those cultures and all those belief systems across Imeriel… with all the warriors and skalds and historians… all the people who have dedicated themselves to learning *something* in the name of being worth more than they were when they were born…why the blades would the Old Ones call Ehryn? *Ehryn!* She's not even of Alathi blood!" The words were so suddenly biting and bitter that Ehryn recoiled on reflex, feeling like she'd been slapped in the face.

Tendaji's face was stern when he replied. "Namaoii. You may not like it, but Ehryn saved all of us on the boat. Do not forget that we all owe her Call our lives."

"Is that what you want me to call her? Our savior?" the Wolf Pup demanded.

"I didn't—" Ehryn started, but Namaoii was already standing over her, eyes flashing with a deep unspoken hurt.

"That's right, you didn't. You didn't *do* anything. Things greater and stronger than you saved us. You were passive then and you're passive now and you'll be passive again if Jaladri or one of Her Sisters comes back. Why did Alathi pick *you* of all people?"

"Namaoii," Tendaji said reproachfully, but Namaoii shook her head.

"No, Faoli. It's not fair. Some of us train our entire lives to be worthy of the gazes cast our way. Some of us work constantly just for the honor of being useful to Clearwall. To Imeriel. Ehryn here has never picked up a sword, never held an allegiance, never tried to be anything more than what she was born as—worse, she actively tries to hide from a world that would lay everything at her feet for the *chance* that her unseen patrons might look upon them in favor—and yet she's the type of person that Alathi would Call? Alathi, whom my ancestors worshipped and revered for centuries, yet died out as a footnote in Imeriel's history? Alathi, Goddess of Justice?" She clenched her fist and Ehryn thought she saw tears in the princess's eyes. "What the blades could be just about that?"

"I'm sorry," Ehryn said, pulling her knees up to her chest. Namaoii wiped her eyes angrily and stood.

"I don't want to hear it. Leave me alone."

Namaoii stormed to the other side of camp, her back turned towards the others but still within the circle of firelight. Tendaji watched her go.

"You should go talk to her," Ehryn whispered. "She would respect what you had to say."

"I will give her a moment to regain control of herself. While you and I do not mind such displays of humanity, I get the feeling the princess will see her own tears as unbecoming of the Wolf Pup."

Ehryn nodded. Tendaji was probably right.

"Tendaji…Did you feel Alathi's presence when She spoke? I didn't know there was anything in existence that was that deep. That old. I felt Jaladri, and She was made of the same things that all of Imeriel is built on. The oaths and the traditions and the… the rot. But Alathi was deeper. Older. And Namaoii's right. I don't know why She chose me. Namaoii would be better. You would be better. Why didn't She pick someone else?"

Tendaji put a kind hand on Ehryn's shoulder. "What happened on the Starlit River was unexpected. Jaladri hasn't come close to our side of the Tapestry for a long time. Only the Elisians talk about the Sisters' awakening, and most of Imeriel assumes their sermons are fanatical delusions. You could not have expected anything like this from your kintar. You did the best you could."

But Ehryn's eye was drawn to the old warrior's fantoii, and the Voices on the Wind whispered sweet promises in her ears.

You must wield it.

You will be Her arm.

Help us.

Ehryn shook the Voices away. Violently.

Tendaji offered her a waterskin. "Do they hurt you, Ehryn? When they speak?"

"No… They want me to be someone I'm not. There are a lot of people who could be the person they want me to be, so I don't know why they didn't choose someone else. I… I want to help them, Sir. I do want to see this through and help them and then go home. I want to be worthy of the Call. But I don't want to lose who I am along the way."

"The kintar is supposed to be about growth, Ehryn. Many people discover things about themselves they did not expect to." Ehryn felt herself drawn to his fantoii again.

Ask him about it.

Build the foundation for your destiny.

You will wield it.

"I want to grow," Ehryn whispered. "But not like that."

Ehryn didn't know if Tendaji had seen her eying his blade or not, but his smile was genuine as he held her eyes. "Then, perhaps, Ehryn, we are all very lucky that you were Called and not someone else."

12

Alathi strode across Her mountains, and Her warriors followed.

They had grown over the centuries. For a time their minds grew more quickly than She'd expected, and they swam through a sea of uncertainty and doubt, powerless to control their own fates, begging the universe for guidance and order in a cosmos that offered none. They clawed at the dirt and sky and their sanity, begging for some sense of direction in the storm. Some promised that things would work out if they worked hard enough or fought well enough or did as the universe instructed.

The mortals called for Guidance.

And Alathi heard them.

Her Wolves were Her favorite. They modeled themselves after Her visage. Felt the power in Her icy call and crafted their swords to be Her tools. They stood proud and fierce and tall against lesser tribes that swore themselves to Her sisters and brothers, who had taken interest in the little specks of humanity in the centuries since Alathi had first seen them color the Weave. She guarded Her followers with ferocity. She had raised them from mites and beetles, and She would not let anyone take them from Her.

But Her Children feared. They had followed Her and heeded Her words for an eternity, but now others were using the magic She'd taught them. Others were growing powerful through theft and deceit and without following the way She'd shown. Had they chosen wrong?

They had not. She would remind *everyone* of Her name.

Alathi raised Her blades above Her head and called Her storms to the battlefield. She screamed against Her younger brother's forces and reminded Him that She was stronger than He would ever be. That She had carved out this world for Her followers while He had only stumbled onto it after millennia. A moth drowning in Her lake.

His followers yelled their battle cries, and the ground trembled. Lightning flashed and rain fell, mixing with the ice and snow and anger. Alathi smiled.

Her Children had grown past the simple, monotonous yells of their predecessors. She'd taught them to tattoo intricate designs into their flesh. Designs that bonded with the earth and sky and sea and harnessed the power of the Weave in their indigo patterns. There were only so many designs a single body could hold, but Her Children were many.

They howled and lifted their swords to match her stance, and She faced Her brother across the field, rising above the plain, towering down over all that would oppose Her and those who followed Her way.

Her warriors released their howls of victory and declaration and charged ahead, weaving around the tree trunks of Her legs to meet their adversaries. Alathi stepped over them, pulling the ice storm with Her, sinking deep into the mud of Her brother's making to face Him head on. She saw fear in His eyes, but not the ability to back down. Not the strength to admit He had made a mistake. Alathi swung Her swords.

So be it.

Below Her, the strongest of Her warriors—those that had taken Her name in their devotion—tore apart Her brother's forces.

They were the Alathi.

Her Fangs.

13

Ehryn thought that the others would want to talk more about what had transpired on the Starlit River and the very real existence of Jaladri, one of the Sisters. An actual Goddess among mortals. But no one did. They mentioned it in passing, quietly, with reverence at first, but then even that stopped and Ehryn was left with only her own memories. Within a few days, it was almost like it had never happened at all. They were just normal children on normal kintars.

They saw only a fraction of what you did.

The mortal mind protects itself from the unknown, pulls into itself.

Barricades itself from the darkness the same way your societies do.

They will make memories that their minds can comprehend to fill in the gaps they missed.

It is human nature.

…But the warrior should remember.

He saw. He saw!

That one is hiding something.

Be wary.

Ehryn shook the Voices away, glancing towards Tendaji. The old warrior was up ahead, telling an attentive Kant about the life cycles of butterflies. If either were still worried about Jaladri—or even remembered what had happened—neither showed it.

Namaoii fell into step beside Ehryn, forcing her to shift focus. The princess had started speaking to her again the day before, using the maddening tactic of pretending that the biting, tearful conversation next to the campfire had never happened. It remained in the air between them. A thick pocket of hurt and unspoken apologies.

"We're coming up on Crested Fir," Namaoii said as they walked along a well-kept road. "That's where Faoli-Tendaji said he was stabling the horses we'll use going forward."

"Namaoii, about what happened with Jaladri…" Namaoii's eyes narrowed dangerously.

"*Stop. Not another word!*" she hissed, casting fervent glances in all directions. Ehryn recognized the fear in her eyes and finally understood. She wasn't the only one who was afraid of what had happened on the boat, she was simply the only one who would be comforted by talking about it.

After a few minutes Namaoii tried again, with what Ehryn could now see as forced normalcy. The fear was gone, and the outburst joined the bubble of things left unsaid. "I'll be glad to have a good, strong horse under me again. All of this walking is slow and boring."

"I've never ridden a horse," Ehryn said, slightly embarrassed.

Namaoii rolled her eyes. "Of course you haven't. Why am I not surprised?" She rolled her neck and hit Ehryn's shoulder in what could have passed as a friendly gesture. "It'll be fine. I'll teach you. Kant too. Otherwise, this kintar is going to take decades just to get out of Clearwall's shadow."

Crested Fir was a hospitable village, filled with traders and craftsmen who stood behind brightly painted stalls or wagons, holding up trinkets and baubles and smiling as they chatted with potential customers. Storytellers and performers dotted the streets and marketplace, trying to catch the attentions of those who wandered by, and Kant was particularly interested in listening to each tale spun for the gathered children at their feet. It took the group a long time to make their way to the stables. Tendaji seemed in no hurry, however, and only Namaoii tapped her foot impatiently as Kant was distracted yet again.

"It's not even like they're *new* stories," she grumbled to Ehryn. "He does this when storytellers come to the palace, too. He likes when one recital uses a different word or character name, gets all excited. He thinks variances are these great things that philosophers can use to learn about societies and the evolution of customs, when really it's just because normal people can't remember things word-for-word like he can, so they improvise and hope no one notices. He doesn't understand that most of the time there's no greater meaning other than people are dumb and make mistakes."

"At least he finds brightness in the world," Ehryn replied. "Sometimes it's nice to be around people who express joy, even if it's over something you think is stupid. It's comforting. Probably for him, too." She drifted to one of the stalls nearby, looking at its assortment of cards displaying beautiful, colorful paintings of the town and surrounding areas.

"Bring something home with you to your family! Show them everything about your successful kintar when you return!" the vendor said enthusiastically. Namaoii sneered and pulled Ehryn away.

"Don't be naïve. Crested Fir makes almost all of their trade on kintar travelers. They sell items that cost almost nothing to make to   kids

who don't know any better. The kintar is supposed to be your first look at the world, right? So everyone knows you haven't seen enough to not be swindled."

"They seem nice," Ehryn countered carefully. "Friendly. Like they're excited to show young people a little bit of the wider world by sharing a bit of their heritage."

"Heritage? We're not even far enough away from Clearwall to meet someone interesting. I'll bet you almost anything that most of the people here were born in the Maze."

Ehryn pulled her arm away and browsed a few more stalls, partially in awe of the craftsmanship, and partially because she didn't want to give Namaoii the satisfaction of knowing that Ehryn thought she was probably right.

"Fine. Waste your kintar. See if I care." Namaoii stomped away to lean against the stable that Tendaji had disappeared into, but Ehryn saw that the older girl was still keeping an eye on Kant across the market, though she desperately tried to hide that she cared.

Ehryn finished looking at the paintings and went to stand beside Namaoii, also watching to make sure Kant was okay. The storyteller had finished his tale, and Kant waved to Ehryn before stopping to look at one of the brightly-painted stalls. Namaoii was still fuming, but Ehryn thought that might be the princess's default. "I bet a lot of young idiots get this far thinking they've seen the entire world. They buy a bauble for their families and go back home, their kintar complete. What a waste."

Ehryn didn't try to explain that this was further than she'd ever been, and instead watched as Kant offered a few coins to the stall's merchant in exchange for a decorated rattle. He came back smiling as he held it up for her examination.

"Look, Namaoii! Ehryn! Look! Do you think my sister will like it? When she's born, I mean. I want to tell her all about the kintar. Everything I saw and heard!"

"You could have gotten the same damned thing in Clearwall for half the price!" Namaoii scolded. Kant's face fell at her tone.

"But... but it says Crested Fir on it," he said, looking at the little wooden toy with dismay. "The ones at home don't say that."

"I'm sure she'll love it," Ehryn intervened. "And she'll love your stories."

"Yeah, sure," Namaoii replied with obviously false excitement. "You know what? Let's hear one of them. How would you describe Crested Fir, Kant? Now that you've seen it with your own eyes."

Kant frowned a little as he looked around. "It's... a town. Filled with people... wearing clothes... and selling... things. Like this rattle!" The ending seemed to be enough for him, but Ehryn remembered what Namaoii had said before they'd left Clearwall. Kant could echo back any story or conversation he'd ever heard, but he couldn't make up his own. It didn't seem right for Namaoii to make fun of him when he didn't even realize she was doing it.

"Here, Kant," Ehryn said softly, taking his hand. "Let's look around." They took a few steps back into the marketplace, and she let her eyes roam over the town, taking in details she hadn't seen before. "Are you ready?" Kant nodded, still holding the rattle in his other hand. Ehryn smiled. "Crested Fir is a bustling town, filled with people who smile big smiles and laugh loud laughs. They're proud of who they are and what they do, and they find joy in sharing that satisfaction and self-assurance with all the people who come through on their kintars. The villagers wear bright clothing and dresses embroidered with flowers and birds, and every stitch is unique. Sometimes there are small mistakes, but that makes them even more beautiful than the simple dresses and tunics that are mass produced in Clearwall. And there's something homey and comfortable about the worn leather shoes and well-used aprons. Every outfit there looks like it was made by the person who wears it—and therefore it looks exactly like how they wanted it to look. Every seam a declaration of personality. The houses and market fronts have hand-carved banisters and shutters, and most are painted in bright, vibrant colors. Like the people who live in them, each building is unique, and the character of the individuals of Crested Fir give a unique personality to the entire town. But that's not even what Crested Fir is known for. This little town has carved their name and place in the world onto trinkets and wooden animals and stories and, through that, all of Imeriel learns about them through word of mouth from smiling youth who got their first taste of life outside Clearwall. A web of little tales that span a thousand kintars and souvenirs—all leading back to a place hidden in the forest next to the Starlit River that no one would have known about otherwise. And that's where you got this rattle from, Sister. Crested Fir. A place that you'll always know, even if you never go there yourself, just like thousands of people before you. Crested Fir is kept alive by stories… and you're part of that story now, too."

Kant's smile was stretched clear across his face by the time she finished, and he immediately repeated the entire story back to her, even miming handing an invisible baby the rattle when appropriate. By the end of it, his grin was even bigger, though Ehryn wasn't sure how that was possible, but it made her smile, too.

"Like that?" he asked excitedly. Ehryn couldn't help but laugh as she nodded.

"Just like that, Kant. Do you think she'll like it?"

"I think she'll love it!" Kant exclaimed. Then, before Ehryn could say or do anything else, he had his arms wrapped around her waist. "Thank you so much, Ehryn!"

Ehryn hugged him back, and for a moment the world felt a little nicer than it had before when it was dimmed by Namaoii's pessimism. When they broke off from each other and returned to the stable, Namaoii looked like she was about to say something, but decided against it and looked more brooding than ever. They waited in silence until Tendaji came out of the stables, leading four horses.

"I hope you've all gotten what lessons you hope to from Crested Fir, children. There is so much more to learn. Mount up, and we will begin."

As much as she was glad that she'd been able to help Kant a few moments before, now Ehryn was self-conscious again. She looked at the gelding that had been saddled and was waiting sleepily in front of her. She had never ridden a horse before. Though she'd worked with the donkey her mother owned, she doubted those were similar. Her brother had been a strong rider in his youth, taught by one of his friends, but he'd never had the chance to teach her.

She hoped Dhruv was still watching over her, either from the Elisian enclaves or somewhere else. She hoped he could help her not make a fool of herself. Ehryn looked to the skies hopefully, but there was no sign that anyone had heard her silent pleas. Even the Voices on the Wind only chattered quietly in excitement about the coming journey.

Biting her lip, Ehryn watched Tendaji mount, then tried to mimic what he'd done. But even when she got her left foot into the stirrup, she couldn't push up hard enough to swing the other leg over. Next to her, Kant couldn't even reach the stirrup to begin with.

Tendaji turned in his saddle to watch them, and Ehryn couldn't read the expression in his eyes. Namaoii looked on with annoyance, already mounted and frowning impatiently. Ehryn tried again, both embarrassed and afraid. She didn't want to be a burden. She didn't want to be trouble. And she really didn't want Namaoii to make fun of her.

Somehow, miraculously, she got her leg over the saddle. Rather than pride, however, she only felt relief. She lifted her eyes to the sky, silently thanking whatever deities were listening.

Kant was still struggling, and Ehryn didn't know how to help him. She didn't want to seem pretentious if she tried to give advice when it seemed so obvious that she'd only succeeded a moment before by the grace of some merciful Goddess. It was Namaoii who finally said, "Kant. Lead her over to that fence and use it to mount." Kant's eyes lit up, and he did as instructed, the mare plodding behind him. Once positioned, he scrambled onto the fence and into the saddle, grinning brightly.

Once she was sure he wouldn't just fall off again and delay them further, Namaoii nodded to Tendaji. The old warrior looked past the towering young woman to Ehryn.

Ehryn's heart thundered in her chest. Was she sitting wrong? Had she messed up somehow? She met his gaze uncertainly, waiting for whatever admonishment might come.

"Well, Mistress Ehryn." Tendaji's voice was cool, but not unkind. "Where should we go?"

Ehryn's eyes widened, and her heart thumped harder. "...Sir?" she shook out. She thought that their course was already plotted. That there was somewhere specific the Royal Arcanist would want to send them. "Wh-where does the Royal Arcanist want us to go?"

Namaoii urged her horse forward until she was directly in front of Ehryn. Her eyes were like clouds before a storm. "You really want to wait until some old man tells you where to go? This is *our* kintar, Ehryn. We go where no others have decided for us. Even my mother wasn't able to order you anywhere when you stood before her in the throne room. She could only make suggestions. There are very few in Clearwall who hear the Voices on the Wind like you do. The Alathi are gone, and any others that heard them once have already left Clearwall. My mother is curious. Kant and I are curious. Thus, we've agreed to follow wherever that pull leads. You said the other day that it is North. Is that still true or not?"

Ehryn remembered saying that, but now she regretted it. She didn't want these people to look at her for answers. She'd been lost and scared and overwhelmed by what had happened on the boat. It was a mistake.

Wasn't it?

But the Voices were still chattering excitedly. Calling her forward.

The world awaits.

There is so much to see!

Help us.

"It… but…What if I'm wrong and the Call doesn't actually go anywhere?"

"Then we follow something else!" Kant beamed, leaning all the way forward on his mount so he could see Ehryn from around her horse's head. "But I don't think it will lead nowhere. Isn't it exciting? To be called forward by the voice of a Goddess?"

From far away the Voices on the Wind whispered again.

Help us.

Ehryn shuddered. She wasn't sure it was excitement that she felt. But the others were still looking at her. Kant with unbridled enthusiasm. Namaoii with impatience. Tendaji with no emotion at all, but a gleam in his crystalline eyes she thought was comforting.

Ehryn swallowed hard and closed her eyes, focusing on the pull that laced through the earth and sky. It was everywhere.

Everything. But the tautest threads led in the direction of the ghostly whisper.

"What if it's dangerous?" she finally asked, crystallizing the doubt that made her so indecisive.

"Then we'll face that, too," Namaoii responded sternly. "Better to follow it and be prepared than to hide from it. Stop stalling, Ehryn. Are we going North or not?"

"Yes," Ehryn squeaked. "North."

No one questioned her. Tendaji simply nodded and turned his horse towards the northern road. Kant pumped his fist into the air and followed, though it took several kicks to get his horse to move. Namaoii motioned for Ehryn to move forward first, then followed behind as they left Crested Fir, following unknown voices into unknown futures.

Help us.

14

Mavrikal turned Her face to the moon. The moon She and Her sisters all shared. Had shared? She didn't know. It was different now. One sister too few. Was the moon, the one constant through all the Tapestries, through all the halls and threads and existences, still present in whatever realm Illindria had gone to once Her thread was cut?

Cut by a mortal. The Betrayer. The mortal who killed a Goddess and loosened the trap.

It could be the beginning of Their downfall.

A rush of anger and hatred stormed through Her at the thought. Spikes of venom and shadows erupted from Her back, Her shoulders, Her fingers. They pierced the veil She slunk behind, and a deer on the other side fell, shuddering in darkness. Mavrikal barely noticed.

She had to find Her sisters. Let Them know what They had missed. What She had found.

The blade. The Betrayer's blade. Getting closer to the trap. To the end.

Everything They'd set in motion might be undone.

But Mavrikal wasn't sure where Her sisters were. They spent Their days between the different Weaves. Flowing with the magic They'd harnessed, following it across space and time. Sleeping in the halls where the Tapestry stretched infinitely on all sides, reaching into oblivion. Where mortal walls and mazes did not disrupt the flow. The life.

Her Sisters didn't know what had been built in their absence. The walls and cities and mazes that rattled Mavrikal's mind, blinding Her from the Tapestry's twists and turns and colorful strands. The mortal world stole Her sanity with their cities and machines. Just as they'd stolen Illindria's sanity by the end.

More than Her sanity. They'd stolen Illindria's life.

It would not be the same this time.

Illindria's death had opened the trap. Not enough to release Their ancient enemies, but enough that those They'd locked away could be heard. Followed. So Mavrikal watched the mortals. Killed those who got too close. They could not afford a repeat of what had happened with Their youngest sister.

Illindria had been Mavrikal's favorite, but She'd been weak. And now that She was gone, a corner of Their carefully-laid trap was loose. Most mortals didn't realize it, so intent on their miserably short lives, but if they'd stop to look, they would notice that more had changed in the past century than their ancestors had experienced in millennia.

And some were beginning to follow questions they shouldn't know how to ask. They were growing and adapting quickly. Too quickly. Quicker than they realized. Quicker than even Her sisters knew. It was too fast to be seen from the Goddess halls, where years seemed like moments or where lifetimes passed in seconds. It was too much to see from Their sanctuaries.

So Mavrikal watched from here.

She'd been on the mortals' side of the Tapestry for longer than any Goddess to come before Her. On the plane closest to their walls and trees and lives. But it was okay. She had to do it.

Someone had to do it.

The humans were becoming dangerous. Growing outward, upward, into themselves. Capable of love and invention and insight their ancestors had never showed. They were smart and resourceful enough that Mavrikal knew they had the power to ruin everything if She did not stop them.

So She did. Every time. When they drifted too close to the trap She guarded. And after they fell, She fed false dreams to those who would send more. None approached the trap without Her knowledge.

Mavrikal tasted the air, lapping the scent of the new group that had left the confusing barriers of Clearwall. She thought She'd sensed them before, but had lost their scent on the Starlit River. But now She knew they were there. And they were… different. Wrong. From Her perch across the veil, She could not quite pinpoint all of them. Two were certain. Two were… harder. She tried again, focusing. She could smell the strange two now, barely. A hint of blood She wouldn't notice if She hadn't been looking for them. If they'd left alone, just the two, She would have missed them completely.

She peered at Clearwall through the Tapestry's threads. Two of the mortals had obvious Weaves. One was strong and powerful and might color generations. The other was barely a strand of silk. But the other two… they didn't appear at all.

What is this?

The two ghosts smelled strange, now that She had caught their scent. Not siblings, exactly, but also with the sibling thread. She'd never seen that. It was new. Different.

Dangerous?

She licked the air again.

She didn't know.

But She could taste something else, too.

Hollowed.

Tonicloran.

The convergence of all We've waited for.

This was it.

She smiled.

She would follow.

The inland paths leading north from Crested Fir were not what Ehryn had expected. While Queen Isolde had worked hard to clean up the Starlit River and rid Clearwall of the dreck and garbage that had littered the streets in the past, there was a level of industry in Clearwall that Ehryn had always known, even without recognizing it. The factories that used steam to power great machines that automatically manufactured nails, horseshoes, and other daily necessities did not pollute the river like people thought it might, but all of the moving, working parts gave the air a metallic taste. A slightly iron feel. There was always the sense of movement in Clearwall, even in the middle of the night. Things were always chugging steadily forward.

Ehryn thought she had felt the world outside of Clearwall when she'd sat next to the Starlit River in the darkness, or when she'd gazed upon the waters from the boat they'd taken from her docks, but now she realized that she had always experienced Imeriel through a slightly tinted pane of glass. For the first time, it felt like the world and its magic wasn't broken up and piecemeal because of the Starlit River and the twisted walls of the Maze. For the first time in years, Ehryn felt like she could breathe.

Almost. Because there was something else in the air, too. Something that Ehryn had only vaguely sensed in Clearwall. It reminded her of the rot she'd always felt below the streets, but it was more than that. It was dark and cold and deep like Jaladri had been. It slithered after them like a shadow, and, as they rode further north, Ehryn realized something she'd never thought of before.

She'd always considered the Maze a mistake. An inconvenient consequence built from a lack of foresight and city planning. But Clearwall had been a bastion of safety for its people from the first days when peasants had stacked rocks upon each other and built a ring of torches to fend off the darkness.

No leader in history would purposefully build their city so that its people would be burdened. Where their magic would be stunted and their commutes difficult.

Not unless there was more protection in that than harm.

The Voices on the Wind chittered together in frightened whispers.

You've left the trap. She follows.

Tell the warrior.

No! He'll turn back. He won't understand.

Take his blade.

Keep going. Don't stop. Don't fear.

Help us.

Sometimes it would get so bad that Ehryn would almost cry out for Tendaji to wait. To look for whatever followed them. But just before she could, the… *thing* that slunk behind them would dissipate like it had never been there. She'd search for it again, worried that she was going insane, but by then the rot was gone and there was only the bright connection of the entire world stretching out from beneath her horse's hooves. The Eternal Tapestry and all its threads thrumming out around her, connecting her to everything that had or would ever live. Of course she would sense some darkness in something so huge. Right?

But the Voices on the Wind were still whispering at her not to be afraid, and she wondered if they would do so if there was actually nothing to be afraid of.

15

They traveled north for weeks, and Ehryn finally began to understand why Faoli-Tendaji had been asked to join them on this strange trek. She'd already figured out that he was a warrior who could see and protect them from things that normal people couldn't, but there was more to him than being a guardian and a guide. Tendaji was a teacher. Ehryn didn't know anything about destiny other than she wanted nothing to do with it, but if anyone in the world was destined to help others learn about the world and themselves, it was Tendaji.

"This is your kintar," he would remind the children. "Yes, Clearwall wants you to bring new information and creations back with you, but the journey is about learning for yourself as well. To make your life better when you decide where you want to go with it. Allow me to teach you."

And he did. He spent hours every day sparring or discussing politics with Namaoii while Kant and Ehryn explored the fields and farmsteads and forests they'd never seen before, talking with people they met along the way. Most of the settlers within a few weeks' ride of Clearwall were used to kintars, and they were happy to share stories or recipes or traditions. Ehryn was particularly excited to meet a family of beekeepers one day, and she spent hours with them, learning their trade. She wondered if this was the same family from whom her mother got her candlewax. She wondered if her mother would be pleased if she learned how to do it herself. Maybe if she brought this knowledge back home with her, Everly would forgive her for having left.

At nights, Tendaji would stay up for hours next to the campfire, whispering to Kant, filling the wide-eyed boy's bottomless mind with stories. Namaoii and Ehryn would often listen, too, but much of it seemed to be ancient history, spoken to Kant so it would not be lost. The two girls almost always fell asleep before the tales were finished.

"Where are you from?" Ehryn asked one day after the old warrior finished telling them about a southern spring festival while they rode. "You know so much about so many places."

Tendaji shrugged one shoulder. "I'm not from anywhere, Ehryn. A tiny community to the north. We were once quite isolated, so any time I had the chance to learn about other cultures beyond what I knew, I took it. I've always found it fascinating. So many little pieces of a mosaic that together create a world. It's an honor to share it with all of you."

Ehryn frowned, trying to remember the conversation they'd had after she'd woken on the beach next to the Starlit River. The memory was hazy, but the Voices on the Wind caught it too.

Be wary.

Lies and half-truths.

He is hoping you will not remember from before.

He let his guard down then.

Do not trust him.

"You're from north of here? Will we see where you grew up?" Kant asked, standing in his stirrups awkwardly to see Tendaji over his horse's ears.

"I'm afraid I don't know, Kantilieh. Ehryn is the one who is guiding us, after all."

Ehryn tried to imagine what growing up like that would be like. They were already further north than she'd ever been, and even the daylight hours were starting to get uncomfortably cold. She shivered on her horse just thinking about it. Even with the Starlit River, it was rarely this cold in Clearwall, and her home had always been well-heated by the silkstrand furnace that her mother had installed in the kitchen.

Tendaji must have noticed her sudden shivers, because he smiled and motioned to her saddlebag. "I packed a wool cloak for you before we left. There are gloves and thick socks in there, too, when you need them. You too, Kant. It will get colder as we reach the mountains."

Ehryn turned awkwardly in her saddle and pulled out the cloak, wrapping it around her. The Voices on the Wind chittered in her ear.

He knew?

He knows more than he should.

Be wary.

Ehryn wrinkled her nose, but the cloak's presence bugged her, too. She thought she could voice her uncertainty without mentioning Jaladri or Her Sisters—something that she'd tried on several occasions but that Namaoii had always shut down immediately.

"Wait," she said. "The saddlebags were already packed before we met in the square. Long before you asked me which way we should go. How did you know we were going to head north?"

Tendaji shrugged again and gave that easy smile. "I didn't, really. But I suspected. When the young Master—" Tendaji chuckled and tried again. "When the Royal Arcanist called upon me to be your guide, I assumed he had some idea of where you'd want to go, and that he'd send someone familiar with the terrain to accompany all of you. I've been further north than most people he could call on, so I made a guess. There are headwraps in there, too, if we had gone south instead."

"How far north?" Namaoii joined in. "Did you train at the Monastery of the Fallen Star? Is that where you earned your ascension?"

"No, but that is a very educated guess. Most people outside the Order do not know the names of the monasteries or where they are." He gave Namaoii an approving smile. "Your mother will be pleased to know you've been studying the locations of our allies, Namaoii."

Namaoii almost smiled at the compliment. "I've been studying the location of our enemies, too. Or those who haven't decided which side they're on. Mother should know I'm old enough to know what goes on outside of Clearwall."

"Of course she does!" Kant exclaimed. "That's why you're on your kintar! That's what it's for! We're learning so many things!"

"Except for where we're going," Namaoii carped, giving Ehryn a pointed look.

"I'm sorry," Ehryn said. "I don't—"

Black feathers.

Wild birds.

North. North.

North.

Tell them that's where you need to go.

Tell them.

Come.

Help us.

"I know you don't. But would it be too much to ask for—
"

"Is there a town called Black Feather?" Ehryn cut Namaoii off, distantly pleased that the princess got a chance to know how it felt.

If Namaoii was angry for being interrupted, the feeling gave way to curiosity. "Black Feather? Not that I know of." The older girl turned her entire body in her saddle to look Ehryn in the eyes. "Why? Did you hear something?" Ehryn couldn't tell if she was excited or scared.

"There's no town called Black Feather, but there are the Blackfeather Wilds!" Kant broke in. "I saw it on a map. A huge empty area north of here. There aren't any towns or anything! Just landmarks and rivers and mountains! Do you want me to tell you about it? Here! Let me tell you!" He didn't even wait for them to reply, and instead dove directly into a somewhat monotonous recall. "Little is known about the Blackfeather Wilds. Once the home of the exiled Order of the Croeli, the borders of this inhospitable land remained guarded and uncrossed for untold centuries before the Godfell War. Explorers that have traveled there since the frontier has reopened have found little but overharvested fields with eroded soil and gnarly, inedible native foliage, leading many to revere the capabilities of the Croeli that had survived for generations in this harsh environment." He beamed proudly. "That's from an introduction I read once."

"Nothing grows there at all? No one lives there?" Ehryn frowned, thinking of all the planning and supplies that would be needed to venture that far.

"The tonicloran used to! Here! I know about that too!" Again, Kant's voice took on a monotonous tone. "The tonicloran is a highly-discussed plant among scholars. Having been eradicated during Elise the Queen of Dark Iron's rise to power, little is known about this mythical vine except that ancient Faoii both feared and worshipped it. In the next three chapters we will discuss—"

"Enough, Kant!" Namaoii burst out. "Why does all this matter, anyway? Why are we even talking about the Blackfeather Wilds? No one lives there. Nothing grows there, and what does isn't helpful to Clearwall. We don't even send our scouts that far. There are old treaties from the time of my ancestors, when the Croeli were first brought back into the fold after the Godfell War, but they have never been renewed. There's no one to renew them with. It's a blasted wasteland."

"That's where the call is coming from," Ehryn asserted to a sudden cry of excitement from the Voices. "I know it. I don't know why, but there's something there. A thread that needs to be untwisted."

Namaoii knit her brow. "We don't have the supplies or mounts prepared for the Blackfeather Wilds. Blades, most of us don't even have the training. We'll die if we go there. Or you will, anyway. At the very least, we'll be forced to turn around before we can travel past any of the explored areas. Voices on the Wind or not, going that far is a terrible idea."

The Voices on the Wind wailed in despair. For a moment Ehryn couldn't hear anything above their cries. Those gray clouds of hopelessness that had nearly drowned her in Clearwall slithered back behind her eyes. Ehryn scrounged for something—anything she could say. She wouldn't go back to that emptiness she'd only just escaped. She would go to the Blackfeather Wilds by herself and die first if she had to.

But if she could, she'd rather not go alone. She tried to keep her voice calm and to silence the Voices on the Wind when she spoke again. "Queen Isolde wants to find out where the whispers come from, right, Namaoii? What better way to prove your abilities than to give her the information no one before you has found? By going where no one else has ever gone?" She looked around the group almost desperately. "There have been other Called, right? But none of them have searched for the source. They all went on to follow the bidding of the Voices away from Imeriel." She pulled a phrase that Namaoii had used the day they'd met. "They abandoned Clearwall. Are we not better than that? Shouldn't we at least try?"

Namaoii looked uncertain. "We'd do better to go west. Try to reach whatever's left of the Danhaid. There are rumors that a few pockets of them have been spotted in the plains, and they might have more information on the Blackfeather Wilds that we can use for a later expedition."

That's too late.

There's not enough time.

Help us.

And then Alathi's demanding boom:

Fight her, Child! We will not be ignored!

It took everything Ehryn had not to topple from the saddle and clutch her head at the command. She thought she heard someone say her name in concerned tones, but she didn't know. Couldn't concentrate on anything other than the immense power swelling up behind her eyes.

"Maybe it's too far," she whispered, barely able to hear her own voice around the reverberations in her skull. "Maybe we won't be able to make it and we'll have to turn back. Maybe the trail will grow cold, or the thread will be cut before we get that far, or we'll arrive and there will be nothing there. Maybe it's just a trick played by unknown spirits. But…" She took a deep breath and steadied herself. "But I'd rather the trail go quiet and end in disappointment or try and learn my own limitations than live forever feeling this pull I never sought out. I can't go back. I'll go by myself if I have to, but I will see the end of it, one way or another. With or without any of you." She breathed out again before she realized how stern and strong her voice sounded. There was no hint of Alathi in it, though, as she'd expected. It was, completely and definitively, hers.

Everyone stared at Ehryn for a long moment, and there was the sound of howling on the wind. The faintest smell of yarrow. Then, suddenly, Namaoii barked out a laugh.

"Broken Blade! I'm almost impressed, Ehryn. That was the most spine I've ever seen you show. And it was *your* voice, not anyone else's. For a moment there you were almost… assertive. One might even say worthy." She laughed again before settling back in her saddle. "You want to see for yourself that there's nothing in the Blackfeather Wilds? Fine. My mother does want to know where your Voices on the Wind will lead you, and I can learn to fight from the Faoli no matter where we go. Maybe it'll be a waste of your kintars, but not of mine. North it is. For now. If you're wrong or I think you're going to die, we can turn west instead, anyway. Time is on our side."

But the Voices on the Wind cried at the words, screaming that time was running out.

16

That evening it was considerably colder than it had been before, and Tendaji had them all stop earlier than normal.

"Come here, children. If we are going to continue north, there is something you need to know how to do."

The trio gathered around Tendaji as he carefully stacked an assortment of sticks in a tent-like shape on the ground. "Who here could light this?"

Namaoii's hand went up immediately. After a moment, Kant's went up, too. Slowly, uncertainly, Ehryn raised hers as well. She had lit the fire in the hearth at home a thousand times and had even learned to load the silkstrand furnace her mother had installed. Surely this would not be so different?

Tendaji nodded. "Very good. Now. Who can light it without a flint and tinder?"

All three of them dropped their hands.

"None of us are callers, Faoli," Namaoii said. "Not even fire callers, and those are the most common kind."

Tendaji smiled a little half-smile and sat back on his calves. "Why should it matter if one is a fire caller or not?"

Everyone stared at the Faoli like he'd sprouted feathers. "How else would you call fire if you…can't call fire?" Ehryn squeaked. It didn't make any sense to her.

Tendaji's ice-blue eyes twinkled in the dusk. "That is the question of all magic users, isn't it? And to understand it, we must go back to the beginning: Where does our magic come from?"

This time it was Kant who replied. "In the days of Illindria, Great Goddess of the Faoii, War Watcher of the Danhaid, and False Child of Alathi, magic was a rare and coveted resource, only accessible to those stalwart heroes of the Order, taught and trained within the monasteries that dotted Imeriel. Smaller sects outside the walls were able to perform less miraculous bouts of magic, though the reason for this is often disputed by scholars, some asserting that small drops overflowed from the monastery sieve, while others are convinced that these morsels were doled out by the Great Goddess in a plot never fully recognized by humans. In chapters fourteen and fifteen we will…"

Tendaji laughed. "Skip ahead, Kant. What changed? Why do even those outside the monasteries now have magic?"

"I know this one," Namaoii cut in. "Kaiya the Emancipator struck Illindria down. The Fallen Goddess's magic spread throughout the world after it was no longer contained within Her human vessel. Now, everyone has a special ability, and each new generation seems to be slightly more powerful than the ones that came before."

"I thought Kaiya was called the Betrayer," Ehryn squeaked, ashamed that the other two knew so much more about magic than she did.

Namaoii shrugged. "Most of the time she is. That's what she was called during the Iron Queen's time, and there are no books from before then. But the Royal Arcanist calls her the Emancipator. And if she's the reason Clearwall has magic, then I believe him."

There was something different in Tendaji's eye when he spoke again. A sheen of pride or gratitude.

"Very good, Namaoii. Now tell me: Think back to the legends of the Faoii of old—even the Faoii in the monasteries today—do they only know one type of magic?"

It was such a simple question that Ehryn was astounded she had never recognized it before. While few people had ever seen the inside of the Faoii monasteries, everyone knew of the nearly-mystical protectors of Clearwall. The Faoii were everything a person could be—healers, warriors, diplomats, smiths, inventors. The best of all citizens were brought into the coveted ranks. And no one had ever assumed that those astonishing women and men were only capable of one skill. One power. The Faoii were more than any regular person. Capable of so much more than any commoner. But Ehryn had never questioned why. The others must have been thinking the same thing, because they all slowly, uncertainly, shook their heads.

Ehryn thought that if she saw Tendaji's half smile one more time she'd go mad, but his face was completely serious. "If you know this, children, then why do you assume we are all worthy of only one gift? Why can only callers call fire and only healers heal? How do you think the Faoii learn more than the one spark of magic they discover within themselves during their youth?"

"They train," Namaoii said, a tiny bit of excitement creeping into her voice. "They learn. They teach themselves all the things that they want to know." She slammed a fist into her other hand. "They prove that they're more than what the Goddesses assign."

"Exactly," Tendaji replied, his eyes shining. "Know this, children: there are very few unlearnable magics in the world. One can learn to do almost anything with a tutor, practice, and dedication. It may be difficult—so much more difficult than your innate gifts—but there are tricks you can learn, too. The Faoii use songs, the Danhaid use dances, the Alathi use tattooed symbols. There are so many ways to access the Weave, and it is both your right and your honor to learn the paths you wish to take. Never let anyone tell you otherwise. Do you understand?"

They all nodded and watched as the old Faoli lifted a twig in front of their faces. With a quiet hum, his eyes flashed silver, and it erupted into flame.

They all stared at the little blaze until Tendaji extinguished it with a flick of his wrist.

"Well? What are you waiting for? Pick up a stick, children. It is time to learn."

17

Ehryn was worried that the others would be angry about the slow going and the increasingly cold temperatures as the Voices led them north. But no one seemed to mind. They practiced new types of magic under Tendaji's watchful eye and learned about the world around them as they traveled. Soon, even Ehryn had almost forgotten about the harrowing opening to their kintar. She was glad she'd chosen to come. Wanted to show her parents all she'd learned when she returned.

Kant apparently felt the same way. "I can't wait to show my baby sister how to call fire! Look how good I'm getting!" Kant hummed the little song Tendaji had taught them, and his eyes flashed. A tiny flame appeared on his finger, and he whooped happily. Ehryn was happy for him. She could create a spark if she concentrated, but only on a stick or campfire, and not usually an entire flame the first time.

Kant snapped, and the flame went out. He smiled again before turning to look at the clearing where Tendaji and Namaoii were sparring. "You know? We could probably learn to do that, too, if we wanted to. But I don't think I'd like that very much." Ehryn nodded and turned to watch the warriors practice. The Wolf Pup of Clearwall had been a formidable fighter when Ehryn had met her in the square, but she'd used their kintar to hone her technique under Tendaji's tutelage.

The two still had drastically different fighting styles, however, and while Ehryn had no desire to learn to fight herself, she was fascinated watching them. Namaoii was like a hurricane, all power and speed and flurries of relentless attacks with her blade. The princess's arm moved so quickly that Ehryn almost missed the intricate twirl that brought the tip of the fantoii around towards Tendaji's collarbone.

But as quick as Namaoii was, Tendaji was wraithlike in comparison. He flowed around her movements like water around a rock. Like eddies in a stream. Namaoii might as well have been attacking a shadow, and as Ehryn watched, she realized she was. Tendaji wasn't there like he should be. His movements weren't natural. He was there—but he also wasn't.

It was a magic she'd never seen before.

"That's not fair!" Ehryn let out without realizing what she was saying. Namaoii jolted at her sudden outburst and lost her footing. Tendaji smacked the princess hard in the side with the flat of his blade.

"Stay out of it!" Namaoii hissed, rolling to her feet. But Tendaji raised his hands to waist height and placed his sword on the ground at his feet, their spar evidently finished. The Voices on the Wind chattered excitedly the moment he put it down.

Pick it up, Ehryn.

You must wield it.

Help us.

Ehryn shook the voices away and tore her eyes from the sword, focusing on Tendaji as he approached her.

"Why did you say that, Ehryn? What made you so upset?" the warrior asked quietly.

Ehryn's face reddened. Tendaji and even Namaoii had often offered to train her in swordsmanship, and she had refused. This wasn't her place to butt in. She never should have said anything.

"It's… it's nothing, Sir," she finally whispered.

Tendaji shook his head. "No. Please tell me. You are always silent when we spar, but I know you watch. What finally made you speak?"

"It… it wasn't fair. The way you were moving—Namaoii can't do that. She can't match you. There's no way for her to keep up, so she'll always lose. Sparring is supposed to be about learning. It's supposed to be fair."

Namaoii stomped her way towards them. "So what? Do you think our enemies will think like you do? That a real fight is going to be 'fair? Are you stupid?"

The words stung. Ehryn hung her head.

"No. I—"

"If you want to survive in this world, you need to start thinking like a survivor. Whatever comes against you, or us, or Clearwall, or Imeriel—there will always be *something* we didn't foresee. Something we didn't plan for. Half of being prepared is knowing you aren't, Ehryn. It's why we almost died on that boat. It's why Tendaji and I keep practicing even when you won't pick up a blade to save your own skin from the danger you put us all in. Either join and help us or stay out of it, but don't talk about fair."

Ehryn was surprised. "I didn't… I thought you forgot."

"How the blades could one forget about something like that? We're not dumb, Ehryn. We're careful. The Weave ties all things together. Don't talk about what you don't want to draw from it lest something hears. And if you do—" she brandished her sword angrily— "you'd best be at least willing to face what you call. But you aren't, are you? You never are."

Tendaji put a hand on Namaoii's shoulder, and the older girl quieted. After a moment, he addressed Ehryn. "Namaoii is not completely right, Ehryn, but I understand where she is coming from. Do you want to try fighting? We would be happy to teach you. Perhaps that would put everyone's minds more at ease."

Ehryn didn't raise her head, only shook it. *No.* She had no desire to fight anyone. She didn't want to know how it felt to hold a sword in her hands. The Voices on the Wind cried their disapproval.

You must! You must!

You will wield it.

We will help you.

It's your destiny to pick up that blade.

Help us.

"No!" Ehryn yelled, trying to be louder than the calls. Everyone around her jumped at the outburst and she tried again, softly this time. "No. Thank you, Sir. But no."

Namaoii scoffed. "Useless. If you won't even pick up a blade in your own defense, then you're a liability to Imeriel. Luckily, there are others out there who care enough to do the hard work for you. Don't get in our way." She huffed and turned her back on Ehryn, then fisted both hands in front of her and bowed her head towards Tendaji. "Faoli-Tendaji. I'd like to try again."

"In a moment, Namaoii. I want to know first whether you believe what I was showing you before was adequate training or not. Do you agree with Ehryn? Was it unfair?"

"No." Namaoii's response was immediate and biting.

"Why not?"

"Because I paid attention to your lesson when you taught us how to call fire. No magic is unlearnable." Ehryn didn't need to look up to know that Namaoii had redirected her piercing gaze to stare into her soul. "Show me again, Faoli. I want to learn."

"Very well," Tendaji responded, returning to his blade and stepping into stance again. "But be aware, Namaoii. No one can learn to Blink anymore. No matter how hard you want to learn, I cannot teach you."

"Then I'll learn how to fight against it. Come on. Let's go again."

"What makes it unlearnable?" Kant piped up, earning him a withering glower from Namaoii as she clenched her sword in both hands. Tendaji just barely succeeded in hiding a smile before she noticed.

"There used to be a plant that the Faoii both revered and feared. Of all the living things in Imeriel, it was most closely tied to the Gods. It allowed you to see the Tapestry through Their eyes and step between the threads."

"The tonicloran!" Kant nearly yelled. "The bane and strength of the Faoii!"

"Yes. It was powerful, but it was a curse as well. Be grateful it is gone." His eyes were haunted as he stared at something the children couldn't see.

"So be it," Namaoii hissed. "But if I can't join you, I can sure as blade rust learn to beat you. Let's go again."

Tendaji came back to himself quickly, shook his head once, then got back into stance.

"Very well. Shield up, Namaoii. Let us see how you do."

After Namaoii and Tendaji had finished their session (again with Namaoii being smacked with the flat of Tendaji's blade, but after a much longer and harder fight than the first time), Tendaji came and crouched next to Ehryn as she practiced calling fire to twigs before shaking them out and tossing them aside.

"I didn't mean to ruin your lesson," Ehryn whispered, not looking up.

"You cannot ruin a true lesson, Mistress Ehryn. Only change its direction." Ehryn nodded but didn't respond. Tendaji let the silence spread for a few moments before speaking again. "May I ask you something, Ehryn?"

Ehryn shrugged. "Sure."

Tendaji leaned back until he was sitting on the ground and looked at the sky. "Now that we are out of Clearwall, what do you feel?"

Ehryn frowned and turned her head to face him. "Sir?"

Tendaji gestured vaguely around them. "It is not meant to be a difficult question, Miss. I want to know what you feel. It can be anything. The earth and the grass around you. The air or the sun on your skin. Maybe just tell me what the wind feels like. But tell me—is it different now that we are no longer behind the walls of the Maze?" Ehryn frowned at Tendaji, but his look was so earnest that she finally leaned back and breathed in.

"It's… cleaner here. The factories and the dust and the dead fish from the docks… It all kind of builds up in Clearwall in a way that you don't notice if you never leave. But it's there. And it feels more crowded in the city, even when you're by yourself. The wind doesn't move like it should, broken up by the houses and the walls and the Maze. But here it's… open. There's nothing stopping the calls or the cries or the wind or the birds."

Tendaji didn't respond, but something about his silence weighed on Ehryn. She took another deep breath and focused on the unease his stillness brought.

Don't do it. Ignore it.

You'll drown in it.

Help us.

Ehryn withdrew from the tickling sensation at the back of her mind as the Voices on the Wind begged her not to scratch at the wall. She'd noticed it before when she thought she'd felt something slithering behind them in the darkness. But now that she really focused, unafraid, she realized it was bigger than that. She peered into the shadows that always seemed to be in the periphery of her consciousness, into the darkness she'd noticed beneath the waves even before Jaladri caught up with them. The Voices on the Wind tried to block her, but she pressed through them.

Ehryn couldn't stop herself from crying out at the sudden rush of rot and decay that flooded her senses, tumbling out from behind hastily-constructed walls she didn't remember building. She did not think she'd been the one to build them at all, but now that they were gone, she was suffocating, buried under a swamp that had always been on the edges of her perception.

Ehryn released all the air in her lungs as though she'd been punched in the stomach, and she curled into herself on the grass, forgetting for a moment that the rot wasn't as real as the earth and the sky and all the things around her physical body. Next to her, Tendaji already had a hand on his fantoii, the other on her shoulder, his eyes darting in all directions as he peered at the trees surrounding their little camp.

"Ehryn, are you alright? What is it?"

Ehryn shook her head, breathing heavily. "It's nothing physical," she finally gasped out. Tendaji released his fantoii and waited for her to continue. "It's nothing bad… or real… But it's both those things, too." Ehryn wrapped her arms around herself and fought back tears. "There's a weight on everything. We've all lived with it so long that we don't even notice it anymore. It's like a sponginess beneath the earth. A rot just below the surface that sometimes climbs up enough that we can smell it, but we bury it so quickly that people just… forget it's there. But it is. And no matter how much we work, no matter what we build or who we help or how free we make our cities… it's all built on this crumbling rot that no one acknowledges." She looked at Tendaji, distraught. "How can we make anything lasting if the foundation is a dried husk of what it should be?"

"We cannot," Tendaji replied kindly. "Deep breaths, Ehryn. I'm sorry. I did not realize what my question would bring."

"No… no. I think I needed to see. I think I should have a long time ago, but they didn't want me to. And I don't know why."

"They? The Voices on the Wind?" Ehryn nodded. "Do you know where the rot stems from? Where it manifests?"

"I… I don't know. Should I?"

"I'm not sure. Those who hear the Voices on the Wind, or the War Watchers or Those Who Speak in Dreams… whatever name you choose for them, the Called have information the rest of us do not, and it is my job to help you break it apart and examine it, Ehryn. To help you understand the things that only you can hear. The Queen wants to know, and it is my duty to ask. But more than that, I want you to be able to go home after this without being buried by the things you can't see or control. I want you to know happiness."

Ehryn closed her eyes again. She knew she should do the Queen's bidding, but she didn't want to follow the sickness that touched upon the edges of her mind like decay. She didn't want to wrap herself in the sludge that their entire civilization was built on.

We tried to keep you from it.

We told you not to open the door.

But now you have. So if not you, then who? Who else will look?

No turning back.

We are with you.

We need you to see.

Help us.

The voices at the edge of her mind were soothing, but there was a sternness in them, too. A finality. And for once Ehryn felt a strength to push herself forward of her own volition rather than through the anxious desire not to disappoint someone else.

Nearly gagging, she used the Voices to steel her and dove forward. Into the muck and dreck and darkness that she'd avoided all her life, even though some part of her always knew it had been there.

"It's… in all of us," she finally whispered. "The beliefs we've built the world on. They're tarnished and broken. They're falsehoods prettily painted on dark shadows of what once was. Those we call the goddesses… are not."

Ehryn's heart hammered in her chest. What was she saying? The Goddesses were not a forefront in most people's minds, true, but no one doubted Their existence.

You know. You see.

The False Children.

Help us.

Tendaji raised both eyebrows at Ehryn's declaration, then settled them again. Ehryn thought he would answer, but the silence spread out between them for what seemed like hours.

"Please say something," Ehryn finally whispered into her knees.

"What would you have me say?"

"That I'm crazy. That the Faoii and the legends and the stories that our world is built on are right. That a thousand years of tradition holds more weight than… than whatever that was."

"Is that what you believe?"

Ehryn wanted to believe it. She wanted to go back to Clearwall and live the life she'd been living with her parents before everything had gotten so twisted. Where she made her prayers to the goddesses on holidays and hung her trinkets in the window and where the twists and turns of the Maze muffled the voices that called to her. If they were muffled, it was easier to pretend that she didn't know what they were trying to say.

But she remembered the fog that had nearly suffocated her in those days when she'd been paralyzed by indecision and uncertainty. If she went back now, it would be worse. She had to see this through. She couldn't ignore the rot under her feet anymore.

"No," she finally mumbled. "And… and the world needs to know if we want to fix any of it."

That last bit of truth was the hardest to swallow. To tell people they had been wrong for generations? Who would not dig in their heels against such nonsense from the shy daughter of a chandler and a launderer?

Tendaji must have understood her thoughts because he squeezed her shoulder. "That will be a difficult thing to convince the world of, Ehryn."

"I think it will be impossible."

"You may turn back if you wish. We are still close enough to Clearwall that you can return home. Pretend you never felt these things. Rebury your senses in the twists of the Maze and live a full life in whatever manner you choose. Perhaps you could even learn to be happy."

"What will the Queen say to that?"

"Nothing." Namaoii broke in, sitting down across from them. Ehryn had enough sense to appreciate that the princess had maintained her distance until now, only coming close when the conversation turned in a direction she understood. "Mother will take the information you've provided and mark it down with whatever other information previous Called have given her. You won't get a statute or a crier in the square telling your story, but sometimes people come back from their kintars with snippets of something bigger. Eventually, there will be enough to tell the whole tale. There are always more Called, Ehryn. Maybe it will take generations, but if you can't do it, someone else will see it through when   you   couldn't."

But Ehryn knew that wasn't quite true. Maybe it had been once when people other than the Royal Arcanist could see the Weave and manipulate the strands in a way that gave one more than a lifetime to learn. But something had changed recently. The Voices that called from beneath the Weave were louder now than they used to be, and the threads around them were untangling. And the rot beneath their feet was getting worse. She didn't think time was on their side anymore. More than that, though, she knew she'd never be able to forget the truth now that she had acknowledged it. Spoken it. And she would not drown in that despair again.

"No," she whispered. "I want to keep going."

18

Mavrikal followed.

She still didn't know what She followed. A group of little mortals. Two of them were definitely human. But the others were different, and She still could not quite figure out why. They didn't appear in the Weave like they should. Their threads seemed strong and sure and like they would color the entire Tapestry if left uncut. But She couldn't quite see them like She was supposed to. They were only visible in Her peripheral vision.

Not good. Not good.

The Betrayer had been like that. Had been hard to see in the Weave until the moment when she was all that there was. A blinding thread carrying a screaming sword. They hadn't realized quickly enough that this abnormality was dangerous rather than a defect. They'd thought it was because she had no great role in the Tapestry, when really it was because she spent so much time outside of it.

Illindria had thought She could use the little mortal but had miscalculated. Then the Betrayer had remade the entire Tapestry in an image that did not have Them in it.

Were these humans the same? The two She could not quite see as She slithered after them in the shadows? Or were they like so many of the others She had tasted on the air and followed? Who'd fallen and died before they could reach their destination?

She wasn't sure. She didn't know. She would have to look with Her mortal eyes. See what was right in front of Her.

So She slid from the shadows as the group of four gathered around their campfire. She scoffed. They were nothing. No one. She could kill them now or later or never to no consequence. Just plain children and an old man.

But then She saw the sword.

The sword.

Her sword.

Mavrikal's eyes burned with fury. That was different. That was a problem.

The threads were made to bind mortals. Not objects. Never objects.

Except for one.

She could not risk it. They were getting too close to the trap. There were too many variables.

They were better off dead.

She gathered Herself. Posed to strike. Take the one with the blade out first. The children would fall easily.

Ready…

Ready…

"Mavrikal… wait."

Mavrikal spun. Tasting the air. Watching the darkness of Her side of the veil. No one had been here in… longer than She knew. No one had ever said Her name. She blinked. Hard. Tried to focus black eyes on the darkness no one else had ever broken.

Saw Her. Knew Her. Blinked again. Tried to remember how to make Her voice work. Her mouth. When was the last time She had had to speak?

"Jaladri?"

Her older sister flowed out of the darkness like water. The strands of Her hair moved like seaweed around Her shoulders.

She's left her Hall? Her sanctuary?

"Mavrikal. The mortals. They are stronger than you know." Mavrikal saw now that Jaladri looked small. Weak. The shine in Her eyes was gone. Her hands trembled. Mavrikal thought for a moment that She felt fear at the sight of Her older sibling's vulnerability. She'd forgotten what fear felt like. "They have help, Mavrikal. We must be careful."

Mavrikal blinked again. Used her tongue to taste the flavor of Her sister's voice. Jaladri was sincere. Who could make a Goddess fear?

"Help?" Mavrikal moved close to Jaladri, riding the shadows like a snake's trail. "What help, Jaladri?"

Jaladri's eyes were deeper than Her oceans as She looked back across the millennia They'd ruled.

"The Old Gods."

19

"**May I ask you a question?**" Ehryn asked one day after Namaoii had finished practicing her sword fighting and Kant was a few lengths away studying a green bug with six wings. Tendaji was at the lake nearby and had given them all the choice to learn how to fish or to practice a few new types of magic he'd demonstrated that morning. None of them had opted for fishing.

Namaoii rolled her eyes and took a long pull from her waterskin. "Besides that one?"

"Yes."

"Fine."

"Why aren't you at one of the monasteries, learning to be Faoii?"

Namaoii frowned and opened her mouth to reply, then shut it again. This happened several more times before she finally threw down her waterskin and sighed.

"I could. Everyone tells me I should. Even my mother named me 'Namaoii' as a call to the sacred Order. Becoming a Faoii is basically expected, and everyone knows I'd be good at it." She didn't even look at Ehryn as she stood up and began to pace, speaking like she'd run out of time or be interrupted. "And there *is* honor there. Tradition. Strength and unity. Everything a woman should want, right? I've heard it all. I know it would make the most sense."

"So… why don't you?" Ehryn prodded.

"Because what if there's something more out there? How would I ever learn what else I'm capable of if I just do the first thing I know I can?"

"But battle magic is your gift, isn't it? Wouldn't you want to hone your greatest skill?"

"What if it isn't, though? What if I know battle magic because I've woken up at dawn to train for as long as I can remember? What if everyone assumes that my one gift is being a warrior, but it isn't a gift at all? It was just what I put the most effort into?"

Ehryn considered that and thought about her parents, who contributed happily to society with their washing and candlesticks. Sometimes she forgot that they could have been anything or gone anywhere. But instead, after their kintars, they'd decided to return to Clearwall to do the simple things that they loved. That they were good at. She didn't think Namaoii had that option—to be happy in a simple life with simple magics. The only freedom Namaoii had was to choose to be great in a way her mother hadn't laid out for her—but she would be required to be great, nonetheless.

Namaoii was still looking at Ehryn, and Ehryn tried to at least offer some comfort. She knew from experience that Namaoii opening up like this was a rarity, and she didn't want the older girl to regret it.

Ehryn stood and quietly took both of Namaoii's hands in hers. "I hope you find something of worth on this journey, Namaoii. For right now, you don't have to be anyone other than you."

"Thanks." The response sounded genuine. "Really. I mean it. I'm trying not to put too much stock into this… Call you feel," Namaoii said, her voice grave. "I don't want to put our path and destinies fully in the hands of old deities and deny that we have any hand in it at all. But it's hard not to feel at least some hope that we find something at the end of it."

"If the Royal Arcanist is right, how could we not?" Kantilieh piped up. Namaoii gave him a hard look, and he shrank back again. It happened quickly, but Ehryn caught it and frowned.

"What do you mean?"

"The Royal Arcanist likes to say that adventure finds those who seek it," Namaoii cut in. "But he says that our kintar has the power to change the Weave. If we want it to."

Ehryn frowned. Jacir had made it sound like their journey was of no great consequence. Just a chance for her to learn and grow. Had he told the others something different?

"I've returned, children." The three spun around and bowed their heads as Tendaji approached. "Have you practiced the Danhaid steps I taught you?"

"We have, Faoli," Namaoii lied, "but we have not seen any rabbits."

"Magically called or not, they'll still be frightened by conversations." Tendaji laughed. "Do not worry, though. I was able to catch several fish. Sit down, and I will show you how to gut and clean them."

Namaoii wrinkled her nose but accepted one of the knives that Tendaji doled out to each of them. Ehryn felt a tiny bit of pride. She, at least, knew how to gut a fish.

"Faoli, can I ask you something?" Namaoii said as the old warrior slit one of the white bellies.

"Of course, Namaoii. How can I serve?"

"Tell me about your fantoii." Namaoii motioned to the glistening blade at his side, and Ehryn's heart beat a little faster. She'd wanted to ask about the blade many times before now but had never had the courage. She didn't even know how to start. The Voices on the Wind cheered and babbled in excitement now that the conversation had been broached.

It is your destiny.

You will wield it.

Listen carefully. You will learn.

But Namaoii was talking again, and Ehryn tried to listen without looking like she was too interested. "The best blacksmiths in Clearwall have sent weapons to my family, and I've always had the best pick of the lot. I know my sword, Faoli. You know I do. But I've never seen anything like that before."

Tendaji considered for a moment, setting his knife down next to the fish before unsheathing the blade in question. "I doubt I could explain how it was forged," he replied. "As far as I know, it is the only of its kind, made in an ancient hybrid style that no one teaches."

"By whom? What blacksmith?"

"No blacksmith. My sister created it. In the Monastery of the Eternal Blade. In fact, it's the second blade I've wielded as a hand-me-down from my younger sibling. Funny how the Tapestry weaves sometimes."

A sword made of magics no one knows.

The only one to cut down the usurpers. The False Children.

They call it the Eternal Blade.

It is MINE.

The last voice was that of Alathi, and it quaked with anger and demand. The other voices silenced, and even Ehryn was left shaking in the aftershock of the declaration. No one else seemed to notice, and Namaoii creased her brow. "There is no Monastery of the Eternal Blade in Imeriel. I've been to all of them. Know each of their symbols and Preoii. It doesn't exist."

Tendaji smiled easily. "Sometimes the monasteries change their names to honor events or people. But we were discussing the fantoii, were we not?"

Namaoii frowned again, still looking at the gleaming blade. "It's... superb. Beyond superb. Why did she learn to craft such an amazing instrument and then not share its design with others? Faoii usually believe that the knowledge of one is then the knowledge of all."

Tendaji's eyes looked a little sad when he replied. "She never got the chance. My sister's life was quite extraordinary, filled with tales that were never told. She had both too much time and not enough, and the world is lesser for what it has forgotten in her passing."

"Not if we pass it on!" Kant yelled. "Tell us about her! About how she made it. Let us carry it forward!"

Tendaji laughed. "Young people are always so excited to do grand things. It is honorable but out of balance. Tomorrow we might learn to forge great swords. Today, however, we gut fish." He resheathed the blade (much to the ire of Alathi's distant howl) and picked up his knife again. "Pay attention, children."

The fish were cooking over the campfire when Namaoii cleared her throat again. "We're getting close to the Monastery of the Fallen Star," she said. "I want to stop there. Speak to the Faoii inside."

"Why?" Ehryn asked, turning the stick sporting her cleaned fish over. "I thought you said you'd been to every monastery in Imeriel."

"Why do you care? It's on the way, and we're bound to learn something better than gutting fish," Namaoii snarled, still trying to wash fish pieces off her hands in the grass. Ehryn was a little surprised by the princess's outburst, thinking that they'd been on better terms a few hours before, but when she looked at Namaoii's slightly green tint, she felt sorry for the royal and let it go. Namaoii handled discomfort and embarrassment poorly. "We're wasting our kintar on peasant work," Namaoii added under her breath, confirming Ehryn's suspicions.

"That's not true!" Kant yelled gleefully. "Look!" He held a stick aloft, hummed a short tune, and it sparked into flame. "I've learned so much!" Tendaji gave the young boy a nod of approval, and Kant's smile widened even more. "This is the greatest kintar ever!"

Ehryn couldn't help but laugh. Kant's excitement was so genuine. So pure. He laughed at her laughing, and soon they were both giggling uncontrollably, though neither was really sure why. Even Namaoii finally broke into a grin. The tension lifted.

"I have been there before," she finally said. "But it was with my mother. I'd like to go back without her there. There are questions I wanted to ask before but couldn't."

Ehryn tilted her head to one side. "I didn't think you'd be the kind of person to keep secrets from the Queen."

"I'm not! It's not like that!" Namaoii shot back. She huffed through her nose and rolled her neck, forcing her next words to come out more softly. "There are … things my mother doesn't think I'm ready to learn. But I am. And my kintar is the place to prove it."

"I don't see any reason why we cannot stop by the monastery," Tendaji said smoothly. "Ehryn, you still feel called to the North?" Ehryn listened to the Voices answer in the affirmative and nodded. "And you have no reason to disagree?"

"No," Ehryn replied. "I actually like the idea. I've never seen one of the Faoii monasteries. I've always wondered what they were like."

"Good," Namaoii said, plucking her cooked fish from the fire and taking a bite. "First thing tomorrow, then. If we push the horses, we might be able to get there before they begin sparring practice."

Ehryn laughed again. Of course sparring practice would be high on Namaoii's list of priorities.

The Monastery of the Fallen Star was far grander than Ehryn thought it would be. While the entire building was very utilitarian in design, there was a graceful, organic curve to the structure unlike anything she'd ever seen before. Everything in Clearwall was either made of straight, efficient lines or a jumbled, hectic mess like the Maze. This was the best of both extremes. It was probably the most beautiful building she'd ever seen.

The Faoii at the gates evidently recognized Namaoii, because they fisted their hands as though grasping an invisible hilt and bowed their heads at her approach. Namaoii and Tendaji both mirrored the gesture, and one of the two sentries dashed inside.

Ehryn wasn't sure how long the guard was gone, so enthralled was she with the twisted metal vines that had been sculpted onto the sides of the monastery walls. She thought they looked hollow but couldn't figure out what the purpose of that would be. There were hollow pipes in their home that carried heat from the silkstrand furnace through the rest of the house, but these didn't seem to serve that purpose.

"I read about those," Kant said at her elbow before his voice took on its monotonous tenor. "'Faoii monasteries traditionally combine beauty and function. While intricate and pleasing to observe, most monasteries sport hollowed, carved vines along their exterior. These decorations are crafted to carry boiling oil down on enemies in case of a siege. In this chapter we will…'"

Ehryn froze, her fingers almost touching one delicate petal. How could something so beautiful be made for something so deadly?

"That's enough, Kant," she whispered. Kantilieh went silent next to her.

The massive door opened again, and a towering woman approached. Her bronze breastplate was nearly blinding in the morning light, and the iron rings woven into her long braid struck against it as she descended the monastery steps. She looked surprised for a moment when she sighted them gathered at the base of the stairs but masked it quickly.

"Hail, Brother," she said to Tendaji, ignoring the others gathered. "May the Goddesses guide your footfalls."

"Hail, Preoii. I am grateful for your blessing, but I am not the one who has sought you out. I bring guests to your hall." He motioned to Namaoii, and the tall woman turned her eyes on the girl.

After a moment of consideration, she spoke again. "Princess Namaoii of Clearwall. Welcome to the Monastery of the Fallen Star. What does the Starlit Throne want with the Faoii?"

Namaoii bowed her head slightly, surprising Ehryn. She'd never seen Namaoii show that level of respect to anyone other than Tendaji. "Preoii-Victoria. I have reached kintar age. I've come to your monastery to seek knowledge about the Faoii and their ways.

I hope that a better understanding of Clearwall's oldest allies will benefit both of our people when I ascend the Starlit Throne."

Preoii-Victoria tilted her head to one side, studying the girl. "You wish to join the Order? Study our ways here in the Monastery of the Fallen Star?"

Namaoii shook her head. "No, Preoii. This is only a stop on our journey. If you'll grant us a few hours of your time."

The Preoii looked over each of them slowly, and Ehryn felt like the towering woman could see into her soul. "You understand that there are some rooms the unascended are not allowed to enter, and that this applies to all of you as well?"

"Yes, Faoii. Though I would be grateful for information about the rite of ascension, if you will share it." Namaoii bowed her head at this request, fisting her hands one over the other in front of her chest as she did.

Preoii-Victoria gave a slight half smile at that. "Very well. I will have a Faoii stable your horses. Welcome, travelers of Clearwall, to the Monastery of the Fallen Star."

20

The grand hall of the Faoii monastery was extraordinary. Ehryn was so fascinated by the sound of their echoing footfalls reverberating off the high beams that she didn't hear anything of what the Faoii was saying to Namaoii as they walked. Kant seemed to be paying rapt attention, however, and Ehryn knew she could ask him to repeat it later if she decided it was something she wanted to learn. Until then, she wanted to experience the Faoii's exclusive world in her own way. Even the Voices on the Wind were quieter than usual, giving off an air of… reverence? Ehryn didn't know, but it sat comfortably on her soul. She didn't want to forget anything she saw here, in this place of peace and strength.

She was memorizing the way the firelight illuminated the triangle and spiral design on their sconces when something to one side of the grand hall caught her eye.

"Wait," she said, just loudly enough to make the others stop and turn towards her. "What is that?"

There was a statue in a recessed alcove off the main passageway, framed by a window on either side. It was so plain in comparison to the towering marble figure that dominated the far end of the grand hall that Ehryn assumed most people wouldn't have even noticed it. But there was something about the three flickering candles, two over the statue's head and one at its base, that had caught her eye, and now that she had seen it, Ehryn was unable to look away. The woman depicted looked so strong, so fierce… but also incredibly sad. Her bronze breastplate was cracked and marred, her braid disheveled so that thick curls framed her pained eyes. The fantoii in her hand was held limply at one side, barely held by weary fingers. It was not a powerful pose, but Ehryn thought that was part of what made it so striking. She understood this woman in a way she didn't realize she could empathize with an inanimate object. Could feel the cloud that had nearly suffocated her draped around the statue's sagging shoulders.

Preoii-Victoria stepped up behind her, gazing thoughtfully at the piece. "This is a depiction of Faoii-Kaiya the Emancipator. You might know her as the Betrayer."

"Why the blades—" Namaoii stopped herself and tried again. "Why would you choose to have her shrine in the same room as one of the Goddesses? Won't that anger Them? She killed Their sister and started all those wars."

It was Tendaji who responded. "Because whether you believe what she did was right or not, Faoii-Kaiya's actions colored the Eternal Tapestry's strands in ways that no one can ignore or undo. For better or worse, the monasteries must recognize her hand in what they are today." Ehryn glanced over her shoulder at the old warrior. His ice-blue eyes held the same sorrowful gaze as the statue.

Preoii-Victoria nodded. "Exactly. We cannot condone or decry what Faoii-Kaiya the Betrayer did in her life, only acknowledge that everything the Order now is owes itself, in some way, to her." The Preoii set one hand on the statue's base. "Faoii-Kaiya came from this monastery. She was raised on these grounds. Her breastplate and ivy helm were crafted in our armory. We must all be prepared to shoulder the responsibility of our actions, knowing that they might one day hold as much weight, while constantly maintaining vigilance so that they never do."

"Tendaji! She looks like you!" Kant said, pointing and smiling. Tendaji gave a half-smile to the boy and set a hand on his shoulder.

"Let's hear what else the Preoii has to say about the grand hall, shall we?"

The others turned away from the shrine, but Ehryn stayed for a few minutes longer, staring at Faoii-Kaiya's mournful gaze, trying not to listen to Alathi's whispers.

Look carefully, Ehryn of Clearwall. You will be My arm, and you will follow in her footsteps. I will make you worthy of her gaze.

Ehryn's eyes fell on the statue's fantoii hanging at Kaiya's side. She could feel its weight in her hand.

She shuddered in a sudden, icy wind from the North.

21

Alathi stood beside Her favorite brother. The little mortals had caught many of the Gods' eyes, and They had eventually come to watch them. Mold them. Try to raise some of them as She had. Alathi let Her siblings squabble amongst each other. Let some of Them take and lead those little mortals that had not dedicated themselves to Her. But even Her tribes were growing numerous. They had fractured amongst themselves. Her Danhaid had broken from the Alathi of Her namesake, using Her dances to live in harmony between the land and sky, far to the west. They were as capable of fighting as any of Her Wolves, and yet they preferred not to raise the beaded spears She'd gifted them. Alathi did not hate these deserters, but she did not consider them perfect. They were Her wayward wings, but she did not need them. Should they choose to return to Her, She would accept them back, but they were no longer Her focus.

Instead, Her eye was drawn to the pinnacles of Her tutelage. Those who took Her word as law, who had distilled Her teachings into a single, glorious Oath and used what they'd learned to build something marvelous.

Her brother nodded in approval. The little mortals had done more than any who had come before. They'd traveled across the sea and built monasteries in Her image. They focused not only on the war and guidance She'd shown them in the past but centered themselves now on a new doctrine that was both sword and shield. That balanced the scales and colored the Weave with glorious threads that shone and glittered and emitted a light unlike anything Alathi had seen before. And they searched the skies and the weave and the Oath for a balance no one else had sought.

The mortals called for Justice.

And Alathi heard them.

She responded with something She'd never considered before: A treaty. A balance to the scales that mirrored what Her followers had finally grown up enough to perceive.

She called upon Avanli, Her favorite brother. The Shield to Her Sword. Together, They reigned.

And the little mortals were finally strong enough to understand that both were important. They started writing down their histories. Started protecting their past, their future, their neighbors… even their enemies' stories. They made treaties and laws and defined morality with words. The little mortals started to care for the well-being of those outside their walls, whether the outsiders worshipped Alathi or not.

For once, Her children cared for the world as a whole, and that inspired Alathi. Enough for Her to seek an ally of her own in this existence where She'd fought Her siblings since the dawn of time. Avanli came, and they worked in tandem to guide these little mortals to the balance they sought.

Alathi and Avanli. Together They were Justice. Balance. And They were worshipped by the strongest of the mortals.

They were the Faoii.

Their Sword and Shield.

22

Ehryn tried to stay out of the way as the others toured the Faoii monastery. Kant had evidently read many things about the Faoii, and he prattled endlessly about forging swords and making breastplates and how different plaits symbolized different things for different women. Preoii-Victoria seemed conflicted when he talked about the connections between the Faoii and other Illindrian factions across Imeriel, but Namaoii was intrigued.

"Wait. Say that last part again," she instructed.

Kant smiled and started again without missing a beat. "A close look at the different sects of religious groups across Imeriel and Alathi give us unique insight into the development and relationship between the cultures over time. The Alathi, Danhaid, Croeli, and Faoii share many of the same roots, despite a conscious effort by some or all of the groups to differentiate themselves from each other at different times. Besides the obvious connection of accessing magic through the Goddesses and the Weave in a way those outside the sects could not do, we can see evidence of this cultural evolution in hairstyles and language. The Alathi skalds have the same designs in their beards as the Cleroii have in their braids, suggesting that the two groups, despite their separation of gender, time, and continent, played similar roles within their organizations. So can we, too, see distinct developments of Alathi, Danhaid, and Croeli naming patterns, with the newly-developed Faoii altering from this convention as a way of distinguishing themselves from the ostracized and perceived enemies of their Order…"

Ehryn tried to act interested, but she was already lost. Tendaji, however, seemed genuinely pleased at the boy's excitement. "You know, Kantilieh, there was a time when no one knew any of these things, and you could be killed or worse for implying that any of these groups had the same roots. I'd thought these histories were lost forever. It's nice to hear you sharing them."

"I think…" Kant scrunched up his face, trying to choose the words for a thought his brain wasn't quite capable of formulating. "I think that…. That nothing's lost forever if you know where to look. Even the things that go extinct are really just… waiting. Until we have the knowledge and the understanding and the tools to bring them back."

Something about the way he spoke reminded Ehryn of her childhood. Something about the way she and Dhruv had grown impossible plants in their little garden. About looking for seeds… Him leading her home… Something about birds?

But then they were being ushered outside to the Faoii courtyard, and the thought vanished.

"While the Faoii get the majority of their food supplies from common citizens outside our monasteries, young herbalists are often brought to the Order to become Cleroii. Our gardens are cultivated to offer our unascended everything they need to hone their craft for the betterment of the Order," Preoii-Victoria said, speaking over Kant until he fell silent.

"And all of Imeriel, yes?" Namaoii asked. Preoii-Victoria glanced at her.

"Of course. The Faoii serve. We are the strength of the weak and the voice of the silent."

Namaoii looked like she was going to say something snarky in reply, and Ehryn cut her off. It would look bad for all of them if they were forced to leave.

"What is that?" she asked, pointing to a boxed-off plot at the center of the garden. It was barren.

Preoii-Victoria pressed her lips into a thin line. "A reminder. And to some Faoii, a hope."

The tonicloran.

Help us.

Ehryn shook off the icy chill again and followed the others. Many of the warriors on the grounds were warming up to spar, and Namaoii was almost giddy in anticipation. She did her best to remained poised, though, and Ehryn thought she was doing a good job. The Preoii obviously noticed, however, and almost smiled when she turned to the Wolf Pup.

"Princess Namaoii, you've been trained by ascended Faoii, haven't you? Would you care to join the unascended?"

Ehryn thought that Namaoii would jump out of her own skin in delight, but the princess only fisted her hands and bowed her head. "It would be an honor, Preoii." Ehryn was impressed by her decorum.

"Very well. The unascended do not practice with live steel. Tevli will help you find a practice sword. He will be your shield mate during practice." Preoii-Victoria called over a young male warrior and gave him instructions. Namaoii couldn't repress her smile as she followed him towards the field.

For some time after that Ehryn and Kant sat to one side of the training grounds while their companions practiced with the Faoii. Namaoii was treated like the other soldiers sparring, her title holding no meaning within the monastery walls. However, she was not treated like an outsider, either. Ehryn didn't think she'd ever seen Namaoii look so… content. At peace. Joyful. The royal seemed to be in her element, and she thanked the Faoii each time they finished a match, regardless of who won. Except for the difference in armor and hairstyle, it was easy to picture Namaoii as one of the unascended. The princess could have been at home here.

While Ehryn and Kant were mostly politely ignored and Namaoii was treated like a sister amongst the unascended, Tendaji was revered with the utmost respect. There was no questioning that he was held in as high regard as Preoii-Victoria, despite being from a different monastery. He was so revered, in fact, that Ehryn finally hailed a young warrior as she passed.

"Excuse me, Faoii. May I ask you something?" The girl turned towards Ehryn, looking at her plain clothes and unbraided hair uncertainly.

"I'm not sure how much I can tell you, citizen. You are not of the Order. Would you like me to fetch one of the ascended?"

"No. I just… Everyone is being very respectful to Tendaji. Do you know anything about him?" The Faoii looked over to the old warrior that was standing straight and tall next to Preoii-Victoria at the head of the ranks.

"He is a Faoli," she stated simply. "You can tell by how he moves. How he stands. He is ascended enough to have his rank before his name. I admit, I've never seen a Faoli before. They are… rare."

"Why?"

The Faoii looked around uncertainly. "Both women and men are allowed into the Order. For the first time since the Faoii and Croeli split into two groups over interpretations of the Oath centuries ago, all people are welcome within the Faoii ranks. Technically… Technically, all unascended here are equals and are as likely as their sisters to earn ascension. But old traditions die hard.

For a man to earn his rank is not common. He must have had to push through some of the biggest obstacles imaginable and then still kept going. It is truly an honorable thing. It gives us all strength." The Faoii looked admiringly over at the warrior once more just as Preoii-Victoria yelled out across the field.

"Faoii! Form ranks!"

"Sorry, I must go." The Faoii dashed away, and Ehryn refocused on Preoii-Victoria with Tendaji standing next to her.

"Faoii, today we have a demonstration from Faoli-Tendaji of..." Preoii-Victoria paused, glancing to the taller man. Tendaji smiled.

"The Monastery of the Blessed Tendril."

Lies.

Be wary.

If there was something strange about the name, Preoii-Victoria didn't seem to notice, because she nodded. "Faoli-Tendaji of the Monastery of the Blessed Tendril. Watch and learn, Faoii. You hold your blade above all..."

"Because it protects all and shall be part of me," the gathered Faoii said in unison, fisting their hands in front of them before turning their gazes to Tendaji. The Faoli half-smiled and drew his glistening blade. It sang with the might of gods and demons.

The Eternal Blade.

The Goddess Slayer.

You will wield it, Ehryn.

You must wield it.

Help us.

The unascended watching Faoli-Tendaji were as awestruck as Ehryn and Namaoii had been when they'd first seen him move through the steps of his sword dance, his fantoii gliding through the air with an almost supernatural ease. They gasped at the way he flowed across the training ground, wraithlike even without Blinking sporadically like he had while training with Namaoii in the woods. And when he finished demonstrating, the Faoii who had been trained since childhood to be warriors seemed like newborn colts in comparison.

"Lift your blades, Faoii," Tendaji said kindly. "I will walk you through the steps."

The Faoii students practiced for hours, never showing weariness or distress. Whenever it seemed that the line would waver, either Tendaji or one of the Cleroii would offer a song of healing and strength, and the wall of bodies would straighten again. It was captivating to watch so many people dance through the wraithlike movements that Tendaji demonstrated again and again. And while the unascended could not match his grace, there was something awe-inspiring about seeing a hundred bodies move as one in their deadly, beautiful dance.

At the end of practice, a swarm of young, eager unascended flooded towards Tendaji, heads bowed and hands clasped. Even Ehryn wanted to go and tell him how impressive his display had been, but something else caught her eye. Namaoii, instead of pushing through to stand next to her mentor in front of dozens of warriors that would have given anything to be in her place, walked dutifully across the grounds, aiming for Preoii-Victoria. The set of her shoulders carried commanding power, and Ehryn followed out of curiosity, taking Kant by the hand and leading him forward.

They arrived just in time to hear Namaoii ask a pointed question. "Preoii-Victoria. How many Hollowed are here within the monastery?"

Ehryn's mouth went dry. *Hollowed? Here?*

But of course they would be. Where else would the Queen imprison Imeriel's most dangerous and heartless citizens? Where would be better than within the safe confines of a Faoii monastery?

Preoii-Victoria still faced the training grounds, her hands clasped behind her back, seemingly focused on the unascended as they gathered around Tendaji asking questions and requesting additional training. But Ehryn could see the Preoii give Namaoii a long look from around her ivy-covered helm.

"Your mother the Queen has all our most recent reports on the status of the Hollowed in our care, Princess. If you are worried about the safety of your people, I can assure you that the Faoii stand as the shield wall against corruption, now and forever."

"I'm not asking about the safety of Clearwall," Namaoii said, also aligning herself to face the training grounds, hands clasped in a similar fashion. Ehryn noted that the Wolf Cub was taller than Preoii-Victoria. "I am asking about the well-being of the Hollowed."

This did draw a reaction from the Preoii, who swiveled her head to raise an eyebrow in Namaoii's direction.

Namaoii stood her ground. "Hollowed or not, they are my people. The days of Imeriel's citizens rotting away in dungeons, injured and dying, are over, Preoii. Are they not?"

"Of course. Your mother's instructions were very clear."

"Show me."

For a minute, Ehryn thought that Preoii-Victoria would refuse, but with a steady step, she led Namaoii and the others to a building separated from the rest of the monastery. It had heavy doors and the windows were not as large and beautiful as the ones they'd seen in the great hall, but it was not a blemish or cage like Ehryn assumed the Hollowed chambers would be. The Faoii posted at the entrance clasped their hands together at the Preoii's approach, and the Faoii leader led Namaoii inside. Ehryn and Kant followed quickly.

The long hallway was pungent with the scent of incense and herbs. Ehryn recognized the smell of chinol, one of the common herbs her mother put into candles for healers. A Faoii in soft leathers rather than the bronze breastplate approached, her eyes kind. Preoii-Victoria fisted her hands.

"Cleroii-Ashvu, this is Namaoii of Clearwall. She has questions about your patients."

"I will answer as I can. Greetings, Namaoii of Clearwall."

Namaoii didn't respond and pushed past the Cleroii, approaching the first door in the long hallway. She peered into the high barred window. Ehryn stayed behind, keeping her hands on Kant's shoulders when he tried to follow Namaoii. If Namaoii noticed their uncertainty or even that they'd followed her inside, she didn't say anything. Instead, she called through the small, barred opening.

"You there. Stand up. How do they treat you here?"

It seemed like a long time passed before a frail, emaciated face appeared in the opening. Even from across the room, Ehryn withdrew on reflex, every fiber in her being screaming at the carved X on the Hollowed's forehead.

She and everyone in Clearwall had been trained their entire life to fear the Hollowed more than wolves and bears and invading armies. They were rare, fortunately—but the instinct was there. To cast out the few people in the world whose gifts were broken, tarnished, wrong. Who could negate another person's magic with will and thought alone. It was assumed that the effect was temporary, but no one really knew. And the idea of losing your magic, no matter how small or insignificant it seemed, was something that shook most people to the core. A person's gift was a huge part of their identity. That someone could take that away was... terrifying in a way nothing else was.

Namaoii didn't seem afraid at all. The tensing of her shoulders seemed to be from anger rather than fear, and the Wolf Pup forcefully eased her stance before speaking again. "What's your name?" she asked softly. Ehryn raised an eyebrow. Namaoii's voice was... kind. To a Hollowed. Everyone knew that the Hollowed were devoid of emotion. Of sanity. No one was *kind* to a Hollowed.

And yet... and yet the Hollowed responded.

"Amati, Ma'am."

"Amati. How do they treat you here?"

The Hollowed was quiet for a few moments before responding. "Better than they treated me on the outside. I… I am fed. Three times every day. The food… the food is good. Nourishing. The Cleroii set the bones that the elders in my old village broke. Healed the infected lashes on my back. They… they even let me go outside, if I ask. I get to see the sky and sun. Breathe the fresh air. But I am… afraid. Of the guards. I hear them whisper."

"Who has threatened you? What did they say?" Victoria barked, apparently as angry at this news as Namaoii was. Amati didn't respond.

"But no one has mistreated you?" Namaoii asked again. "You are well-fed and cared for?" The Hollowed nodded, but Ehryn could see the woman's pallor and jutting cheekbones even from across the hall.

"It's true," Preoii-Victoria said sternly. "We follow the Queen's instructions. The Hollowed are well-kept while they are in our care."

"She's barely skin and bones!" Namaoii's voice was shaking.

"This one has an illness I haven't been able to cure," the Cleroii said quietly. "She does not eat. Whispers in the night. Were she not a Hollowed…" Cleroii-Ashvu went quiet, looking almost embarrassed.

"Speak," Preoii-Victoria demanded. "What were you about to say?"

"If… if she wasn't a Hollowed, I'd almost believe she was one of the Called. The things she says… we had a Called amongst our ranks, once. They disappeared into the North. This one… Amati. She sounds like he did."

"No one from outside the monasteries has two blessings," Preoii-Victoria sneered. "And certainly not a blessing and the Hollowed curse. This is nonsense."

Cleroii-Ashvu clasped her hands in front of her and bowed her head. "I know, Preoii. That is why I never reported it. Her words are simply the ravings of a madwoman. But we are of the Fallen Star. No one is beyond help."

Something from deep within Ehryn's memories pulled at her. From a time before she heard the Voice on the Wind. From when she and Dhruv played in the garden... When he'd led her home after they looked for seeds...

But then Amati was screaming, and the thought was lost.

"It's the blood! The power is in the blood! She wants it. But I won't let Her have it! I won't eat the food! I won't be strong enough to be sent to Her! I'll die here first! She can't use me if I don't let Her!"

This time Namaoii spun completely around to face Preoii-Victoria, and the Preoii actually *tensed* in the fury that rolled off the Wolf Pup. Ehryn doubted anyone had ever made Victoria tense before.

"What is she talking about?" Namaoii demanded.

The Faoii's voice had the faintest tremor when she spoke. "I assure you, Princess. I do not know. No one is allowed to approach the Hollowed alone, not even me. Blood magic is forbidden within the Order. And even if it weren't, without the fabled tonicloran, no one alive knows how to practice those dark magics. Whatever she thinks she's seen, it was not one of us."

Namaoii opened her mouth to respond, her fists clenched, but a sudden, fierce cry from the cell forced her to turn back to the Hollowed again.

"No! Not her. She is nothing compared to She Who Comes at Night. She sees us. Watches us. Waits for us. And now She has seen you, knows you. She will follow. Something is coming, and She Who Drains the Blood carries it forward!"

"Who are you talking about? Who is hurting you?" Namaoii and Victoria said in near unison.

But Amati didn't seem to hear. "Listen to me. Listen! She needs the blood of the Hollowed. She craves the power of erasure. The Hollowed in the monasteries are not safe from Her for long. *None* of them. *None.* Mavrikal's servant knows where we are sent. Knows where our thread is cut! They work in unison, and in our fall will be yours, too!" The terrified intensity with which she spoke made Ehryn shudder, and she could see the hair on the back of Namaoii's neck stand up.

"Amati. Let me help you. Let me—" Namaoii started, but she jumped back in surprise when the Hollowed suddenly thrust her hands through the bars, screaming about demons in the night and eyes in the stars.

Neither Namaoii nor Ehryn even had a chance to react when the Faoii who had been standing at the door were *there*, binding the Hollowed's hands and wrists in thongs of leather.

"Don't hurt her!" Namaoii yelled. "She can't... she didn't touch me. It's fine." But Ehryn heard the way her voice shook as she spoke.

Preoii-Victoria's voice, on the other hand, was hard as iron. "If you're *quite* satisfied, Princess, I'd prefer to return outside. We have obliged you until now, but I do not want harm to come to you within the monastery walls. The Faoii have no desire to anger the Starlit Throne." Preoii-Victoria's tone offered no room for argument.

"Yeah... Yeah. We're done here." Namaoii turned away from the crying Hollowed and returned to the courtyard, rolling her shoulders. "She's wasting away. Even if she's insane, there must be something you can do for her physical health."

"I was not aware that she was choosing not to eat. We will find out what she is doing with her rations and make sure that she is properly nourished. Her mind will not heal if her body does not," Preoii-Victoria relented.

"And… I know the incense hides it, but it still smells terrible in there."

"That is impossible to avoid in any barracks that are constantly occupied," Preoii-Victoria replied, the lines around her eyes showing the barest hint of annoyance.

"You don't have every cell filled, do you?" Victoria shook her head. "Rotate the Hollowed between cells more often. Thoroughly clean the cells between rotations. It should help with the smell and might help with… with whatever has her so anxious." Victoria seemed to consider this for a moment.

"We can do that after each Hollowed is healed and sent on," she finally replied.

Namaoii stopped walking, her brow creasing. "Sent… on? The Hollowed are sent away from here? That wasn't something born of the poor girl's madness?"

Preoii-Victoria looked surprised. "Of course. We are only to find the Hollowed throughout Imeriel and provide for them until they are well enough to be sent into their servitude. Your mother was very clear on this."

"And… and where do they go to become servants?"

The faintest hint of fear or uncertainty on Preoii-Victoria's face. The quick glance of indecisiveness as she tried to determine if this was a trap or a test.

"Surely you are aware, Princess—"

"Tell me!" Namaoii's voice was filled with steel and fire.

The Preoii's eyes darkened, but she did not back away. "Why, to the Elisian enclaves. Where they go from there I do not know, but all Hollowed are conscripted by your mother's hand. For the greatness of Imeriel. The greatness of Clearwall."

Namaoii's shoulders tensed, but she did not speak. Preoii-Victoria's eyes were still dark with seething rage at having been commanded by someone outside the Order. Ehryn could feel the tension sparking between them, like the sky right before a thunderstorm.

"Namaoii," she said quietly, stepping between the two warriors. "Maybe we should go."

"That might be best. Is there anything else, *your majesty?*" Preoii-Victoria stressed the last part, and Ehryn was suddenly very aware that the Faoii had no obligations to obey the Throne other than courtesy and whatever treaty Queen Isolde had set up between them. Namaoii's actions might could wear that relationship thin very quickly, if they hadn't already.

Namaoii seemed to figure it out too, because she released the tension in her stance. Deliberately, she clasped her hands in front of her and bowed her head. "Thank you for your hospitality, Preoii-Victoria of the Monastery of the Fallen Star. The Starlit Throne is honored by our alliance and hopes to maintain our friendship for generations to come. With your blessing, we will leave now to continue our kintar."

Preoii-Victoria stared at Namaoii for a long moment before she relaxed and returned the gesture. "It was our... honor to host one of the royal family. It would be our honor to invite you to dinner, as is customary between the Faoii Order and the Starlit Throne."

Namaoii shook her head. "I'm afraid we must decline, Preoii. We have much to do before we return to Clearwall."

"Then may the Goddesses guide your footfalls. Please give your mother my regards."

Namaoii promised to do so, and Ehryn was impressed by the dance she'd watched the two perform with only words. She and Kant also offered their goodbyes before Namaoii led them back out to the courtyard.

Tendaji must have seen something in Namaoii's face, because he separated himself from the unascended and drifted over until he was walking next to the young warrior.

"We are leaving." He did not frame it like a question. "Are you alright, Namaoii?"

"I'm fine. But there's something dark happening here. I want to be far away from here before nightfall."

No one argued. Ehryn's head still reeled and her limbs quaked in fear at the thought of that carved X on Amati's forehead. She'd never been so close to a Hollowed before. She hoped never to be again.

They were almost to the gate when Cleroii-Ashvu ran up, face grim. "Princess Namaoii," she said as she reached them, "there's something you should know."

"What?"

"I might be speaking out of place in your customs, but not in ours. The Queen's private operations are not of the jurisdiction of the Faoii, and we have brokered a peace with her. Several of the Hollowed I have treated were far worse off than I could attribute purely to poverty. They spoke of a mine. A mine filled with conscripted Hollowed, worked past exhaustion and often left unburied in a labyrinth. They... they often spoke of having seen the Queen there. They fear her greatly. I don't know if such a place truly exists, but whatever your mother hid from you, she is fully aware of how they are being treated. These mines seem to be the end of the thread for those Hollowed that do not somehow make it back into my care."

"Where is this mine?" Namaoii demanded.

Ashvu shook her head. "I don't know. I wasn't sure it was real, and I never asked for more information. I was just trying to make those poor people more comfortable."

Namaoii's eyes narrowed, and she rose to her full, intimidating height. "More than one person told you of the same torture camp and you thought it was just a fever dream? What kind of excuse is that? That's below your Order, Faoii. You should be ashamed."

Rather than looking admonished, Cleroii-Ashvu squared her shoulders. "I did not have to tell you at all, Namaoii of Clearwall. You've trained with some of our ascended and you've learned our history, but that does not make you one of us. Do not presume to speak for the Preoii when I was only trying to help you."

Something in the words filled Ehryn with a deep, irrepressible rage. It wasn't until she smelled blood on the wind that she realized the anger was not her own.

Lend me your voice, Child! Alathi's command thundered through her head and made it clear that it was not a request.

Almost before Ehryn could give her control to the Goddess, it was wrested from her, and a booming declaration of rage and demand burst from her throat in a voice that was not her own.

"SHE PRESUMES NOTHING, SMALL FAOII WHO HAS FORGOTTEN THE WAY. BEFORE YOU WERE YOUR PREOII'S PETS, YOU WERE *MINE*. BEFORE YOU WERE THE FALSE CHILD ILLINDRIA'S, YOU WERE *MINE*. YOU WERE THE SWORD AND SHIELD I HANDED TO THE PEOPLE WHO COULD NOT DEFEND THEMSELVES. YOU WERE THE OATH I SWORE TO UPHOLD. YOU DARE OFFER UP PALTRY EXCUSES ON WHY YOU ARE LESS THAN THAT FROM WHICH I FORGED YOU? KNEEL NOW BEFORE THE ETERNAL BLADE YOU SWEAR UPON AND TELL ME THE OATH I GAVE YOU IN YOUR BIRTH."

Ashvu's eyes were wide and her face ashen. With knees bent by a force beyond her understanding, the Faoii fell before the power of Alathi's demand. She trembled on the ground, nose bent to the dirt at Ehryn's feet.

"That voice… that… My Goddess. You are the foundations on which our Order was built. The ties to an Oath that is older than these walls or these grounds. You… I… I don't…"

"I GAVE YOU A COMMAND. REPEAT THE OATH ON WHICH I BUILT YOUR ORDER. THE OATH I CARVED INTO YOUR PREDECESSORS' BONES."

Ashvu didn't even bring her face up from the dirt. Words rolled from her tongue in a steady stream. "I am Faoii. I am the harbinger of justice and truth. I am the strength of the weak and the voice of the silent." Next to them, Tendaji looked uncertainly between Ehryn and Ashvu, then fisted his hands in front of him, but did not speak. "My blade is my arm, and as such is the arm of all people. Wherever I am, there will a weapon against injustice always be. And with this weapon, I will protect the weak and purge all evil in the land. I will be ready to perform my duty for the weak at all times. And through this, I shall remember that all things are sacred and all souls worthwhile. But my blade will be held above all, for it protects all, and shall be a part of me. For I am Faoii."

There was a deep and awesome power in the Faoii Oath, and it rippled out from the ground beneath Ashvu's repeated phrases. Others nearby turned their heads to see what was happening. They fisted their hands and joined the chorus. "My tongue will never forget the words of truth, for when I speak, then will the Goddess hear, and I am only Faoii in Her presence. We are the Weavers of the Tapestry. We see the threads through all the world and guide them with the Goddess's eye. Above all, we are Faoii."

Preoii-Victoria was approaching now, and Alathi did not give her the chance to speak. "JOIN YOUR SUBORDINATE OR BE SILENT." Ehryn's throat was dry, and her entire body ached. Preoii-Victoria's head snapped to the side like the command was a physical blow, and then she, too, hit her knees and matched Ashvu in the Oath. Still more followed her example.

"Our blades will sing with the voice of every throat that has cried out against injustice and dance with the steps of every innocent child. We will lead the choir, and the voices of our swords will deafen the ears of our enemies. For we are Faoii."

The wind around them picked up, cold and strong like a gale through mountain peaks as they repeated the last line again, in unison, tied together by a thread that felt to Ehryn older than the Tapestry itself. "We are Faoii!"

The Oath exploded across the monastery grounds, and the silence that followed was so absolute that no one missed Alathi's next words when She spoke again. "TELL ME, FALLEN FAOII OF THE FALLEN STAR—WHICH PART OF THAT OATH WOULD YOU SAY YOU FULFILLED WHEN YOU LEARNED THERE WERE PEOPLE ENSLAVED WITHIN RIDING DISTANCE OF YOUR MONASTERY AND YOU DID NOT RAISE A BLADE TO HELP THEM?"

Ashvu was sobbing into the ground, and it was Preoii-Victoria who responded. "My Goddess. My Queen. The... the Order was decimated by the Queen of Dark Iron. We are barely within the first few generations of Faoii with which the Order is to be rebuilt. We must focus on strengthening our numbers and training our warriors before we can blindly go to help others who are not of the sisterhood. Those outside our walls must defend themselves for a time before we can return to the protectors we once were."

Ehryn thought her jaw would break or her eyes would bleed with the scream of Alathi's response. Her entire body was shaking now, but she could not break free. "YOU INSOLENT CHILD! AS LONG AS ONE FAOII STANDS, THERE *MUST* BE JUSTICE. A SWORD THAT IS HUNG ON THE WALL IS USELESS TO THE FARMERS WHOSE CROPS BURN. A THOUSAND DANCES LIKE THAT WHICH I WATCHED TODAY ARE WORTH NOTHING MORE THAN A CHILD'S FIRST STEPS

IF YOU'D USE THEM ONLY FOR SELF-AGGRANDIZEMENT WITHIN YOUR PRETTY WALLS. HOW *DARE YOU!*"

If Preoii-Victoria responded, Ehryn didn't hear. She was burning alive from the inside. She'd become a cauldron moments before it boiled over. One of Jacir's sky fish that got too full. She felt her body trembling, felt the sweat beading on her forehead, but she could do nothing. She couldn't even clench her teeth together to stop Alathi's tirade.

Tendaji must have noticed something was wrong because suddenly he was behind her, hands on her shoulders. They made Ehryn feel grounded. Connected.

"Enough," he whispered. "Let her go."

Ehryn didn't know if the "her" was referring to herself or Alathi, but she didn't care. She wanted to be free. She ached and her throat was dry and harsh. She felt like she'd been fighting against tied ropes for an eternity. She wanted Alathi to say Her piece and leave her be.

Ehryn felt Alathi consider Tendaji's words, and when the Goddess finally released Ehryn's vocal cords, there was a very distinct impression that She was doing so because She chose to and not because Tendaji's whispered plea held any sway. Ehryn gasped out when Alathi receded back into whatever darkness She came from, and only because of Tendaji's strong grip on her shoulders did she remain standing. The Faoii, on the other hand, were still kneeling on the ground before them, sobbing into the earth.

Ashvu finally found her voice again. "I'm sorry… After the fall of Illindria… we were taught to honor the idea of the Old Gods, not the… not the Goddess Herself. But there's so much open to interpretation. I didn't know. I didn't…"

"Faoii," Tendaji cut in, his voice now laced with a power that Ehryn knew stemmed from the same threads that Alathi used to command. A thinner strand, obviously, but his voice colored the air in the same way, held people's attention with the same chord. The congregated Order lifted their heads to look at him. "The Faoii Order was built on strong foundations of which you've only just begun to scratch the surface. You have discovered deeper columns today, and they will topple all of what we've built if we ignore them again. Do not forget what you heard here or the Oath you've sworn. Do not forget She who wove it into the Tapestry and bound us all to Her blade. The future of the Faoii Order and Imeriel depends on it."

"And send word to Queen Isolde," Namaoii said. "Tell her that her daughter wants to meet her at these mines."

23

Mavrikal slithered back and forth, impatient. It was taking too long. She needed Teilithia *now*.

Jaladri was supposed to get Her. They were to stop this group of wanderers with their Eternal Blade and Voice of the Ancient Sword. Mavrikal still didn't know what they were, but they'd bested Jaladri in Her own element. Perhaps the Goddess of Oceans had forgotten how to fight in Her centuries away, but that they could dispirit one of the Sisters, however out of practice? It shouldn't have been possible.

Mavrikal thought it best to simply destroy them all. But Jaladri had convinced Her to wait. They might be useful, these beings of blood who smelled like siblings when there was no sibling and like erasure when there was no Hollowed. The blood that smelled like tonicloran. This group held everything The Goddesses needed to restrengthen Their hold on the Tapestry. To subjugate the mortals who were growing too powerful too fast.

Mavrikal thought it wasn't worth the risk. Better to destroy them all and drain the blood slowly, as She had done for decades. She'd been ready to strike the entire group down the moment Jaladri had stopped Her. But Jaladri had told Her to wait.

And now it was too late. Alathi had reawakened Her pet Faoii. Had strengthened the dangerous little group.

A day ago it wouldn't have mattered. The silly Order had been rendered harmless since the Old Gods' fall. They'd been crumbled and rebuilt over and over again. Merely shadows of what they once had been, even with all the Weavers they had staring at the Eternal Tapestry. The Faoii had become pathetic.

Until now. Because now they'd found the threads from which Alathi had woven their Order. They were once again a part of the Weave in the way they were meant to be. She remembered what it had been like to be tied to the Weave in Alathi's name. How hard it had been to break free of Her influence. Jaladri had let an ancient threat reemerge in Her inaction.

It wouldn't do. Mavrikal would not return to what was! With or without Teilithia, She would end this. Reclaim the blood for Their purposes. Restrengthen the trap. Reforge Their grip on the Tapestry.

Her sisters feared these mortals, but they had lived too long away from them. They'd let Their dreams rebuild the little humans into the memories of what They once had been.

But the mortals were nothing without a Goddess to worship. They looked for reasons to bow. She'd prove it.

She'd remind everyone.

24

Ehryn dreamt of Dhruv. Of the forest they visited in their youth, looking for seeds. Of somewhere far away and yet right beside them all the time. She could feel his love across time and space. His hope for her. For a moment it seemed almost like--

Wake up.

WAKE UP.

She's coming.

Help us.

Ehryn rolled groggily in her bedroll, the dreams and her brother's presence vanishing. It was still dark. The camp was silent, wrapped in a heavy fog. Her head still hurt from the day before. There was no reason to be awake yet.

But the Voices on the Wind screamed at her from far away. Ehryn tried to drown them out, but they were insistent.

Hurry, Ehryn!

Hurry!

The strong, commanding voice that usually stood in front of the others was absent. Instead, the chitters only came from the smaller, quieter whispers that usually backed the Call.

Wake up.

Wake up!

She comes!

She comes, Ehryn!

She's coming!

The urgency in the last sentence finally shook Ehryn fully awake. She sat up in her bedroll, shivering. The air was colder than it should be, even for being as far north as they were. The fire seemed distant. Dulled. Blearily, she looked around the camp.

Everything seemed normal. The others were asleep in their bedrolls. She could hear Kantilieh snoring. Even Tendaji was sitting beside one of the trees, whittling something she couldn't see. Ehryn felt certain that he would know it if anything so much as a mouse entered their little camp. They were safe.

Weren't they?

No. Something was off. The Voices on the Wind chattered nervously as Ehryn peered into the darkness.

There.

It wasn't so much a thing as…an absence of one. A shift in the air that wasn't quite visible. A smell of rotting meat that didn't quite reach her nose. But once Ehryn perceived it, there was no denying its presence.

It's Her.

The Middle Child.

She Who Drains the Blood.

We didn't recognize Her.

She's changed so much. Shifted between planes for far too long.

Run!

RUN!

No! Hide! Running won't help.

The False Children have found you.

Ehryn wanted to move out of her bedroll. She wanted to scream to the others to wake up. Shout at Tendaji to protect them. But she was frozen. Moonlight filtered down through the trees, barely illuminating the shape in the distance that dripped darkness and unease. It oozed along the edge of muted firelight, slithering between moonbeams.

Ehryn stared, any sound she would make stuck in her throat, her breath frozen in her lungs. She felt trapped. Helpless. All of the parts of her bones that had learned to fear the dark woke up in unison, begging her to flee.

The Middle Child.

The False Children.

Usurper!

Mavrikal.

Ehryn's mind heard the words, but they meant nothing. She couldn't think of anything beyond her own internal screams. She feared whatever crept in darkness at the edge of their camp, her mind writhing in uncertainty at what was and wasn't possible.

She felt something familiar there. Something old and dark and rotten.

The corruption beneath Clearwall. The rot the world was built on.

The shape at the edge of camp reeked of it. The decay and slime slid off it in wet chunks. And now that she'd smelled it, Ehryn could no longer ignore it. She gagged.

The shadow turned towards her. Ehryn wasn't even aware it had had a face until it looked at her, wide eyes and wider grin stark in the darkness. It hissed something that Ehryn almost understood, and the smile grew wider.

Move.

Move!

You must move!

Run!

Don't let Her get you.

Run! Run!

But the chittering Voices on the Wind that normally pumped blood into Ehryn's legs or pulled her into action had no effect on her now. Ehryn sat in her bedroll, frozen, gaze fixed on the wide, mad eyes that swirled with gray and green as they came closer in the darkness. The creature stepped into the little circle of firelight—that little flicker of illumination that seemed so small and paltry here in the blackness of night—and Ehryn wondered if this... *thing* had ever tried to come to Clearwall, only to be forced out of houses and taverns where even the deepest corners were so easily lit by candles and hearths.

There was salvation and protection in fire. But more so in communities. Here, isolated in the wilderness, their little fire was barely enough to illuminate their bedrolls and, instead of making the inky figure feel more real as it became more visible, made it appear like the flickering figments of Ehryn's imagination. Of her fear.

Finally, the figment stepped between Ehryn and the campfire, and she could see Her for what She was. The firelight touched upon Her tattered dress and sinewy arms. She was beside Kant's bedroll now, and Ehryn wasn't sure whether she'd rather he wake up and see this thing made of fog and instinctual fear or stay asleep and be free of the horror it brought. Why wasn't Tendaji helping? Why was he still sitting there, whittling away while terror incarnate invaded their camp? Why couldn't she feel the warmth of the campfire?

The chittering Voices had turned into screams at Mavrikal's approach, but as the Middle Sister took another step, they fell suddenly, eerily silent. Ehryn had never felt so alone. She tried to curl into herself, tried to breathe past the smell of rot and panic.

Finally, the thready voice of Alathi broke through, sounding weak and tired.

If you will not run, you must fight. The creature before you is an abomination while you are perfection. Face Her. Beat Her.

Then save us.

The thought of having to face this creature alone was enough to break through the ice around Ehryn's throat and limbs. She didn't know how to fight. She didn't want to learn. Alathi had already faded back into the darkness, unable to even take control. Ehryn wasn't the one to face this monster. But she knew someone who was.

"Tendaji!" she screamed, scrambling backwards. "Tendaji!"

The Middle Child grinned wider, taking another step forward. Ehryn could feel the chill that rolled off Her wispy, smoky robes. Her black hair danced with a nonexistent breeze and Her piercing eyes were made of shifting, poisonous clouds.

"Strange little mortal." The woman's voice curled through the air like the smoke that lifted from Her fingers, caressing Ehryn's cheek. Ehryn shivered and tried to scream again, but her trembling voice could only squeak. "How did you find your way here?" Mavrikal sniffed Ehryn's hair, a too-long tongue slipping out between Her teeth. "I know that scent. Did a sibling guide you?"

Ehryn shut her eyes, tears leaking out of the corners. They almost burned against the chill of her skin and Mavrikal's icy breath on her face. She wasn't going to get out of this, and she knew it.

Then there was a sudden, earth-shaking battle cry and the sound of a howling blade. Ehryn's relief almost toppled her. Tendaji was here. Tendaji would save her.

But the iciness did not dissipate, and there was a smoky laugh next to her ear. Ehryn opened one eye. The Middle Child still stood in front of her, still grinning Her pointed smile. But now She had one talon-like finger lifted to Her mouth.

"Hush, little mortal. Shhhhhh."

Ehryn's stomach filled with ice water.

"Tendaji…" she whispered, her entire body shaking. Tendaji's eyes flickered in her direction. Looked down at the bedroll at her feet.

"Ehryn? Where are you?"

Ehryn gazed past the woman's shoulder. Everything else in their little camp was blurred. Misty. And she realized now that it was not the fog she thought it was when she'd first woken up. This was…different. Something she thought she remembered from a long time ago. But those wispy memories didn't help her now. Tendaji shifted in and out of her vision, trying to watch everything at once, his blade ready as he called her name.

He couldn't see them.

Everything around Ehryn seemed… off. Out of focus. She could still see Tendaji, head swiveling in the firelight as he searched for her, but there was also the faintest outline of a different forest. If she squinted, she could almost see a grand, marble hall where the shadowy Goddess stood, Her impossibly long hand pressed tight against   Ehryn's   mouth.

The Goddess's eyes shifted, and She tilted Her head. "Why can't I see you in the Tapestry? What are you?"

"Nobody," Ehryn whimpered, the sound muffled by the palm against her lips. "I'm nobody."

"I thought as much. Not even the Tapestry cares about you. History will not know your name. The threads don't even acknowledge you enough to paint you into the Weave. You are an anomaly." She shifted until Her lips were right next to Ehryn's ear again. "But bow before Me and I can make you *great*."

Ehryn could only smell the rot that threatened Clearwall. She wanted to scream. To cry. To do something and let her last moment be one that would save the others. *Run,* she would cry. *Run and save yourself.* But her insides were frozen, and she could only stare past the upheld finger and grin made of teeth and whispers. Up into the eyes that had gazed upon the Tapestry for all of eternity, slinking across a mortal plane where Her sisters would barely tread.

It was the face of madness.

"You follow a man who feeds you lies and leads you to your doom, little mortal. Help Me, and you will sit at the right hand of a Goddess. Nothing will ever be hidden from you again. The world will be set right. But We need you." She leaned in closer. "Help us."

Ehryn shuddered when she heard the Dark Goddess whisper those words that the Voices on the Wind had repeated a thousand times, and she squirmed, screaming into the night. The ghostly hall shrieked with a nonexistent gale as the Voices on the Wind screamed with her.

The Dark Goddess's face contorted at the sound, and she slammed the hand that was covering Ehryn's mouth backwards, striking her skull into the marble pillar that was both there and not.

"No! You will not bring Them back! We will NOT GO BACK!"

The Middle Child was towering above Ehryn now, pressing down on her, filling her mouth and lungs and veins with smog and ink and venom. But Ehryn's cry had broken through the veil, and her comrades were stirring on the other side of the fog. "What's going on?" Kant asked groggily, sitting up in his bedroll. He cast bleary eyes towards Tendaji brandishing his sword at nothing.

"What is it? Where'd she go?" Namaoii was there now, too, eyes focused on the space that the dark queen occupied. Almost. She frowned, and Ehryn watched the Wolf Pup's eyes, grateful for something—anything—else to focus on besides the spark of insanity in the Middle Sister's gaze.

"Namaoii… please," Ehryn whispered. In front of her, Mavrikal's features softened, and Ehryn recognized a hint of fear where the madness had been.

"No… No. Those Voices of the Old Ones lie, little mortal. In ways you cannot possibly understand. If you follow Them, They will bind us all to stones we cannot break and sink us below seas we cannot swim. But swear yourself to Me, and I will pull the poison from your ears and teach you the truth of how things once were. No snippets of information. No control wrested from your grasp. You will be My Chosen. Herald of the Sisters." Even with the Goddess's grip released, Ehryn couldn't breathe. Couldn't hear anything except the silky whisper that reverberated long after Mavrikal stopped speaking.

"What the--? What is that?" Namaoii asked into the darkness, her eyes narrowed. But then she met Ehryn's terrified stare, and Ehryn could only cry with relief that someone at least saw her.

Namaoii reacted to that look of fear with *rage*. "Tendaji! Move!" she screamed, reaching out into the darkness, her eyes flashing in the firelight.

Namaoii's massive hand connected in a way Ehryn didn't think possible, striking the thin veil between the worlds that still shimmered between the Goddess and the campsite. And suddenly, with the sound of twisted metal, the hall, the forest, the spaces between the strands that some forgotten part of Ehryn remembered exploring with her brother… all of it was gone. Namaoii gripped the Middle Child by Her tendrils of limp hair and yanked Her back into the camp and the little circle of light.

The Goddess screamed, Her teeth gnashing as She spun. "How did you--?"

But Tendaji's war cry and screaming sword drowned Her out as he swung his fantoii towards Her too-long neck. She slid out of the way, a blur of white skin and black eyes and talon-like fingers.

"That sound…That sword. It *is* you!" The dark Goddess materialized fully a few paces away, Her thin tongue sliding across Her teeth. "You live. We always thought you walked Imeriel still. Never saw you disappear onto the life pool's farthest shores. The infamous brother. The Betrayer's confidante. I even tried to pull you from the shadows in the aftermath of my youngest sister's fall. I twisted the Call the Iron Queen heard so she would track you and all your worthless Order down instead. But We could not find you. Could not follow that lovely sibling blood the way We should have been able to. A pity. I would have given anything to slit your pretty little sister's pretty little throat. To gift that sword to Teilithia."

Tendaji's face twisted in a snarl of rage, and he spun back to face the Middle Child. Then he took a step to the side and was *gone*.

Ehryn's mouth fell open, sure that she was seeing things, but then the old warrior appeared next to the Dark Goddess, his blade screaming in fury. The Middle Child flinched away from the sound and Blinked away from him, appearing on the far side of camp. She curled in on Herself, wary, like a cornered beast.

"I've heard the sound of your blade across the Tapestry. I know what it is," She hissed.

"Then you know what it can do."

Tendaji Blinked again, but She reacted in kind, staying just out of his reach.

"You've come out of the shadows, Tendaji of the Fall. Even Jaladri did not recognize you for who you are. But She will know, now. And when She wakes Teilithia, you will remember the true power of the Sisters. I will use your blood to bind all of Imeriel back to its place at Our feet. You are a creature of deceit and lies and secrets, and you will lead these children to their fall like you did to all those who came before." She flicked Her eyes over to Ehryn appraisingly, flitting out of Tendaji's reach again as he appeared next to Her. "As for you, little mortal. The Voices you hear were locked away for good reason, and he is but a puppet to Their wills. We will not allow you to release Them again. I've called My own servants to ensure it is so." She was suddenly beside Ehryn, filling her vision with the sharp teeth in Her wicked smile. "My previous offer still stands, though. Follow Me and I will make you great. Join My servants and you will be held above all mortals. They will show you the truth. And I will return for you." The honeyed whisper filled Ehryn's head again, until she couldn't hear anything else. Couldn't think past the silken words. "Remember."

"Enough!" Tendaji Blinked again and swung his sword at Mavrikal's head.

But the Dark Goddess was gone.

Ehryn felt the wind of Tendaji's sword tip sweep across the bridge of her nose, and she stood there, shaking, in its wake. The group waited uncertainly, watching the shadows with tense, fervent gazes. But the Middle Child didn't re-emerge, and after a few moments, the sounds of the forest returned with the calls of birds and crickets. Ehryn's legs refused to hold her, and she sank to the ground.

"What was that?" Namaoii demanded, still focused on the edge of the firelight.

"The... Middle Child? One of the False Children?" Ehryn squeaked out, trying not to cry, encompassed by cold and fear.

Tendaji's face, which had once again become a cool slate of stoicism, showed the faintest hint of concern. "Ehryn, can you stand? Can you ride?"

"Give... Give me a moment," she whispered around chattering teeth.

"We may not have that long," Tendaji replied. With quick, decisive movements, he began to pack up camp.

"Where are we going?" Kant asked, fully awake now and looking like he wished he wasn't.

"Back to Clearwall. This kintar has ended."

"No!" Even Ehryn was surprised that the word came from her own mouth in her own voice. Everyone turned to look at her. "No," she repeated. "Just… just let me think."

Her teeth were still chattering, and her heart felt like it would give out. She was dizzy and nauseated and unsure of everything. But now both Alathi and Mavrikal had warned her of Tendaji's lies, and he wanted to take her away from where all the answers were coming from. Her stomach knotted in uncertainty and anger. Part of her wanted to go home. Missed the safety of their hearth and the smell of clean linen and soap. But something deeper called to her now, awoken at the sight of She Who Demands the Blood. She didn't trust Mavrikal. Knew she could never follow that madness, no matter what parts of Her whispers had rung with truth. But she didn't know how to trust Tendaji anymore, either.

Mostly she was afraid. Afraid of what Mavrikal had said, afraid of what might come from their journey, afraid of what the Voices on the Wind actually were and what could make something as powerful as Mavrikal show fear. But more than anything, she was afraid of having seen the face of darkness and knowing they'd let it go again. It would follow them home. Follow them back. Her family, Kant's mother and soon-to-be baby sister, Queen Isolde… none of them were safe if Ehryn let them lead the Middle Child back to Clearwall. She took a deep breath.

"We… we can't go back. It will only get worse if we go back. It will follow us. I know it will."

The Voices from beyond the veil screamed their approval, demanding her help. Ordering her to fight back against those who had created that rotting crevice in the world deeper than she could fathom. Ehryn knew they weren't telling the whole truth, either. Every one-sided discussion left her with more questions than answers and the vague feeling that Alathi didn't *want* her to know the entire story. But Ehryn had to find it. They were close, now. She didn't think she'd ever be able to quiet the Voices on the Wind if they didn't see this through. She would go mad before they got back to Clearwall, deafened by the continuous cry, the unfinished riddles. The vague shapes she could almost make out in the mists around her mind.

"We have to keep going," Ehryn said firmly. "Mavrikal was afraid of the Call. She was trying to scare us away from it. For all Their power, the Sisters—the False Children, the Usurpers, the Goddesses—whatever They are, Alathi is more powerful than They are. We need to find out what happened. We need to stop the rot beneath Imeriel and see what it has to do with bloodlines and Hollowed and power. We need to set it right. And the only way to do that is to keep going."

"Ehryn, I can't in good conscience continue leading you North," Tendaji said firmly. "You all could have died here. I must bring you back to Clearwall."

"What if she's right? What if it follows us home?" Namaoii demanded. "Clearwall depends on us. We cannot lead danger to her gates. Especially if we can eliminate that threat before the regular citizens even know it's there. And there are still the prisoners at the mines who need our help. Who else will care about their fate if not me? Us?"

Tendaji was the closest to frustrated Ehryn had ever seen him be. "Tell me, Namaoii—what makes you think that this group is better prepared to stop the Sisters than Clearwall's armies or the Faoii?"

"Princess Namaoii broke through the magic between the veils! No one else in Clearwall can do that!" Kant piped up, apparently the least concerned of all of them. "And Ehryn… Ehryn is the only one who knows how to get to where the Old Gods are trapped." He pumped his little fist into the air. "We're small and we're fast and we're smart. We might be young, but that just means people underestimate us."

Namaoii crossed her arms over her chest. "We're the first people in history who might be able to stop that… thing and Her sisters. If The Sisters are walking the world again, we need to find out why *now* before Jaladri sinks more boats or Mavrikal attacks more travelers. Things have changed since we left Clearwall, and it is our duty to see our mission through. Clearwall Keep has sent out hundreds of young people on kintars. None have ever had something like that happen before. And none of the previous Called have actually been led towards Alathi and the Old Gods. We might be the only ones to ever have this chance."

Tendaji looked like he was about to say something else, but he refrained. His eyes were impossibly sad. Ehryn heard something equally heart-wrenching on the wind.

Lies. We've called others. And they found only Her. The Middle Child. She's always there. Lurking. Watching. He knew.

But you will be different.

Help us.

Ehryn wanted to ask Tendaji about the others that had come before. Wanted to know exactly what he was hiding from all of them, but Namaoii was speaking again, her voice filled with power and command. "Faoli-Tendaji. In the name of the Crown and for the greatness of Clearwall, I demand you accompany us further north!"

Namaoii's voice was like iron striking stone. It made the firelight brighten and the leaves on the trees shake. Ehryn and Kant recoiled on reflex, and even Tendaji closed his eyes against the force of her order.

When he opened them again, his blue eyes were the color of frosted steel.

"No."

Namaoii gaped. Ehryn wondered if anyone had ever denied her before. If anyone had ever been able to. Tendaji pulled a length of rope from his pack.

"I am sworn to greater forces than you, Namaoii of Clearwall. I am sworn to return you safely. And if I must bind you to do it, I will. But we *are* going back. It is up to you what level of humiliation you wish to endure on the ride."

Namaoii's fists clenched and unclenched. Her dark eyes swirled with thinly-veiled threats. "You've seen what I can do, Faoli. What I really am. Your magic will not get me back onto that horse."

"I think we both know that I don't need magic, Princess."

"Don't call me that!" Namaoii's fist moved more quickly than Ehryn could see, aimed for Tendaji's nose. But all it hit was air. Namaoii spun, the adrenaline from the fight and this humiliation building. But Tendaji wasn't looking at her anymore.

"Children, get behind me."

Ehryn followed his gaze. She saw the torches first, blinking closer. Then there were shouts of excitement that barely overcame the ominous buzzing of an ongoing chant. Her heart dropped.

Mavrikal had said She'd called others. And as frightening as the Dark Goddess was, She was not the only thing that had drummed fear and loss and uncertainty into Ehryn's heart.

She should have known. She should have recognized that the fanaticism and the rot and fear that underscored Clearwall were connected. They'd come into the square a dozen times and each time had declared that the rot was borne from disbelief and disobedience.

Of course they would come when She called.

Elisians.

25

Ehryn remembered her mother's final plea. *Don't go to the Elisian communes. I don't know what happens in there, but I don't think people come back out.*

Now the fanatic group with their Goddess symbols and ongoing chants were bearing down on them, and Ehryn didn't pretend to think it had nothing to do with the Middle Child and Her whispered threats.

Tendaji and Namaoii had their swords out, standing back-to-back as they watched the Elisians advance. But the fanatics didn't get within reach of their blades, and none of them seemed to have any weapons save their holy symbols and smoky braziers. The Elisians stopped several lengths away from the little group, and an aging woman stepped forward.

"Travelers." Ehryn was surprised that she could hear every word perfectly over the continuous chanting from behind the

Elisian leader. "Our Weavers in the enclave saw you on the threads. One of you has been touched by Mavrikal, the Middle Child. She's called us forward to worship at Her Chosen's feet."

Ehryn didn't trust this group that came on Mavrikal's heel. Didn't trust their braziers or their symbols or their melodious muttering. She could still hear Mavrikal's honeyed whispers behind her eyes, wheedling deeper and deeper into her skull. She couldn't hear the Voices on the Wind that would have offered her encouragement or advice. Everything—her eyes, her ears, her skull—was filled with the sweet haze of the braziers and the rolling melody of the cloaked worshippers.

"Stay away from her," Namaoii snarled, scowling through watering eyes. The leader of the Elisians turned toward her, haloed by torchlight and blue smoke.

"We know you, Namaoii of Clearwall. I assure you, there is no reason to fear us. We want to help those who are plagued by lies and false whispers. We want to save the world from the lies of the Old Gods. If the Chosen can break free of Their hold, it will be a great victory for all mortals. It will be a great symbol of strength."

Ehryn wondered what the Voices on the Wind would say to that, but she could not hear them over the Elisian chant. "No, thank you," she said, trying to sound as forceful as Namaoii might have. "Go back to your enclave and let us leave in peace." Next to her, Kant was coughing, and she pulled him to her.

"Can you lay off with the braziers?" Namaoii demanded, still not putting down her sword. "You heard her. Get out of here."

The Elisian frowned. "What a pity. There are so many things we desire to learn from those few that the Middle Child reaches out to. You are so special—next in line to divinity, in a way. We would make you very comfortable in our commune."

"Again. No." Tendaji's voice hardened, the faintest bit of power lacing the words, and the torches and braziers flickered. The woman at the front of the group seemed unfazed, but the change made Ehryn feel dizzy. The chant that a few of the Elisians had been singing under their breath was louder now, but the words ran together, sounding like a river or the wind.

"Ehryn," Kant said through his coughing, "I don't feel…". But then the little boy was listing bonelessly into her side. She tried to yell out, but she couldn't breathe through the smoke in her lungs, couldn't convince her sluggish body to respond. Everything was spinning and foggy and far away.

"Faoli! I can't break it! It's not magic!" Namaoii was coughing too, her voice filled with rage or fear. There was the sound of a scuffle further away. Yelling. The constant, overpowering sound of chanting. The smell of brazier smoke. Nothing.

Ehryn came back to herself slowly. Her mind was finally clear, and Mavrikal's lingering whispers were gone. She stood and tried to get her bearings.

They were in… not a dungeon, like she'd expected. She was on a soft bed, and the room around her, while windowless, was not unpleasant. There was a wash basin and a plate of food on the table to one side. It would have been a comforting place to wake if not for the heart-wrenching sounds of Kant's sobbing somewhere nearby.

"Kant?" Ehryn called. "Kantilieh? Can you hear me? Where are you?"

A sniffle from the other side of the wall to her right. "Ehryn?"

"Yeah. It's me. Are you okay? Did they hurt you?"

"No. I…" He sniffled again. "I thought I was alone."

Ehryn wondered about how trapped Kant must have felt before she'd woken. A head filled with every possible scenario and story, and no way to direct that knowledge. All of the fear of a terrible tale but none of the comfort that came with a known resolution. She tried to soothe him through the wall.

"I'm sorry, Kant. I'm here. We're okay. Can you tell me about where you are?" Ehryn looked around her own quarters again, eyes resting on the door at the far side of the room. Cautiously, she tried the knob. Locked.

"It's… a bedroom. It's bigger than the one Papa built for the baby back home. It has a bed… a table… Food!"

"Wait!" Ehryn tried to keep her voice quiet, but it came out sharper than intended. "Wait, Kant." She thought about the brazier smoke and the way it had muddied their minds in the forest. "I think they drugged us before. Don't eat anything, okay? Just… hold on. We'll be okay."

From the other side of the wall, Ehryn heard Kant sniffle again. "Promise?"

"I promise," Ehryn said, hoping that she was worthy of Kant's trust.

There was a groan from the wall on the other side of her little room, then a steady stream of colorful and bawdy curse words. Ehryn sighed, relieved. "Namaoii? Are you okay?"

"Broken, dirty blades. No, I'm not okay! Where the sky cursed woven Hell are we?"

"I don't know. One of the Elisian communes, maybe?"

"Why—" Kant couldn't even finish his question before Namaoii's booming voice and the sound of her pounding fist on the door drowned him out.

"Hey!" the princess hollered, banging obnoxiously. "Hey! Elisians! Get over here and let us out! NOW!"

Namaoii didn't have the same level of magical command that the others in her line had, but it didn't matter. The Wolf Pup of Clearwall had the voice of someone who was used to being obeyed, with just enough power in it to make one notice. Ehryn was not surprised when she heard a scuttle of feet from the hallway outside her door.

"There's no need to yell, Princess," a sweet young voice called from outside. "I can't let you out, but if you'll give me a moment, I'll fetch the Madame First."

"I don't care what it takes, get this door opened *now!*"

"I'm… I'm sorry, Princess. I can't. The First can answer your questions. I was only told to report when you were all awake. You are, and I must go." The scuttle of feet faded as the woman left.

"Get back here!" Namaoii demanded, banging on the door so loudly that Ehryn's wall shook.

"Wait. Did she say all? All of us? What about the Faoli?" Ehryn didn't wait for a response and started her own call through her barricade. "Tendaji! Sir! Can you hear us?"

There was no response. Ehryn tried again. Nothing.

"Knock it off, Ehryn. He's not here," Namaoii snarled from her side of the wall.

"I hope he's okay," Kant said, barely loud enough that Ehryn could hear him. She frowned. She hoped so, too.

They waited in a silence that was only broken by Namaoii's infrequent curses, wondering what was to come.

Eventually, there were new steps outside their doors, along with the jangle of iron keys. "A moment, Children, and I'll unlock your doors. We have much to discuss, I think." This new voice was almost syrupy sweet, and it made Ehryn uncomfortable. From somewhere far away, the Voices on the Wind chittered, but not loudly enough for her to understand. They were muted. Quiet.

"Where's Tendaji?" Kant demanded as soon as his door was open, surprising Ehryn. He spoke with more strength than Ehryn thought he'd be able to muster from his small frame. "What did you do to him?"

"Nothing, Child. Give me a moment. We'll talk once everyone is comfortable." The sound of footfalls and the rattle of keys moved to Ehryn's door, and she heard the lock click open. She opened her door cautiously and found herself before a tall woman who was barely beginning to show the first streaks of gray in her hair. She wore the simple, woven robe that all Elisians wore, its only adornment a Goddess symbol—an inverted triangle with a clockwise spiral at its center—woven onto the chest.

The Elisian turned toward the last door in the hallway, sliding a large iron key into the lock. Ehryn moved to stand beside Kant, taking his hand in hers. He squeezed her fingers.

Namaoii didn't even wait for the woman to move away from her door, kicking it open the moment the key turned in the lock. The Elisian stumbled back, arms flailing wildly as Namaoii stormed out, pushing their captor against the wall.

"Where's Tendaji?" the Wolf Pup demanded. "Why did you bring us here?" The Elisian regained her composure quickly, apparently unperturbed to have Namaoii's arm against her throat as she spoke in the same sickly, syrupy voice as before.

"Please, Princess. I'm sorry for the deception before, but we really do need to talk to all of you if we want to save Clearwall from the rot beneath her streets. We were prepared to have the Faoli here as well, but he was gone before we could even speak to him. Just gone. In a blink."

"Blades take you." Namaoii's voice dripped venom as she pressed her arm harder against the woman's neck. "Tendaji would never leave us behind."

"No? Please take a seat. We have much to talk about." The Elisian still sounded calm as she spoke around Namaoii's pressure on her throat. "I promise that it will be enlightening. If you do not like what I have to say, I have no doubt you could overpower me again, Wolf Pup." She was sounding properly strangled now but tried again when Namaoii still did not release her. "I promise you have nothing to lose but everything to gain. It truly is for Clearwall's benefit, I assure you."

Namaoii seemed to think it over until the woman's face was nearly purple. But when the woman did not fight back and no one else came to her rescue, Namaoii finally released the Elisian with a violent jerk of her arm. "Fine. We'll hear you out. But if I don't like what you say, I *will* kill you."

The Elisian doubled over, coughing and trying to catch her breath as she motioned to several chairs placed around a circular table in the center of the long room. No one moved towards them, and it was a few minutes before she finally regained her composure.

"That's fair. I understand your wariness. But it's okay, children. It's okay. My name is Madame Tessil. We're just going to talk, and then you may be on your way if you desire. If you'll take a moment, you'll notice that you have come to no harm and are still in possession of everything you had when we brought you here. Except for your fantoii, Princess, which is over there by the wall. I'm sorry I had it removed. I expected something like this would happen when we finally met face-to-face."

Namaoii moved to the designated wall without turning her back on the Elisian, checked that her fantoii was undamaged, and buckled it around her waist. She did not take her hand off the hilt.

The Elisian didn't seem to mind. "As you can see, we have no intentions of fighting or hurting you. I only wish to talk. Take a seat. It'll be okay. I promise."

Namaoii and Ehryn looked at each other uncertainly, then took a few cautious steps toward the table. Kant was the first to sit, and Ehryn pulled a chair close to him, once again taking his hand in hers.

"It's going to be okay," she whispered to him, wishing that her voice sounded as sure as Madame Tessil's did.

Namaoii refused to sit. "If you just want to talk, why did you have to drug us to get us here? Why'd your damned Goddess try to kill my friend last night?"

Madame Tessil stirred a lump of sugar into a porcelain teacup as calmly as though Namaoii had asked whether or not she expected rain. After a moment she took a sip, set the cup down, and smiled again. "I know you must be worried. I know that what happened seems like we're the bad guys in this story. But you must understand—we Elisians are some of the few who can hear the Goddesses. They often try to help us guide Imeriel to something better, though so many think it is madness and fanaticism rather than the command of the Sisters. But I swear to you, children, the path you were going down—the path that man was leading you down—would have been your doom. And you would have never known if we had not separated you from his aura of power. From his spell."

"What are you talking about? Tendaji's never tried to control us. And he's definitely never tried to hurt us. Mavrikal tried to *kill* Ehryn!"

"Did She?" The woman smiled slightly, seemingly sure of the answer.

"Of course! Tell her, Ehryn." Namaoii elbowed Ehryn hard in the side.

"Yes, Ehryn. Please tell me. Did Mavrikal try to kill you when you met Her?"

Ehryn wanted to argue, to fight, but something about Madame Tessil's voice made her pause and think back. "No... She wanted me to worship Her. At first... at first, She wanted to know who I was. How I got... to wherever She was. She wanted me to bow before Her. It wasn't until She heard the Voices on the Wind that She got angry."

"Ah. Yes. The Old Gods. Tyrants that the Sisters locked away. Can you blame the Middle Child for being afraid? For trying to stop you from working with those ancient monsters that use magic to control Their subjects?" Tessil took another sip of her tea. "The Voices on the Wind and the Faoli you followed have been lying to you, Children." Ehryn thought that the Voices on the Wind would protest, but if they did, she could not hear them.

"That's not true!" Namaoii declared.

"Of course it is. Who would know better than a Goddess? Mavrikal can see the entire Tapestry. She knows what is true and what is false." Tessil closed her eyes for a moment, still smiling. "Surely, Children, you've noticed that your previous guard's story did not always line up like it should? Surely you recognized the holes in what he said?"

Namaoii glowered, and Ehryn remembered the questions the princess had asked about the monasteries and his glittering blade. She thought about all the times he'd dodged their questions as easily as Namaoii's strikes in sparring practice. She hated that the Elisian's words made sense.

Namaoii looked conflicted, too, but shook her head. "Faoli-Tendaji might be cautious with what he reveals, but he'd never hurt us. Or leave us. I know that much. He was about to take us back to Clearwall before you all came along. His only goal was to keep us safe."

Madame Tessil nodded. "Ah, yes. Back to Clearwall. I grew up there, you know. I, too, once thought it was the safest place in Imeriel. But there's a rot beneath its streets. A darkness." She focused on Ehryn. "You've felt it, haven't you? You didn't want to go back, did you? None of you did. But he would have forced you."

None of the children had it in them to respond, and Madame Tessil nodded. "I thought as much. The Middle Child saw that you would be returned to Clearwall one way or another. There, you would have been beyond Her help. Beyond our reach. She called us to you so that we may at least speak before your return. Give us a chance to at least introduce you to the truth. I'm sorry for the deception. That horrid man had you under quite a spell. If we didn't release you from it, you would have fought beside him, and we might have hurt you in the resulting struggle. It was only after he realized his hold was broken that he disappeared and we brought you here. We just needed a chance. A chance to talk. We have that now. And when we are done, if you still want to leave, you may." She smiled again. "Do not fret. It's going to be okay."

"That's rich, coming from an Elisian," Namaoii spit. "You're all as crazy as the psychotic witch you got your name from."

The Elisian's eyes darkened a tiny shade, but her smile did not waver. "You know a distorted version of our history, Princess. Madame Elise was the best of us. She heard voices and Whispers on the Wind—knew there were ancient beings stronger and grander than even the Betrayed Goddess Illindria. She was the first to hear Mavrikal. She tried to bring all of Imeriel back to the worship that would save us from the rot that leaks from the Old Gods' prison, now that the trap has loosened with Illindria's death." Her eyes fell on Ehryn and softened a little. "We know now she was the first to hear Mavrikal's voice. The first of Her Chosen. Not so different from one of you, after all." Tessil's voice took on the syrupy sweetness she'd had before. "Illindria's death was the catalyst. It undid the edges of the trap that keeps us safe from the ancient tyrants that Mavrikal fears. The echoes of Illindria's dying cry woke Mavrikal and the others from Their slumbers. And They saw what had happened to Their people. Saw the rot that seeped from the opened corner of the Old God's prison. Called upon Madame Elise to mend the chasms between those who worshipped and those who did not. To repair the rifts. Madame Elise tried, but she was brought down in the name of 'progress' before her work could be complete. We follow where she led. That is all."

From far, far away Ehryn thought she heard someone yell *Lies!* but she could not think of who it might be.

"Madame Elise was a fearmongering, myopic *fool*," Namaoii growled. "And her Proclaimers were the same. The strongest of our people were burned at her stakes. We lost generations of gifts that we haven't seen a resurgence of yet. Our Weavers were nearly decimated. And she worshipped the Old Gods, not the Sisters."

"Did she? Then why go after the sect of fanatics that killed Illindria, the youngest Sister, if not in vengeance for those she worshipped? It seems that whoever wrote your histories might have had an agenda. Can I assume it was Jacir, the Royal Arcanist, who silenced Elise from speaking the truth? The man who shredded her mind? Imprisoned her and forbid her to preach until she died?"

Namaoii narrowed her eyes, her words dripping with malice. "Jacir should come and do to you what he did to her."

Madame Tessil sighed. "There is so much old anger. No one wants to see what we're trying to do now. But I suggest, Wolf Pup of Clearwall, that you ask those who hear more than you. There is a rot beneath Imeriel, and none of your machines and inventions are fixing it. In fact, it seems to be getting worse. Something is wrong. Something is decaying. What else could cause that other than the displeasure of the Sisters at Their trap being undone?"

Namaoii scoffed and turned to Ehryn, silently demanding a decry of the Elisian's proclamation. But Ehryn could not bring herself to lie, though she hated agreeing with the smug fanatic who peered at her above a smile that did not quite reach her eyes.

"No, Namaoii… she's right. There's a rot in the earth, and it's getting worse. Everything our society is built on is based in something… wrong. I don't know what's caused it, but—"

"Of course you do!" Madame Tessil cut in. "It started building when Illindria died. It seeped out of the prison that the Sisters built to contain an ancient evil. And the Old Gods grow stronger with every step you take towards freeing Them, so the rot grows deeper. Your little band and the Voices you follow so blindly are the root of it all! But we can fix it, together. Fix the trap and heal

Imeriel!" Her eyes glinted with fire, a blaze that could only be lit by true devotion. "You'll see. We'll help you to see if you'll let us. If you'll just stay for a little while."

"You can't keep us here. Queen Isolde will burn down every one of your communes if that's what it takes to retrieve me. To retrieve us," Namaoii stated pointedly. Tessil reset her perfect smile and turned it towards Namaoii, but Ehryn saw it twitch a little on the edges.

"Ah, yes. Queen Isolde. Your mother. The same mother who has lied to you and kept things from you your entire life? Who put laws into place that would imprison you if she only knew? Who has already imprisoned dozens like you and forced them into mines, where they die and remain unburied until their bones are bleached white by the sun? Is she so much better than me that you will not at least sit and listen?" Namaoii's face darkened. She clenched one fist but didn't respond.

"Namaoii? What is she talking about?" Ehryn whispered. Namaoii refused to even look at her while Madame Tessil purred quietly.

"Come now, Ehryn. You hear the voice of the Middle Child. One of the Great Goddesses. Surely you know more than what you let on. You cannot be as naïve as the others of your age, even if you haven't completed your kintar. What have you learned from Mavrikal's voice?"

"That's... that's not who I hear," Ehryn said, though she had to pry the memory of the Voices on the Wind from deep within the recesses of her mind. "It's not. She almost killed me when She realized I was hearing someone other than Her." She tried to say it with conviction, but it felt like the wrinkles in her brain were filled with honey. Sap.

"Are you sure?" The priestess smiled. "Think back."

Ehryn thought about the night before. The voice that had seeped between the inky black lips and dark teeth that smelled like blood. *Help us.* And she shuddered. Because the voice *did* sound like what she'd heard her entire life. Not the chattering smaller voices, no. But the deep one. The strong one. She couldn't remember Her name anymore. Maybe it had been Mavrikal, after all.

The First was speaking again, her smile unwavering. Her voice sweet and thick and perfect. "There's a rot under the earth. Under Clearwall. It's deeper than everything—crumbling the foundations of the great city whose walls you hide behind. Whose twisted streets and barricades block out the voices of the Goddesses. Only the precious few can still hear Them through the midst of all of that. Only the privileged. The Chosen." She reached out and stroked Ehryn's cheek. "You've felt it, that chasm. That rot. Do you know what causes it?" Ehryn shook her head.

"That's the absence of the Goddesses." Ehryn thought that Tessil had said it was something else before, but she couldn't remember. Couldn't imagine anything so deep and powerful as to create that chasm other than the Sisters. Madame First nodded and continued. "Clearwall no longer worships like it should, and the darkness is spreading. But here, in our enclaves, it's different. Here we've built our lives on stronger ground. And there are no twisted walls to block out Their voices. Mavrikal speaks to us every day. Soon, Her sisters will too." And Ehryn could almost see it—see the serenity that would come with donning the simple frocks of the Elisians. Working together to heal the separation between Gods and mortals. And if enough of them listened for long enough, if enough people followed, the Dark Goddess would retake Her previous visage. Anger had warped her into the thing they'd seen last night. Mavrikal could be whole again.

Madame Tessil smiled, her hands reaching comfortingly for Namaoii and Kant now. They looked serene. Even Namaoii's snarl had slackened into a content, blank canvas. That made Ehryn happy. Namaoii had been so angry for so long. This was better. This was…

"You all have so much more to learn, children. Let us talk to you. Fill in the gaps between what you learned in your city of walls and lies. Afterward, you are welcome to leave if you want to. But at least let us try to give you what we know."

The Madame First looked at Kantilieh specifically here, and Ehryn put an arm around him on reflex. He would remember everything he heard here with perfect accuracy. Kant had the potential to be the greatest gift of the unheard.

Kant's magic is a priceless tool, she remembered someone saying long ago.

…That some people would turn into a weapon.

Namaoii's warning from the very beginning of their kintar—Namaoii's devotion to her duty and her city and her friends—broke through the fog that had dampened Ehryn's mind. Her heart hammered in her chest as she looked—truly looked—at the woman sitting in front of them. The priestess was still moving her lips, still speaking in that calming, sweet voice. And Ehryn believed her. Believed everything she said.

But then the strong voice that sounded like Mavrikal cut through the sweet whispers.

RUN!

The voice was deeper and stronger and greater than anything in the commune they stood in. Greater and deeper than the roots on the trees outside or even the rot that Ehryn could feel under all of their feet. It was even deeper than the threads of the Tapestry that tied river and sky and earth together. To think that she'd attributed such a deep well to Mavrikal was an insult.

RUN!

The Voice—*Alathi's voice,* she remembered now—pierced a veil that had wrapped itself around Ehryn's mouth and eyes and throat like a shroud. She hadn't realized that it was suffocating her, but now that she was free of it, she could breathe again.

"It's magic!" Ehryn gasped out, scrambling away and pulling Kant and Namaoii with her. "Don't listen to her! It's not real!"

Namaoii stumbled a step, blinking like she'd been asleep. Then her face twisted in a scowl and she screamed, slamming her open palm into the Elisian's chest with incredible force. There was a spark and the sound of twisting metal. The older woman fell away with a cry.

"Run!" Namaoii ordered, shoving them both towards the door at the end of the hallway. "Go!"

Ehryn gripped Kant's hand and pulled him towards the door at the far end of the room, wondering with all her heart how she could have forgotten her mother's orders. How she could have fallen into the same trap that Dhruv must have years before.

Don't go to the Elisian communes. I don't know what happens in there, but I don't think people come back out.

26

Ehryn gripped Kant's hand like their lives depended on it. She didn't know how much the Elisian's honeyed words had affected him, didn't know if they could repair the damage of her lies, didn't even know if Kant still trusted her as much as he had learned to trust Madame Tessil in a few short minutes, but she was determined to get him out of here in one piece so she could find out. Kant, blessedly, squeezed her hand so tightly she thought he would have broken it were he any bigger. She thought that was a good sign.

Namaoii had already taken the lead, shoving her way through door after door until they found themselves in a large room filled with occupied tables. Namaoii didn't even stop as she charged through, looking for another escape route in the hall.

It took the Elisians a second longer to realize what was happening, to hear the distant cries of their Madame First. The little group had almost made it to the far door before robed men and women began jumping up from their meal to apprehend them, clutching Goddess symbols and whispering eerie chants, their eyes alight with fanaticism and dark promises.

"Namaoii! Duck!" Ehryn screamed as one of the Elisians reached the Wolf Pup. The man's hand shot out, fire dancing on his fingertips, tiny flames sparking towards their heads. Ehryn wrapped her arms around Kant, waiting for the pain and smell of burning flesh, but Namaoii was already striking the outstretched hand with a spark and sound of twisted metal, batting it away. The Elisian fell backwards, mouth gaping.

The other Elisians didn't even falter, pushing their way forward. The air was filled with incense and battle songs. With spells and chants and magics that felt inky and black like Mavrikal's whispers. "We can't get through all of them!" Ehryn screamed.

"We don't really have a blade-cursed choice, do we?" Namaoii yelled back, drawing her fantoii. "Stay behind me!"

Ehryn kept Kant close to her and stayed in the wake of Namaoii's onslaught. The Wolf Pup of Clearwall didn't flow through the Elisians like Tendaji would have. Instead, she crashed into them like a tsunami against a weathered dock. The fanatics tried to dodge out of her destructive path, and a few even moved with battle magic, but few were fast enough to escape her twirling blade. Namaoii had been sparring with Tendaji for months, and no movement, however enhanced, could compare to the way he Blinked in battle. Next to the great Faoli, the Elisians were like untrained recruits.

Even with Namaoii's training and strength, however, the fanatics just kept coming. There were too many of them, and even the Wolf Pup couldn't cut a straight path to the door. Hands and songs and spells reached out for them, causing cuts and burns and mind-numbing fear. Whispers of promises and threats slithered through their minds. Vows of change and calls for Mavrikal to come and finish Her work.

Overwhelmed, Ehryn looked around frantically for something to rescue them. Anything.

Is this the end?

Like so many before you.

Help us…

"Get away from my friends!" Kantilieh suddenly screamed, brandishing a candle he'd plucked from the wall behind them. "I said *GET AWAY!*" And the little, quiet, mouselike boy shrieked the tune that Tendaji had taught them in the early days of their kintar. The little hum that seemed so simple, but that, with enough focus and power, could spark twigs alight.

The candle blazed upward in a solid wall of flame that even the fire callers in Clearwall's square had never demonstrated. The Elisians fell back away from the sudden heat, screaming as their robes and hair caught alight. Kant brandished his candle with one hand while squeezing Ehryn's fingers with the other, still screaming at them to leave his friends alone. Namaoii took the opportunity to kick through the door they'd been trying to reach and yanked them all through.

"Did you see me, Namaoii? Ehryn? Did you see what I did?" Kant panted, all smiles and pride as Namaoii swung the door closed again, leaning heavily against it as Elisians pounded on it from the other side.

Ehryn tried to tell him that she was proud of him, but a sudden, devastating blast of force against the door made her shriek instead. Together, she and Namaoii shoved a heavy shelf filled with tubes and bottles against the shaking barricade.

"What do we do now?" Ehryn breathed once the shelving was in place.

"How the blades should I know?" Namaoii hissed, ramming her fist into the wall. "Everything's gone sideways." She pressed her shoulders against the barrier as it shook again. "We need to find a way out of here. Look for another door. A window. Anything! I'll hold them back."

"Maybe she'll know," Kant piped, pulling on Ehryn's hand. Ehryn turned away from the door to see where he was pointing.

A withered husk of a person was laid out on an iron table in the room's center. Ehryn's heart caught in her throat and her mouth filled with bile at the sight. At first, she thought the girl was dead, but then the poor creature turned her head towards the intruders, her skin limp and hanging off her skull.

Somehow, it made the X carved deep into her forehead even more glaring. Ehryn stifled a gasp and pulled Kant behind her on instinct, her insides flooding with terror. *A Hollowed.*

"Help… me."

Namaoii turned at the sound, her face blanching at the withered shell of flesh and bone. She let out a curse, kicked the door once in unbridled fury, and rushed to the table, unshackling the woman's limp wrists with fingers that shook with rage.

"Namaoii!" Ehryn shrieked. "That's a—"

"I know what she is! Keep them off me for a minute!"

The door budged a little and the contents of the shelf clattered and fell, shattering against the floor. Ehryn and Kant tried to push back, listening to the Elisians' shouts echoing in the hallways.

"We need them! Mavrikal demands it!"

"There's power in the blood! We need to drain the blood!"

Namaoii pulled the limp woman across her shoulders and turned back to the others. "Okay, I have her! Let's get out of here!" she bellowed.

"How?" Ehryn nearly cried as another thump on the door rattled her teeth.

"There's a knife here. Are you ready to become a fighter yet?"

You must. You must.

Ehryn shoved the Voices back down, shaking her head.

"What? No! They'd tear me apart!"

"I thought so. Then you take care of her and I'll handle them." Namaoii's eyes were filled with steel and fire, and her wolfy smile was frightening as she squared her shoulders and aligned her fantoii with the door.

"There's too many of them!" Ehryn argued, pressing her shoulders into the shelf that threatened to topple down on her.

"Back up! Grab her. *Now, Ehryn!*"

Ehryn and Kant released the door and scrambled back behind Namaoii. Ehryn pulled the emaciated woman down and dragged one bony arm across her shoulders. She shuddered again at the sight of the X carved into her forehead. She knew that symbol. She'd been trained her entire life to fear that symbol. Couldn't believe that she was willingly getting this close. Willingly touching the cursed skin of a Hollowed.

But Namaoii was already releasing a battle cry, and she hacked and cleaved her way through the sudden wave of bodies that tried to shove through the door, filtering into her reach, their hands outstretched. Her fantoii took care of most of them, but when someone got too close, Namaoii would stretch out her arm to grasp and rend and claw at chests, arms, faces. Amidst screams and that sound of twisting metal, the pulse of bodies began to fall away.

"She *is* one of them!"

"Her blood! We need her blood!"

"Grab them both!" the Elisians screamed.

Namaoii didn't need the commanding power of her lineage when she yelled over her shoulder to her companions. In that moment, Ehryn and Kant would have followed any order she gave. "Stay on me! Now!"

The Wolf Pup of Clearwall pushed through the door, trampling the people still in front of her, pushing the others back with blade and outstretched hand.

Ehryn didn't even question. The fear of the woman leaning against her was nothing compared to being left alone in this enclave without Namaoii to lead the way. Kant was already moving forward, his melted candle outstretched. "Come on, Ehryn!" he yelled.

Ehryn hoisted the Hollowed as best she could and followed.

27

"Ehryn! How do we get out of here?" Namaoii yelled as she pulled her blade from an attacker's stomach.

"How should I know?" Ehryn cried back. An Elisian stumbled towards her, clutching his bleeding neck with one hand, grasping for the Hollowed with the other.

"We need her… Mavrikal demands the blood," he gasped. Ehryn pulled the dying woman out of his reach, kicked the Elisian as hard as she could, and followed after Namaoii.

"We've been following you since Clearwall!" Namaoii thundered. "You must have some idea! Tell us which way north is if nothing else! Give us something!"

"I touched a Hollowed! I don't know anymore!" Didn't Namaoii know what everyone said? Just touching a Hollowed was enough to lose your powers forever. How could she connect with the Voices on the Wind without magic?

"Don't give me that!" Namaoii shot back. "That's just your own fear and a lifetime of lies talking. Now *focus*, Ehryn, or so help me I will leave you here to die!"

Ehryn tried to do as instructed, but she couldn't tell where the Call normally came from. There were sounds everywhere, too much magic that crashed against the walls. Too many Elisians screaming in the wake of Namaoii's destructive path.

"I don't know! I don't—"

Hear me, Child. Focus.

Help us.

And suddenly she *did* know. Alathi's Call shot through the smoke of the Elisian braziers like an arrow through a pane of glass. And as the pane shattered and cracked, Ehryn could feel an icy breeze from distant mountains on her cheek. She followed the Call like a river, powerful and sure. "There!" she screamed, pointing to a door to one side of the room.

Namaoii didn't have to be told twice, herding them to the exit. By now the Elisian resistance was thinning with most of the fanatics staying out of arm's reach, doing little more to impede their progress than shouting and praying.

It still felt like hours passed before they made it, though, and the Hollowed was barely conscious as Ehryn tried to carry her forward. Then Namaoii was kicking open the final obstacle, and they found themselves in an open courtyard, all fresh air and the scent of carefully cultivated herbs. At any other time, Ehryn would have found it idyllic, but she couldn't appreciate the beauty amidst the sudden, shrill cry of fear and demand that nearly deafened her. Here, in this courtyard at the center of an Elisian enclave, the Voices on the Wind were louder than They'd ever been before. And something was wrong.

Ehryn stopped, yelling for Namaoii as the other girl broke for the gate at the end of the lawn. Because there was another scream she'd heard above that of Alathi and the others.

A scream she recognized.

"Namaoii. I think Tendaji is in that barn!" Ehryn pointed desperately, knowing that she'd heard correctly. Knowing deep in her bones that the barn in question dripped with the inky goo of Mavrikal's dark whispers.

"What? How do you--?" But there was no more time and suddenly there were more Elisians in the garden, carrying nets and chains between them. Namaoii growled and pulled the others at a dead run in the direction of the barn. The Elisians behind her raised their voices, the cacophony almost deafening, ordering them to stop. But then they were through the door, and Namaoii was sticking a gardening hoe through the handles to keep it closed.

"That won't hold them for long. You'd better be right and not have just led us into a—" Namaoii froze, wide eyes following Ehryn and Kant's equally-terrified gaze.

Tendaji was there, his skin gray and his face distorted in pain. He was strung from the barn's loft, arms and legs spread apart, braided hair twisted until the top of his head was yanked backwards toward the rickety beams above. There, spread-eagled, he twitched in and out of focus, his body flickering like a candle's flame in a breeze. His ice-blue eyes tried to lock on the little group as they entered, his tongue working to say something--but the flickering grew faster, and whatever he was going to say was lost in a scream.

"Tendaji? What did they do to you?"

"I... don't know." The flickering got worse with each word, distorting his voice. He shut his eyes, his entire body rigid. Sweat and blood dripped from his skin, and from each droplet a spindly, twisted plant sprouted from the earthen floor beneath him, only to wilt again within moments.

"Hold on! We'll get you out!" Ehryn's eyes roamed the chains that held Tendaji. The restraints flickered in and out of existence, too, but not in sync with his torn body that dripped thorny vines that wilted into ash.

"They're… using his blood. Like they used… mine," the Hollowed breathed in Ehryn's ear, her voice full of sorrow. "The…magic…of his blood…binds him. They want… something from…him. Are trying… to pull… magic…from the blood."

Namaoii cursed under her breath and reached out with one open palm. "Faoli, I'm sorry," she whispered. "But I don't know what else to do."

"Do… it," Tendaji ground out, his voice thick. He opened his eyes again, pained gaze locking with Namaoii's. "Please."

Namaoii nodded and took a step forward until her palm connected with Tendaji's forehead. There was a grinding sound and a spark. The air around them dropped in temperature until Ehryn was sure she'd be able to see her breath if she weren't holding it. Somebody screamed.

Ehryn looked to Tendaji. He was still in front of them, pale and shaking, but solid. The contraption that bound him had stopped flickering as well, and Namaoii went to work on freeing their friend and guardian.

Once released, the old warrior dropped to the floor, breathing heavily. Namaoii knelt beside him, her face more worried than Ehryn had ever seen it. "You okay, Faoli?"

"They're breaking through!" Kant suddenly cried, eyes focused on the door that was shaking under the force of blows from outside. Ehryn tensed. With everything else, she'd forgotten where they were.

Tendaji looked to the shuddering door, then set his gaze on Namaoii. "How long will it last?"

"I don't know. I've never stuck around long enough to find out."

"Even if it is forever, then I am grateful. I know you are not Faoii, but today you are worthy of the title." Tendaji moved to stand, and both Ehryn and Namaoii reached out to steady him. Ehryn saw a sort of sparkling in Namaoii's eyes. A shade of pride and gratitude. Tendaji looked around at the wilted tendrils near their feet. "They failed. They couldn't get it from me. There's still time."

But the Voices were screaming, and Ehryn didn't think that was true anymore.

She comes.

Her trap failed and She knows.

There's no time! No time!

Take what She wanted. Use it!

Help us!

Ehryn's eyes fell to the withered tendrils at Tendaji's feet, and she once again had a fleeting memory of the garden she'd cultivated with Dhruv.

No magic is unlearnable.

Nothing is lost forever.

"They're going to break through any moment. We'll have to fight," Namaoii bit out, squaring her shoulders and raising her blade in the direction of the door. "Can you?"

"I will for as long as I can. Whatever happens, Wolf Pup of Clearwall, you three must escape. Do you understand?" Namaoii nodded, and Tendaji straightened a little. "Kant, get my sword. It was tossed in a chest there." Kant scrambled to obey.

Get it. You can wield it.

You're ready.

Help us!

But Ehryn didn't want to wield the sword. Another plan, far more within her tastes, was scratching at the back of her head. If she could just have a minute to *think*.

The door splintered again. Tendaji lifted his fantoii, but it did not scream with fury and bloodlust. He looked at it uncertainly before squaring his jaw. "Namaoii, promise me you'll get them out. Tell Jacir and Isolde what happened here."

He's done for.

It's almost over.

At least they won't be able to get it from him.

But we need it too!

Help us.

He'll die here.

Leave him.

"No!" Ehryn screamed so loud that the beating on the door momentarily quieted. "No! We have to keep going! All of us!"

No one answered. No one even looked at her. Something deep in her heart broke. "Please," she begged. "Please."

Even the Voices were quiet. The silence in the barn was palpable, shattered suddenly by a wrenching of wood as an axe head suddenly broke through the door, snapping the hoe's handle. Everything started moving again at once. Ehryn looked around wildly. It wasn't supposed to end like this. This wasn't how it was supposed to go. The Voices on the Wind screamed and cried around her, wicked in their demand and terror. All yelling for attention. All trying to tell her what she should do.

Then, Alathi's unwavering voice broke through the din.

Do you trust me, Child?

"Yes! Yes! Whatever you want! Please!" The others looked at Ehryn like she'd gone crazy, but she didn't care. "What can I do? I'll do anything!"

"What makes it unlearnable?" Kant's voice asked from across time and space. Ehryn remembered Tendaji's answer:

"There used to be a plant that the Faoii both revered and feared. Of all the living things in Imeriel, it was most closely tied to the Gods. It allowed you to see the Tapestry through Their eyes and step between the threads."

The Voices on the Wind howled with approval.

Yes! Yes!

The tonicloran!

Restore Our power. Receive Our gift.

Help us.

"But it wilted! It's not here! It's gone!" Ehryn cried.

So were all the other plants in your garden, Alathi whispered.

And Ehryn remembered that she once had magic before the Call. Before society had told her to focus on one gift and could not believe she'd had another.

All she had to do was reach through that veil. Like she had with Dhruv. Like she had in her dream before Mavrikal had found her. Like she had with the pen in Jacir's study or any of the other hundreds of lost objects and forgotten plants she'd ever looked for in her life. It was so easy.

She reached, trying not to focus on the screaming behind her. The sounds of fighting and triumph.

And suddenly a single stalk of tonicloran was in her hand.

"Grab on to me!" Ehryn screamed, wrapping her fist around the innocent-looking plant. She felt the thorns cut deep into her skin.

"Ehryn! Don't!" Tendaji's voice. Filled with horror.

But it was already done, and Ehryn was screaming as her mind and thoughts and soul scattered through the broad, flat leaves that twisted and turned between the spaces in the Weave. The entire universe spun around her in sickening, glorious circles. There was nowhere to focus. No way to gather herself back together.

Do you trust me, Child?

She couldn't remember how to answer. Couldn't figure out who was talking or what they wanted or how to speak. Couldn't remember her own name. But she felt the hands on her arms and the smile in her mind and some part of her screamed that she'd agree to anything if it would *just stop.*

Yes! Yes! Please!

Then let go.

Ehryn did.

28

Everything hurt.

Ehryn thought her head would split open and the parts of her mind that were scattered all across the world would spill out of it. Or maybe it already had, and they already were. She tried to open her eyes but couldn't remember how. Doubted she would see anything even if she did.

"Where am I?"

She didn't hear the words. Didn't know if she'd spoken them. But something answered in the darkness. A voice she had heard a million times before and had just barely learned how to fear.

Somewhere forgotten. I am near, but still so, so far. But there are echoes here. Reverberations across the life pond. Your friends are safe. You made them safe. I will help you get back to them. But first I want to show you something.

Ehryn opened her eyes to the nothingness around her. It was similar to the forest she and Dhruv had found in their youth. Similar to where she went when she dreamed, when she followed rivers to oceans and threads across time and space.

Similar, but not the same. Ehryn followed the voice that led her gently outside the bubble of emptiness she'd woken in. Found herself surrounded by marble columns and endless windows. She remembered this place from her encounter with Mavrikal. It was serene and beautiful now that the Dark Goddess had vacated its rooms.

Almost. There was a pool in the center of the hall, and things writhed and twisted underneath its surface.

Ehryn feared whatever was beneath those waves the same way animals feared fire. The same way deer knew to run when they caught the scent of a predator on the wind. She feared Them as humans feared the darkness outside their ring of torchlight. But she also recognized those beings that cried out from beneath that mirrorlike pool. Had heard Them on the wind for years.

So, as much as her very soul told her to run, she could not. Would not. She would see the end of this, one way or another.

Alathi's voice sounded proud when She whispered again. *Very good, Ehryn. You are growing. Stay. Let me show you the truth.*

Ehryn stood at the edge of the pool, and several shifting, out-of-focus figures appeared in a circle around the hall. Ehryn recognized Mavrikal and Jaladri in the group, and, while she didn't know the others, figured she could guess.

The Sisters.

"Why do they no longer worship Us, Sister?" one of the gathered women asked in a voice that brought to mind rich, green jungles filled with vines and giant leaves. Her hair was adorned with flowers the color of sunsets. "What changed while We slept?"

"We lost the tonicloran." The tallest figure bent at the waist as She replied. She smelled of pine trees and mountain air. When

She rose again, Her willowy arm was extended until it almost reached Ehryn's incorporeal body, holding up one of the twisted vines that Ehryn had seen sprout from Tendaji's blood. But, just as it had on the barn floor, the stalk wilted and disintegrated in Her fingers. She brushed the ash away carefully. "When We originally bound the mortals' blood to Our blessed stalk, their offspring felt the compulsion, too. But now they hear beyond Our songs. Beyond Our commandments."

"They've even learned how to tap the bloodline power for themselves," Jaladri interjected in Her voice the color of shells. "One commanded entire armies with Our rite. Bent minds to his will in the ways only We should be able to."

"They've become so powerful," the Goddess of Vines and Jungles said in Her tropical whisper. "Can We rebind the mortals as We did in the beginning? When We ascended?"

"We can if We can find more of the blessed tendril. If the Betrayer did not succeed in destroying all of it," the Eldest replied.

"We can! We can!" Mavrikal smiled and circled the pool, Her eyes darting this way and that. "I found it. Found him. Tendaji of the Fall. The tonicloran is in his blood." The Sisters closest to the Dark Goddess drew back a pace at her inky whispers, but Mavrikal didn't seem to notice. "The Betrayer took it from Us. But she did not realize that she returned it when she forced the tonicloran upon her sibling. Cursed him in the same way she was cursed. And now, after all this time, it has resurfaced. My worshippers will extract it. It will be Ours again. Soon."

A woman wearing a veil the color of desert sand looked uncertain. "Teilithia, is it true some of the humans can hear whispers? *Their* whispers?" Her voice was like baked clay.

The Eldest Sister narrowed Her eyes. "It does not matter if humans can hear the Old Gods. Mavrikal has destroyed everyone that's ever gotten close to Our trap. Let Alathi whisper all She wants to. We will not go back to what We were before. I swear it."

Alathi laughed mirthlessly. *Illindria said something similar. But She heard Me call from beneath the threads for eons, and I wore Her down. I demanded justice, and She responded by trying to unite the Faoii and Croeli. She misunderstood My orders, but it led to Her downfall, and I was able to get the smallest foothold upon Her death. With you as My arm, Ehryn, these usurpers, too, will soon know My justice.*

Ehryn shuddered at the deep rage in Alathi's voice. The ancient hurt that had festered for millennia. She started to respond, but Mavrikal was speaking again.

"Several of those that travel with Tendaji of the Fall have useful magic in their blood," She hissed, Her smile too wide, Her lips spread too thin. "My worshippers know the magic of My whispers. They are already reminding these little mortals how to worship properly. I can bring them back to Us willingly, without having to waste a drop of their precious blood."

"Why should the mortals worship You above any of Us, Mavrikal? Look at You. Look at the way staying on the mortal plane has warped Your vessel. You are no longer worthy of their veneration." The Goddess of Tides turned to face Teilithia. "If this group is as useful as Mavrikal says they are, We should bind them to one more worthy, Sister. Make sure the effort is not wasted."

Mavrikal flared, rising up in a cloud of ash and smoke. "I don't see You—any of You—venturing outside Your halls to watch the mortals and guide the threads they color. You dare say that I have not earned this? I'll throw You into the oceans You cower beneath, Jaladri!"

Jaladri, too, grew in size and matched Her sister's glare. "I was the first to face the mortal who hears Alathi's Call, Mavrikal! I'm the only reason that any of us know that the Old Gods are strong enough to be heard! That They're this close to being released! Without My warning, We would have no plan to realign the mortals to Our will at all!" Jaladri's eyes sparked with lightning and crashing waves. "You've been on this plane too long, Mavrikal. You've lost yourself like Illindria did. You will fall as suddenly as She, and Your death will release the Old Gods. One way or another, You are about to be Our end."

Mavrikal shot toward Jaladri in a cloud of fire and smoke. The other Sisters shouted encouragement or dissuasions, Their voices crashing against each other like sandstorms and fires and tsunamis. Ehryn felt like all the worst parts of nature were coursing through the infinitely long room, clashing in imminent disasters that could level cities. She cowered on reflex. Alathi laughed softly.

No. This is good. They are fracturing already. We can set it right. You can set it right.

Ehryn didn't know if she found the ancient Goddess comforting or not.

Finally, Teilithia, the Eldest, held up Her hand again. The others fell quiet. Mavrikal moved to Her original spot, seething silently.

"We used the tonicloran once, and it worked better than in Our wildest dreams. We can see the Tapestry now and know that the tides have changed. And We can use that to Our advantage. Mavrikal has already started Us on the path." The Ocean Goddess opened Her mouth to speak, but Teilithia gave Her a hard look. "She has. And We have learned how to move forward. While once the matriarchs of the family held the most weight, the threads have shifted. The power now lies on the shoulders of siblings."

Mavrikal slithered in Her dress of smoke and lies. "Yes. Yes! I've already started draining sibling blood. It reweaves what was broken when Illindria fell. Keeps Our nemeses in Their oubliette. And when We are ready, We can use the sibling bloodlines to put all of the mortals back under Our control!"

"But we need the tonicloran to rebind them all to Us," the Veiled Goddess of the Desert said again.

"I told you, I found Tendaji of the Fall. It's in his blood. The magic in the blood. My devoted are extracting it from him now. Soon it will be Ours again."

That made everyone smile, and They laughed in voices that sounded like fires and sands and streams and jungles. Only the Sea Goddess crossed Her arms over Her shell-laden chest.

"It took centuries to bind the mortals to Our will the first time. And the humans unwove that command with a single stroke of a sword. If We hadn't wrested control of the silver-clad one and had her destroy all of the powerful mages in Imeriel, the mortals might very well be worshipping the Old Gods now, with magic too strong for Us to combat. That was too close for Us to be this confident."

Ah. Elise. She heard Me too. Heard My cry to restore justice. She followed Me in her youth, before these usurpers drowned out My Call. Even at the end, she still thought she was following My whispers. A shame.

"Then We will take it from them. Make them dependent on Us for their magic, as the Faoii were beneath Illindria's gaze," Mavrikal replied, licking Her teeth. Teilithia frowned and turned to Her mad sister.

"You have a plan, Mavrikal?"

Mavrikal twirled Her too-long fingers. "Yes. Yes! My pets. Those I visit in the night. My Hollowed. They can drain the magic of their brethren. Leave behind empty shells that We can decide whether or not to fill again. Make them worship Us out of need."

Jaladri narrowed Her eyes. "And You already have access to these... Hollowed? You're prepared to drain the mortal lines with their blood?"

"Yes! Yes! They are already Ours. Locked away until We need them. Parceled nicely for Our convenience. And in exchange, all We must do is allow one small human to maintain her throne."

The Oldest of the False Children smiled, and Ehryn heard the ice break beneath the stream of Her voice. "Perfect."

"Do You want Me to return, Sister? I left them in one of my enclaves. I will gift them to You, and You may do with them as You wish."

"Return, Mavrikal. Use the tonicloran and the Hollowed blood together to drain all those We can reach through the sibling bloodlines. Force them to need Us again."

"There will still be enough mortals left to try and fight back," Jaladri protested. "If She starts this, everything will move very quickly, Teilithia."

"Go with her, Jaladri. Use the Elisians that already worship Us and lead the Hollowed to those You cannot access through the Weave. The mortals will be divided. Weak. It will be easy to take that magic away from them when they are alone and afraid. And once they are without magic, they will do anything We ask just for the chance to have it again."

There was a chittering of laughter and excitement around the pool. Then, like fireflies, the False Children blinked out of existence.

Ehryn found herself in the desolate hall again. She could feel the rot and decay and sickening *wrongness* in the spaces where the False Children had stood.

Now you know Their plan. I will send you back to your friends. You brought them closer than anyone has before. The other Weaver—the last one who stepped into these halls—did well in preparing the path for you. You are almost invisible to the Mad One. Almost. You must move quickly. She will look for you. And if you cannot move quickly enough, Her Sisters will join in the search. If that happens, then nothing will save any of Us.

All hope rests on you, Ehryn of Clearwall.

I will not have the strength to save you again. Not unless you free Me.

Follow your brother's strand.

Help us.

"Wait!" Ehryn cried, but she was falling through space and time, her mind stretched in every direction, pulled apart and reassembled over and over.

Then there was only darkness.

29

When Ehryn opened her eyes again, she gagged. The fire was too bright. The trees above her seemed to spin and twirl, getting bigger and smaller as she tried to focus. She closed her eyes again and whimpered.

"Easy. Easy." Namaoii's voice. Rough and… concerned, maybe? Did Namaoii even get concerned? "What the blades happened back there?"

Ehryn shook her head. Didn't know how to explain the way her mind had stretched and bent and pulled and how they'd ended up in a hall that couldn't possibly exist and that she'd stood above the trap that held the Old Gods when They weren't actually there.

The overwhelming feeling lessened by degrees, and Namaoii didn't push as Ehryn got her bearings. It felt different now.

There was crisp air and the smell of earth and pine needles. "Where are we?" Her throat was dry. It hurt to talk.

Namaoii put a waterskin up to her lips. "Damned if I know—drink it slowly—one second we were in that barn and the next we were… here. Wherever here is."

"Did you hear Alathi in the pool? She's trapped beneath the pool!" Ehryn wanted someone else to help everything make sense. Wanted to know she wasn't crazy.

"What?"

"The pool. The tonicloran showed me. It spreads everywhere. All over the world… but not the world. It pulls you all along it in a million different directions, and none of them are here." The words poured from Ehryn's mouth in a tumble. "It's so big. It spreads all across the Weave, and through it. Under it. You could follow it anywhere. To any place or point or time or even places that don't exist here at all. The Voices on the Wind are trapped below it, and the Sisters want it and the world needs it, but it's too powerful and everything is so wrong and perfect and beautiful and terrifying all at the same time with it, and if we bring it back so much good can happen or the Sisters can use it to enslave us all again, and I don't even know where the Voices *are*, but I know the Sisters fear Them and locked Them up and maybe we need to get Them back out, but if we focus on that we might run out of time before the Sisters use the Hollowed to… to…" Ehryn finally had to take a breath and it turned into a wracking, laughing sort of sob. Because all of this was only a tiny fraction of what the tonicloran had shown her as she spun back across the Tapestry to land here in this desolate forest with its little camp.

Ehryn felt a hand suddenly against her forehead, and it was cool and grounding. She leaned into it, and the overwhelming cyclone of thoughts and memories stilled. After a moment, Namaoii pulled her hand away. "Well, you don't have a fever, but I think I'd better go wake Tendaji up. You… you don't seem well."

"No! Don't go yet." Ehryn didn't know why, but she was terrified of being alone with only her thoughts and the memories the tonicloran had filled her mind with. "Just… just give me a minute to process everything before we get the others, okay? Just sit with me for a while. Please?"

"Okay. Drink some more water, though." Namaoii pressed the waterskin into her hand again, and Ehryn took a few more cautious sips, focusing on the crisp night air and the sound of the crackling fire and Namaoii's breathing nearby. The two stayed in amicable silence for a while before Ehryn finally felt grounded enough to open her eyes and sit up. Namaoii watched her closely, concerned. "I'm fine now. Really," Ehryn assured her as she wrapped her blanket around her shoulders. "What about Tendaji? Is he okay?"

Namaoii frowned and looked at one of the bedrolls on the other side of camp. "As okay as someone can be after…that, I guess. He's slept more in the last two days than I saw him sleep during our entire journey. I'm not really sure what they did to him, but I'm glad we got him out."

It took a moment before Ehryn could sort out her real memories from the ones the tonicloran had introduced, but then she remembered Tendaji hanging from the rafters in the barn and shuddered. "Those chains. That barn. All of it. That was dark. Did you notice how it was here and wasn't here? Did they… did they pull that ability from his blood?"

"You should know. You've been like that for the last two days. Shifting in and out like he does. I… I wasn't sure you were going to come back completely, and Tendaji couldn't even go in and lead you out again. We… we really thought we might lose you."

Namaoii's voice shook a little, but then the Wolf Pup cleared her throat and added gruffly, "Kant was the most worried, of course. About you, and about everything that happened in the enclave. We spent a long time answering his questions, trying to break through the lies that Tessil leaked into his brain. It hurts him, not knowing what's true and what isn't. He takes everything at face value and doesn't understand that some people hide things or lie. I hope that talking to you later will help. If anyone can find a way to ease his mind, it'll be you."

Ehryn nodded. "I hope so. I'll try to find the right words to say."

Namaoii leaned back and looked at the stars. "Heh. 'Find.' That was your gift, wasn't it? Some of the Called said they had other magics before they heard the Voices on the Wind. Never guessed you'd have something useful like returning what's been lost. Explains why you always find my whetstone when I misplace it. But pulling the tonicloran through the veil? No one else could have done that."

"I'd… I'd forgotten I had it. My brother and I used to find amazing plants when we were young. Even the Royal Arcanist had me locate a pen before we left. I guess I never really lost that magic. I just… didn't know it was still there."

Namaoii sighed. "I should have known you were special. Maybe I didn't want to believe it before. Maybe I didn't want you to have a bigger role to play in the world than I did, especially when it seemed like you didn't even want any of it."

Ehryn reached out and placed a hand on Namaoii's arm. "I'm sorry. I would have given the tonicloran to you if I could. Let you move like Tendaji does. Let you see… everything. Clearwall needs that."

"Clearwall already has that." Namaoii shrugged. "We have Jacir, after all. As amazing as you might think you are, you're no Royal Arcanist." Ehryn thought that she should be offended, but Namaoii gave her a wink, and the pain faded. "Besides," the Wolf Pup continued, "who knows what would have happened if I'd been the one to touch the tonicloran? I might have sapped the power from the Goddess plant or worse. Maybe it's better that it was you."

And it *clicked.* Everything she'd seen Namaoii do with Mavrikal and the Elisians and with Tendaji. The conversation with Amati in the Faoii monastery. The dropped sentences and doubt and cynicism when they'd talked about their magics.

Without even realizing what she was doing, Ehryn yanked her hand off Namaoii's arm as though it had burned her and scurried back on her bedroll until her back hit the tree behind her.

"You're one of the Hollowed!" she gasped, instinct taking over. The fear was there again. The terror when she'd seen the X across the other woman's forehead. All the legends and stories and hatred that had been ingrained in her since childhood. Years' worth of distrust distilled into a primal, unshakable terror.

Namaoii watched as Ehryn scurried away from her but didn't move. Only gave a pained, infinitely sad expression as Ehryn pushed herself backwards into the tree.

"Yeah. Run," the Wolf Pup whispered, her pained voice taking on an edge of anger. "It's not like we were friends up until now, were we? It's not like a *Hollowed's* magic saved you back in that enclave. Blades." The Wolf Pup stood and turned away from Ehryn, tears in her eyes, and started walking in the other direction. Her voice shook when she spoke again. "Tendaji wanted to talk to you when you woke up. I'll go wake him."

"Wait!" Ehryn cried, shame overpowering her fear, her heart clenching at Namaoii's expression. "Wait. I'm sorry, Namaoii. I'm sorry. I know I owe you my life and more. I… I didn't mean it. It's hard. They teach us to hate… hate people like you from the minute we can walk. I didn't realize how deep that hatred was."

Namaoii tensed again but rolled her neck. "Don't I know it," she whispered, still not turning back to Ehryn.

"Can… can we just sit for a moment? Before you get Tendaji? Let him sleep a little longer? Let me try to decide what I want to say to him? What I want to ask?"

Namaoii's stance didn't soften, but she turned her head enough to look back over her shoulder. "What do you mean?"

Ehryn took a deep breath. "I… I know the Elisian was using magic, but… but some of what she said did ring true. About Tendaji, I mean. There have been secrets. A lot of holes. She was right about that."

Namaoii barked out a soft laugh. "Yeah. I've noticed it, too. I have a few things I want to ask him myself." Stiffly, she sat down again, though not as close as she had before. "I think he knows we've figured out that there's more than he let on. I think that's why he wanted to wait until you were awake. Get us all on the same page together."

Ehryn nodded. She wrapped her arms around her legs and stared at the fire, thinking of everything she'd heard from Mavrikal, from Alathi, from dreams and visions and Calls and lost echoes that had never made sense. There were too many questions. Too many uncertainties. And she couldn't quite look at Namaoii, no matter how hard she tried.

Namaoii must have noticed, because she sighed. "You're still thinking of the Hollowed thing, aren't you?"

"I'm trying not to."

"Well, you're terrible at it. Just say what you want to say. Might as well get it over with before Kant wakes up. He doesn't understand why it makes a difference what I am, and Tendaji doesn't care. So I can at least figure out the hatred with you right now."

"I don't hate you," Ehryn objected.

"Yeah. You're only afraid of me. Those two things usually go hand in hand."

"I'm sorry," Ehryn whispered.

"Of course you are." The remark was biting. Namaoii visually forced her shoulders to relax, but deep lines creased her face in the firelight. "Just ask what you want to ask, Ehryn. I'm too tired to play games." Ehryn realized that Namaoii had probably been keeping watch for most of the last two days, even after all the fighting she'd done in the enclave. Those deep lines in her face carved sorrowful ravines into Ehryn's soul, but she had to know.

"Why… why aren't you at one of the monasteries? All… all of them…you… are supposed to be at the monasteries."

Namaoii bristled. "You can't even call us people, can you? Can't even imagine us being anywhere but locked up like Amati was." She sighed deeply. "We have names, Ehryn. All of us. But everyone stops thinking of us as human the minute someone calls us 'Hollowed' instead. Of course the first thing you'd want to know is why we aren't locked up."

"I'm sorry," Ehryn whispered again, but it sounded weak, even to her.

Namaoii shook her head and pointed at a still bedroll on the other side of the fire. "My name is Namaoii. It always has been and I'm not any different than I was three days ago. That poor girl's name is Khalista, but you didn't even bother to find that out. Just called her 'Hollowed' like everyone else. Like my mother taught everyone to, without even realizing what she was doing. And you're right, Ehryn. My mother locked that poor girl up to make you feel better. And she wouldn't hesitate to do the same to me."

Ehryn's face fell as what Namaoii was saying dawned on her. "She doesn't know," she whispered. "Queen Isolde doesn't know."

"Of course she doesn't know! Do you think I'd let her find out? Let her imprison me or work me to death in the mines like everyone else? Just because of who I am? How I was born?" Namaoii threw a stick into the fire. "She doesn't know, Ehryn. And she can't know until I'm ready to tell her myself and face her and everything she's done. You saw how terrified Khalista was when we mentioned Mother's name. Until I see those mines and confront

Isolde myself, I won't understand completely, but I know there's a reason my people hate the Starlit Throne."

Ehryn shuddered at how Namaoii called the Hollowed "her people." Until now, the Wolf Pup had only used that phrase to describe Clearwall. Could she stand for both groups? Could anyone?

"My mother thinks I'm gifted in war, and that's only because I train every day just to keep up the illusion. I've learned the stances and how to make my voice commanding like the others in my line, but I'll never be as good at it as they were. Or… I don't think I will. As far as I know, no other Hollowed has ever been allowed to learn other magics. Though it's not like any of them were given the chance to try."

"If we talk to Queen Isolde, maybe she'll understand," Ehryn tried. Namaoii didn't even offer her mirthless laugh. Just stared into the fire.

"She can't know, Ehryn. Not yet. The very idea of me dismantles everything that the precious Faoii have built their supremacy around for generations. She'd have to lock me up. Or at least keep me out of the public eye. Secret me away and use me for whatever she uses the others for." Namaoii glanced towards the other Hollowed's—*Khalista,* Ehryn forced herself to remember—bedroll. "But I guess we know what that is now, don't we?"

"The Sisters need Hollowed blood," Ehryn said. "They want to use that and the tonicloran to drain everyone of magic. Make us dependent on Them again." Namaoii looked scared at that, then angry.

"And my mother is giving Them the Hollowed They need. She sends them to the monasteries to be plumped up and healed so the blood will flow. Makes them work themselves to death in the mines, where no one notices if a few go missing."

"Maybe she doesn't know everything. Maybe the False Children have been deceiving her." Ehryn didn't believe her own words, but she tried to sound optimistic.

"I doubt it. We've learned enough to know she stands behind this barbary." Namaoii threw another stick into the fire with an angry flick of her arm. "When I ascend the Starlit Throne, I'm going to change the narrative for the Hollowed. They never asked to be what they are. They deserve more than what they've gotten up until now. Khalista deserved better than this."

Ehryn looked over at the occupied bedroll. "How is she?"

"Do you actually care?"

"I wouldn't have asked if I didn't."

Namaoii thought about that for a moment. "It's a start. Maybe a start for all of us." She shook her head and looked over at the still blankets. "She's hurt. Bad. Weak and sick. They *tortured* her, Ehryn. Nearly drained all of the blood out of her. My mother will pay for it. And after that, I'll make sure the Sisters she swore herself to will pay for it, too. We're going to free all of them." She looked Ehryn in the eye, her gaze filled with iron and thunder. "All of them, Ehryn."

Ehryn bit her lip. The idea of The Hollowed being free to live wherever they wanted to? Of possibly having one as a neighbor? Her mind fairly screamed in terror.

"I know I'm on the sideline of this, but—"

"Damn it, Ehryn! Don't you understand? There are no sidelines! Not for people like me who get locked up or killed if they stand up or they sit down or they kneel or they grovel or they hide. You think you can sit by and not make an impact. But we *see* you. *I* see you, Ehryn. I know which side you're on when you try not to pick any sides at all."

"Namaoii, I—"

"No! Everyone thinks we're all in the same boat—we all get what we get when we're born, and we have to make the best out of what we have. But it's not like that, Ehryn. You're not even *in* a boat. You're on a shore and just watching the rest of us sink or swim. You're watching the clouds and the waves and thinking that it's a shame you can't stop the storm, but you *can*. We all *can*. But no one does." She clenched her fists, and Ehryn shrank back on reflex. "You think the storm won't affect you, but it does. And every person who doesn't do anything at all is just adding to the waves." Ehryn shut her mouth, considering what Namaoii had said. The other girl grew silent, staring at the campfire.

Finally, Ehryn did something she'd been told her entire life *never* to do.

She reached out and took Namaoii's hand in hers.

They sat there together, silently, and Ehryn saw the look in Namaoii's eyes. A look of relief. Acceptance. Pride. She'd seen that look before, too.

"The other day… when you saved Tendaji. You weren't proud because he called you Faoii, were you?"

"Is that what you thought? No. I don't give a whetstone about that title. I don't care about being a Faoii, even though that's what everyone wants for me."

"What was it then? I saw the look in your eye. It was like you'd seen the sun for the first time."

Namaoii smiled, remembering. "I care that I'm one of the Hollowed. I've always been a Hollowed. But that was the only time anyone has ever considered my magic as anything other than a contamination. Where someone saw me as a Hollowed *and* a person."

Ehryn squeezed the other girl's hand. "I'm glad you were there, Namaoii. No one else could have saved him. Not from that."

"It's still a long way from over, though. Isn't it?" Namaoii asked.

Ehryn nodded and stood. "I think so. And I think it's time we wake Tendaji up. That vine that came from his blood? The tonicloran? Both the Sisters and the Old Gods want it. And I think I pulled it from somewhere They couldn't get to on Their own. We need answers. We need a plan. What happens in the coming days is going to depend a lot on what we learn in the next few hours." She held Namaoii's gaze as the older girl stood up. "And, Namaoii? I'm sorry, too. For everything."

Namaoii stared at Ehryn's outstretched hand. For a minute, Ehryn thought she would walk away, but finally the Wolf Pup took it. "Then prove it. Let's find a way to make it better for everyone."

30

As they went to wake up Tendaji and Kant, Ehryn once again noticed the weariness in Namaoii's shoulders and knew that no one had come back from the Elisian enclave completely unscathed. Their minds and bodies had been pushed to their limits, and the group had learned more in a day than they had during their entire kintar up until now.

Ehryn wondered if they would be ready for whatever came next, though she didn't know what that might be. This had become bigger than a simple kintar or even the fight against the fanatic order of the Elisians. Two factions of beings greater than all of Imeriel—literal gods—were fighting a war that had lasted millennia, and she didn't know if her little group could do their part to end it and still come out the other side.

Ehryn waited for the Voices on the Wind to give their suggestions and encouragement. To tell her to pick up Tendaji's sword and be more than she was. To urge her to reach her destiny and protect her friends. To whisper "help us." But since she'd reached across the veil to grasp that thorny stalk no one else could find and visited a hall that no one else could glimpse, the Voices on the Wind had been silent.

Ehryn had had the company of Alathi and the others for as long as she could remember, and now, without the Call, she felt alone. She didn't regret what she'd done to save her friends from the Elisians, but she'd felt Alathi weaken in the hall. Had felt Her drift away at the end. She didn't know how to bring Her back or if that was even the right thing for Clearwall. The uncertainty made her feel cold.

Their entire mission on this kintar had been to follow Alathi's Call. Now it was gone, and Ehryn didn't know where to go. Was she worth anything without the Voices on the Wind? What was she if she was not Called?

But then, she'd had magic before the Call, hadn't she? Dhruv had known of her gifts. So had her parents. They'd been proud of her long before she'd heard the Whispers on the Wind. "Destiny" was just a word. She was worthy even without the promises of Goddesses. Right?

But she could still imagine exactly what Tendaji's blade would feel like in her hand. And she knew that even if she was worthy now, she could be truly great.

Ehryn shook the thought away. Great by others' standards, not her own. It wasn't the same. It was too big of a tangle to unweave on her own. The others would help. She wasn't as alone as she felt, after all.

Ehryn leaned over Kant's bedroll and shook him awake. He groggily turned to face her.

"Ehryn! You're okay!" Kant fairly jumped from his blankets, hugging her as tightly as his little arms would allow. "I'm so glad you're here. Everything was so confusing. Madame Tessil said they were the good guys, but the Elisians tried to hurt you. Us. And what they did to Tendaji..." He pressed his face into her shoulder. "I was so scared. Thank you for saving us."

"Of course, Kant. I'll always be there to save you. Well, if Namaoii isn't there first, anyway," Ehryn smiled into his hair and hugged him back. "Come on. We're going to talk about what happens next. I want you to be there."

Kant scrunched up his nose. "I'm not good at decisions, Ehryn."

"I don't think anyone ever really is. We just do the best we can with what we know. And you know more than all of us combined." Ehryn took Kant's hand and led him closer to the fire. Namaoii and Tendaji were already there, and Ehryn was able to look at the Faoli for the first time since the barn. The old warrior was thin, his cheekbones prominent, but his eyes sparked with concern and fear.

He stood and made his way to Ehryn. He grasped her hands, bringing them close to his face, eyes worried over the deep scars that twisted around her fingers and palms where the tonicloran had pulled her down into the vast emptiness of eternity.

"Ehryn? Are you hurt? Are you whole?"

Ehryn nodded, though the Faoli did not look away from her scarred palms.

"I'm okay. We're all okay, Tendaji, Sir. It worked."

Tendaji shifted his gaze to study her face. "I was afraid you'd get lost in the Weave with no one to help pull you back. And I couldn't even go to the other side to guide your way. I'm so sorry, Ehryn."

"I had help. Alathi guided me. She helped me not get spread across... everything." Ehryn took a deep, steadying breath as the memories of the Tapestry and everything within stretched into an infinite chasm at the edges of her mind. She pushed it back and tried to smile. "It was worth it. I don't regret anything."

Tendaji looked sad and squeezed her hands again before sitting. "Perhaps. But I can see eternity behind your eyes, Ehryn. I will help you however I can. I promise. You are not alone in this."

"Thank you, Tendaji." Ehryn took a seat, too, and Kant perched beside her. "It saved us. That's all that matters. I'll take everything else as it comes and pay whatever price I have to pay for it later. But for now… that's enough. That has to be enough."

Tendaji sighed. "Yes. It… *you* did save us. We could not have gotten out of there alone, and I do not doubt that the Elisians would have called forth She Who Demands the Blood if they hadn't already. Who knows how long we would have had? And your… sacrifice jumped us across the Weave. She will have trouble finding us for a while at least, until we start on our path again and start to reweave the shining threads where She can see them."

"Can't Ehryn just jump us across the Weave again if one of the Sisters gets too close?" Namaoii asked.

Ehryn wanted to say that she could try. That she'd do whatever it took to keep them all safe. But even as she tried to form the words, the endless chasm yawned in front of her, deep and imposing and filled with promise. She thought she'd go mad with the infinity of it, caught within the generations and miles and endless secrets that all promised haven if she so chose, but within each pinprick of light a million possibilities poked through, all with the Sisters' dark shadows creeping at the edges. Searching. Waiting. She didn't know where to go to save them. Didn't know how to tell Namaoii about everything she saw. The campfire was gone, and her friends' voices were distant. She was already lost in its gaping maw of endless possibilities.

Then Tendaji was in front of her, hands on either side of her face, staring at her with ice-blue eyes that had seen such darkness before and had still come back from it in one piece. She held his gaze until the Weave faded into the background again.

"Stay with us," Tendaji whispered. Ehryn only nodded. It was several more seconds before Tendaji seemed satisfied. He released her gaze and returned to his spot by the campfire. Ehryn's head swam, and she focused on the ground beneath her feet. Kant, next to her, took her hand.

"I'll take that as a no," Namaoii finally said. "You could have just said so."

"I'm sorry," Ehryn whispered. "I thought I could do it."

"All magics take time to master," Tendaji said kindly. "I've heard that it's harder when the choices are infinite. Going in without a set path makes it easier to get tangled in the strands. You might be able to bring us all to a pre-determined destination that you know well, but Mavrikal would be able to follow such a path easily. Anything else will take training and time."

"I didn't think the tonicloran would be so powerful," Ehryn whispered. "I didn't know anything could hold that much inside of it."

"It is the greatest of all gifts and curses," Tendaji said sadly.

"You know more about it than you've let on, don't you?" Namaoii said, the smallest hint of authority and demand creeping into her voice. "You've had the time to learn. There's no way you're as young as you pretend to be."

Tendaji frowned. "I've never pretended to be a young man, Namaoii."

Namaoii's eyes darkened when the Faoli sidestepped her questions yet again. "Stop with the pig shit, Tendaji! We're past secrets! Whatever happens from here on out, we need to know *everything*, or none of us are making it back to Clearwall." Namaoii crossed her arms over her chest. "There are things you're not telling us, 'Tendaji of the Fall.' You once said your sister was part of the Monastery of the Eternal Blade, which is fine. I thought maybe your father was old when he conceived you. It was *just* possible that you could be related to someone from that long ago. But then you said she was your younger sister. You talk about the Blackfeather Wilds like you grew up there, but that's not possible, either. You're older than you say you are. Older than you could possibly be. Jacir, too. What is actually going on?" Tendaji nodded slowly.

"You're perceptive, Namaoii. You truly are worthy of the Starlit Throne."

"No. No flattery. No dodging questions. Just tell us the truth."

Tendaji nodded. "Very well. I owe you that much. Both of you. All of you. Please know that the things I kept from you were supposed to be for your own protection. The things we're going to unbury next to this campfire are usually best left forgotten. But not here. Not tonight. You all need to know."

"Start with the tonicloran," Ehryn whispered, the scars on her hands aching as she said the word. "What is it?"

Tendaji sighed and stared up at the stars for a moment before responding. "It's a plant made from beyond the Weave. It ties all the strands together. Past, present, future. All aspects of the world are connected to its tendrils. But their roots are tied to the Sisters, not the least of which is Mavrikal, and Their magic. Destroying it weakened Them greatly, loosened Their hold."

"And now They want it back. They want to use it to restrengthen Their control. Make us need Them again," Ehryn said.

Tendaji nodded. "It seems so. Mavrikal tried to pull it from my blood. She failed because of Namaoii's magic, but that will not stop Her from trying to get it from you instead. We will have to stay out of Her sight. I'll try to teach you. But…" His voice grew a little gruffer. "But Ehryn, I wish I didn't have to. The tonicloran is a curse for anyone who touches it. We live our lives like shadows, ghosts. We watch all the people we love die. We watch our work get undone and tarnished. The world was better without it. Humans do not deserve such darkness in their lives."

Ehryn tried to smile for him, but the deep sorrow and hurt in Tendaji's face made her heart clench. "I… I saw a lot in the tonicloran tendrils. In the Tapestry threads that spread out in every direction further than I thought my mind could go. And… and you're right. There was a lot of darkness there. I think it would be easy to only focus on the dark spots. But there's beauty in it, too. Even in this, right? There has to be some good in it. There has to be."

Suddenly Kant piped up, his face made of all the brightness and joy Ehryn was talking about. "That's right! You've been here longer than any of us, Tendaji! You must have seen things that you couldn't even imagine when you were my age! Just like my sister is going to see things that I can't picture now! What's your favorite thing? Do you know? Can you pick one?"

"Now's not the time, Kant!" Namaoii barked. But Ehryn squeezed Kant's hand.

"No, I think it's the perfect time. Tell us, Tendaji. In all the things you've ever seen, what do you think is the most beautiful?"

Tendaji stared at her for a long moment. "There are so many other things we should be focusing on, Ehryn," he started.

"I know. But I also need to know that there's at least some good in that infinite darkness. That when someone has the opportunity to look at everything, their heart can still find hope. Please, Tendaji. I want to know that I didn't lose who I was when I took the step to be who I'm going to be."

Tendaji tried to smile, and Ehryn saw something in his eyes sparkle. "I know I've said this before, Ehryn, but we are all very lucky that it was you who was Called and not someone else." He leaned back and looked at the stars. "Very well. I've never actually looked upon the Tapestry. I've let better people than me gaze across all the threads and decide which is the best to follow. But you're right. I've watched entire generations rise and breathe and thrive. There have been truly beautiful things in the world while I've lived in it."

"But what was your *favorite*?" Kant pressed.

Tendaji smiled wistfully. "The stories, Kantilieh. My favorite thing has always been the campfire stories. Of what has been and what we dream might be."

Kant seemed content with this answer and smiled. After a moment, Tendaji turned back to Ehryn, his expression less pained. "Maybe that is part of the tonicloran's curse, as well. But you're right. I've seen things I never would have expected. In my youth, I could not believe that the Faoii and Croeli would merge as one. I did not think we could ever work as equals. I never thought I would see a world where everyone has magic. Where everyone might have been equally capable and deserving of taking the tonicloran's curse. But so few want it, and that, too, is beautiful. Because for the first time in history, people are more willing to stand on their own feet and depend on their own abilities than ask to borrow magic from deities and ancient pools. We live in our own light, and that is… that is magnificent."

"Is that what I did? When I pulled the tonicloran across the veil? Did I take power from the Sisters?"

"I don't think so. I think They lost the tonicloran in Their sleep. Or Kaiya and Jacir ripped it from Their grasp when they followed the Weave in ways no one else can do. I think you used a different type of magic entirely to find the tonicloran, and then Alathi used its power to amplify that ability." He looked at her thoughtfully. "You've always had the ability to move between the planes, haven't you? That is not something the tonicloran provided."

"I just thought I was dreaming," Ehryn whispered. "I don't even know if I could tell you when I was here and when I wasn't. Where the curtain actually was."

"We call that curtain many things. It's part of the Tapestry, the life pond, the Weave... whatever you want to say, it's all the same. That little piece of reality that separates our world from wherever the Gods and magic come from. The tonicloran is of that world. But it sprouts here, poking holes through the curtain, climbing and twisting through the Tapestry, making great cracks that shouldn't be there. It is very powerful, the little plant, but it's not actually meant for little beings such as us. And, for all of its potential, it seems to be used most often as a means to control others. Kai tried to destroy all of it so that no one else would have to experience its curse. I thought she had succeeded. You must have pulled it from somewhere even she could not go."

"Who's Kai?" Namaoii asked.

"My sister. You... you saw her statue in the Monastery of the Fallen Star. Her old monastery. Though they renamed it sometime in the last century." Tendaji chuckled. "I must have missed the ceremony."

Namaoii's eyes widened, but she only gaped, evidently struck dumb by this revelation. Only Kant piped up excitedly. "I told you she looked like you!"

"You did. That was very perceptive, Kant."

Kant beamed, and Ehryn leaned forward.

"Your sister destroyed all the tonicloran. But we saw some of it in the barn, beneath... beneath where they had you. It wilted immediately, but it was there."

Tendaji released a deep sigh. "Our blood carries magic. It always has. And in the days when tonicloran was used in blood magic, it became part of us as much as we became part of it. We could travel through all the world and all the threads as easily as its vines twisted through earth. Once, there was a Faoii deep in the ground who used her blood to make it grow. To make it spread. I assume that the Elisians were trying to do something similar, and thankfully they failed. I did not realize that some of the twisted plant still lived on through me. It's good they weren't able to extract it like they'd hoped."

"They'll still come after Ehryn, though. We have to stop Them," Namaoii declared. "We can't let Them make us all into Their slaves."

"How, though?" Ehryn asked. "You and Tendaji almost defeated Mavrikal together, but She was only one of the Sisters. Jaladri has already woken the others up. We're not powerful enough."

"The Old Gods are," Namaoii said pointedly. "You saw how scared Jaladri got when She heard Them in your voice on the boat. All Alathi had was your vocal cords, and She was able to push Jaladri back into the sea."

"Then we need to find Them. Undo the trap the Sisters made below the Tapestry." Ehryn frowned, rubbing her forehead, trying to remember everything she'd heard in those disjointed minutes between the barn and the forest. "That's where the Voices on the Wind call from. The trap. It weakened when Illindria died, and Alathi has been gathering strength. But She's gone now. It took everything for Her to help me with the tonicloran. I don't even know where to look for Her anymore. And I don't know if freeing Her will be enough."

"She didn't give you *any* idea on where else to go? We can't just keep walking north forever."

"She said…" Ehryn thought back to those hazy seconds in the hall before she'd lost consciousness. "She said 'follow your brother's strand.'"

"What does that mean? I didn't know you had a brother," Namaoii said.

"I don't. He… he disappeared on his kintar. His traveling partners said he joined one of the Elisian enclaves, but we never found him."

"Oh. You're one of those," Namaoii said awkwardly.

"One of who?"

"A victim of the firstborn curse. You know how rare it is to see a family with three kids, right? For as long as Clearwall's taken a census, there's always one or two kids—on very rare occasions three—but that's it. That's all we have. But in the last fifty years or so, there's been a strange increase in deaths of the oldest child. Some sort of freak accident after their sibling is born or… or a kintar gone wrong." She looked apologetically in Ehryn's direction. "It doesn't happen in every family, but it happens enough. Enough that my mother never risked having a second child, even before my father died. It might not be as obvious from the Maze, but when you have all of the numbers… there's a lot of dead or missing firstborns." She turned to Kant. "Never repeat that to anyone." She held his gaze until he promised.

Namaoii was right. It wasn't common enough in the Maze to cause a commotion, but Ehryn knew there were whispers of the firstborn curse. Ehryn thought of Dhruv and wondered once again what had happened to him. Now that she had seen the Elisian enclave, it didn't surprise her that he could have been sucked into something sinister there, words dripped into his ears like honey until he forgot who he was. But what if it was even more ominous than that? She looked over to Kant and was suddenly grateful that he wasn't able to make the connection himself when he talked so excitedly about his coming sister.

"What happens to them?" Ehryn whispered.

"We don't know," Namaoii responded. "It's one of the great mysteries. But if Alathi said something about your brother's thread, then it probably has to do with the Old Gods or the False Children, doesn't it?"

"Probably, but I don't see how." Ehryn rubbed at her eyes. Her head hurt. The fire seemed too bright again.

"Queen Isolde once said that siblings are a beacon and that the Tapestry is often carried on four shoulders," Kant piped up. "It was when they were discussing the census four years ago after—"

"That's true, she did." Namaoii cut in. "She says that a lot. My ancestors Aurelius and Lucinda were siblings, and they brought Clearwall from the clutches of the Iron Queen and her Proclaimers. The Royal Arcanist and his sister changed the face of the Weave together. The Betrayer and..." She paused and motioned to Tendaji. "You and your sister brought magic back to Clearwall. The Tapestry's strongest Weaves are almost always carried on four shoulders. That's got to mean something, right?" She directed the question at Tendaji. He answered slowly, carefully.

"Yes. There's something magical about the way siblings work together and trust each other and build worlds with four interconnected hands. Their energies connect and weave around each other. Make everything stronger. The Faoii were able to create something close to this when they built the monasteries. Shield sisters could create a bond that was almost as strong. And it was marvelous. But it came only with long, endless trainings and hard work. It wasn't quite the same, though. Not like what we see here. Not like when two siblings live and breathe and work together from childhood."

Something nagged at the back of Ehryn's mind. There were no Voices on the Wind any longer, but Ehryn was suddenly sure that if they could, the Voices would whisper something about Tendaji and lies. About the way his words sounded like he was dancing.

"You know, don't you?" she said suddenly, turning to the Faoli. "You know what happens to the siblings of Clearwall. You know why Alathi told me to follow Dhruv's thread."

Tendaji frowned and looked to the North, his eyes the color of an iced-over river. "Years ago, Jacir suspected something, though he could never see what was truly happening. That was the worst thing, in those early days where he thought he could see everything on the Weave in a way no one else could, but then discovered there were shadows he couldn't pierce. He followed the darkness beyond any of the places where a human mind should go. Past the edges of madness and hope. I don't think anyone else in the world could have done it and come back whole, not even my sister. But he did. He went to wherever the Eternal Tapestry spirals from. To the center of all the threads and all the chaos and all the dreams of gods and man. And in those corners, he found Mavrikal and Her Sisters, drawing upon the magic of the Weave to twist the threads to fit Their desires. But so much of what They want is dependent on a trap that takes more to sustain than They alone can muster. So They use the magic of sibling blood to keep it in place. They seal the gate with the sacrifice of firstborns. He does not—cannot—know Their full plans, but he knows the False Children use sibling blood to keep the Old Gods trapped beneath the Weave."

Ehryn thought she was going to be sick. For years she'd been clinging to the hope that she might eventually find Dhruv again. That he would be in one of the Elisian enclaves. Brainwashed, perhaps, but alive. Maybe even happy. That he was gone, drained of blood by Mavrikal to keep the Old Gods sealed beneath the Weave… She buried her face in her hands and sobbed, the memories of their garden and his laughter shattering around her like glass. Next to her, Kant squeezed her hand and rubbed her back, trying to make her smile.

"I'm sorry, Ehryn," Tendaji whispered.

"I don't understand," Ehryn said through her sniffles. "If Dhruv is gone, then why did Alathi tell me to follow his thread?"

"Because the Old Gods have tried to do some good with the blood that holds Their cage closed. Have tried to use the drops that reach Them. Of all the people that have disappeared, a small portion of the younger siblings have gotten a specific gift shortly thereafter. And it's the only time we ever see this particular magic appear at all."

Ehryn swallowed hard. Because she *knew*.

"The Call." Ehryn's breath caught, her entire body quaking with a cold that seeped into her bones. "Those of us who hear the Voices on the Wind."

"That's right. No one else ever hears them, except for a random handful of those who lost an older brother or sister to the Sisters' thirst for blood and power."

"What? That's why she's special? That's what makes a Called great?" Namaoii sounded hurt and angry, but not nearly as much as Ehryn.

"Why didn't anyone tell me?" she nearly yelled. "Why didn't anyone say anything?" Her heart was beating in her ears, but there were no chittering voices from far away to prattle about what didn't matter. And still Alathi, the one Voice that might possibly answer for what She was and where She came from—was gone.

"Because knowing you have a sibling by your side or at your back—that faith and hope and love between two of the same womb—is what makes the thread burn bright, Ehryn. You were invisible to the False Children when you didn't know you still had the blood of your sibling working through the Weave. If you'd found out before the tonicloran removed you from the Tapestry… They would have found you easily, just like They found everyone else Jacir sent forth."

Ehryn felt cold as the anger and shock seeped from her body. Her mind felt stretched. Thin. She felt hollow in a way that she didn't think a person could. "So there were others before me?" she finally whispered, already knowing the answer.

"Of course there were." Namaoii sounded indignant. "You've heard the criers tell their tales. About how they abandoned Clearwall."

"None of them abandoned Clearwall, Namaoii," Tendaji said quietly. "Their journeys did not end well."

"Then why would my mother send me with another Called on this kintar if it was just going to end in disaster? If it's that dangerous?"

"I don't think she knows," Tendaji replied. "Queen Isolde so often talks about hearing of the Called exploits through dreams and messengers. Jacir has not tried to dissuade her, letting the False Children think They have the upper hand. But he believes that Mavrikal feeds the Starlit Throne false information so that your mother will continue to send those who pose a threat directly into Her clutches."

"Then… what really happened to the other Called?" Ehryn wasn't sure she wanted to know, but some part of her *needed* to.

"Jacir told them what he knew. That the Voices came to them only after their siblings had died. That the Voices on the Wind were tied to their brother or sister's thread."

"And?"

"And they set out on the journey thinking they could save their loved one. Thinking that they would be unstoppable with their older brother or sister to guide them. And their thread burned as brightly as their hope."

"The False Children came for them." Ehryn tried to picture how differently she would have acted if she'd known everything from the beginning. She looked back on the glimpses of the Tapestry she had seen and knew that her thread would have been obvious had she marched forward with a sense of purpose and determination. She would have been just one more beacon for the False Children to chase down.

"Yes. Mavrikal would meet them before they found the trap She and Her Sisters had set. The previous Called fell at the hands of a threat that even Jacir could not stop or foresee. That was the first time he knew someone else was plucking the Tapestry's strings.

Where he knew that there was something darker going on. That's when he called upon me to be your guide. He and I are the only two alive that have ever dealt with the spaces beyond the Weave before. Or we were." He looked at the deep scars on Ehryn's hands, his eyes haunted. "So I came. We thought I could protect you or prepare you more than others could. That maybe this time would be different."

Ehryn mustered up all the energy she had and smiled at her guide. "It is, Tendaji. We've gotten further than anyone that came before us, right? We're going to see the end of this. We're going to make sure that no one else has to lose someone with only a strange Voice to console them. I just... I just need to follow Dhruv's thread."

I'll follow you, Big Brother. I don't know how yet, but I'll find your thread. One more time, you're going to guide me home.

31

Ehryn stared at the fire and considered their options. Tendaji didn't know which was stronger—the tonicloran's ability to mask someone on the Weave or the beacon that came from Ehryn's knowing her brother's blood was guiding her. So they did not know how safe they were here, or whether Mavrikal would be able to find them again now that Ehryn was firmly back on this plane.

"You're sure you don't feel the Call anymore? You don't know where to go?" Namaoii grumbled.

"No," Ehryn whispered. "Pulling us through the tonicloran took all Alathi's strength. She might not be back."

"What about the others?"

Ehryn had to concentrate hard before she barely made out the whisper between the trees.

...Help us...

"They're there, but distant. There's no pull. I want to help Them, though. If the False Children imprisoned the Old Gods for power, then maybe the Old Gods will be able to help us now."

"They failed the last time They went up against the Sisters," Namaoii pointed out.

"Yeah! But they didn't have us!" Kant proclaimed.

"A lot of good that does," Namaoii huffed under her breath. "What about your brother's thread? Can you focus on that?"

Ehryn shook her head. "I know it's supposed to be obvious, but I don't feel it. I can't see it. I don't know what Alathi wants from me."

Namaoii exhaled slowly and rolled her neck. "I've never felt so lost before. It's not a fun feeling."

Lost.

Ehryn thought about Dhruv again. About the pen Jacir had been looking for. The plants in her garden as a child. The tonicloran.

"When I was young… Before Dhruv died. We had a garden. We spent hours searching for seeds and bulbs in the farmers' fields and on the docks of the Starlit River. Places where we never should have been able to find anything special. But we did. We always brought impossible new plants back home, and we grew so many amazing things. I… I stopped after he died. Then I started hearing the Call, and everyone said that that was my gift. Everyone focused on that. And I forgot about all of it."

"That's… interesting, Ehryn, but you told us that already." It was obvious that Namaoii was trying to sound kind. "I don't really see how gardening is going to help us."

"Not the gardening. Finding the seeds. Finding the pen that Jacir was looking for or the whetstone you lost last week. Finding the tonicloran. I… I pulled them all from *somewhere*. I know I did. I think I've always been able to pull things from beyond the veil. See lost creatures the size of ships in oceans that don't exist in this world. Pull forgotten plants from soil I couldn't walk on. But now that I have the tonicloran… maybe we can *go* there. And maybe if we're not on the Weave itself, we'll be safe. Safe until we decide where to go next. And if I'm going to find Dhruv's thread… I think it would be there. That was *our* place. I think I can find it." The endless Tapestry stretched out before her, but it didn't feel so imposing now that she had a specific target in mind. She didn't know exactly where it was, but she could almost sense it, just on the other side of the curtain.

"But Mavrikal can go to the spaces between the Weave, too. Won't She follow us?" Namaoii demanded.

"There are more pockets outside the Weave than stars in the sky, Namaoii," Tendaji said kindly. "And no map to guide you there. It is not like the Tapestry where, while it is infinite, has clear threads one might follow. If Ehryn can reach such a place, it could take millennia for Mavrikal to find us there."

"Can *you* reach any of these pockets beyond the Weave?" Kant asked excitedly.

Tendaji shrugged one shoulder. "There's a hall I know how to find. I think it is the closest to our Tapestry, as everyone who has ever brushed the tonicloran has been there at least once. It was Illindria's hall before She was struck down. It makes sense that all of our magics spawn from there, and that we can most easily follow the currents back. But, no, I do not know of any others. This seems like a magic that Ehryn was gifted specifically."

"How do I… what do I do?" Ehryn asked.

"How did you do it before?" Namaoii quipped. "Can't you just do that again?"

"Every time I found something that was lost, I did it without even noticing that I'd done anything special at all," Ehryn replied. "And when I moved us all from the barn, I had help."

"I had help the first time I did it, too, as did Kaiya. I don't know how much help I can be now, without magic of my own, but I think we must try. We are not safe here."

"And I'm not sure Khalista will make it much longer if we try to move her again." Namaoii motioned to the bedroll that Ehryn had forgotten was occupied, it was so still. She swallowed hard.

Tendaji looked thoughtfully over at the bedroll and then back to Ehryn. "I understand if you do not want to try Blinking again. We might be safe here, Ehryn. And finding somewhere else that is safe might be very difficult to do. However, if you want to try, I will teach you as best I can."

"I want to try," Ehryn said firmly.

Ehryn tried to do as Tendaji instructed. Tried to push aside the veil that she had inadvertently crossed an unknown number of times in her life without ever realizing it was there. But she didn't know how. And without being able to go forth and pull her through, Tendaji was unable to help beyond giving simple suggestions. "Breathe deeply, Ehryn. Picture the rift in your mind. Or focus on the Great Tapestry. The destination is not important if we cannot first find the path."

Somewhere behind her, Namaoii made a frustrated sound, but she stifled it quickly. Ehryn didn't blame her. She was frustrated with herself, too. It had been hours already, and the threat of Mavrikal finding them hung over everyone's heads. Even if she and Tendaji were hidden, Namaoii and Kant were not. And even though she was exhausted, she didn't want to give up. She wanted to bring them somewhere safe until they could refocus on the Call. She wanted a place to think about Dhruv and the threads and the Hollowed and the False Children. She wanted a moment to breathe.

Breathe. I'm supposed to be focused on my breathing.

Ehryn tried to realign herself, once again looking for the rift that she used to find without knowing she was looking for it.

"You know, Mistress," someone close to her whispered, "you, in particular, are best at finding things you don't actually realize are lost."

The voice was kind and familiar, but Ehryn still gasped in surprise. Her eyes flew open.

She wasn't where she'd been before. The campfire and her companions were gone, and she was standing in the marble hall.

"Jacir!" A tidal wave of relief, hope, and comfort cascaded against her when she saw the Royal Arcanist. Finally, someone who could guide them. Who could answer their questions. Who could make everything make sense.

She jumped to her feet, nearly running to the Royal Arcanist, but stopped when she saw his face. This wasn't the Royal Arcanist she knew. He was young. Really young. Barely older than her.

"Are you…? How?" she whispered, suddenly afraid.

The boy cleared his throat, looking sheepish. "Ah. We already know each other, I guess. Sorry about that. I promise you that I am the same Jacir you've apparently already spoken to. Though my guess is we meet sometime far in the future when the False Children are close to whatever Their end goals are."

"Yes… yes." Ehryn said slowly. "Yes! They're going to—"

Jacir held out his hand with the faintest hint of power, and Ehryn's mouth shut with a snap.

"I'm sorry, Mistress. I hope I didn't hurt you. But you can't tell me what you know. If you tell me now when I am young, then I will know of Their plans in the future, and it might very well change how you and I and all of Clearwall react to the threat. I've gotten pretty good at looking at the Tapestry, and I assume the me you know is better at it still, and the threads always begin to unweave completely when I get close to knowing what the False Children have planned for Imeriel. So I'm afraid you have to leave me in the dark. I hope I at least gave you a guide or some assistance, though? Someone to make the journey easier?"

"Yes. Tendaji, Sir. He's been very helpful. I don't think I would have made it this far without him."

The young Jacir scratched his head. "Tendaji? I don't recognize that name, but I'll remember it. Make sure he's ready whenever you are. Whenever that is. I don't suppose you can tell me what year it is where you are?" He shook his head before she could reply. "Nah, better not. If I'm too sure that you'll do something I might mess up my wording and push you away when we speak. Then we'd really be in a bind, wouldn't we? Nothing mucks up a destiny like pretending there's such a thing as destiny." He laughed, but Ehryn didn't see what was funny.

"If you don't know anything about where I'm from, then why... how are you here?"

"By carefully planned chance, Mistress. I've watched all of the threads a thousand times and have looked for when those who inadvertently come across the tonicloran make their way here. It was something I begged for help with when I was young, so it was one of the first things I learned how to do. I've guided dozens of mages like yourself to safe passages. Or... I will, maybe, depending on how you see time." He smiled and looked around. "You're taking this really well, though. Like you've been here before. Did you just find the tonicloran or am I late?"

"I did, but..." Ehryn swallowed hard, looking around for the False Children in the shadows of the hall. "But you weren't the one who helped me."

"Ah. That was you then. I saw someone on the Weave once but couldn't pin them down. That was a strange thread that pulled you along. I didn't recognize it."

"It was—"

Suddenly the hall began to shake and break apart, and Jacir held his hand up again.

"Again, Mistress Ehryn. I do not—cannot—know."

"Then… then at least know that we're not safe here!" Ehryn blurted out. "You have to believe me that the False Children will find us if we're here too long. Mavrikal will find us!"

Jacir shook his head sadly. "Ah. You've already run afoul of Them. Then we cannot stop here to rest and to answer questions. Nor can I train you in the best way to navigate the Weave to come to this place—or whatever place you're going." He gave Ehryn a conspiratorial wink and held out his hand. "But I can have you trained by the same woman who trained me. And by the same way I will train your guide Tendaji when I pull him forward across the threads to your time. Be lively, now, it can be a bit jarring at first."

Ehryn didn't know what to do or how to respond. But, even with all the secrets and uncertainties, when she looked into Jacir's eyes she knew she trusted him. She reached out, took his hand, and they Blinked.

Ehryn and Jacir stood at the bottom of a dark pit. It was cold, dingy, and smelled of vomit and blood. There were three others with them, two alive and one dead, but no one seemed to notice their presence.

"Want to see a neat trick?" Jacir whispered. "It'll only be disorienting for a second as you go in and come out again." Before Ehryn could respond, he tapped her forehead.

She was Faoii-Kaiya of the Monastery of the Eternal Blade. She didn't know how many times she'd tried to obey Vonda's orders. *Open your mind's eye. See the Goddess's world. Open it. Open it!* She had seen Illindria's world unbidden so many times before, its ethereal images dancing across her vision in a superimposed ballet. But she had never forced it to happen. It wasn't something she knew how to control.

She sagged, sweat dripping from her forehead as she gasped on hands and knees. She tried again, prying at the door she could just barely sense in the center of her forehead. It cracked ajar, threatening to slam shut again even as she pried. Straining, she pushed harder…

There. It snapped open with an almost physical blow as, for the first time, Kaiya purposely coerced her mind's eye to obey her will. The images shook in her vision for a moment before breaking apart. The door slammed shut again, and Kaiya's head reeled as she gasped for breath. Vonda scowled from her chained dais.

"No, no! You're using your innate abilities. You must use *me.*"

"I…I can't," Kaiya gasped out, her arms shaking.

"No? And why not? Come on, Faoii! You've already accomplished the impossible just by seeing those fading images! Your mind is there. The next part is easy. Even the brain-dead Croeli can do it."

Kaiya hung her head.

"You can do this, Faoii! So why don't you?"

Kaiya knew the answer, but she didn't want to admit it. Fear clawed at her like inky tentacles, wrapping around her face in a suffocating scarf. She couldn't. It was too overwhelming. She was too helpless in that world of endless possibilities—endless mistakes.

"I…" She let her voice taper off, hanging her head. Bile rose in the back of her throat, and her stomach rolled. "I…"

"Faoii, look around you!" Preoii-Vonda spoke with the full power of the Order, making Kaiya's head snap to attention. "Your world and everything in it is *dying!* Your friends are walking to their deaths, and they will fall painfully by my hand. I cannot save them, but you… you have the power to keep them alive, and you let your own fear control you?"

Kaiya heard the unspoken question: *How dare you?*

It was the power and the humiliation and the soul-deep desire not to disappoint the chained Preoii that snapped Ehryn back out of Kaiya's mind as she thought of her friends who were still in the camp without her, possibly with Mavrikal lurking in the darkness, waiting to strike.

Even without being there, she saw their downtrodden expressions and realized they'd been keeping strong faces for her benefit. Now they sat, staring at flames, waiting for her to come back and lead them. Namaoii without her pride, Tendaji without his stoicism. Even Kant was quiet sitting next to the other two, his unbridled excitement dampened by their melancholy. It was all so different than she was used to seeing. And it hurt her heart.

"Their hope," she whispered. "They've lost their hope."

"Then it's a good thing you're good at finding things, Mistress!" Jacir laughed from far away. And Ehryn realized she wasn't in the oubliette anymore. Jacir was no longer beside her.

"Jacir! Where are you? What's happening?" But there was no answer.

Panic overtook Ehryn's senses. She was alone. She didn't know where she was, and she was alone. Her friends would be lost without her. Without Dhruv's thread. Without hope. And she didn't know how to get back to them. Everything was lost. Everything was...

But then there was grass under her feet. Trees up ahead. She felt like she recognized the air here. There was a distant song on the wind. The scent was familiar.

And at her feet was one of the seeds that she and Dhruv had found in their childhood.

She'd done it. She'd found the pocket between the threads that her brother had shown her in their youth. And now that she focused on the Tapestry without fear, like Kaiya had learned to do hundreds of years before, Ehryn could see the tiny space between the threads that held this refuge. She could bring her friends here. It would be okay.

As she was about to dive back through the Weave to the little campfire in the woods, Ehryn heard a quiet, serene singing in the forest behind her. Ehryn thought she should be afraid, but she wasn't. Little snippets of her childhood floated back to the surface of her memories, and for a moment, as Ehryn went back into the threads to retrieve her friends, she wondered exactly what Clearwall had lost over time, and what would happen now that she'd helped find it again.

32

Alathi frowned, and Her brother shook His head. The Faoii Order was fracturing, and neither knew if it could be healed.

Alathi and Avanli went to Their northernmost monastery, where the loudest of Their harbingers screamed for Their attention. Teilithia stood there, strong and straight and tall. Her eyes were steely and filled with fire, and she shook her fantoii at Alathi when the Goddess of Justice approached.

"Now You answer? After we begged for Your guidance for so long?" There were tears on Teilithia's cheeks. "How dare you!"

Alathi narrowed Her eyes, towering over Her favored servant. "You dare threaten Me, Faoii?" She demanded. Her blade formed in Her hand and power gathered behind Her words. The hall in which they stood turned cold. "Remember who stands in front of you, Faoii-Teilithia."

Avanli, standing next to Her, set a hand on Alathi's arm. "Let her speak, Sister. See if her anger is justified before You decide whether or not to cut her down."

Alathi lowered the tip of Her sword but did not dismiss it. She could see Teilithia's breath when the little mortal spoke but was surprised when her voice did not shake.

"Now You come? When our monastery has fractured into pieces? We begged for Your guidance, Alathi. We begged for You to tell us which interpretation of the Oath was the correct one. And You did not respond. We have cut off the limbs that fight too readily and without consideration. We have fractured the Order. And all You had to do was tell us which of our factions were correct!"

Avanli tilted His head to one side. "Both."

"That's not an answer!" Faoii-Teilithia cried. "We've followed You since the beginning of time, but now that we've started asking questions You do not answer! You were supposed to make us great!" The little Faoii's eyes were filled with tears. "You should have used Your eyes to look upon the Weave. You should have answered our questions when we called! Whatever this is, it is not justice!"

Alathi and Avanli rose menacingly at her accusations, and Avanli's shining shield appeared in His hand. Teilithia stood in front of it, staring past her reflection and into the eyes of her Gods. "It is not justice," she repeated. "I will not be intimidated into believing it is."

"You know nothing of Justice," Alathi and Avanli said in unison. "We are the balance of the Tapestry you've woven. We are either side of the loom. Your actions here demonstrate clearly that you are not capable of greatness without Us. You are not ready to exist without Our guidance."

"But You don't guide us even when we beg! You can look upon the Tapestry and see which answers lead to the best outcomes for everyone, but you do not!"

Alathi narrowed Her eyes. "We do. And that is why you have come as far as you have. Your questions just do not hold the weight you feel they do. You are yet too small."

"Stop mistaking small for insignificant! You just don't want us to grow outside of Your influence!"

"You are not able to. Not yet. Follow as We lead, and someday your descendants will ask the questions that will truly shape the universe."

"No! It's not enough! We *begged* you for answers. For guidance. For understanding. And you gave us only pieces as You saw fit! You could have shown us the one true path and we would have *all* followed it! But You were too weak to lead us all. You lost the Danhaid to the West! The Alathi across the sea have all but died out! And now half of our Order will stay here, and the other half will move south to Imeriel. We are supposed to be unified in Your image, but You have failed!"

Teilithia's eyes were wild with anger, hurt, and a fanaticism Alathi did not trust. "We need a new image," Teilithia whispered, her words filling with power. "A way to align everyone under one goal. I will make sure that everyone marches in the same direction. No one will seek guidance ever again. They'll never know what it's like to walk outside of destiny's shadow. You and all Your lack of insight are nothing."

Alathi unfurled Her fiery wings in indignation. "You insolent, tiny piece of dust! You will *never* be capable of walking this life unguided. You demand Our help and then throw a tantrum when you do not get it in the manner you hoped? Look at you, a child against Gods."

"Enough. At least my followers will not know what it's like to walk alone without a path."

"How will they find undiscovered treasures, then?" Avanli asked genuinely. "How will they grow?" Teilithia only laughed at Him in response, and something about the sound filled Alathi with rage.

The Lady of Justice screamed Her fury at this insolent, pathetic, ungrateful infant and swung Her sword… but the power that She normally drew from the earth, the air, the Weave…was absent. Her sword slowed while Teilithia laughed harder. Unable to move, unable to speak, Alathi could only move Her eyes. For the first time in her existence, She felt fear.

And from the dark corners of the hall they stood in, Teilithia's Faoii sisters emerged from the shadows. Alathi recognized their stances. Recognized the Danhaid steps from one, the Alathi tattoos on another. The Inklam hand waves, the elaborate Mevami'am drawings. Teilithia's Faoii song. Everything She'd ever taught, tied together in a complex spell Alathi didn't recognize. Didn't know was possible.

Thorny vines that Alathi had never seen before sprung from the marble floor at Her feet. Tied themselves around Her ankles. Pulled Her down hard. Her blade fell from Her hand.

Next to Her, Avanli raised His shield, gathered His power, grabbed for Her, pulled as He could, but fell away. His screams echoed in the hallway and were lost.

Alathi struggled against the vines, but She could feel the way they sucked the magic from the ground all around them. They slithered through the earth and between the fabric of the Tapestry, sapping power, draining life force. From far away She heard Her other siblings scream in fear. Felt Them pulled down below the ground She stood on. Below the plane any of Them existed on. She tried to break free but could not.

Teilithia stood over Her, now, impossibly tall, shining with an incredible light that looked too much like the glowing threads of the Eternal Weave. "From now on, we will decide who is worthy of magic. We will watch the Weave, and there will never be a question of which path is the correct one forward. We will be everything You were not." She crushed Alathi's fingers under her heel, but Alathi did not feel the blow. Couldn't feel anything anymore. Could barely see. There was only darkness and cold and emptiness as She was pulled further into the ground.

Then, before the darkness enveloped Her for an untold number of centuries before She'd find Her voice again, Alathi was left with one final declaration from Teilithia the Usurper. The strongest of Her Children.

The mortals screamed for power.

And Alathi heard them.

"You failed us, Alathi. You must pay for that. We will assume Your visage and lead Your people as they were meant to be led. This is Justice."

They were the False Children.

Her Usurpers.

33

Ehryn stumbled to one knee, her head spinning and every piece of her body and mind aching as she pulled the last of her companions, Tendaji this time, through the veil into the secluded corner of… she didn't know where, exactly. It was not part of the Weave that they knew. It stood outside of time and space, between the threads that so many mages used to trace patterns and people across the eons. They were not completely invisible here, she didn't think, but the Sisters wouldn't know to look between the threads. They would be safe here for a while at least.

Or she hoped so. Tendaji was already helping her to stand, and the world spun sickeningly as her head moved. But she pushed it away and fought her way to her feet. Tendaji wasn't doing much better than her. Even Namaoii was exhausted, though she would never admit it. And Khalista looked far worse than any of them.

"I didn't expect there to be trees," Namaoii said as she looked around. "I thought you said this place was outside the world we know."

"It is," Ehryn assured her. "Look. I don't think I've ever seen trees like that before. Have you?"

The entire group gazed around at their surroundings, awestruck. There was something primordial and beautiful about the great trees, with roots as thick as Tendaji was tall twisting around each other and through the earth, making huge caves the size of houses or entangling so tightly they looked like bands of rope fit for giants. The entire area pulsed with power deeper and stronger than any that Ehryn had experienced before. It didn't even feel like something she could direct or absorb or learn like the other things that they had studied and practiced and seen on their kintar. But at the same time, it felt familiar. It felt like the Weave they all tapped into every time they drew any magic at all forward.

Life. The entire pocket hidden between the threads felt like life. Life that had been able to flourish to its full potential. It was gorgeous and overwhelming and pure. For a long time they all just stood there, breathing in and feeling safe for the first time in days.

"Are the trees… singing?" Kant asked quietly. "Can they do that?"

Ehryn cocked her head, listening. The same melody she'd heard before was drifting from deeper in the trees. "I don't think so," she said. "I recognize that sound. I don't… I don't really remember. But I think it's a woman."

"I thought we were safe here!" Namaoii hissed. "If there are others here, we don't know what to expect! We could be in more danger now than we were in the other forest!"

"Not from Mavrikal, at least. She doesn't know to look for us here. And… And Dhruv and I came here before. Possibly many times. I don't know. But I think we're safe." She reached out and very deliberately took Namaoii's hand. She looked from their linked palms back into Namaoii's face. "Trust me."

Finally, Namaoii nodded. She gave Ehryn's hand a quick squeeze and bent over to pick up Khalista. "We've followed you this far, I guess. Lead on."

"Before, you were following the Call," Ehryn pointed out.

"Nah. It was always you."

Ehryn felt humbled by that as they walked through the towering, alien forest.

⬧

They didn't have to go far. They'd barely made it through the roots of the nearest organism before they heard the sounds of movement up ahead. Tendaji stopped first, peering into the gray twilight all around them.

"Ehryn, take Khalista," Namaoii ordered. Ehryn did without question, no longer afraid of the girl or what the X on her forehead symbolized. "If something happens, get her through first. Then Kant. Then come back for us. Can you do it?"

Ehryn's stomach knotted at the thought of Blinking again so quickly, but she agreed anyway. She'd find a way if it came to that.

Namaoii nodded, satisfied, and she and Tendaji moved in the direction of the sounds, back-to-back like shield mates. Ehryn tried to spread the dead weight of the Hollowed over her shoulders and reached one hand out for Kant. They held their breath and waited.

The people that emerged from the trees did not come across the ground or roots like Ehryn'd expected but appeared on branches high above the little group's head.

Tendaji and Namaoii seemed surprised as well, unprepared for this possible outcome. They tried to regroup, but neither seemed particularly prepared to fight enemies from above.

"Don't worry," someone said in a sweet voice that Ehryn seemed to remember from her childhood. "We have no desire to fight you."

The group looked up into the branches and met the soft gaze of a tall, tanned woman wearing a sleeveless dress and no shoes. She descended the tree deftly, using the great, twisted roots and branches as easily as if they were boardwalks.

"My name is Birdie," she said when she reached them. "Are you lost?"

"We… I don't know." It was Ehryn who spoke, and Birdie turned her kind brown eyes on the girl. "It's not that we're lost. We came here on purpose. Just…we just need to rest. To hide. To think. Please."

"Well, we'll start there, then." Birdie smiled at looked Ehryn over. "My, how you've grown. How is your brother? Is he here too?"

The question surprised Ehryn so much she took an involuntary step backwards, nearly dropping Khalista in her haste. "You know me?"

Birdie laughed, but it did not seem out of malice. "You used to come here often as a child, Ehryn. Looking for seeds and bulbs and great beautiful things that you and your brother could grow in your garden. Don't you remember who helped you find them all?" She smiled again. "I'm glad your brother finally taught you how to walk through. It's been so strange only sensing you here without you stopping to say hello. We've quite missed you."

"I… Dhruv didn't. He… died. A long time ago."

Birdie's face fell, and she glided forward to set one

hand on Ehryn's shoulder.

"I'm very sorry to hear that. But I'm glad you're here now. Completely here. I saw you recently. You came through and took the only sprig we had of a very powerful little plant that we've had trouble replanting. Did you bring it back with you?"

Ehryn looked down at her hands as though she might have been holding the tonicloran still and just not have noticed. But her hands were empty, and she looked between Tendaji and Namaoii.

"You didn't have it when we landed in that forest. You must have left it back at the barn," Namaoii stated. Tendaji looked visibly shaken by that, and Ehryn's heart sank.

"Then Mavrikal already has it. Or she will soon."

"Ehryn," Tendaji hissed nervously. "We have to go back!"

But Ehryn saw how much his body shook. Closed her eyes and knew she couldn't get them all back to the Elisian enclave if she tried, and even if she did, they wouldn't have the strength to take back what she'd lost. It seemed hopeless, and she didn't know how to fix it.

Namaoii seemed to be having similar thoughts, and her shoulders sagged. "We can't get it back now, Faoli," the Wolf Pup said wearily. "We're not strong enough. But maybe… maybe we'll still be okay. Goddesses or not, it will take Them time to start Their ritual. We need to rest. To plan."

Tendaji still looked uncertain. Birdie walked up to him and placed her hands on either side of his face. "You've been through so much. Rest here. Let's get you and your friends somewhere comfortable. You can tell me everything or nothing later." She smiled at everyone and motioned them all forward. "Don't worry. You're not the first lost travelers to visit. Maybe we can help you find your way."

Others came from the trees, then, throwing rope ladders down over the branches to the weary travelers, climbing down as deftly as Birdie had to help the newcomers ascend the canopy. None seemed afraid of Khalista as they took her in their arms and gently carried her into the treetops with the others.

Ehryn and her companions didn't know what else to do. They followed Birdie and the others through a twisted path of boardwalks and bridges that spread across root and bough, snaking through the trees. Ehryn gasped at the place they eventually came to, nestled deep in the impossible forest.

Huge, towering, colorful trees spread in every direction, shrouded with vines and leaves and animals that Ehryn had never seen before. Leaves as long as her arm spread across the canopy, and glowing vines twisted around the thick branches, bearing fruits and flowers of every color. So amazed by the foliage, Ehryn almost didn't recognize the handcrafted landings and dwellings hidden amongst the trunks on every side. Here, women and men spun thread from the vibrant fibers or lifted trilling bird calls to each other. Every now and again a strange catlike creature would bound from the trees and nuzzle up against one of the humans before flitting away again.

"What… what is all this?" Namaoii asked, eyes wide. While Kant looked excited and overjoyed at everything around them, Namaoii looked frightened. She unconsciously reached for Ehryn's hand.

"A sanctuary," Birdie replied. "A place where kindhearted, often lost souls have gathered the endangered plants and animals from across all the Weaves. We're in a sort of gap between all of the Tapestries here. A place where all the threads pass nearby. Avanli, Ancient God of Refuge, built it as a place to hide His siblings, but was too late. And in His sorrow, it has grown into a place to gather all that is lost or will be lost. We are the final library of scrolls that no one knows how to translate. The final whispers of songs people no longer sing. The final sanctuary where all lost things are remembered."

"Wow," Namaoii breathed. "I can't believe Ehryn used it to find misplaced pens."

Ehryn rolled her eyes and was about to bite back, but Birdie laughed. "I remember that pen showing up on my writing desk one day. I think a mutual friend of ours put it there on purpose. Though, whether he did it for amusement or because doing so somehow influenced your actions in the Weave, I cannot say. Usually such small, insignificant items don't end up here. We watch the Weave and look for items of importance that have colored the threads in the past or might again in the future." Her gaze rested on Tendaji's sword for a moment. "But sometimes little things *will* appear, usually left by certain old men with childlike mischief."

"Are you talking about the Royal Arcanist?" Namaoii asked, but Birdie and Kant had already burst into giggles together and refused to say anything more about what they found so funny.

Birdie ordered someone to take Khalista and to fetch one of the healers, then led the group to a large platform supporting a central fire. They sat on soft pillows, surrounded by leaves and flowers and vines. Fuzzy creatures crept up from the overhanging branches and curled themselves into their laps, vibrating happily. For the first time in days, Ehryn felt herself begin to relax, the weight of an entire world easing from her shoulders.

"I know you're all tired. Rooms are being prepared for you. Sit with me and rest," Birdie said.

Ehryn looked at their hostess. She recognized the long braids that had been twisted and folded on top of the woman's head. The simple, seamless dress. The open smile.

"I remember you," Ehryn finally whispered. "Kind of. From when I was young. I'd forgotten about you. About all of this."

"And yet you brought your friends with you? You're either very foolish or very brave, Ehryn." Birdie smiled when she spoke, and there was no malice in the words. "I remember you, too. I once told you all about myself and this place—the Between." She smiled and reached out to touch Ehryn's arm. "It was such a joy to have you and your brother here without us guiding you forward. Such a rarity in this sanctuary that neither the False Children nor mortals can find. But the birds can. Cats see us, watch us in the darkness with wide eyes and twitching tails. Dogs will sometimes growl when they sense us beyond the veil. Cows will low, and donkeys will put back their ears and refuse to move if we get too close. I'm sure you've seen our unintentional handiwork." She laughed when the others mutely nodded.

Ehryn swallowed nervously. "But you're mortal? Humans like us?"

"Of course."

"Why don't you live with us in the cities, then?"

"We were tasked not to by the God—the true God, not the False Children who have claimed the title more recently—who made this place. We were to become the protectors of those who would be forgotten. To give voice to all those who might be lost. He was so worried that others would disappear like His kind had."

"Are you Danhaid?" Tendaji asked softly.

Birdie turned her face to the old warrior. "Some of us were, once. Some of us were Alathi. Some of us were Inklam and Mevami'am and Kistiu. But none of those tribes exist any longer as they did, and it's rare for someone other than the animals to know we're here. Little Ehryn and her brother were some of the first in a very long time. We thought it might mean something, but then they stopped coming by." Birdie smiled at Ehryn. "What made you decide to come back?"

"We needed a safe place to rest. To hide."

"Safe from whom?"

"The Elisians. And Mavrikal."

Birdie shuddered. "Mavrikal. We've seen Her. She has spent more time on your side of the Tapestry than any of Her sisters ever have. It seems that She's started to go quite mad. Even the threads tremble at Her hands."

"It happened with Illindria, too," Tendaji said quietly. "There's a reason the Tapestry separates the shores. No one from one plane does very well for very long on any of the others."

"Ironic, then, that they were human, once. To forget who you are and then be tasked every day with facing it… I suppose I would go mad, too. I was not born yet when Illindria walked Imeriel. I hope She is saner now that things have been set right again. Before your sister set it right again. If only we'd realized there was so much left to do." Tendaji looked surprised, and Birdie nodded to the blade belted at his side.

"I know you, Tendaji of the Fall, though you lived before my time. I was taught to search for that blade in the Tapestry in case it resurfaced again. My predecessors said that in many of the threads, you or your sister threw it away. They watched the Weave so that we might retrieve it and keep it here in the Between should you decide that it be lost, but eventually it just disappeared. The Weavers say it still has a role to fulfill. I always wondered what happened to it."

Tendaji looked at the sword thoughtfully and turned it slowly, the light catching its polished surface. "I thought about discarding it many times. But I could not bear to part with it. My sister wielded this sword in a war to save our world. At the time, it was the only item we knew of that had its own destiny and thread in the Weave. In the end, she was despised for everything she'd done. Before I faded into the darkness at the edges of her life, she asked me to get rid of it. To destroy it. She wasn't sure she had the strength." He paused. "I always convinced her to keep it, to use it to forge a brighter future for Imeriel. But when she bequeathed it to me through the young Jacir, I understood the power of it. The danger of a blade that could slice through the very threads of the Eternal Tapestry. But I never had the strength to destroy it, either." He stared at the hilt of the sword like there was writing there that only he could see. "It cried with me the day I picked it up. And then it sang."

It did. But not anymore. Now you must wield it, Ehryn of Clearwall.

Ehryn jumped. The whisper was not the same as what Ehryn had heard her entire life. It was not the voice of Alathi or the other Voices on the Wind… but it was similar. A male's voice. And it seemed to be right next to her ear. She whipped her head around to face the speaker, but there was no one there.

No one else seemed to notice, and Namaoii was speaking now. "I didn't want to believe it before. But it's hard not to believe in the impossible while we're sitting on top of a tree that doesn't exist in a world outside the Tapestry's strands. Your sister really was the Emancipator? The Betrayer?"

Tendaji's eyes grew cold, but his voice was soft. "No. My sister was Kaiya. She was strong and brave and would do anything to save her friends. The world turned on her and shackled her with a title she never deserved. But I remember her. And now you do, too."

"Yeah we do!" Kant exclaimed. "We'll tell her story to everyone! Build statues like the one in the Faoii monastery!"

Tendaji gave Kant a heartwarming smile. "That would be nice, Kant. I'd like my sister to be a symbol of hope again. And I'm tired of hope coming in the shape of a sword."

But that whisper came again, right next to Ehryn's head, so close she was sure she felt lips against her earlobe.

It must. You will wield it.

"Statues are nice, but monuments won't bring down the False Children before They enslave us all," Namaoii said pointedly.

Everyone's face fell into a dour expression at that, but Birdie's smile didn't falter. "Things are always easier after a peaceful rest and a hot meal. You've all been through so much and need to sleep. When you wake again, we can discuss what you need from the lost, what we need to protect for the future, and what all of it means for the False Children." She stood in a single, graceful movement, stretched until her bare toes were pointed beneath her, then turned away from the circle.

"Come along. Things will seem better when you wake. You'll see."

Ehryn once again felt the presence of someone at her side, and she wasn't sure that she believed the promise.

34

With the perpetual twilight of the Between, Ehryn wasn't sure how long they'd sat beside that pleasant fire, breathing in the soft, sweet smells of exotic trees while stroking fuzzy kits that buzzed and purred. By the time they stood again, however, she felt refreshed in a way she hadn't expected. She still looked forward to sleep, but there was no doubt that everyone walked a little straighter as Birdie led them down one of the treetop paths.

The accommodations were not large or extravagant. A pile of furs heaped on top of each other to form a bed. A basin for water and a chamber pot. The free-standing huts had walls for privacy and quiet, but there were no roofs, only the over-arching canopy of leaves and a starless twilight sky. Ehryn looked confused as Birdie opened her little door. Birdie smiled and shrugged. "Why create roofs in a place where there are no elements? Sleep well, Ehryn. You are safe here. Soon we will discuss your next steps. Avanli grant you rest." Then she was walking away, leading Kant to the next hut over. Ehryn waved at him, and for a moment the mousey boy looked like he would stop and turn around, but he only waved back before going inside.

Ehryn knew she was tired both physically and mentally, but she could not sleep. She drifted close to the blissful edge of unconsciousness, but in doing so her mind skirted the Tapestry she now had access to on a level she'd never thought was possible, and the enormity of it jerked her back awake. She'd always felt the Call pull her over rivers and across mountains, begging her to be more than she was and go further than she could in a near-constant cry for aid and mercy. For years she'd watched the Starlit River wistfully, wondering what lay beyond its waves. And now she had the ability to go beyond anything she'd ever dreamed of. She could go anywhere.

And all she wanted was to go home.

Ehryn missed her parents. She missed helping her mother pour candlewax and the smell of clean linen. She missed sitting next to the Starlit River and watching ships from far-off lands sail into the docks. She thought she'd been jealous of inanimate objects—they had a purpose that would bring them to unknown places. But now she had a purpose that could take her anywhere, and she was afraid.

She knew now how her mother felt. Dark things lurked on the edges of human society, and no matter how bright they made the torches or how far out they built their walls, those things were always there. They always had been. And they did not like being pushed out. They would do whatever they could to re-stake their claim on the will of humankind. They would force everyone to kneel in submission again.

Unless Ehryn could get to where the Voices cried out for help. Maybe not even then. Alathi had failed once and had been locked beneath the Weave. There were no guarantees she could succeed where They had not. There were no guarantees that Mavrikal and Her sisters would not start Their ritual before Ehryn could find her brother's thread. Now that she knew that somehow her brother's life and legacy was still twined around hers, she wanted to make sure that it was used for something great. But it was so dangerous, and there were so many different ways she could fail.

Ehryn thrust her head into her pillow and sobbed. She'd never felt so alone before.

Dhruv. I'm sorry you loved me so. I'm sorry that we worked so well together and came here so often and always had each other's backs. Because if we hadn't—Mavrikal never would have found you. I'm so sorry.

Ehryn knew she wasn't the only person to lose a brother. The False Children had made it so common that it had become an unspoken curse. The idea of the Sisters targeting siblings twisted at Ehryn's heart. It was so... evil. To separate a pair in the name of power. Mother always made her candles in pairs, hanging them by their conjoined wicks over the table to dry. To look at two such beautiful things and choose one in each group to burn entire cities with... Ehryn sobbed again.

She didn't want this. She was okay with being the conduit. To lead better people to greater things and then go home. She didn't regret saving her friends—it might have been the only good thing she'd ever do—but she didn't want to be the one to decide everyone's future.

"What do I do?" She sobbed into the darkness of her room. "What am I supposed to do?"

"The problem with that question is if you always ask it to others, you never learn to answer it yourself."

Ehryn shot up in bed, a scream caught in her throat. The person standing in front of her held up a gauntleted hand. His horned helmet covered His face, but even without seeing His features, Ehryn knew He was something more than human. He was older and deeper and more powerful than the Sisters or the oceans or the sky. The hairs on her arms stood on end.

"Who are you?"

"You know my sister, Alathi. The Sword. I am Avanli, the Shield. I created this hollow in Our Tapestry to save Her and My other siblings when Our followers revolted. I was not fast enough, and now She is trapped beneath the Weave. I've waited here for Her release, for She is Vengeance, and the world must hear Her call."

The figure was motionless as He spoke, and His voice was without emotion. Ehryn frowned. Alathi was so passionate in comparison. A storm of fire and ice. "What if I don't want vengeance?" she asked. "What if I just want to make things right again and go home?"

"Justice and Vengeance are often hard to separate, but the False Children must answer for what They've done, lest They look for other ways to enslave your kind. I do not think it matters what any of Us want, only what must need be."

"Can you help me stop Them?"

"Alathi can. She has wielded a sword since before the stars knew how to shine. She is the gale in mountains, and She will bind the Usurpers to rocks of Their own making and let the poison of Their lies seep into Their eyes for an eternity longer than They thrust upon Her."

Ehryn frowned and hugged her knees. "If we free Her, will Alathi make us worship Her as They did? Will it be the same as it was before?"

"Perhaps not. She is Justice. There was a time when humans needed Us to teach them what We were and what We stood for. But you seem to have stood for your truth many times without My sister to judge it."

"You mean Vengeance."

"And Justice, yes."

"And you think She'll just… let us go? After we free Her?"

"If She sees that you've outgrown Her definition of Herself… perhaps. I do not know. I only know that I need to see Her again. And you, of all mortals, have come closest to making that happen. I have faith in you, Child."

"I don't understand. How can someone outgrow a Goddess?"

"By adding to what We were without Our demanding it. We set the groundwork. We placed bricks and stones upon the Earth and showed you what it meant to walk amongst them. We built Our halls, and since then you have built entire cathedrals. Cities. Empires. You took the blossom We gave your ancestors and made entire gardens, and I have wept in joy at watching you be so much more than I or My sister planned. It is marvelous. It is unjust that She cannot see."

"Where have You been, though? Why haven't You freed Her on Your own?"

"I could not face the False Children alone. It took much of Me to make this pocket in the darkness, and I do not know how long I was here before I found Myself again. Before one of you little mortals found Me and helped Me don this form. It is why I have not lost Myself to insanity like She Who Demands the Blood. And it is why I have seen that you can be so much more than We thought you could without Our guidance. My sister will see, too, once you save Her. For She is Vengeance, but she is also Justice."

Ehryn was uncomfortable with how black and white this ancient being was. How unlike Alathi He seemed. But at the same time, she could see Him standing beside His sister. Balancing Her passion with His poise. She could see the two siblings dancing Their graceful steps across eternity. "If she is Vengeance and Justice, who are You?"

"Loyalty. Protection. I am the Shield to Alathi's Sword. I heard My sister call to you across the threads and have followed your path. I watched you play here with your brother when you were young. It was I who handed My sister his thread when Mavrikal cut him down. We are all part of the same Tapestry. And I, like you, am strongest when My sibling calls."

"My brother didn't actually call, though," Ehryn said bitterly. "You just tricked the thread into believing it."

"No. But leave it to Vengeance to build upon the sacrifices of the fallen to enact change." Ehryn bit her lip and didn't respond. After a few moments, Avanli spoke again.

"Rest here, in this place I made for My siblings too late. When you are healed and ready to continue, I will help you. I will hold Mavrikal back while you free Alathi and the others. When you free everyone from the False Children's grip. When you become the hand of Justice."

Ehryn opened her mouth to reply, but the Old God tilted His head to one side. "Someone comes." He brought a gauntleted fist up to His chest. "Think well on what I've said. The world is shifting, and the False Children's grip *will* loosen."

Then the figure was gone, and Ehryn was left in an empty room without a roof, sitting motionless under a perpetually twilight sky.

It was too much. The last—*day? Week? I don't even know how long it's been*—was just too much. Too much had happened. Too much had changed. Too much had been dropped into her lap and into her head and into her life. Ehryn didn't even have the energy to cry anymore. So when there was a knock on her door a few minutes later, Ehryn couldn't do anything else except for stand, walk woodenly across the room, and open it. Kant stood on the other side.

Ehryn's first reaction was to tell Kant that she was tired and wanted to sleep, but the little boy looked so sad she couldn't bring herself to turn him away. A part of her was even grateful for this change in focus. This, at least, was something she was probably qualified to deal with. "What's wrong, Kant? Can't you sleep?" Kant shook his head without looking up. Ehryn frowned. "Can I help?"

Kant nodded mutely, still without looking at her. He fidgeted from one foot to another and pulled at the hem of his tunic. Ehryn put a hand on the little boy's shoulder. "Hey. It's okay. Whatever's wrong, we'll figure it out. After what you did for us back in the Elisian Enclave…" Ehryn froze, suddenly embarrassed. "I never even thanked you for that, did I? I'm sorry, Kant. I should have thanked you earlier. You were so brave."

Finally, Kant looked up at her without lifting his chin. "Actually, Mistress Ehryn, that's kind of what I want to talk to you about. Could… Could I come in?"

"Of course." Ehryn held the door open, and the younger boy scuttled inside.

They sat on the edge of the bed together, and it was several minutes before Kant finally seemed to relax a little. He took several deep breaths, pulling his eyebrows together as he gathered his thoughts into words.

"Ehryn… When we return to Clearwall, people are going to ask me what happened. I'll tell them everything, and they'll write it down into big books and put them on high shelves and someone like me will dust them once a week. It'll be accurate and useful and Queen Isolde will like it, but I know it won't be… pretty." He swung his legs in a circle over the edge of the bed for a minute and hung his head. "I've read dozens of books about poetry and prose. I've seen descriptions of people and places that made my heart beat faster and made me smile until my cheeks hurt. Someday, if Queen Isolde wants, she'll pay someone to take what I say and say it again, but… better. They'll tell Princess Namaoii's story in a way that inspires other people. In a way that's going to be remembered. But my story won't be part of those histories."

"Oh, Kant…" Ehryn began, but he held up a hand.

"I don't mind, Ehryn. There isn't anyone I want to hear my story, really. Except… except my sister. When she's born. I want to be able to tell her what I did. I want her to know that I mattered. And when I tell it to her, I want it to be pretty. I want it to sound like the stories I'll tell her out of the books I read. But I can't do that by myself." He fidgeted with his hands again. "I was… I was wondering if you would help me tell my story. Like you helped me in the market square in Crested Fir. I want it to be true; I don't want to lie to her or make her think that I'm something I'm not. But I want it to be like a real story. And… and if you can help me with it once I'll remember it forever. Please?"

Ehryn smiled and pulled Kant towards her until his head rested on her shoulder. They sat on the bed in the quiet of twilight under a starless sky.

"Of course. Are you ready?"

Kant nodded.

"There once was a hero named Kant…"

35

After Ehryn'd tucked Kant safely into his own bed, content and smiling in his slumber, she returned to her room. The story had lightened her heart, and she finally, mercifully fell into a dreamless rest of her own.

Now, after an untold number of hours that wasn't helped by the perpetual twilight of the Between, she felt… not prepared, exactly, but less hopeless than the night before. There were still so many threads to untangle, and it was hard not to feel like a leaf caught in the hurricane of the Sisters and the Gods that had started a war when her ancestors had barely come to Imeriel. But even in such huge and overbearing circumstances, Ehryn finally felt like she could breathe. Like maybe she wouldn't be crushed by the things outside her control.

She should have known better. She shouldn't have trusted those few moments of calm and surety. Because as a howl of hurt and loss carried across the quiet canopy, Ehryn's heart tore in two.

She recognized that voice. Knew that deep sound of sorrow.

Barefoot, heart pounding in her chest, Ehryn rushed out of her room and across the swinging bridges, already knowing that she'd find Namaoii in the hut at the other side.

"She didn't make it," the Wolf Pup nearly screamed when Ehryn burst through the door. "We did everything we could, and Khalista didn't make it, Ehryn!" Ehryn's heart fell, and she hugged the sobbing princess who didn't try to push her away. "Is there no justice?"

"I'm sorry," Ehryn whispered, though she didn't know if Namaoii even heard her. Didn't think it mattered if she did. Ehryn held her friend as the Wolf Pup howled at the perpetually twilight sky, her gleaming breastplate rattling with the wracking sobs.

Ehryn was ashamed of the distrust she'd shown for Khalista in the beginning, and now she felt guilty that she didn't feel the pain and hurt at the loss of an innocent life the way Namaoii did. Some part of her brain was still conditioned to see this as a positive, and that hurt her. Clearwall had forgotten the value of a human life. The Gracious Queen had not sentenced someone to death since before Ehryn was born, and yet their society still believed that death was an acceptable end for the crime of being born a Hollowed.

Surrounded by the pained, wrenching howl of Namaoii's sorrow and fury, something hardened deep in Ehryn's heart. It wasn't *right*. They'd gotten to the girl. They'd pulled her from that table of torture and death. They'd escaped the Elisian enclave and the Blood Goddess. They'd brought her somewhere safe, where healers of every forgotten art had been able to tend her.

And it still wasn't enough.

Some part of Ehryn had always believed, however illogically, in a universal justice. She'd listened to the Goddess of Justice's voice her entire life. She'd believed the promises and the stories and the laws. She'd believed that good things happened to those who did good. Who put good out into the world. And those who were greedy, spiteful, cruel… they ultimately got what they'd earned and lived miserable lives surrounded only by the memories of what they'd done and all they'd pushed away. That's how the stories went, and even though Ehryn knew that life wasn't quite so black and white, she'd believed in the overall strength of the word "justice." A just world wouldn't have failed Khalista.

But they had. And as her heart hardened around the hurt, callousing in a way that even the depressive cloud she'd experienced in Clearwall hadn't prepared her for, she pushed away the faint whispers of the Call that tried to wriggle up from their distant prison.

"Justice," they'd cried her entire life.

But Ehryn didn't believe in justice anymore.

But those weren't the words that Namaoii needed to hear right now. "I'm sorry, Namaoii. I'm so sorry," Ehryn whispered over and over again. "I didn't know Blinking would be so hard on her. I didn't think—"

Namaoii turned a hard look on Ehryn, her dark eyes fiery through her tears. "This is *not* on you," she growled. "You might have done the only kind thing that girl ever saw."

"But she… she didn't deserve this. Any of this. I'm sorry I didn't see that before."

Namaoii deflated a little bit, worked her throat for several minutes before trying to speak again. "It's really easy to see the X. People don't realize that they're carved into the heads of children. Children who are then taken—not even taken, thrown out—and brought to the monasteries. I didn't know what happened after that. I didn't know they went to the Elisians. To the mines. To that… thing that's following us."

"You couldn't have known. No one knew."

"Someone did." The fury returned to Namaoii's eyes, and she straightened next to Ehryn. "You saw the fear when we even mentioned Mother's name. The Starlit Throne oversaw everything, and during at least one part of the process the so-called Gracious Queen was physically present—enough to drive terror into that poor girl's heart." Ehryn tried to picture what it would be like to find out her own mother hated and tortured people like her. Tried to understand the fire and hatred in Namaoii's eyes. "She's going to pay for this, Ehryn. Khalista deserved better than this. Clearwall deserves better than this. I'm going to give them something better."

And in that moment, clad in unpolished armor in a roofless room that smelled of chinol and death, Ehryn could *see* the ruler that Namaoii would someday be. It would be hard, and she would make mistakes, but even as Isolde put Imeriel above all else, Namaoii raised every *person* in Imeriel to that rank. It would be nearly impossible, but if anyone could do it, Namaoii could.

"What are you going to do?" Ehryn whispered, not sure she wanted to know the answer.

Namaoii released a heavy sigh. "I don't know yet. I want to go to those mines and free my sisters and brothers, but it won't mean anything if we don't stop Mavrikal first. We've already sent the Faoii that way. It will have to be enough until we straighten everything else out." Namaoii rose and paced in front of Ehryn, her eyes wet but angry. "It has to start with removing the rot Mother's built her throne on. If my mother has become powerful at the Dark Goddess's feet, then removing the Middle Sister is still the first step to repairing the damage. But… but before that, I think it starts with honoring those she never did."

She turned and took the cold, pale hand from beneath the blanket laid on Khalista's deathbed. "I'm sorry, Khalista. I wish I knew a better way to say it."

An idea struck Ehryn, and she took Namaoii's hand. "Come with me," she said. The older girl gave her a quizzical look but nodded. Together they walked to Kant's little hut, and he opened the door with a smile, the uncertainty from the night before evidently   gone.

"Kant," Ehryn said softly. "We need your help."

Kant's face brightened a little. "Really? Both of you? You think I can be helpful?" He looked mostly to Namaoii, who at last nodded. His face split with a smile. "What do you need?"

"We want you to help us find a dirge that honors someone who died unjustly," Ehryn said. Namaoii tensed at the words, then softened and squeezed her hand.

"Yeah," the Wolf Pup said quietly. "I think that's exactly what we want."

Kant opened the door a little wider and motioned them inside, where he sat cross-legged on his bed. "I know a lot of dirges! They're sad, but people use the most beautiful language for their loved ones when they know they won't get another chance to say it again. Come sit down with me. We'll find the perfect one." Ehryn smiled at Kant's enthusiasm. Maybe he didn't truly understand death. Maybe he never would. But there was something heartwarming about the little boy finding the most beauty in someone's twilight, and his irrepressible joy at repeating words borne of love. Even Namaoii's lips twitched upward as they followed him inside.

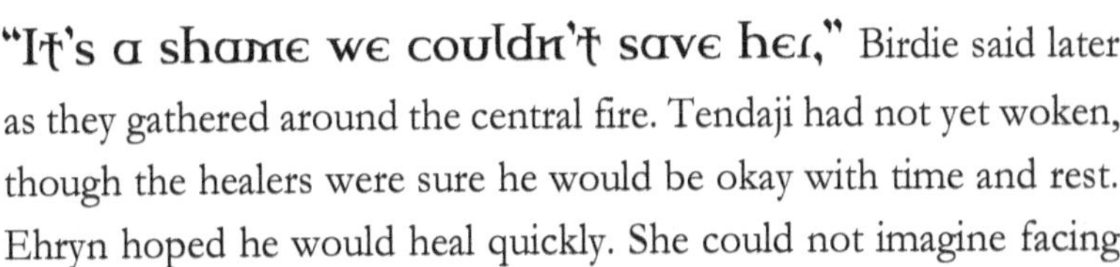

"It's a shame we couldn't save her," Birdie said later as they gathered around the central fire. Tendaji had not yet woken, though the healers were sure he would be okay with time and rest. Ehryn hoped he would heal quickly. She could not imagine facing the False Children without him at their side.

"The others are taking it hard," Birdie continued. "Though none of us knew Khalista, we feel her loss in the community. In the Weave."

"Others?" Namaoii brought her head up a little too quickly. "What do you mean?"

"Why… the others. All we saved from being forgotten. Clearwall has built an entire industry on lost children. We were able to save a few from the mines before Mavrikal took them."

"You mean… there are…" Namaoii seemed to fumble with her words.

"I believe you call them Hollowed."

Something broke in Namaoii's expression, but it was a crack of power and fire. Lightning in a too-dark sky. She was on her feet in an instant. "Show me. Can you show me?"

"There are not many, and those we do have are currently preparing a service. Practicing songs and prayers that have not broken through their exiled communities," Birdie said before turning to Kant. "I would ask that you attend the funeral, young scribe. I know you have prepared your own offering for Khalista's farewell, but I also think it is important that someone outside the Hollowed know their songs."

Kant nodded vigorously. "Are there a lot of those here?"

"They have names, Kant!" Namaoii hissed. "They're not 'those.'"

"Do they? I'll make sure to learn all of the names, too! Usually they're just recorded as 'dirge' or 'wedding song' or 'sonnet!'"

Namaoii looked confused for a moment, and Birdie couldn't help but laugh. "I think he's talking about the songs, your Highness."

"Of… of course," Kant looked around nervously, like they were playing a trick on him that he hadn't quite figured out. "What else would I be talking about?"

Namaoii didn't respond, still looking stunned. "I didn't realize they'd have their own songs. Their own stories. But of course they would. Cut off from everything else… they had to find hope somewhere."

Kant saw Namaoii's sad face and reached for her hand across the table. "Do you want to go practice our song again? Make sure that Khalista and your sisters and brothers will like it? Make sure it offers hope for them, too? When you save everyone else?"

Namaoii looked at the hand like she wasn't sure how it got there, then up into Kant's bright eyes. "Yes, Kant," she finally whispered. "I'd like that very much."

Ehryn watched them walk away. She still didn't think she believed in justice… but in that moment, she thought she remembered what hope was.

She wondered if it was enough.

36

Ehryn wasn't sure what she expected a funeral in the Between to be like. Birdie said they were rare in this world where people didn't age, removed from the Tapestry and its threads that marched forward without slowing down or worrying about who was dragged towards oblivion.

The entire village gathered to mourn the loss of the woman none of them had known, and Ehryn was amazed by the variety of people that stepped from their little huts. There were several tall, bronze warriors who called themselves Danhaid, their copper hair lined with shells. There were a few of the broad-shouldered Alathi with their blue tattoos and wolfish grins—they'd come to fight alongside the resistance in the war against the Iron Queen. These in particular drew Namaoii's eye as she stepped up to help take one of the ropes that secured the pallet they would use to carry Khalista. Ehryn could see the similarities in Namaoii's features and remembered once again that Isolde had conceived the Wolf Pup with her Alathi consort before his death. She wasn't sure if there'd been any other Alathi in the palace during Namaoii's lifetime.

The people who truly caught all of their attention, however, were the Hollowed. A handful of women and men stepped forward with sad eyes and lamenting cries to help pull on the ropes that would lift the corpse of their fallen sister. The corpse of someone who had committed no crime other than being born. They did not try to hide the X carved on their foreheads, and no one drew away from them. In a world that hated the Hollowed—that shipped them to monasteries and enclaves and mines like vicious dogs—it did not surprise Ehryn that they chose not to leave the Between after being saved by those who gathered what was lost.

Ehryn glanced at Namaoii and saw the determination in her eyes as she looked at each carved X. Then, with a nod to the others, she lifted her rope across her shoulders, and they brought Khalista up between them.

"Namaoii of Clearwall. You knew her best. Would you like to begin?" Birdie asked.

Ehryn knew that Namaoii was not one for words, and she thought that the princess would ask Kant with his flawless memory to sing the dirge they'd chosen the day before—a song of loss and of people begging for forgiveness when they could not save their dearest child from a fire. It was not a perfect analogy, but Ehryn had felt the pain and sorrow in the song, and she knew that Namaoii wished she could have done more for Khalista. That she could have saved her from her mother.

Ehryn took Kant's hand and began to walk beside the procession. Tendaji had finally woken, and he walked behind them, looking old and worn. Namaoii didn't even look in their direction. Instead, she lifted her voice that had always seemed to Ehryn to be made of iron rings… and sang. The others walked in silence and helped to carry Khalista's emaciated frame down through the boardwalks and towering roots, past the cleared pastures of pigs and goats and horned beasts with flaring nostrils and broad heads that Ehryn couldn't name. Past the fields of wheat and grain and plants that she and Dhruv had once coaxed from their little garden. All the while, Namaoii's voice was as thick and full as a cloud heavy with rain that had not yet fallen.

When her song was finished, another Hollowed in the line began, his dirge about the curse of the carved X and of an afterlife that awaited those who carried the burden for both too long and never long enough. The other Hollowed joined him.

They carried Khalista across the forest until they came to a huge tree of shimmering green and silver, stretching upward into the perpetual twilight as long glowing tendrils drifted down to barely kiss the ground at their feet. Ehryn and Kant stared up at the gorgeous, living monolith with wide eyes that reflected the motes shifting and shimmering on the branches. The great tree seemed to breathe in at their approach, and Ehryn couldn't believe that such a thing had ever existed and then been forgotten.

Between the soft dirge being sung around her and the idea of such incomparable beauty being lost to everyone else that walked or would walk across the world, Ehryn felt like she was being crushed. The sudden weight of everything that had already happened and what would happen and what might never happen overtook her. Her eyes filled, and she sobbed. She tried to stifle the sound, afraid to interrupt the singing or to draw anyone's eyes to her rather than to the covered face of Khalista… a girl who had also been so lost that no one in her world even knew she'd existed. The waste was too much. It wasn't fair.

Kant squeezed her hand and Tendaji put a heavy hand on her shoulder. "Are you all right, Ehryn?" he whispered to her, his voice barely carrying over the song around them. More people had picked up the melody, calling and crying into a void that did not hear them. There was hurt there, and anger, and fear, but mostly there was only loss. The feeling you get when you close your eyes at the top of a canyon—open and gaping and hollow all around you, with nothing to fill it but screams and cries and uncertainty.

"It's not fair," Ehryn whispered. "The world doesn't even know she's gone. No one even knows… knows that they lost someone who had all of the potential to be amazing or beautiful or strong, but never even got the chance."

"They will," Namaoii growled. A few of the others that had gathered turned to look at her, catching the lightning and fire in her eyes that burned even more brightly than the glowing leaves of the ancient tree. "We'll make them see."

The group lifted Khalista's empty shell into the reaching tendrils of the great light tree, and Ehryn realized with a shock that there were suckers on the ends of the glowing leaves, like the underbelly of a squid. It wrapped its grasping vines around Khalista's withered frame and drew her body back into itself until there was only the motes of light and a soft *shuck* sound from deep within the growth.

"She's going to be the last one," Namaoii said resolutely as she turned towards the others gathered beneath the beautiful carnivorous branches. "She Who Demands the Blood will have no more of us. We will cut the False Children off from the magic They hope to twist and taint. We will ensure that *no one* uses us as a weapon or a slave ever again." Her voice rose in pitch, almost to a frenzy. "We will march on the enclaves and rescue every person they've enslaved for our blood. And then we will march on Clearwall and make the Queen rue the day she chose to sell her subjects in the name of fear."

"And who are you?" someone called. Namaoii's eyes glinted.

"I am Namaoii, the Hollowed Wolf Pup of Clearwall."

The words rang across the gathered mourners like flames across a dry field, and Ehryn could see the heir to the Starlit Throne march back on her home with these people at her back—ready to tear down the walls and prejudice and fear.

The fear.

"Namaoii," Ehryn said quietly, her voice still hitching. "Is marching against Clearwall really the best way? Don't people already fear the Hollowed enough?"

There were quiet murmurs and nods from the few Hollowed with their carved foreheads. Namaoii pursed her lips.

"What else is there? The people need to know that we're here. They need to know what happened while they looked the other way."

"We came here when Birdie and the others asked because we did not think it was possible to break through to those in Imeriel. The Clearwall you have held in your mind—that shining jewel of advancement and open-minded scholars—was lost long ago," one of the Hollowed whispered, one hand absently reaching up to brush the carved scar on his forehead.

"That's okay!" Kant piped up. "Because we have Ehryn, and Ehryn is great at finding things!"

As always seemed to be the case when Kant spoke, the unease in the air fizzled and evaporated, and a few of the tear-streaked faces smiled. Even Namaoii released the tension in her shoulders.

"There will always be traders if someone is willing to buy," a tall Hollowed woman said. "Close a market stall and another will open. Ban the trade, and smugglers rise. The only way to eliminate the need for goods is to go after the buyers."

Birdie nodded. "Your mother has no small hand in this, Namaoii, but she is not the root of this evil. Or the largest threat."

"She still must answer for it. For all of it." Namaoii stared into the tree where Khalista's body had been enclosed.

"Yes. And she will. But all branches fall if the trunk is chopped."

Namaoii took a deep breath. "Then… then we have to go after Mavrikal. She Who Demands the Blood. Keep Her from taking any more of us, and definitely keep Her from using our gifts to suck the magic from the Weave." Several people quaked at the mention of Mavrikal's name, but others nodded. Namaoii huffed out a sigh. "Then we go for the Old Gods. Release Them and enlist Their help against the False Children. End this madness." She turned to Ehryn. "What do you need from us?"

Ehryn looked around nervously, still trying to stifle her tears. "Namaoii, are you sure this is the best time?" she whispered.

"Yes," Namaoii said definitively. "We're here to honor Khalista's life, but if we really want to do that, then we need to make damned sure that she's the last one who gets laid in the ground over what someone carved into her forehead in her childhood." The others behind her murmured in agreement, and Namaoii stepped close to Ehryn, towering over her. "If we need to stop my mother, fine. If we need to cut down the Sisters, we'll figure that out. If we need to release the Old Gods to stand with us against the False Children, then we'll make it happen, and if it turns out that it's just releasing a snake to catch a mouse then I'll fight them, too. But this has to stop."

Some distant part of Ehryn that wasn't terrified by the fire in Namaoii's eyes smiled at that. Leave it to Namaoii to know what was right and want to fix it but to reach for a sword when she didn't know how. But the steel in her heart was there. And as others straightened their shoulders and rose to their full heights at the Wolf Pup's back, Ehryn thought that the princess was truly worthy to lead.

"There are warriors here," Birdie said quietly next to them. So softly that most of the people gathered couldn't hear. "Most are the final followers of ancient doctrines or codes, invited to the Between as a way to pass on or preserve their knowledge. They still practice their treasured techniques or styles every day to keep them from being lost forever. A few even call themselves Faoii, remnants of the monasteries that have been built and destroyed and rebuilt again over the centuries, most recently during the Godfell War and during Elise the Iron Queen's reign. If it is justice you seek, they may yet follow." She cast her sad brown eyes in the direction of the tree that had enveloped Khalista's remains. "Justice is the one thing we are most afraid of losing here in the Between."

Namaoii held Ehryn's eyes for a long time, either daring or begging her to rise to the occasion. But Ehryn could not. "Fine," Namaoii growled before turning her back and bellowing at the gathered mourners. "Faoii! You who call yourselves the harbingers of justice and truth! Who will follow us to fix this? Who will help us stop this injustice?"

The Hollowed stepped up immediately, as did a few of the other warriors that Ehryn had seen gather for the procession. Everyone moved to the side, however, as five women came forward, moving like water around rocks, their presence so filled with power that it took everything for Ehryn not to cower before their gazes. Namaoii held her head high and faced them, but they looked right through her, instead focusing on Tendaji, still standing behind Ehryn.

Ehryn thought that Tendaji would be angry or hurt by the presence of these women with antiquated breastplates and rings of iron in their braids—they had, after all, ended up here instead of in the wars of loss and sorrow that his sister had waged. But, when they ignored Namaoii completely and instead turned to face him, he fisted his hands in front of him like he was grasping an invisible sword hilt and bowed his head.

"Goddesses guide your footfalls, sisters. I wish we could have met at a more appropriate time." The little group of women returned the gesture.

"No, the child is right. This is exactly the time and place to make the world better in memory of those that have fallen," a tall warrior said, her long black braid the color of raven feathers in the light of the glowing tree.

"We knew that one day we would be asked to leave this place and fight again," one of the other Faoii said. "We've heard the whispers of Avanli through these leaves and know that our Order was based on lies woven by the False Children for centuries. We were carefully manufactured puppets created to make mortals dependent. The Horned God told us of your arrival and that change is near. We have waited for the one who would release His sister and set things right."

Tendaji looked uncomfortable. "I'm not the one you've been told to wait for, Faoii." He paused, uncertain. "Have you cast off the title of the Sisters' false Order?"

"Not at all," the first Faoii replied, her eyes sparking with fire and starlight. "We are Faoii. We are the harbingers of justice and truth. Now more than ever before it seems we might truly become worthy of that title."

The others around her were nodding. "That has always been our call. Across every monastery across every Weave we have seen. We did not know that Our true Goddess was unjustly trapped beneath the Weave, or that the truth had been buried with Her."

A woman with her hair filled with beaded braids stepped from the group. She was shorter than the others, and her accent was slow and quiet. "Some of us have waited here since we opposed the False Children in the first Faoii War. Back when the Faoii and Croeli were one. When the Alathi were more than myths and ancient treaties. When the False Children first sucked all the magic from the land and left only rough hellscapes of poison and barren fields. They decimated us in those early days when we had to learn how to fight without magic or war cry or Alathi's blessings. So few survived to bow before Their new Order, where They pretended to be both Alathi and Avanli—Great Goddess and Horned God. It was blasphemy. A few of us were brought here to preserve the truth.

Few are left now. So many times before now we thought we might be able to replant the truth in the world. We were wrong." The others squared their shoulders when she held Tendaji's gaze. "Is it different this time?"

Tendaji looked like he was going to reply, but Namaoii stepped in front of him, forcing the Faoii to meet her gaze. To acknowledge her.

"It has to be. The Hollowed are dying in mines as we speak. The False Children are close to cutting everyone off from magic again." She spoke specifically to the shorter Faoii with beaded hair. "If you lived through that once, you understand why I won't let it happen again. We're going to stop the Sisters, and then we're going to cut Them down."

The Faoii looked at her through narrowed eyes, their noses scrunched up as though they smelled something rotten. "With what, Child?" one of them asked down her nose.

Namaoii bristled. "With whatever we have! Tendaji and I nearly cut down Mavrikal when She surprised us in the forest. We *can* do this with your help! We've already called on the Faoii of the Monastery of the Fallen Star to meet us at the mines. Your sisters need you!" Most of the Faoii straightened at this, their bodies unconsciously shifting into fighting stances. The tallest Faoii looked unmoved, however.

"We are here to preserve the truth until we know it will not be lost again. There are no others to hold it if we should fall. We will not lose still more to rash actions if the time has not yet come," she said. "Your fight sounds just, and we wish you well, but we have been told to wait for she who wields the Eternal Blade, and we will do so." The Faoii turned to walk away, but stopped to offer a softer, "I am sorry for your loss."

Namaoii's face crumpled, and her shoulders drooped. The others that had stood so readily behind her before began to fidget and break away. And Ehryn realized that the best chance they actually had at succeeding was about to fall apart.

"Wait!" Ehryn cried. "We have the Eternal Blade!" She turned to Tendaji frantically. "Show them, Tendaji! You have to make them see!"

Tendaji frowned and drew his fantoii from its sheath.

But the blade was listless. Silent.

Ehryn stared in disbelief. Every time Tendaji had drawn his blade before, it had sung with the chorus of a thousand angels. It had been glorious and terrifying and had always made her feel a little braver than before. But now, in its echoing silence... she felt empty. Cold.

This wasn't right. This wasn't how it was supposed to be!

The short woman with beaded hair clucked her tongue. "Times change, child. We said *she* who wields the Eternal Blade. Even if that's it, the wrong hand holds it."

Both Namaoii and Tendaji looked to Ehryn. "That's you," Namaoii said without anger. "We all know it. You're the Called. Pick it up or we lose them." Ehryn hesitated, and Namaoii grabbed her by the tunic. "Pick it up, Ehryn!"

And for the first time since the barn, the Voices on the Wind cried their approval. They were muted and distant, but their whispers caressed Ehryn's ears.

Take it.

Take it.

It is yours.

The time has come.

The Faoii who had started to walk away turned to watch the unfolding scene. Ehryn shivered as Tendaji unclasped the sheath from his waist and offered the worn scabbard to Ehryn.

"Ehryn of Clearwall, I believe this is yours," he said in the sudden silence.

Ehryn hesitated.

"Lift it, and the Faoii will follow you," the woman with

raven hair said.

Take it.

Wield it.

Help us.

The pull of the Voices was nearly overwhelming, but something tugged Ehryn's limbs in the other direction. She didn't want the blade. She'd *never* wanted the blade.

And she heard her brother's laughter from across the Weave. His joy. And she knew he never would have wanted her to pick it up, either. She'd found his thread. And she would follow it.

But not if it meant losing herself along the way.

"No!" she nearly yelled. "I… I don't want it. I'm not a warrior."

"You must be." The beaded Faoii's eyes gleamed with magic and knowledge. "It's your destiny."

Destiny.

Destiny.

Help us.

But the words rang hollow to Ehryn. The Voices cried out across millennia, but this feeling was deeper than that.

Ehryn had always trusted the Voices on the Wind. Had always trusted what others said about the Weave. Had trusted that smarter and older people knew what was best for her. But in this moment, she finally realized that she should have trusted her heart more than any of it.

She remembered her father's words. "I want you to know that it's okay if you only ever bring one person happiness, my daughter. And I would be proud if that one person was you."

Destiny.

"No." Her voice was firm and strong. Stronger, she thought, than even Alathi could have made it. "Destiny doesn't mean anything to me. Give it to Namaoii. She's been training to be worthy of that sword her entire life. It should go to her."

"It doesn't work that way," Namaoii growled. "If Alathi, Tendaji, *and* the Faoii say it's supposed to go to you, then that's what's supposed to happen. Doesn't matter what either of us want."

A coldness filled Ehryn. "Why not? If that were true, then why are we even fighting against the demands and dreams of the Sisters? Why are we fighting to keep our own magic instead of just accepting what They'd give us? Aren't we fighting for the lives we want, rather than the lives They say we're destined for? Isn't that why you're not already in those mines?" The Voices on the Wind grew louder, and Namaoii opened her mouth angrily, but Ehryn would not be deterred by any of them. She let her own voice get louder still, drowning them out.

"I'm so tired of living in a world where our worth and our destiny stems from things beyond our control. The gifts we get at birth or the families we're born into or whatever else. We can't just blindly follow words like 'fate' forever. We can't just sit idly by and wait for Weavers or Arcanists or Goddesses to tell us what to do. If we want a world where the people who work for something actually *get it,* then we have to make it. And that starts now." She took Namaoii's hand and squeezed the older girl's fingers. She consciously softened her voice. "Namaoii, you've worked your *entire* life to be what you are. Tendaji's seen it. Kant and I have seen it. You're more worthy of holding that sword than anyone else, destiny be damned."

Namaoii looked conflicted, and she stared almost mournfully at the scabbard in Tendaji's hands. "You can't deny destiny," she finally said, though her voice was hoarse.

"I'm not denying destiny," Ehryn replied. "I'm *correcting* it."

Ehryn took Namaoii's hand and laid it on the fantoii's hilt. "Namaoii. This sword belongs to you."

And the sword *screamed.*

37

It didn't seem to Ehryn that they were returning from a funeral as the group walked back to the village of treehouses together. But she also thought it might be better this way, filled with hope and anger and a demand for change rather than the heart-wrenching melancholia that had burdened them all a few hours before. Rather than dirges and tears, there was a bristling readiness from those gathered as they whispered about freeing humanity—freeing themselves—from the False Children. Namaoii was crafted of steel and promise, and she pumped her fist in the air and led in war chants, her new sword's cry rising with its own fury and bloodlust. A call for change. For justice. You could feel the power gathering in the air.

Ehryn watched Namaoii in her re-found strength and determination, and while the Voices on the Wind whispered their dismay that it was not she who led that group back to the village, Ehryn held no regrets. Her heart felt light. If she had to change who she was at the core in order to be a leader, then she wasn't the right person to lead.

You will learn though, my Faoii. I will show you what you can be.

Follow your brother's thread to the mines. I will wait for you.

Help us.

Ehryn stopped at that, her entire body prickling in uncertainty. The main voice—Alathi's voice—had returned.

And She called her Faoii.

When they made it back to the village, Namaoii was already ordering people to prepare, taking control of the communal table near the central fire.

"You're sure?" she asked Ehryn.

Ehryn nodded. "Yeah. Dhruv's thread leads to the Blackfeather Wilds. Alathi says to go to the mines there. Stop the False Children from using the Hollowed blood."

"Then that's where we go," Namaoii declared. "Has anyone here been to the mines before?" One of the Hollowed nodded. "Great. We need a map."

Birdie laughed. "There are thousands in our archives here. I'm sure we can find one that will suffice."

"Perfect. Let's see if we can find one. And anything at all about the Hollowed, the False Children, the Old Gods… anything. Weaknesses, strengths. How this ritual the Sisters are planning might work. How we can stop it. There's got to be something. Find it and bring it to me. Then get as much sleep as you can." The people around her nodded and dispersed.

Finally it was just Namaoii, Tendaji, Ehryn, and Kant sitting at the table. Namaoii wiped a hand over her face and looked at each of them.

"Ehryn… thank you. I didn't have a chance to say anything before. But what you did… You didn't have to. They would have followed you and I would have helped in any way I could. We still would have made it."

"It's better this way," Ehryn said. "We needed a true leader. The Eternal Blade should be yours."

"But be careful, Namaoii," Tendaji said quietly. "That rot that Ehryn warned us about is everywhere, and it's flammable. It took very little for you to light this first spark, but you must direct which way the flames go. Like the tonicloran, that blade is both a blessing and a curse. Many people will look to you for guidance while it is in your hand. As they once did Kaiya. As they once did me."

Namaoii looked at her fantoii for a long moment before turning to Tendaji, her face crumpled in a mixture of regret and pride.

"Faoli. I'm sorry. I'm so sorry," she finally ground out.

Tendaji gave that understated smile and shook his head. "You have nothing to be sorry for, Namaoii. We own nothing in this world. We are only borrowing things from future generations. That sword sang for you, and I am honored to relinquish it to one as worthy as you."

"That's not what I mean," Namaoii protested. "I… I know why the blade doesn't sing for you, anymore. Before, when I…" She fumbled and shook her head. "I didn't know how much it would change things. For the first time, seeing you, I… I actually understand why we're feared."

Tendaji made a sympathetic sound. "There is no gift in the world we should fear, Namaoii. You and those like you have been treated poorly for too long. That is why we're gathered here now and why you have dozens of people scouring archives of forgotten lore as we speak. To keep the rest of the world from being cut off from the magic of the Weave. It is… not a pleasant transition. I would spare them that if we can." He looked at Namaoii, who was tracing the lines of his face with her eyes, looking torn. "Do not look so sad, Namaoii. I do not blame you for anything and am still grateful to you in ways you cannot know. If this is my life now, I will live it well with no regrets. Perhaps now I may see some of the things in life that duty kept me from before."

Namaoii's face softened, and after a moment she actually laughed. "If we get through this, I'll help you pick a vacation home, Faoli."

Ehryn and Tendaji laughed too, and for the first time in days the shroud of doubt seemed lifted. Almost. Because one voice at the table was still silent.

"Kant, what's wrong?" Ehryn asked.

"I'm… thinking," Kant whispered.

"I thought I smelled a furnace overheating," Namaoii said under her breath. Ehryn shot the older girl a hard look.

"What are you thinking about? Can we help?" But Kant was standing, facing Namaoii with all the rage his little body could muster.

"You know I can hear you, right?" Kant demanded. "You always talk about me like I'm not here. Like I don't understand. Like I'm a piece of furniture built for the convenience of you not having to hold a pen. But I can hear you. I know you say I can't think things on my own or figure anything out or make my own choices. But… but I deserve to be allowed to try without you making fun of me."

Namaoii looked surprised and opened her mouth to respond, but Tendaji held up one hand. "That's fair, Master Kantilieh. What choices are you considering?"

"I…" Kant scrunched up his face in concentration. "Tendaji, can you explain again how the tonicloran is different now than it was in your time?"

"What?" Namaoii nearly yelled. "*You're* asking someone else to repeat something? Why?"

"I told you. I'm thinking."

Namaoii started to laugh, but even Tendaji gave her a look this time. Namaoii caught it and rolled her eyes but was silent. Tendaji considered Kant's question for a minute before giving a cautious reply.

"It used to cause painful blisters that—"

"No," Kant interrupted. "I mean, how is it different in the Weave."

"Magic used to follow bloodlines through descendants. With the right blood or starting point, you could watch someone's ancestry for generations. With the right spell or ingredients, you could control their descendants."

"And… now?" Kant still hadn't opened his eyes, his face twisted in concentration.

"Now it seems that the tonicloran and the strongest threads are focused on siblings. Two strings that twist together that are more visible than all the ones that are around it."

"How did… how did you save your sister from that? How did you remove your thread from hers?"

"Kant, if you're worried about your unborn sis—"

"Please tell me."

Tendaji sighed. "The Royal Arcanist removed me from the Weave."

"With the tonicloran. You used it to run in that area parallel to the Weave. And your sister's thread grew quiet."

"Yes. For many years she was all but invisible in the Tapestry. She lived for more than a hundred years without anyone knowing she still existed. Without anyone being able to find her. Until she chose to direct the threads again with the young Jacir."

"I still don't know why you're asking all this," Namaoii snorted. "You know you're better at recalling information than—"

"Shut *up*, Namaoii!" Kant yelled. "Let me *think!*"

Namaoii gaped. Ehryn didn't think she'd ever been told to shut up before, and *definitely* not by Kant.

"Kant," Tendaji said, quietly. "Even if you wanted to do what I did in order to save your baby sister from the False Children, I don't know where to find more tonicloran. And... and you saw what happened to Ehryn. You don't want to go through that, do you?"

Kant shook his head. "An eternity of remembering every story I ever heard? No. I don't think it would all fit in my head. I don't want that at all."

Tendaji knelt and placed both hands on Kant's shoulders. "Then what do you want, Kantilieh?"

Kant suddenly opened his eyes and smiled. It was the biggest smile Ehryn had ever seen. His face looked like a candle that had just been lit in pitch blackness. His eyes twinkled when he spoke.

"I want to stay here with Birdie. I want to go and tell stories and learn more and stay in the Between to save my sister and... maybe someday, when I'm ready, I'll give myself to that tree we just saw. I think it would be nice to be part of this place for eternity."

Namaoii sputtered for a moment. "Goddesses' girdles. He came up with something on his own. Something he *wants*. I didn't think it was possible."

"Are you sure, Kant?" Ehryn asked softly. "If we can stop the False Children, you won't have to hide.   This place won't be necessary anymore."

"I think it will always be necessary. There will always be *someone* who covets that power. Who will try to enslave others for their own gain. And even without the tonicloran, people have already started noticing the power of siblings. Queen Isolde wasn't the first person to say that the Tapestry is carried on four shoulders." He took a deep breath. "I want my sister to have a story she made herself, without fear that someone else will see its opening pages and try to write it. I'll never be the type of person who can write his own tale—but maybe someday, if I wait long enough, I can tell hers." He smiled and looked around the forest and its steady twilight sky. A cow lowed in the fields outside the village. "Birdie treats me like a colleague, not like a servant or a piece of furniture. And I *know* that I can save more songs or stories or poems from being lost than anyone else here. I think this is where I'm supposed to be. Which is funny. I've never felt that way about anywhere before."

The others stared at the boy, who didn't seem quite so little anymore. He smiled at them. "Don't worry. I'm going to come with you when you finish this. I'm going to watch and listen and carry the story forward. Help Birdie write it if I can. I'm going to go home and watch my sister be born and tell her everything I learned. I'm going to hug my parents and thank them for everything. And I'm going to make sure they know that this is what I want and that this is what the world needs from me. Then I'm going to come back. And I think we're all going to be a little happier for it."

Everyone else was quiet for a few moments, and Kant sat there, smiling to himself, looking for all the world like someone who had just won a coveted prize. Even Namaoii looked at him with a respect she hadn't shown before.

"You know," the princess said quietly. "It'll be a little bit before the others come back with maps and news. Maybe you could tell us a story, Kant? The one about the scaled monsters with ruby eyes."

"Of course! I'd love to!" And Kant started an animated tale about far-off worlds and magnificent beasts. Under the twilight sky, the others listened, aware that, if this was a gift that they were going to lose, at least they could appreciate it while they had it.

38

Namaoii stood in front of the table, surrounded by maps. The firelight bounced off of her newly-polished breastplate, and warriors flanked her on either side. There were many gifted painters in Clearwall, and Ehryn reminded herself to remember this moment so she could ask one of them to immortalize it for Namaoii's inauguration. Or maybe she would learn to paint, herself, when this was over. When she was safe in her home surrounded by the scent of soap and candlewax. She thought she could learn to paint, with time and practice. No magic was unlearnable, after all.

It was hard to tell how long had passed in this world between time. It seemed like years had come and gone since they'd left the Faoii monastery and run afoul of the Elisians. But Birdie assured them that the Faoii were still making their way north, to follow the orders Alathi had given them. And no one had seen any activity from the False Children.

"The mines are here," Namaoii said to the others, looking over the maps they had of the region from before the Blackfeather Wilds had become a wasteland. "We can get there, free the Hollowed, and then escort them back to the Faoii who are still coming up from the south. Hopefully that will give us enough time before the False Children come to find out what's going on."

Ehryn gazed over Namaoii's shoulder. The maps were all evidently of Imeriel, but none were exactly alike. Towns were present in some and not others, the names and courses of rivers changed over time, coastlines and mountain ranges were slightly different as cartography evolved. Ehryn found it fascinating. It reminded her of the stained-glass windows she'd seen in Clearwall Keep. A collage of images all telling the same story.

The oldest Faoii looked as well, the beads in her hair rattling as she nodded sagely. "It makes sense that we're going there," she said, indicating Namaoii's marker. "That's where the monastery was."

"Which monastery?" Namaoii asked.

"The only monastery. The Faoii monastery. We only had one back then, before the Sisters drained the entire place of magic with their spell. Those are the grounds we fought Them on, magicless, scared, unable to hear Alathi for the first time in our lives. Many of us died. Many more threw down their fantoii and worshipped the Sisters, begging for mercy. They gave it. And from then on, only the Faoii had magic at all."

"Until Kaiya cut one of Them down," Tendaji said slowly. "All of the years I lived there, I never realized its significance. A plain laid bare by magic thousands of years before I walked away from it. Watched over by a false Goddess who pretended to be something She wasn't so that my ancestors who split from the Faoii would not cease their worship."

"We only ever knew of the Goddess," one of the Faoii said. "Who did you worship in the north? Or… who did you think you worshipped?"

"Me."

The word was so deep, so old that it reminded Ehryn of cave echoes that still whispered the secrets of those who had once painted on their walls in clay. It sounded like stones that had gathered sand on the wind for so long that they eventually became dunes.

But she knew that voice, and Avanli was suddenly there, His silver armor brighter than a reflection of the firelight could possibly account for, featureless behind His horned helm and planted shield.

The warriors behind Namaoii fell to their knees, gripping their hands in front of them as though grasping an invisible hilt, their eyes on the ground. Even Tendaji was out of his seat and kneeling faster than Ehryn could see. Not as quickly as he could when he could Blink, but with a power and training that had nothing to do with magic.

The Old God looked at His kneeling worshippers and spoke. "I told you all to wait until you found she who wields the Eternal Blade. She who will release My sister from Her prison and right the injustice of millennia past. The blade has screamed, and it will herald justice. Our Usurpers already have the cursed plant that bound My siblings below the Weave. They already have the blood that will strip your kind of the magic We gifted you in your infancy. It all must end where it began—on the ground where My sister's temple stood. Where She was betrayed. Where She was trapped."

He looked at them all, one at a time, through the dark slit of His helm. "The Usurpers will follow you, will try to hobble you… but fear not, little mortals. My Sister taught you what it was to be Justice. My Sister gave you weapons and strength when you were but mud and ash. You are strong, and in those moments where you are not, I will be there. I will remind the world that Justice is of two scales, and that even Their attacks are nothing against the Shield.

"You are Our Ascended. Our Vengeance."

39

Mavrikal lapped the air with Her tongue. She knew that taste. That scent.

But it wasn't here. She drifted across the veil, to the hall She'd claimed as Her own. Wondered briefly about the God who had lived here before. She knew His name once.

She licked the air again. Closed Her eyes and focused. It was still there. Faint. As faint here as it had been on the other side.

She drifted back. Parts of Her mind felt stretched like taffy, but She'd forgotten what it felt like not to be that way. The scent was so close, but also far. Was it broken up by one of the cities? One of the mortal bubbles with its twisting walls that humans had learned to build a thousand years before when they were new? When Her sisters still walked Their planes and shifted the world to Their desires? When They had still been afraid?

No. It wasn't in the cities, or across the sea. Nor was it in the halls and cathedrals They had taken upon Their ascension.

Where? Where?

She knew that scent. That thrum against the Weave. That terrible power made of darkness and light and all things that were primal before She had even been born. The humans had learned to fear Her kind just as Her kind had learned to fear *Them.*

She couldn't wait. Couldn't find it. She knew the human Tapestry better than any of Her Sisters. But this wasn't on the Tapestry. It wasn't in Their halls that housed the Tapestries of Their worshippers. It was somewhere else.

Below it? Have They come?

Maddened by fury and something deeper—a terror She'd forgotten how to feel—Mavrikal dove through the threads, following currents that had nearly run dry. Her Sisters pulled so few strings anymore. Were content with Mavrikal doing the work.

But Mavrikal could not do this.

"Teilithia!" she cried, appearing in a room of vines and flowers, open to a forest that spread infinitely in every direction. "Sister!"

Her Sister rose from the mossy bed She'd been lying on, moving a sleeping fox from Her lap. She carefully stepped over the new, twisted stalks She'd been tending, but the vines reached out to brush Her ankles, their broad, flat leaves growing at Her touch.

Mavrikal flicked Her tongue, Her eyes bouncing around the room. The tonicloran drowned out almost everything else, here, but She could still smell it. Could still taste it. The power. The fear.

"Sister. One of Them is out from beneath the Weave!" And as She said it, She knew it was true. How? How? After all this time? Was that possible? But She knew that thrum.

Teilithia's eyes darkened, and the flowers in Her hair closed to pointed buds. "What has happened?"

"I don't know! The trap is still in place! No one has left it. But I know what I felt."

Teilithia cocked Her head to one side and inhaled deeply.

She spread Her fingers, and the green slip of Her dress ruffled as She probed the edges of Her hall. Of Her threads. The tonicloran at Her feet rose and twisted around Her calves, Her arms, amplifying Her power. After a moment, She opened Her eyes again.

"We missed one, all those years ago. He hid well for Us to have never sensed Him before now."

"What's changed, Sister?"

"He's revealed Himself to the mortals. He's played His hand. But He already has too much power. They will follow Him instead of Us if We do not strike."

"Follow Him? A nearly silent God that the mortals have forgotten? When We taught their very bones to fear Us instead?"

"Yes, Sister. Because that was not fear you felt at the edges of Your mind just now. It was something stronger. Our ancient master has invoked *reverence.*"

"What do You want Me to do?"

"Come with Me. We will gather Our Sisters and begin. It is sooner than We would have liked, but We have enough Hollowed, now. And this tonicloran will have to be enough. When the mortals realize that We hold the power of their magic, they will abandon Him quickly. And they will remember why fear rules Imeriel."

Mavrikal hissed in excitement, and Teilithia's Hall was empty.

40

Ehryn didn't understand the magic that Birdie normally used to move between the outside world and the Between, only knew that she didn't have the ability to move everyone herself. No one else seemed to be concerned, however, and Birdie in particular seemed unfazed. Instead, the soft-spoken, barefooted woman gave each of those gathered a hug as they met in the field beyond the twisted trees. "I will see some of you again soon, I hope," she said, smiling at Kant in particular. "Make sure that the world remembers what it has lost. Plant the seeds of memory back into the soil. I cannot wait to watch them grow."

"This is a battle for the fate of all mortals," Avanli responded, His voice rumbling from beneath His horned helm. "All other objectives are secondary. We must stop the Usurpers." He cast His gaze across the group He towered before. "Be prepared, warriors. We cannot fail."

Then Avanli whispered a song that Ehryn didn't recognize, the patterns on His breastplate glowing blue… and suddenly she was falling, clutching Kant's hand as the world and the Weave and the universe fell away under their feet. They spiraled through oblivion before finding themselves suddenly on solid ground. The air was cold and the ground bare, and a few of the gathered warriors were on their knees, pale and groaning. Next to them, Avanli wavered in and out of existence.

"Finish your task," He ordered from behind His flickering helm. "I will reserve My strength and return when you call." Then the God of Balance was gone.

"I know this place," one of the Hollowed whispered, her voice shaking. "This is… this is where they brought us. This is where we almost died."

"Show me," Namaoii demanded, straightening. The others stood too, and the Hollowed woman pointed to a nearby hill.

"The mines are there. That's where the others are."

"Not after today. We're going to get them all out." Namaoii led, and the procession crested the hill together.

No one seemed prepared for what they actually found atop that mound. "Mines" wasn't the right word at all. They were standing above a valley. A crater. A maze of ramshackle walls and piles of stones that seemed to serve no purpose other than to force long lines of chained prisoners to serpentine through the jumbled mess while moving rocks from one place to another. A dry well sat at its center, dilapidated and forlorn, a symbol of forgotten life and hope in the center of a dusty labyrinth.

Ehryn couldn't believe what she was seeing. Ragged, exhausted, frail women and men plodded through the trenches, nearly bent in half under the weight of the baskets on their backs, which were filled with gravel and stones. They didn't even stop to look at the newcomers who crested the edges of their prison, just stared on with soulless eyes at whatever was in front of them and kept going.

Namaoii released a sort of feral sound and slid down the rocky cliff face, the few Faoii from the Between following behind her. She was not quiet in her descent, and by the time she reached the bottom (with the others stumbling after her), a clean-shaven man was already there, brandishing his spear.

"How did you get here?" he demanded. "What are you doing here?" Namaoii didn't even reply, rising to her full height, eyes sparking with steel and fury. The guard evidently recognized her because he lowered his spear immediately and placed a fist against his chest as he bowed.

"Princess Namaoii! I apologize. Her Highness did not tell me to expect you."

"Well, I'm here now," Namaoii replied with a voice worthy of commanding armies. "Faoii, get down there. Release all of them."

"Ma'am! You can't—" the guard protested.

"Now." The Faoii spread out around the Wolf Pup, moving in the direction of the chained Hollowed.

"Ma'am! We're only following orders! If you send the Faoii down to release our charges, the guards will be forced to fight them. Do my men deserve to die for having followed the Starlit Throne's commands? Please, let us at least talk about this first!"

Namaoii narrowed her eyes, considering. "Fine. Faoii, get down there and get ready. But don't do anything until my say-so." The Faoii fisted their hands in acknowledgement and made their way into the maze. "You." Namaoii kicked the guard forward. "Show me why you're willing to die for this place." The guard nodded, swallowed hard, and led them to a platform overlooking the workers. The Hollowed didn't even look up, only continued their twisted trek through the maze.

"It is the Starlit Throne's command," he said nervously. "There is little useful ore in the surrounding mountains, but there are enough sources of common rocks to continue building the ever-shifting labyrinth the Gracious Queen has commissioned from us. Even for all their deficits, Clearwall is made great by finding use for all her citizens. The Hollowed do important work here, and the rest of our citizens are safe from them. The Queen has declared that this is what's best for everyone."

One of the Hollowed below them fell, was dragged a few steps by his fellow convicts, and forced himself to his feet. "How can you be okay with this?" Namaoii tried to sound the same as she had before, but Ehryn could hear the horror in her voice.

"We trust the Gracious Queen. This is what punishment is, Princess. People must pay for their crimes. Their duty makes Clearwall great."

"This is slavery! These are people who did naught but get cursed with the accusations of *possibly* hurting someone in the future. The system was built against them from the day they were born!"

"Your mother disagrees. And it's a system that you and everyone else has benefited from in any number of ways. Surely this is a small price to pay for the comfort of everyone else in Imeriel."

"It is, indeed," a new voice said from behind them. "You have done well, Charles. The Starlit Throne finds no fault in you, regardless of what this young upstart might say. Return to your duties. I will make sure that the princess and her Faoii cause you no further trouble."

The overseer immediately snapped to attention, putting one fisted hand on his chest. "Of course, Your Majesty. Right away."

The little group spun around to face the newcomer. Queen Isolde the Gracious Queen stepped lightly on the trail that led to the one permanent building further along the platform, the deep blue folds of her skirts barely brushing the dusty ground. She pulled a silk handkerchief from her sleeve and held it in front of her elegantly straight nose as the soldier kicked up a cloud of dirt sliding down into the Hollowed maze.

"Daughter. I would have told you of this place in due time. Why did you have the Faoii summon me here with such urgency? I had to have the Royal Arcanist transport me here. Was this not something we could discuss after your kintar?"

Namaoii seethed as she looked over her mother's unperturbed stance. "Mother. I'd hoped that they were wrong. That you didn't know what was happening here."

"Whatever do you mean? These people are a threat to Clearwall. To her greatness and her citizens." The Queen cast a long, judgmental look at the Hollowed gathered behind Namaoii. "By creating this place, I have removed these abominations from anything that would make them a threat and have gained the favor of the Goddesses at the same time. This place, however unsightly, is a win for us, my child. Mavrikal has seen to it."

Namaoii's face twisted. "You know you're working for She Who Drains the Blood?"

"Of course. Wonderful that She could have use for these despicable creatures when no one else does. My Lady of the Shadows was the one who ordered the maze you see below you. Such a small price to pay for Her blessing."

Namaoii clenched her fists again. "Mother, what have you done?"

"What I had to, of course. You've never wondered why Clearwall has not known war since I took the throne? You've never wondered how I kept all of our people safe and happy even as the Elisians gathered in force? Mavrikal sees to it. Her power is what makes us great. She does not even demand that I force the rest of Clearwall to bow to Her."

"Mother! Don't you understand? She'll force us all to bow at Her feet! You're sacrificing your citizens to feed Her coming tyranny! She's going to use their blood to strip all of Clearwall of its magic!"

Isolde laughed lightly. "How perfectly foolish. Our magic brings glory to the Goddesses. Has it been so long since I brought you to temple, my child?" Isolde placed a gloved hand on Namaoii's cheek. "And what is this of citizens and tyranny? My dear, they're only Holloweds. And they pay for Mavrikal's favor. There is no tyranny here. No cruel demands. Who would not agree to give up a few animals for the safety of tens of thousands of humans?"

Ehryn saw Namaoii stiffen at the word "animals." When the Wolf Pup spoke again, her tone was low and bitterly cold. "You really have no idea who I am, do you, Mother? What I am?"

Isolde brought her hand back down. "Of course, Daughter. You are Faoii. And I see that your kintar has finally taught you as much." She motioned to the Faoii who stood near the chained Hollowed, awaiting Namaoii's command. "I am very proud of you."

"No! You don't even know me! You know nothing of me!" Namaoii went for the fantoii on her hip but stopped and stared past her mother to the line of broken slaves. Her voice cracked a little when she spoke again. "And it seems that I knew nothing of you, either. This is wrong, Mother. This is everything you taught me not to be."

"This is what it is to be a leader, my daughter. You are the Wolf Pup of Clearwall. Surely I taught you to have more teeth than this."

"No! Real teeth would be doing what's right for everyone and standing against any who would tell your citizens they don't deserve even basic dignity, regardless of what gifts they do or do not have. Real teeth are of stronger stuff than this…this slavery. This hiding behind people's fear and burying what they would not want to see." She pointed to one of the guards on the other side of the crater, looking her mother directly in the eye. "Tell them to release these people! Tell them you were wrong!"

Isolde's dark eyes hardened, and she raised her chin. "I will not, and I was not. If you are to eventually lead Clearwall and all of Imeriel, you must learn what it is to make hard choices."

"Hard choices that the *people* support. We are the voice of Clearwall, Mother, but the heart is her people. We should only be a mirror of what is best for them!"

"This is what's best for them, Daughter. Do you not see?"

"I see us using our own citizens who have done no wrong as slaves. The citizens of Clearwall might prefer not to have to see or deal with the Hollowed, but surely they would want better for them than this!"

"On the contrary. People are fickle beings who care little for what they don't have to look at. The Hollowed are out of sight and thus out of mind, and our citizens—our real citizens—live better lives for it. They live in comfortable homes and have all of their needs met. We are truly the Gem of Imeriel. This small freckle is more than a fair price for such flawless beauty, otherwise. Do you not see? This is for the greatness of Clearwall. The greatness of Imeriel."

Namaoii faltered, and for a moment Ehryn *did* see. As Isolde, the Gracious Queen of Clearwall spoke, pride bubbled up in Ehryn's heart. They really were living in the best city in the world, in a country that was beautiful and fair because of their generous queen who protected them from the unsightly, grotesque abominations of the Hollowed. Life was better because of her, and Namaoii was a fool to question that.

"Namaoii, maybe we should—"

But the Voices on the Wind were screaming from nearby.

Child, lend Me your ears.

Ehryn did, but some deep part of her knew what would change even before Alathi blocked out the gentle, silky whispers that wrapped themselves around Isolde's words. Isolde's ancestor,

Aurelius, was known as the Iron Voice. When he spoke, his followers had *wanted* to do what he said. It had made him legendary.

And as Alathi's ocean of power overcame Isolde's thimble, Ehryn wondered how all of Imeriel had not realized that Isolde was the same. The Gracious Queen had the voice of her line, and she used it to carry nationality rather than orders.

Something about it was so much worse than the commands the Iron Voice had wielded. Something slimy in hiding intentions behind patriotism. And as Alathi's power drowned the queen's magic out, Ehryn suddenly wondered if anyone in these mines were not Hollowed so much as citizens who had seen through her screen and tried to stand against it. How easy it would have been to bury them beneath the guise of making Imeriel perfect. Of making Imeriel great.

Isolde was still speaking, and Ehryn heard the words unclouded. "Daughter. You are the strongest of any of us. All of our ancestors have led to the perfection that is you. You are of the same blood that defended thousands next to the Starlit River when Clearwall was but a hamlet on her shores. You will lead our country to a greatness even I cannot imagine. But to do that you must understand that all things come with a price. It is up to us as leaders to determine what price is acceptable and live with those sins so those who follow us do not have to."

Ehryn could see Namaoii's face twitch as she looked for the words to disagree. But her mother's magics slithered into her ears and ate at her resolve. Kant and even Tendaji looked similarly stricken.

Hurry, Child.

Help us.

"Namaoii!" Ehryn yelled, grasping the other girl's arm. "Her words are honeyed. You know they are." Namaoii looked conflicted and shook Ehryn's hand from her arm without dropping her mother's gaze. "Listen, damn you!" Ehryn screamed.

Isolde straightened. "How dare this despicable thing treat you with such disrespect?" she demanded, grabbing Ehryn roughly by the hair. "You let a chandler's daughter speak to you like this? Namaoii, put this child in her place. Clearwall needs to know that you are the rightful leader. They must show you respect!"

Ehryn grabbed at her scalp, trying to pull herself free, but the queen's grip was tight. She blinked back tears enough to see Kant and Tendaji reach out for her. "Do not move!" Isolde commanded. "Bow before the future queen of Clearwall! Before the greatness of Imeriel!" Ehryn felt the power in the queen's words. Watched Tendaji and Kant hit their knees. Namaoii blinked at them like she didn't recognize anyone here. Like she didn't know where she was. The queen turned her attention back to her daughter. "Namaoii! I told you to deal with this peasant. Make her show you the respect you deserve!"

"Of course, Mother," Namaoii replied, sounding exactly like she had when Ehryn first met her. "Ehryn, you've forgotten who I am." She laid her hand on her fantoii.

"The hell I have. You're the one who's forgotten. Damn it, Namaoii! *Listen!*" But Namaoii was beginning to draw her blade, and Ehryn knew that if she heard that sword's cry, it would be the last thing she ever heard.

So she did something she never thought she'd do: she kicked the Wolf Pup of Clearwall directly in the stomach, screaming, "Figure it out, *Princess!*"

Namaoii crumpled forward with a sharp exhale. But when she stood again, her hand was no longer on her fantoii's hilt. "Don't call me that," she hissed. But her eyes seemed clear.

"What are you waiting for?" Isolde demanded. "And now you've let her strike you? What has happened to you on this kintar, my daughter? Who are you?"

"I don't think you even know," Namaoii whispered. She straightened. "Mother, you have always taught me that every person has a place in Imeriel. All gifts are precious and useful."

Ehryn felt Isolde stiffen behind her. Felt the queen's grip tighten on her hair. "Of course. That is what I've been trying to tell you. Even the Hollowed and their victims have a place in Imeriel. You know this."

"Places like this? This is the saw that cuts through the rock to find the gem that is Clearwall?" Namaoii gestured to the maze below them, at the broken people with broken souls carrying broken rocks.

Isolde nodded. "It is not pretty work, I know. But no sapphire is brought forth from the earth polished and set."

Namaoii looked over the people and whispered again. "Mother. I want you to know who I am. What I am."

"I know everything I need to know, Namaoii. You are my daughter. Do as Clearwall requires of you. Put this little beast in her place and leave this desolate ruin with me. Your place will be at the head of our armies and upon the Starlit Throne. You will be the crown jewel of Imeriel, her unbreakable queen."

"Only because of your whispers that shaped the hearts and souls of those we promised to uphold, not change." Namaoii hands were shaking as she took a step closer to them. "Very well, Mother. My place may be on the throne when we finish this quest. But yours… yours should be here."

And then she was reaching out, her broad hand wrapped around her mother's regal face, palm pressed against her high cheekbones.

Ehryn heard the twisted metal sound of the Hollowed touch before she felt Isolde's body tense and fall. The queen's grip loosened, and Ehryn bolted to Kant and Tendaji, their eyes clearing in the echo of Namaoii's gifts.

Then there was only the sound of Isolde's cries as she writhed on the ground. "What have you done? Namaoii! My daughter! What did you do?"

"I freed Imeriel from the weakest of its chains," Namaoii said, turning away. Ehryn saw the tears on her face as she turned to look over the Hollowed maze again.

"Free these people, Mother. Find homes and aid for them until they can heal. The Faoii I've brought will help you. I'm going to help Ehryn free us from those even worse than you. When I return to Clearwall, there will be much to talk about, and we will set your mistakes right and offer reparations to those you've wronged. But for now, I have to fix something else you've broken. You are lucky I do not bring you with us to offer to Mavrikal when we meet Her next."

"No! You can't do this to me! I'll have you arrested! You'll be locked in Clearwall Keep forever! You aren't worthy of the throne!"

Namaoii released a chilling, mirthless laugh. "I have already gathered the Faoii under my banner without your aid. Send every guard in Clearwall after me, Mother. Send your armies that I have trained with my entire life. They believe me Faoii, as you did. I can take any soldier in our barracks. And while I could not take them all at once, I do wonder if they'll follow your command to capture me without that silent whisper of greatness you'd promise them." Isolde fell quiet at that, her eyes widening in realization of everything she had lost. Namaoii continued: "But you are welcome to try. If you are wrong, however—" she turned to look at Isolde over her shoulder—"then they will be my force when I march back into Clearwall. It would be better, I think, to do as I say now. We will work together upon my return. You can make Clearwall into the greatest city ever built morally at my side or not at all." Her eyes softened. "I do love you, but I am not yours to control any longer. No one is."

They stood there together as Isolde contemplated her daughter's words. Then, slowly, woodenly, the queen rose and started making her way to the guard they'd spoken with earlier. Ehryn watched her traverse the maze in her gown of velvet and broken superiority. The maze that twisted like a river. That broke up magic the same way the one in Clearwall did.

And something hit her.

They thought it would dampen the Call.

They learned it from the rivers.

But it's not enough now that you're here.

Help us.

Here, in the center of a maze at the base of a crater that had formed when the Sisters pulled Alathi into the earth, Ehryn recognized how far they'd come. She gazed at the well in the center of the maze. It looked so much like the pool she'd seen before.

"Namaoii. We've found the prison of the Old Gods."

41

"**Y**ou're sure?" Namaoii asked. "Here?" Ehryn nodded.

"It makes sense," Tendaji said quietly, his crystalline eyes drifting over the maze below them. "I never ventured here in my youth. But I knew that the original stalk of tonicloran we had in our temple came from somewhere in this area. It all started here."

"How do we release Them, Ehryn? We're here. What do we do?" Namaoii turned to Ehryn with expectant eyes. Ehryn stared across the Maze, felt the pull from all around her, heard the Voices screaming for release. Felt Alathi's demands.

Help us.

"I… I don't know." Ehryn tried to figure out the next steps. She knew with every fiber of her being that this was where they needed to be to free the Old Gods from the trap the False Children had set, but she didn't know how to unlock the door. Namaoii stared at her in disappointment.

"How can you not know? This is what we came all this way for, Ehryn! This is the one thing we followed you across all of Imeriel for, and now we're here and *you don't know what to do?*"

"I don't know! It's not like there are instructions written on the maze walls, Namaoii!"

Foolish Child. You, who have reached across the veil and pulled things from all over the Weave. You, whose brother's blood seeped through My prison bars and tied your thread to Mine? You can do this. You must do this.

"Release Me."

Everything shifted, then. The Voices on the Wind were all around her, and the air was biting cold. The ground beneath her didn't feel like it was made of rot, and Ehryn knew she could follow the Weave to anywhere in the world from here. Across mountains or rivers or to far-off oceans. Then her vision shifted, and they were in the ancient monastery, with its writhing pool, the blood of a thousand older siblings covering the floor, the walls, the infinite Weave. It was somewhere between the two Tapestries where Ehryn caught the discrepancy. A tiny seam where the threads didn't line up perfectly. A missed stitch on the well, or in the pool, or in both places and neither. "I need to go down there," she whispered. "I can save Her."

The Hollowed were still in the maze, their shackles falling away as the guards and Faoii removed them at Isolde's direction. Isolde looked so small, now. So frail. Ehryn wondered how she could have viewed the stately queen with such reverence when she'd first glimpsed her on the Starlit Throne.

Isolde didn't even look at her daughter as they passed her, following the twisted ravines as Ehryn listened to the Voices that beckoned.

They were almost to the center of the labyrinth when a dark, inky shadow fell across their path.

"What do you think you're doing, Little Mortal?"

Everyone spun to where the voice had come from, but no one doubted whom they would find. Mavrikal's tongue slid out from between Her lips as She slithered from one wall to the other, Her fingers gripping the stones, Her neck twisted at an impossible angle as She smiled.

"Avanli!" Namaoii shouted, drawing her screaming sword. "We need you!"

Mavrikal's smile widened. She tilted Her head, licked the air.

"I don't believe He can hear you. It must be the walls of this place. Creatures that depend on magic forget about their normal senses. Don't know what they're missing when the twists and turns cut them off from everything they know." She smiled again, slithered a few feet further down the wall. "Unless you're used to walking on this plane. Unless you've been practicing. Then all it takes is a little signal to call anyone you want to."

She slid forward a little more, and the group stepped back on reflex. "Or if you're used to whispering into the minds of a mortal despite the twists and turns. Then it's not difficult at all. See?"

Behind you!

Help her!

Ehryn spun but was too late. Isolde was there, behind Namaoii, eyes mad and black and filled with Mavrikal's shadows. The Gracious Queen pounced, wrapping her gloved arms around her daughter's throat with a feral scream. Namaoii twisted and clawed, catching blue velvet between her fingers as her mother scratched at her eyes. But the Wolf Pup couldn't get a grip. Couldn't pry away her mother's bony fingers.

Then Tendaji was there, wresting Isolde off the Wolf Pup, pinning her to the maze wall as she screamed and kicked and struggled. They tumbled together, the two trained warriors working in tandem against the ferocity of a madwoman's fearless fanaticism, a thrashing pile of teeth and savage cries.

It was all Mavrikal needed.

Ehryn tried to get to Kant in time. Tried to cross the distance between them even as the inky shadows wrapped around his torso. Mavrikal's face appeared right beside his ear. She licked the air next to his head and smiled.

"Kantilieh, did you know that yesterday you became a big brother?" the Lady of Shadows whispered.

Even despite his fear, Kant's eyes grew big and bright at the words, and a wide grin plastered his face.

"A big bro—"

But he never got to finish the thought before Mavrikal's pale, talon-like fingers were sinking deep into his chest. His expression morphed from joy to shock for a handful of seconds, and he stared in confusion and fear at Ehryn, reaching one small hand toward her.

"Didn't you say once that you can trace your lineage back to the earliest days of Imeriel? That almost everyone is related to you somehow? How wonderful," Mavrikal hissed. Then She ripped Her fingers back again, Kant's blood spraying across the ground. Ehryn could feel the way the Middle Child and Her control strengthened as She pulled the power from his blood. The power of siblings. And in this spot at the center of the Weave, Ehryn could feel that power spread across all of Imeriel, linked to families and distant relations in a web of shared blood and ancestry. Ehryn was in that net as well, as were her parents. She could feel the magic begin to drain away from her. Could feel the walls that separated her from Alathi grow stronger.

But none of that mattered like it had a few minutes before. All Ehryn could think about was Kant's scared eyes as he fell limply to the ground.

Everything broke at once. Namaoii and Tendaji were screaming, charging at Mavrikal together. The Hollowed in the

Maze released tortured cries and came weaving drunkenly around the corner towards them, their skin shriveling as they fell with twisted faces and sunken sockets. Mavrikal Blinked away before the warriors could reach Her, thrumming a deep, hollow sound across the Weave. And the Voices on the Wind were screaming.

She comes.

She comes.

SHE COMES!

There were sudden cries from far away as well. The screams of Faoii and their blades. Everything was so loud. It was too cold.

The Eldest. My favorite daughter. The first of my Faoii. She knows where you are.

Help us.

Namaoii was yelling too. "Ehryn, whatever you're going to do, do it *now*!" Someone slapped her, hard, and Ehryn realized she was cradling Kant's body to her chest. "Now, Ehryn! We need you!"

There was movement everywhere, and Ehryn finally, frantically searched for the seam she'd felt before. But her magic was already beginning to drain, and there were heavy footsteps coming across the Weave. Deep, powerful movements that shook the entire Tapestry.

Whole threads had been cut and rewoven beneath Teilithia's heel. She had unwoven immortals out of existence and repainted the Weave in Her image. Had bent entire civilizations to Her machinations in the name of being worshipped. Had built this entire maze to keep the trap from being touched. Ehryn had seen the dark desires and madness of the Middle Child and had trembled in Her presence. And Mavrikal was nothing in comparison to Teilithia.

She comes.

There's no time.

"Ehryn! What's happening?" Namaoii was yelling in her ear, but Ehryn had no answer. How does one describe a force so large and imposing to those who barely notice the wind?

The other Sisters were there, now, towering Goddesses of desert storms and jungle vines. The Faoii from the Between stood fast against them, but they were merely children facing hurricanes. The Sisters were too much. Too big.

"EHRYN!" The voice was a deep boom, and it came from so close that it momentarily drowned out everything else. For a moment, Ehryn could focus again, and she turned to face Avanli as He appeared on the edge of the maze, towering above them, His gauntleted fists folded across a round bronze shield that could have blocked out the sun. His voice rang out like steel on stone.

"Free Her. I will hold the Eldest at bay, but you must not falter now. Teilithia was always the strongest of Her sisters. We need the strongest of Mine." He turned to the nearest False Child, Jaladri, sweeping His shield into Her torso, throwing Her into Her sisters. "Go. Now."

"Do it, Ehryn! We'll keep the Sisters off of you!" Namaoii screamed in Ehryn's ear.

"There aren't enough of us! Even with Avanli!" the Faoii with the beaded hair declared, joining Tendaji and Namaoii, pressing her back against their shoulders, her braids soaked with blood.

"Yes, there are! Look!" Namaoii cried, pointing to the top of the cliff walls. As she spoke, there was the sound of a hundred battle cries all around them as a dark line of figures appeared on the edge of the crater in a wall of bronze and iron, their breastplates glinting in the sunlight, long braids hanging over their shoulders. Ehryn wanted to whoop in joy and relief.

The Faoii had joined the battle.

"Do whatever you're going to do, Ehryn! But do it now!" Namaoii yelled. "Tendaji! Help her however you can!" The Wolf

Pup didn't even wait for a response before raising the Eternal Blade above her head and running in the other direction, toward the Sisters who swept down on the figures of the maze with blades of lightning and floodwaters. "Faoii! To me!"

Ehryn focused. She had to figure this out. Had to save everyone. And for a moment, as she begged Dhruv and Alathi and anyone else she could think of for help, she saw the seam between the worlds. Knew she could get there. Knew she could—

But Teilithia, the self-proclaimed Queen of All was suddenly there, standing in the way, taller even than Avanli. Her legs were wrapped in leafy tendrils, Her hair braided with flowers, Her eyes piercing and Her mouth drawn into a thin line. The vines grabbed at Ehryn, and she was forced backwards, nearly flattened by the sudden wave of power that emitted from the Eldest Sister, her eyes and nose and ears bleeding as Teilithia materialized at the center of the Maze.

Tendaji was above her, yelling something, pulling Ehryn backwards as she floundered for solid ground, as she tried to remember how to breathe. She tried to see and hear and speak through the blood and the waves and the mountains. The presence of The Eldest was so overwhelming that even Mavrikal and Jaladri, whom Ehryn had trembled before so recently, were nearly lost in Her shadow.

Then Teilithia raised Her arms, and everything calmed. The Hollowed stop their screaming. The ground stopped shaking. The Faoii battle cries clipped off from their lips and drifted away like cut ribbons on the air.

"Hello, Children." Teilithia breathed. "It seems you've gotten into some mischief while I was gone."

Her voice was calm, but it moved across them all like an earthquake. Like a wave. Like a thousand years' worth of foliage in an instant. This was a voice that had spoken worlds into existence and Old Gods into traps. The trees that no longer existed in the

Blackfeather Wilds rustled at Her word, moved their branches in the direction of Her voice.

And the people trembled. All their talk of war and justice was gone. The Faoii fell to their knees.

Ehryn swallowed hard. They weren't ready for this. They couldn't do this.

You Must.

And Alathi's voice was older than those trees. Older than Jaladri's oceans or Mavrikal's shadows or the Veiled Goddess's sands. Ehryn pulled away from Tendaji's arms, strengthened by the Voice that only she could hear.

Teilithia sensed the change in the air. Felt the vibrations of the Call across the Weave. She turned to Ehryn.

"Ah. The Called. Stand, little mortal. Let Me see you." Ehryn didn't move, but she could feel Teilithia's gaze in her soul. After a moment, the Eldest raised Her chin and spoke again. "I will let you speak for all that are here, Ehryn of Clearwall. I will let you save everyone that has followed you to this desolate place and will grant them mercy in your name. Kneel, Child. And all will be forgiven."

Teilithia's words kissed Ehryn's cheeks like butterfly wings. For a moment Ehryn could feel the sun on her cheeks as she considered the Eldest Sister's words.

"You cannot! You must not!" Avanli's voice sounded the way a shield does when it blocks an axe, and it broke through the honeyed promises, deep and old and powerful. Ehryn felt the compulsion of Teilithia's command fall away from her like unshackled chains. She took another step forward. Didn't look away from Teilithia's eyes. Didn't change expression.

Teilithia barely looked at the ancient Shield as the echoes of His words died around them. She just flicked Her woven hair, and Mavrikal pounced. Several of Her sisters joined, but neither

Teilithia nor Ehryn looked toward the battle that raged across the maze. Neither dropped their gaze.

"I can be merciful," Teilithia purred. "I can direct this ritual of Hollowed blood. I will let those who bow before Me keep their gifts. All you need do is kneel."

Ehryn took another step. Teilithia's eyes narrowed, and the flowers in Her hair closed into pointed scarlet buds.

"Kneel!"

The command was overpowering, unstoppable. Ehryn felt her knees begin to buckle under its weight. She thought that Jaladri had been the strongest force she'd ever gone up against when she'd first met the Goddess of the Depths in the boat on the Starlit River. She'd thought that Mavrikal's hatred and anger were deeper than even the oceans. And neither of those voices compared to the deep, overwhelming demand of Teilithia, the Eldest.

"Kneel!"

Ehryn's legs trembled. One knee bent. Behind her, the Hollowed began their screams again. Avanli tried to make Himself heard but was drowned out by the Sisters, who attacked Him from all sides.

Ehryn could not rise.

The Eldest Child smiled sweetly and approached, holding out Her hand. "Think of what you're doing. There is nothing good at the end of this path, Child. Come back to Me. I will take care of you and your family forever. You will be provided for. You will be warm and safe and happy for the rest of your days. As will your parents. Your children. All those gathered here. All you need do is worship Me."

Ehryn felt the allure of the proposal. She'd spent her entire life doing everything she could to make everyone else happy. This would be such an easy transition. It would be calm. It would be nice.

It will be false.

Ehryn almost didn't hear Alathi's whisper over the deep longing *desire* to do what Teilithia said. She wanted to go home. She wanted to give her family a good life. She didn't want to be Called anymore.

But she heard the truth in Alathi's words, even as Teilithia tried to drown Her out.

Ehryn pictured Kant's lifeless, broken body somewhere behind her.

She smiled as she laid her cheek against the False Child's palm.

"No."

It took the False Child just a second too long to realize that She'd been turned down. A second where Her beautiful face scrunched into a scowl that Ehryn was sure more accurately depicted Her true self. A second too long before She jerked Her hand away from Ehryn's cheek.

A second too long.

Because even as the Eldest Child realized what had been said, Ehryn was already moving, grabbing Her wrist that was tangled with tonicloran and wrenching it forward.

"Namaoii! Now!"

And Namaoii was streaking in their direction, that beautiful, glistening blade held high, screaming its fury into the darkness. The Faoii at the edges of the cliff strengthened at the cry of that blade and released their war songs once more, descending on the False Children. Avanli's triumphant yell shook the ground at their feet, and one of the Sisters screamed in pain. For a moment, Ehryn was sure they had succeeded.

But the Eldest Child was already Blinking away, through the veil in the Tapestry that so many and so few had seen.

Ehryn held on, following Her through, using everything she had to pull the False Child back through to the other side.

Somewhere between the veils, Teilithia screamed in fury. Tried to shake Ehryn's grasp.

"Release Me!"

"Not until you release us!"

"Foolish Child! Mortals are nothing without Goddesses."

"No," Ehryn hissed, yanking the Eldest Sister back onto the battlefield with everything she had. "It's You who is nothing without us."

The False Child fell back through the rift, Her eyes blazing. And Namaoii was there, swinging her fantoii with all of her might.

We've done it. We've done it.

It's over. We won.

But no one could have expected the sudden change as Teilithia's eyes filled with fire and a rage that spanned centuries. An ancient and primal desire that everyone has somewhere within them.

To be remembered.

"You treacherous little beast. Your kind could never forget Me. I will show you what I am."

And the Eldest Sister was growing. The pain and anger and ancient loss of having carved Her place into a world that originally saw Her as nothing, only to be forgotten or dismissed now by weaklings that She had led to glory? It was too much. And Teilithia would not have it. Even before Namaoii could swing her fantoii, Teilithia's body was pushing her aside, Her rage and hatred and need to be remembered filling the space before them, Her scream cutting across centuries.

"You will remember Me forever. I'll make you *all* remember why the Goddesses are to be feared."

Ehryn tried to look for Namaoii and Tendaji in the chaos all around them. But all she could see was Teilithia, towering over everything. Crushing Faoii with Her bare, vine-covered heel. Shrugging off the Hollowed touches like bee stings.

Ehryn's eyes and soul and ears were overcome by Teilithia's honeyed whispers. A mortal couldn't face this. Wasn't supposed to face this. They shouldn't have come here. They shouldn't have tried to topple mountains that had been built long before they were born. They'd made a mistake. This was a mistake.

The Eldest sister stared at her, imposing and impossible in Her glory. She was the roots that bound all of Imeriel. She was bigger than anything Ehryn had ever faced. She was the grass and the trees.

But then…

But then…

Something reached out to Ehryn from across the Weave, and she *remembered.*

The Eldest might have been the trees, but Alathi was the storm.

Ehryn stood, squared her shoulders, and opened her mouth. Alathi didn't even ask for permission this time.

"GODDESS? YOU WERE NOTHING IN THE BEGINNING AND YOU ARE NOTHING NOW. IT IS I WHO WILL REMIND YOU OF EVERYTHING YOU'VE FORGOTTEN. FEAR. GODDESS. POWER. THESE ARE JUST SHADOWS OF WHAT YOU ONCE KNEW TO QUAKE BEFORE."

Alathi's control moved from Ehryn's vocal cords to her limbs. To her heart.

"YOU WILL REMEMBER THE DAY YOU TOOK MY THRONE AS THE BEGINNING OF YOUR END, TEILITHIA, FIRST OF MY FAOII. YOU WILL BE THE STAKE UPON WHICH ALL YOUR SISTERS HANG!"

Ehryn let go, and there was a moment of terror as she was filled with ice and fire. But then it was gone, and Her hands ripped at the ground. Ripped through the threads that these mortal hands had the power to rend apart. She felt the tonicloran in Her blood, magic in Her bones. She tore off the top of the Usurpers' trap and Her siblings clawed Their way from the Earth to join the struggle, taking the vessels They could overpower. Swarming towards the lowly beasts that dared attack Her brother. That dared to call themselves worthy of godhood.

She felt the power of what She was. What She had always been. And She was growing, changing. Taking on the form She'd been forbidden for ages, forcing this mortal body to shift to Her design.

Alathi walked the world again.

42

Alathi felt Ehryn let go. Felt that empty vessel yawn open for Her in a way she never had before.

She'd been weak for so long. The others She'd reached out to had died. But now this child, who was not one of Her warriors, had come further than anyone else. She'd turned down Alathi's commands. Had relinquished Her sword. Had refused to rise to all of Alathi's standards. She was like the dust that Alathi had originally seen in the Weave all those millennia ago. Small. Scared. Alathi thought she'd be powerless. And yet this little mortal had faced the False Children. She'd met the eyes of the Usurpers. Reached where no one else could reach and had gone where no one else could go. All without Alathi's war cries. Without Her guidance. Without Her sword.

But now the little mortal cried out for help.

She called for Vengeance.

And Alathi heard.

Alathi screamed Her dominance as She took the form She'd been denied for ages. As She filled that weak and frightened body that did not know what it was to be powerful and gave form to all of its potential. Looked upon the mud and ash the humans had been formed of and made her great as thoroughly as She'd lifted all those that had come before.

Her four arms stretched towards the skies She'd once controlled. Her wings unfurled behind Her, and She remembered what it was to be the Ice and Storm and Vengeance.

The Eldest Usurper's voice still echoed between Them. Now, however, in the shadow of all that Alathi was, She thought that the little Sister regretted Her words.

If She didn't yet, She would. Alathi's voice was eternal, cold and hard.

"YOU FORGET YOURSELF. YOU FORGET WHAT I WAS. WHO I WAS. WHAT I *AM*."

She was Alathi, The Lady of Justice. She was the Sword. And She rose above them *all*, towering into the sky. Clouds gathered behind Her. Ice and snow pelted against the worn rocks that had confined Her for centuries, blowing Her hair and cloak and furs in all directions as Her piercing eyes roved over those gathered at Her feet.

And She could see that they knew Her. The wind picked up with a flurry of snow. Sharp crackles of ice pelted their tiny arms and faces. She pushed harder, and She saw Her storm claw deep into their bones, deep below the lies and furs and supposed power they'd wrapped around themselves.

Only one Usurper did not tremble before Her. A little thing of anger and madness that screamed in fury and denial, rushing at Alathi with poison in her cries. Alathi did not feel the little needles of her blades, only lifted Her boot and crushed the inky creature beneath Her heel. Tendrils of shadow writhed out across the ground like twisted, dying snakes, shrieking. She did not even remember the Usurper's name.

But She remembered Teilithia—Her favorite daughter. The one whose betrayal had cut the most. And She recognized that Faoii's voice as she screamed above the sound of her sister's dying wails.

"Mercy, Alathi! Please! I ask for mercy! Justice!"

People screamed, tearing at their eyes and ears. Running in the opposite direction. But they could not outrun the blizzard or the booming sound of Alathi's voice.

"I *AM* JUSTICE. HOW DARE YOU INVOKE MY NAME?"

Below Her, the Eldest Child was cowering, lifting her arms above her head, pleading as she had once, long ago. But Alathi would not hear it, and She reached out for the sparkling sword with the power to kill this usurper who had dared sit upon Her throne. A little being gripped it. A little, helpless being that She could topple easily. Alathi reached down to take what was Hers.

But something stopped Her. What was this sensation She'd never felt before?

Doubt?

No. This was not right. This was not Her. There was something… A whisper. A call. The thoughts She had were not all Hers. Glimpses of a world and city She could never have imagined flashed through Her mind. Stronger magic than anyone had ever performed in Her time. Unity borne from something other than worship. Mechanisms She couldn't even comprehend crafted purely by mortal hands without the help of Goddesses or Gods.

What was this? Had the mortals become so much more than She'd believed they could? Had She been gone so long? Had they outpaced their need of Her?

No! I will not be forgotten!

Alathi pushed back the voice of dissent and reached out for the sword again. With it, She could reclaim this world. Take it back from those would-be deities who had locked Her beneath the Weave.

But the small human holding the sword stood her ground.

"Ehryn! If you're still in there, listen to me! This is a mistake! Come back!"

Alathi laughed deep in Her throat. Such a tiny thing to make such demands.

But the voice of dissent stirred.

"Ehryn! Please!" A male this time. One who almost seemed worthy of Alathi's eye. "We didn't come this far to escape the Goddesses just to enslave ourselves to another! She's killing everyone!"

Ehryn. She knew that name. But the little mortal in the back recesses of Her mind was quiet. Distant. She'd given herself over to Alathi so many times before. And each time it had become easier to let go. Easier to take this form that She'd been made for. Each time it had become more difficult to claw back to that weak and scared thing that now hid in the edges of Her mind, cowering in the dark.

"Damn it, Ehryn! Those are *your hands* trying to take this sword. You wouldn't pick it up for any of us, but you'll do it for this bitch?"

And Ehryn looked at her hands. Saw them from far away. Saw them reach for a blade that she'd sworn to herself a million times she would never wield. But they weren't her hands. They were Hers. And She was made to wield that blade. She would change everything.

"You're stronger than this, Ehryn! *Did Kant die for this?!*"

And that final barked cry from Namaoii broke through the crashing in Ehryn's ears. It cracked along the edges of her prison like glass, and for a moment she could almost hear above the Goddess's laughing, aching, screaming power all around her. For a moment, she could almost tell which thoughts were hers and which were not.

NO! I will not be usurped again! This world will know Justice!

Is this Justice? This was our world while You slept. This is just another usurpation.

You NEED ME.

We need to be free of all the chains others have created for us with good intentions.

NO.

Alathi shook Her head. That was corruption. That was the afterbirth of the False Children's wicked schemes. Who knew Justice better than Her? She reached for the sword again, prepared to crush the bug that held it. Still it stood its ground.

"Damn it, Ehryn! GET OUT HERE!"

Namaoii. A Hollowed. Someone who should never have been able to learn any magic outside the curse she'd been given. But Namaoii believed that no magic was unlearnable. Namaoii believed that will was worth more than chance. Namaoii believed that Justice was not cosmic.

Namaoii had taught her that the only thing that kept humans below the False Children was that humans still thought they were supposed to be there.

Why couldn't it be true for any of Them?

No! This is a trick! This is not Truth.

Isn't it?

Again Alathi pushed past the dissenting voice that rang as true in Her heart as Her own need for everything to be righted as it had been. It was a trick. The voice of Mavrikal, who could sound like anything. She pressed Her giant fist against Namaoii's chest, not even feeling the prick of Her prize as it dug into Her thumb. She'd be able to shape the sword however She wanted to once it was in Her grasp. And then this usurper who still sniveled at Her feet would truly know the meaning of Justice.

She pressed harder, and the little bug's shell began to crack. It released a cry.

And something stopped Her.

"I am not a trick! Get off my friend!" Ehryn screamed. "This isn't Justice. This isn't the world you remember! Get *away from her!*"

Alathi tried to push harder. But Her arm would not obey. Then, slowly, agonizingly, it began to pull backwards.

"NO!" Alathi tried to propel the other three fists forward. Tried to take the sword through strength. Tried to command Her wings and Her storms and Her body to obey. But the parasite in Her mind resisted.

"Get back. Go back to where you came from. We will not give ourselves over to another Goddess."

And for the first time since the False Children had trapped Her beneath the Weave, Alathi felt fear.

"NO! EHRYN! MORTAL! YOU DON'T UNDERSTAND WHAT YOU'RE DOING! TAKE THE SWORD! LET ME SHOW YOU WHAT WE CAN BE!"

But She had seen the world that Ehryn's people had built. She knew exactly what they could be… and it was far more than She had ever planned for them.

The uncertainty took hold. Alathi began to shrink. And while some part of Her knew it was Just, the fear was stronger. She did not want to go back into the darkness beneath the Weave. Did not want to be forgotten again.

"NO! YOU CAN'T DEFEAT THE ELDEST CHILD WITHOUT ME! YOU NEED ME!"

"No," Ehryn said, her voice her own again. "We don't."

Her head throbbed. From somewhere far away, Alathi screamed and writhed, but Ehryn steeled herself. She wobbled on her feet but put all the strength into her spine that she could as she turned towards the still-sobbing, terrified Eldest. Teilithia was nothing without her armies. Without the false cloak of godhood she'd draped around herself for centuries.

"Namaoii," Ehryn ground out. "Namaoii, take her."

Namaoii's smile was more pained than pleased, but she stepped forward anyway, her blade raised high.

"With pleasure."

It fell with the screams of angels and forgotten gods.

43

Things were both simpler and more complicated then. Teilithia's head rolled to Namaoii's booted feet, and the fantoii's cry was momentarily drowned out by the scream of the other Sisters that remained. They seemed to lose Their fight then, and Ehryn could feel the locked power that had been held back from all of Imeriel seep back into the ground and world with every cut and slash that landed against Them in the sudden chaos. They fell beneath the Faoii's screaming blades and the towering Old Gods.

The Old Gods. Ehryn shuddered at those giants of power and ancient magic. Each of Them occupied a body that was not Theirs, sucking the magic so newly released from the Sisters into Their own vessels. But none of those bodies were Theirs. Each form was a Faoii or a Hollowed that had been overtaken.

Ehryn watched those grand creatures celebrate Their victory. Celebrate Their freedom. "It isn't fair." She shivered at the recent memories of being trapped within her own flesh as something else took control of everything she was. She'd almost lost herself beneath the will of Alathi. "It isn't just."

We saved you this day. It is a small price to pay for the safety of everyone else in your world, is it not?

Ehryn frowned. The Call did not come from the wind or an outside force. It was within her. In the recesses of her mind.

"You're still here, Alathi?" she asked. "Do you know that's exactly what Mavrikal said?"

She felt Alathi look for a response, but there was none.

"Ehryn?" Tendaji asked from behind her. "Are you okay?"

"Better question. Do you know how we deal with *that*?" Namaoii pointed at the crowd of Old Gods. The Faoii at Their feet were caught between bowing and reforming a shield wall. They looked to Namaoii for guidance with uncertain eyes. Namaoii, in turn, looked to Ehryn.

"If we worship Them, is it any different than worshipping the Sisters?" Namaoii demanded. "Those are *our* people in those bodies. And if it's anything like what happened to you, the original inhabitants don't have much of a say, do they?"

Ehryn looked to the gathered giants and slowly shook her head.

"No. They didn't choose this. They had less of a choice than even I did."

Namaoii scowled. "Damn it, Ehryn! Then we're worse off now than we were before! Our people are enslaved! And we cannot win against literal gods!"

"You may not have to." Avanli was suddenly beside them, and He was not towering above them as He had before. He turned His horned helm in the direction of His siblings for several long moments, then turned back to Ehryn. "Alathi is the Goddess of Justice, after all."

Namaoii and Tendaji were both in a battle stance before He'd finished talking, swords focused on the Shield.

"Avanli. Did you know Your siblings could only be freed if They could take over someone else's body?" Namaoii demanded. "Did you know this was coming?"

"Yes."

Namaoii released a feral growl and looked like she was about to charge, but Tendaji stopped her with one hand on her shoulder. He peered at the Horned God's helm. "Whose body are You inhabiting?" he asked quietly, his blue eyes calculating.

"Someone who offered it to Me long, long ago."

"By Your perception, perhaps." Tendaji furrowed his brow. "But I know Your voice. From someone who came to me when I was young." He took a few steps forward. "Show us Your face."

Avanli removed His helmet. Namaoii and Ehryn both squinted. The features were familiar. The nose with its upturned edge. The mouth with its slight smile… But the face was old. Wrinkled and gray. Ehryn didn't think she knew anyone that old. Didn't think anyone that old could possibly exist.

Until she met his eyes. The eyes were impossible not to recognize.

"Jacir?"

Avanli turned those ancient features in her direction. "Possibly once. But there is only Me now. I have spent centuries with your Royal Arcanist in My mind. He taught Me many things in the beginning. Gave Me insights on how We should speak to My sister. What Justice means in this new world that continued to weave while She slept." He reached out His gauntleted hand, palm up. "Come with Me, Ehryn of Clearwall. There is much to discuss."

Take it, Alathi whispered. But Ehryn did not need Her guidance.

She set her palm in Avanli's, and they Blinked.

Ehryn recognized the grand marble hall with its infinitely long tapestry and impossibly deep pool. She also recognized the two people in front of her, though Their bodies had changed. Alathi stood in Her bronze breastplate and furs, Her hair long and braided and filled with iron beads and rings, Her four arms covered with metal bands etched with all the stories Ehryn had seen in her dreams. Avanli stood silently next to His sister, wearing His horned helm and suit of dark armor. He was taller than He'd been when inhabiting Jacir's body, though. Alathi's eyes were drops of liquid fire as She turned to Ehryn.

"You! You dared refuse Me? Me? After all I did for you?"

After everything that had happened, all that she'd seen, Ehryn no longer feared the Goddess of Justice. She shrugged and did not drop her gaze. "I had to."

Alathi looked like She would snap Ehryn's body in half out of pure rage, but Avanli laid a gauntleted hand on Her shoulder. "Sister. You shared the young mortal's mind. See as she tried to show You."

He reached out and touched Alathi's forehead. Alathi tensed but did not reply. She stared at Ehryn for a long moment, then through her, then beyond all of them. Ehryn felt like the Goddess was looking between the spaces in her bones, up through her thread of the Tapestry, past her parents, her grandparents, her ancestors, all the way to the beginning. Power and knowledge flowed from Avanli's hand into the Goddess until there was starlight in Alathi's eyes when they finally refocused.

When She was finished, Alathi trembled, all Her fists clenched in rage and uncertainty.

"No! It cannot be! I will not be forgotten! The mortals *need* Us!"

"They did once, Sister. But We were gone for so long."

"Because of the Usurpers! I will not be punished twice by those whom I raised to glory with My own hand!"

And for a moment, Ehryn empathized with Alathi. The Goddess truly had done the best She could since the beginning of time. She was not at fault for any of what had happened… and yet She could not be rewarded in the way She wanted to be. Of course it would seem like yet another undeserved punishment.

"I know it's not… Just," Ehryn said softly. "Not like You want it to be. But the meaning of 'justice' has evolved over time, Alathi. Just as civilization has. Enslaving those vessels out there will be no more just than Your own imprisonment was." She thought about the way she'd been able to see everything around her without the ability to fight it or influence it. In many ways, she thought that Alathi's complete obliviousness from the False Children's trap would have been preferable.

Alathi rounded on her, teeth gnashing as she screamed. "You know *nothing* of justice!"

Ehryn shrugged again. "Don't I? A few minutes ago I *was* Justice. But I was imprisoned. That didn't feel like justice to me."

"A few people's suffering for the greatness of all *is* a worthy sacrifice!" Alathi screamed.

"I know. That's why we're asking You to stop this. For the greater good of every person that's out there right now. That climbed higher than You ever thought they could. Your siblings are enslaving people that did not ask for it. Their vessels are sucking the magic from everyone that might yet use it to do amazing things." She squared her shoulders and looked Alathi in the eye. "Surely the suffering of a few beings that have already lived for millennia must be worth the futures of entire generations of people whose magic has just begun to manifest?"

Alathi deflated at that. Her mouth opened and closed, and Ehryn could see that She was trying to sustain Her rage. But it wasn't rage. It was fear. The fear of being forgotten. Of the world spinning on without Her. Of having worked so hard to be free, only to find out the universe had left Her behind.

Finally She whispered, "Show me again. Everything I missed."

Avanli reached out once more and pressed His fingers against Alathi's forehead. She gazed into the nothingness between stars, watched the rise and fall of nations. The infinite individual lives of people who had grown and flourished and found love and fortune without Her influence. Watched people help each other and set up complex judicial systems without Her voice. Without Her name. Watched magic develop and grow, and watched people use their gifts to influence the entire world, one tiny ripple at a time. Without Her. Without Her siblings. Even, for much of the time, without the Usurpers.

The humans were beyond what She'd ever imagined they could be. Beyond what She could have raised them to be, even if She had never been trapped beneath the Weave.

They were glorious.

Alathi's gaze was still distant when she spoke again. "I have not been able to look upon the cosmos since We were trapped. I should have seen them through you, Ehryn. I should have noticed…All the times I tried to convince you to lift the Eternal Blade, you resisted. I thought it was because My call was too weak beneath the threads, but you did it again when I was in all My power. And I was too angry to see."

Ehryn nodded. "No matter what You said or did or promised, I never wanted to be anyone but me."

"Even though I could have made you great?"

Ehryn couldn't help but smile. "Judging by how things turned out when we wrestled for control, it seems I was already pretty great."

Alathi's face went through a range of emotions. From insult, to anger, to hurt, to contemplation. Then mirth. "You're greater than I thought you all could become without Me. Without

Us. I did not think the world could be changed with a softer touch. Can it be that you've outgrown Us?"

"I don't know. You hold a power that we don't. Standing in Your presence in that crater was overwhelming. Impossible. We do not wield that power. But…" Ehryn took a deep breath. "But if we have to find that strength within ourselves to free our people and our futures from Your siblings on that battlefield, we're sure as all the hells going to try. Maybe that means we've outgrown You. Or maybe we've outgrown ourselves, and this is how it ends for us. Either way, I can't let Your siblings keep those vessels."

Alathi looked confused for a moment, and Her immortal eyes scanned the universe again. When Her eyes refocused, shining with colors Ehryn had never seen, She laughed.

"Don't wield that power? Have you not realized, Child? Gods are nothing without humanity. We are only muscles in the body of the universe. We are only as strong as you make Us. The only thing keeping those Faoii trapped is their trained belief that We are strong. Generations of the False Children ingraining it into them, humbling them before the might of the Goddesses."

Avanli clicked His tongue. "Sister, You cannot only blame the Usurpers for that. You taught it, too."

"When I taught it, it was true," Alathi countered. "But look at these humans now. Look at how much they've grown without Us!" She turned back to Ehryn, bottomless eyes filled with joyful tears. "We aren't even threads in the Tapestry. We have no path in this infinite, indescribable Weave you humans have created. Look." She waved Her arm, and the Infinite Tapestry unfurled around them. Ehryn had glimpsed pieces of it before now but had never seen it in all of its magnificence. She gasped at its intricate, impossible patterns. Didn't realize she was crying. Was overwhelmed by the way everything tied together in a way her eyes couldn't follow.

"It's gorgeous," she finally whispered.

"Of course it is. And now I understand why. It's because We had no hand in it!" Alathi's breastplate dissolved into a dress of silver, light, and stardust. Her eyes were deeper now than they'd been when She'd first woken. "Time has changed so much. Justice no longer takes the shape of a sword. Or a shield. But of word. I did not think it possible."

She reached out with one unclad hand and stroked the infinite threads. "Look, Child. Do you see how We appear in dots around its surface, though they are almost always bloody scenes invoked in Our names? Who would have guessed in the beginning that We would be the blemishes?" She laughed, and for once it was not tinged in iron. "Your Tapestry will be so much more beautiful going forward. Grander than I ever thought it could when you—and I—were young!"

Ehryn frowned. "What do you mean? How do you want to change it?"

"I don't! That's the very thing. I do not have a claim to this Tapestry as I did when I first helped your kind build the loom. I thought I did, but you are right. It would not be Just. That word has evolved as much as you have since I first taught you to utter it."

Alathi knelt in front of Ehryn, taking her shoulders in Her hands. "We are Gods because we are made of more than the stardust that created the Weave. We are made of more than earth and sky. But you see, Child—" She pulled at a single thread that, until She plucked it, Ehryn would have never been able to decipher amongst the strands—"Every human has a hint of that divinity in them, too. It is what makes you more than the water and mud your bodies are created from. In the beginning, I had to help you nurture it. Water it. But now you are different from Us only in that We *know* of Our divinity. You are trapped with only your small magics or pre-set destinies up until the moment..." She smiled and placed the colorless strand in Ehryn's hand. As she touched it, Ehryn understood and it filled with color—its splendor overflowing the Tapestry and her soul.

"…Until the moment you embrace it," she whispered. "That's why Namaoii learned more than the Hollowed touch. Why the Eternal Blade sang for her." Alathi nodded.

"And why you were able to overpower Me." The Goddess's eyes sparkled as She laughed. "Welcome to Divinity, My child. It is no different than what you were before. Except now you understand what so many people coloring these threads figured out long ago—you have the power to repaint the world in whatever way you desire. And it will be more gorgeous than anything We could have ever comprehended. More than the False Children could have ever forced you to, no matter Their grand machinations of portraits in Their image. You are free to make it anything."

"We were always free to make it anything, though, weren't we?"

Avanli was the one who answered. "Perhaps. You always *could*, at any rate. But how is a person who does not change the world different from a person who cannot?"

Ehryn smiled. It sounded like something Jacir would say. "They aren't."

Alathi smiled and kissed the top of Ehryn's head. "You are made of Greatness, little human. Live up to that."

"What about the Elisians? And the people like them who will always claim that we're nothing without Gods?"

"They will always exist," Avanli said. "And their words will be mighty. But remember that every deed is committed by the one who carries it out, no matter whose name they say it's in. It is still humanity that holds the greatness, who makes the change, who colors the Tapestry."

Alathi nodded. "No matter who they choose to accredit it to, the mortals who perform the acts are in control. Some of them hide behind Our names. Some of them do great things and attribute it to Us out of humility. But none of them are doing it out of anything other than their own desire to see it done."

Ehryn thought about that for a long time. Her brain felt twisted. Stretched thin. "I... don't understand. I couldn't have gotten here without You. Without learning how to Blink. Without hearing Your voice."

"Someone who loved you very much set the groundwork as best as he was able," Avanli said. "To give you the best chance he could. The Usurpers were always going to try to regain control somewhere along the way. Someone who could watch the Weave put what safeguards they could to make sure you had a chance."

"And it seems We were part of those safeguards," Alathi said. "But think about what I've had a direct hand in, Ehryn. Every part of it was in combating what the False Children machinated. The only thing you *need* Us for is to battle other Gods. We can only be used as a weapon. And I think humanity has had enough of those."

"That's a strange thing for the Sword to say," Ehryn mused. Alathi smiled.

"It is, isn't it? But I've seen the inventions on the young Jacir's walls. His paintings from across the Weave. I believe you're about to outgrow swords, anyway."

Ehryn looked at her feet, her heart suddenly heavy. "Jacir. I don't know how or why, but a lot of this is because of him. He's the one who set everything in motion. Lined up things the rest of us couldn't see. Is he really gone?"

Avanli nodded gravely. "Yes. His mind and Mine merged over the centuries. I know what he knew, but there is nothing left of Jacir Harkins as he once was."

"A shame," a new voice said behind them. "I always said the one thing I'd avoid seeing in the Weave was my own end. But now I guess we know how it goes, don't we? Do you know how old

I was when I reached out to You? Wait, don't tell me. I want it to be a surprise."

Ehryn spun around and the Royal Arcanist was there, exactly as he'd been when she'd left his tower in Clearwall. On impulse she ran to him, wrapping her arms around his robed waist, both elated and incredulous that he was actually there.

"We did it," she said without looking up. "I don't know how you saved us, but I know that so many things fell into place like this because of you."

"Hello, Mistress. It is lovely to see you again." Jacir hugged her back. "I don't even know yet what you're talking about, but we'll figure it all out eventually, it seems. Lots of time for that, still." He released her and walked over to the Old Gods by their pool. "And You? You've decided where You want to go from here?"

Alathi looked around Her at the Tapestry. "This world was different when We walked it. We were important in your beginnings. We taught you things that formed a strong basis for humanity. Strength. Justice. Unity. We helped to mold you when you were young. But you've outgrown what even We expected. You've created and built things We could not have conceived of. And none of it was with Our guidance. We were useful for the foundations, but We would have only smothered you if history had let Us remain in the power We originally set. It is common for parents to release their children when they are ready. But you've shown all of this to My brother already, haven't you? That's how he showed it to Me."

Jacir shrugged. "It definitely seems that way, doesn't it? Must have been an older me, but I'll figure it out someday and let You know."

Alathi smiled, and Ehryn thought Avanli did too, under His helmet. "Then We are ready to go."

"But don't we still need you? Justice? Loyalty?" Ehryn asked.

Alathi laughed. "Do you think those things will disappear when We move on? That you need a Goddess to teach you how to be brave? How to be strong? How to be just? We've been locked away for millennia. How did you know of it when I was unable to teach you?"

"From my parents. From my friends. Sometimes… sometimes I just knew."

"You see? I told you, little mortal. Little Ehryn. You're made of divinity. You're made of earth and sky and stardust. There is nothing We can provide that you can't find yourself. So, We'll move on. Watch for other pieces of dust who start asking questions into the void and give them a starting place to stand. Maybe We will give them more structure with what you taught Us. Maybe We will give them less than what We planned. But I hope, little human, that they turn out half as amazing as you did."

"I hope the future version of me knew how to grant you that, because I'm afraid I don't," Jacir said. "But best of luck to both of You, wherever You go."

"Do not worry. You will learn," Avanli rumbled as He took His sister's hand.

Then Alathi and Avanli, the Sword and Shield of Justice… were gone.

44

"Well, that was stimulating, wasn't it? Quite a successful kintar, I would say." Jacir smiled at Ehryn, taking both of her hands in his and shaking them enthusiastically. "I knew you could do it. I knew you'd free us from the Sisters and the Old Gods and refuse all the offers any of Them made. I'm very proud of you, Ehryn."

Ehryn frowned. "You… knew? You knew what the Voices on the Wind were and what following the Call meant and… and everything?"

"Not at all. The Weave is a complex thing, and mostly I only see patterns in it, anymore. But I saw a thousand people reach the trap of the Old Gods and swear themselves to Alathi when She asked. You were the only one who didn't, so I did everything I could to make sure you were the one who'd make it there alive."

Ehryn pulled her hands away. "Did you know when you sent Dhruv on his kintar? When Mother went to the palace begging for news?"

Jacir looked pained. "Yes. But it was the only way you could hear the Call."

"Hear the Call? The only thing you cared about is making it so that I would hear someone greater than me beg for help, for me to trust that voice my entire life, just for the *chance* that I would survive where my brother did not and reach the voice and then betray it?" Ehryn felt deceived. She couldn't hear anything above the rushing in her ears. She saw Jacir's mouth move. Thought she heard his voice.

"…must find me quite despicable."

And she did. She did find him despicable. But as she roved the Tapestry with her eyes, as she thought of everything that had happened and all that she'd learned, she thought she could forgive him for most of it. Even forgive him for Dhruv if that was the only way to save everyone else. She thought maybe she might have done the same thing.

Almost. But one thing above all seemed… wrong. Cruel.

"You could have told me! You could have told me what was coming. What I was supposed to do. 'When you meet Alathi, don't give in.' Would that have been so hard?" Tears were stinging her eyes as she thought about all the uncertainty. All the loss. "We wasted so much time. If you knew what I was meant to do, why didn't you TELL ME? Why didn't you HELP ME? For all the bricks you laid in place, a single candle would have done so much."

Jacir spoke softly. Kindly. "Ehryn. You were the one who wanted to stop hearing words like 'fate' and 'destiny.' The Voice on the Wind—Alathi—She told you what you had to do every day, and you chose a different path anyway. I would have only been one more voice in the maelstrom trying to control you. And look what you've created without that! Proof that sometimes people can weave strands into the Tapestry more gorgeous than either Weavers or Gods can foresee when they're not directed at all."

He took her hands, and Ehryn didn't pull away. "Think about it, Mistress. Do you think that every child will have a Weaver at their side in the future? Someone to tell them from birth what their threads hold? Do you even want that? For children to be told from their first days what is expected of them, as Namaoii was?"

Ehryn looked for ways to argue, but eventually she could only shake her head. Jacir smiled. "No. We are creating a new world for all that will come after us. After today, even Weavers might doubt their gifts as being all-knowing and rather see themselves and their abilities as… potential. They might not be placed on the pedestals they were before. And isn't that what we want? For everyone to start off on even ground, regardless of what they're gifted with? A reason for people to learn other magics if they desire to, guided by their own souls rather than societal expectations?"

"But…It'll be so much harder for so many of them. They'll feel so… lost. Alone."

"Perhaps. You're right in that they won't all choose that path in the way you did. There will be generations of people stumbling in darkness, completely unaware of what might be ahead of them. But they deserve to know that their lives are worth as much as those who were once told of a grand purpose woven into the threads of their ancestors. They deserve to believe that they're capable of walking a path they cannot see. Otherwise, they would give up before even looking for what calls to them, and instead seek for someone else to tell them what to do.

"But you will be their beacon. Their adversary. The woman who stepped a foot into the blackness and took another step even when she could not see where it would go. Who had all the Tapestry before her but walked off its edge into something more glorious than that which was designed by False Children or Goddesses wrapped only in the hubris of Their own magnificence. So much of the beauty of the world is found in exploring it without knowing what will come. By experiencing it."

"But…" Ehryn frowned. "But I made so many mistakes. There were so many things that I would have done differently if I'd just known! You could have told me, but you didn't! You could have helped me. I could have done so much more!"

Jacir frowned, and he turned to gaze at the Infinite Tapestry. "You've passed the rite of the tonicloran, Ehryn. You saw beyond the Tapestry even without its power. If you truly believe what you're saying, you can do things differently for those who will come after you. You can be kinder to them than I was to you." He looked at her, his eyes sad and infinitely deep. "Do you truly think I was so cruel? Will you stand by the Weave and guide the steps of all the children who will come after I am gone? Is that truly the kinder option?"

Ehryn opened her mouth to respond, but then closed it again.

"I… I don't know."

"The world is changing, Ehryn. The Tapestry will change now that the threads are no longer held by the False Children or the Old Gods or anyone who desires to choose a path for anyone else. But you can take their place if you desire. Because you are doing it of altruism rather than control, perhaps it will even be better. But it will be hard. The world is not kind. It does not lay the path neatly at our feet. There will be others who look to you for guidance. Who watched you carve your own path through the underbrush and stand upon the mountains of your own making without the crutches that your predecessors leaned too heavily on. By stepping off the path woven into the threads, by discovering the rivers we carve when we do not look for the easiest option, you will create a world more beautiful than even what I can imagine in all my knowledge. Than even Alathi imagined with all Her time."

Ehryn looked at the Tapestry and saw the beginnings of the threads he described. "There's so much waste," she said. "So much backtracking, so many dead ends. So much despair. How many people will die or give up before fulfilling their purpose? It seems so cruel."

"Crueler than assigning a child their purpose without them being able to search for one themselves? Perhaps. And it will be frustrating for so many. Millions will live their lives unfulfilled, unaware of the side paths that might lead them to greatness. Unable or afraid to step into the darkness of the unknown. Many will try once and fail, and that will be the end of their stories, their threads written into the mundane and the forgotten. It will be difficult."

"So why force us through all of that? Why curse civilization to such…darkness?"

"But that's the thing, Ehryn. I don't think it is dark at all. It will only seem dark because those who are relegated to such terrible lives will be stuck beneath other's shadows. But there are always stars in the sky. Always pinpricks of blinding brightness from those who break free of the mundane to become something wonderful. All on their own, without the machinations and puppeteering of false gods and prideful beings. And… more than all of that—there will be those who help others to rise above such bland threads. You will be the first. A beacon in the darkness. A lighthouse in the storm. A reminder that, no matter how dark the path is, there is always hope."

"What about those who can't see it?"

"That's where others come in. We have moved past the Tapestry of a single hero's thread dominating the Weave. Of magic being gifted to only a few. Of prophesies and Calls deciding who gets to believe they are great. Now… now we all must move forward together, a picture of a thousand lives all intertwined. We must be more than we've been because we are greater than we were." He smiled at Ehryn. "This is the beginning of something none of us have ever experienced before. All of the magic in all of the world is in each of us now, no longer sucked dry by the False Children and Their trap. We can do anything, be anyone. And I think it's time people knew that." He reached out for Ehryn's hand. "Let's go help the people of the world be worthy of their divinity, Ehryn."

Ehryn looked at his hand, saw the maps of a thousand Tapestries on it. And in that moment, she believed him when he said there could be greatness.

She put her hand in his, and together they returned to Clearwall, ready to forge destinies that even the Eternal Tapestry could not conjure.

Several weeks later, Ehryn fidgeted in the throne room of Clearwall Keep, listening as Namaoii finished talking to one of the criers from the square. The crier looked uncertain.

"And do you want the statue of this Holl—this… Khalista to have the X on her forehead, Your Majesty?"

"Yes." Namaoii leaned back on the Starlit Throne. "She was a Hollowed, but she was also a person. Clearwall must learn that those things are not exclusive. Do you understand?"

"Yes, Your Majesty." The crier bowed low and backed out of the room.

Namaoii ran a hand over her face and turned to Tendaji, standing next to her. "Is that it?"

"It is for now, Namaoii."

"Thank all the—whatevers. Us." Namaoii jumped up from her seat, stretching her arms over her head. "Can we spar now? You look like you're doing well enough that I can switch back to my dominant hand." Tendaji chuckled.

"Very well. But try to go easy on an old man."

"Never." Namaoii flashed her toothy grin and set a hand on Ehryn's shoulder as she passed. "Want to come with us, Ehryn?" Ehryn shook her head.

"There's something I need to do."

Tendaji must have seen something in her face because he frowned. "Do you want us to come with you?"

"Thank you, but no. This is something I think I need to do alone."

"Have it your way," Namaoii said, "but meet me in Jacir's tower this evening. I want to learn more about that airship. Maybe we can be pirate queens, after all."

Ehryn laughed, clasped hands with Namaoii, and made her way out into the bustling city of Clearwall.

Her thoughts grew more somber as she walked through the twisted streets of the Maze. Of all the people she had ever met, there was one who had always felt like he had a little spark of the divine. Who'd made the world better. Lighter. And she wanted the rest of the world to know about it.

If they were going to move forward together, she wanted it to be with knowledge of those who had come before.

Ehryn stopped at the little home and knocked on the door, not sure of what she would say. When it opened, a woman with deep bags under her eyes and disheveled hair stood there, a squirming baby in her arms. The child looked at Ehryn with huge brown eyes that she recognized immediately. For a moment, she thought she might cry.

"Ma'am…. My name is Ehryn." Ehryn paused, not sure how to continue. The woman attempted a sad smile.

"I know who you are. How can I help you, Caller?"

"I…I'd like to tell you a story, Ma'am. You and your daughter. If I may."

The woman smiled wistfully, one tear streaking down her cheek. "It's been a while since there's been any stories in this house. I assumed it would be a long time before there was again. Come in."

A few minutes later, Ehryn sat cross-legged on the floor of the small living room, the squirmy, cooing baby in her arms. She smiled at the wide, bright eyes, letting the little fist grab at the wooden rattle carved with Crested Fir.

"There once was a hero named Kant…"

Acknowledgements

I'd like to thank the Faoii Army for helping to make this book a reality. I will not pretend that my initial road to publication was easy, and there were many times when I wanted to give up. But so many of you convinced me to keep going. I have the deepest gratitude and respect for each and every one of you for picking up a sword when I could not. And for having faith in my that I would see this series through. I am so glad I am finally able to show you the end. Thank you, my warriors.

There are several people who went above and beyond for this final tale in the *Faoii Chronicles*. My husband for being the person that listened to every errant thought, whisper of self-doubt, and curse word I had throughout the entire process of creating this series. It didn't matter what I was saying, he was willing to listen and then edit whatever I finally put to paper. Evan Graham for creating the amazing covers for these books and for yelling at me every time I tried to make my own using PowerPoint. The incredibly talented Carolyn Dubiel who *once again* pointed out that I don't know the difference between "that" and "who," among other things. Without all of you, this series would have never been completed.

Also, thank you to those who picked up their blade on Patreon: Murphy Barrett, Kathryn Canan, Chris Claus, Bridgett Duffus, Jamie Easthom, Sandra Fowler, Evan Graham, Kathleen Hughes, Vincent Mosemann, Alyssa Phillips, and Anton Vasiyev. You keep me creating when everything else spirals out of control.

For More Information
about Tahani Nelson and the Faoii
Please Visit

TahaniNelson.com